The McClane Apocalypse
Book Five

Kate Morris

Ranger Publishing
Copyright © 2015 by Ranger Publishing

Note to Readers: This publication contains the opinions and ideas of
its author. It is not intended to provide helpful or informative
material on the subjects addressed in the publication. The author and
publisher specifically disclaim all responsibility for any liability, loss or
risk personal or otherwise.

First Ranger Publishing softcover edition, November 2015
Ranger Publishing and design thereof are registered trademarks of
Ranger Publishing.
For information about special discounts for bulk purchases, please
contact, Ranger Publishing @gmail.com.

Ranger Publishing can bring authors to your live event. For more
information or to book an event, contact Ranger Publishing
@gmail.com or contact the author directly through
KateMorrisauthor.com or authorkatemorris@gmail.com

Cover design by Ebook Launch.com

Manufactured in the United States of America
Library of Congress Cataloging-in-Publication Data is on file
ISBN 13: 978-0692553626
ISBN 10: 0692553622

Dedication

For the lions who went out in defense of our freedom and never came back, I dedicate this *McClane* to you. Thank you for your selfless sacrifice and my freedom.

Chapter One
Cory

The surrounding forestry is becoming more recognizable. He's on McClane ground again. There is a comfort in the familiarity, a solace that he's on the right track. The Ohio armory group, Jackie especially, hadn't taken it well that he was leaving. But he wasn't leaving them forever.

A few days before he left, he'd called a meeting to discuss his departure. He told them who he really was, gave them a brief history of his family and the farm. Then he asked them if they'd like to move to Pleasant View. Cory was surprised when only about ten people wanted to go. He suggested that they shouldn't split up the group, that strength in numbers was important, but some of them didn't want to leave the safety of the armory. Others were from the area and were hoping that their families would return someday. Cory understood their plight but had tried to get them to see reasoning in the fact that they should be practical and leave for a much safer place. Many still hadn't wanted to leave their safe haven. Jackie and her son agreed to leave, and that's all that really mattered. He hadn't wanted to leave her in a situation that would've given him residual guilt. Cory doesn't have romantic feelings for Jackie, but he likes her well enough. She's smart, savvy and, unfortunately, very vulnerable. Her heart is in the right place, but she's very trusting, too trusting.

Hell, she hadn't known him at all and had introduced him without question into her group. Her life in the apocalypse has been sheltered. She can't believe some of the horrific stories he's told her about how bad it is out there. Sometimes she reminds him of a gullible child. Her little boy is just as innocent. Cory doesn't want to consider them being harmed. He's not sure the remaining people at the armory will survive. It takes a lot of work to gather food, forage, farm and keep up on security.

He'd worked on getting the deuce and a half ready and running, had gone on runs to salvage and steal gas and a few parts, and helped them load it full of supplies. It had taken him a few days, but he'd managed to find a rifle and two handguns that fit the ammo he'd discovered in the bunker. Cory hadn't wanted to leave the stragglers behind without more weaponry. A shotgun and a .22 pistol weren't much to defend themselves if they should be ambushed in their remote location. He'd loaded enough food for their trip and cans of ammo onto the truck along with the few meager possessions of whoever was going. Then he'd told them to give him a four-day head start before he took off on his horse for Tennessee. He'd like to beat them there so that he can explain to the family and the people in town that he's bringing new people in. New people are not always a welcome sight, and he'd like them to be warned by him of the impending arrival. He knows Jackie's group will likely need to stop frequently and that their travel will be slow. He warned them where to avoid and where it was likely safe to stop for breaks. They are traveling with women, children and older people. He was pretty sure even on horseback that he'd beat them home.

He'd made love to her the night before he left and kissed her goodbye in the morning. He'd said his farewells to the rest of the group, as well. He had also made sure that she knew how to use the Glock 9 mill pistol he gave her and made her promise to keep it on her in the truck at all times. He hopes that his words sink in because he doesn't want anything to happen to her or the rest of their small group. They are good people who deserve a second chance.

Damn Dog trots beside Jet, wagging her tail happily as if she too knows they are almost there. She has never been to the farm, but

2

Cory's sure that she must be picking up on his anticipation and eagerness. He passes the first series of human traps that they'd set up years before. Then he carefully avoids a trip-wired area. He pulls his radio out of his saddlebag and calls ahead.

"Tango Three to Bravo One, come in," Cory says into the small box.

He doesn't get a response. It's possible that his batteries are dead. It's not like he's had a chance to charge them in the last eight months. August had come and gone quickly while living at the armory. It's now the middle of September. The family will need his help to bring in the harvest. This fact and his talk with the hooch maker had pushed him to the decision to go home.

"Tango Three to Bravo One, come in," he repeats. Nothing. That's strange for sure. His battery pack seems to be working. He's got a tiny red light indicator in the right-hand corner of the walkie-talkie.

The hair comes up on the back of his neck as he starts imagining the worst. It's the middle of the day, not even dinner time yet. They should be there. Someone should have answered, and this causes his stomach to do a sickening flip. Has something happened to them? Has someone overthrown their farm and killed them?

Jet snorts and tosses his head beneath Cory. Likely he is just picking up on his master's mounting tension. He's less than two clicks out now. The barns should come into view soon. Damn Dog stops dead in her tracks and growls. Shit. Something's definitely wrong.

Cory yanks Jet to a stop, jumps from his back and flings the reins over a tree branch near the path. His dog cries once in agitation.

"Stay," he tells her. She whines. "I said stay." This time, his tone is firm, almost scolding. He doesn't need the dog running ahead and alerting anyone to his presence. She lays down next to the horse as Cory pulls his rifle free of the scabbard.

He starts forward on foot, moving cautiously. He comes to the next trip-wire and steps carefully over it. He sure as hell isn't going to go blasting through the woods like a noisy oaf should someone be near. He stalks quietly and slowly, methodically making

3

his way closer to his home. A cow moos in the far distance. He knows that it's from their farm. He's close.

When he crests the next small hill, he spots movement at the bottom of it near the creek. Cory hits the deck. He pops his head up quickly for a sly peek. Good. The person near the creek has their back to him. The sun casts a glare, making the person nothing more than a shadowy silhouette. He doesn't look particularly big, but Cory isn't taking any chances. He's going to sneak in and take him by surprise.

Spotting no other men gives him a bit more courage. Getting to his feet, he comes about just slightly and flanks. He purposely slides four feet down the steep hill, making as little noise as possible as the fallen leaves cover his shuffle. Then he stalks closer. When he's within ten feet, he decides to announce his presence.

"Hey, motherfucker, trespass much?" he calls out angrily. His family could all be dead because of this prick. None of his family is anywhere around. This is definitely not one of the family.

The man spins about in shock, even stumbles and falls down on his butt. However, it's not a man. It's clearly a woman. She wears a blue bandana on her head, tied around her forehead holding back her hair like Aunt Jemima. Except that she's not a cherubic black lady on a syrup bottle. She's a tall, skinny redhead with light-colored, cold eyes. Cory takes a second to peruse her from head to toe. She jumps to her feet with a frightened cry. Then she takes off. Damn!

He hadn't anticipated her running. He really hadn't anticipated her running so damn fast. He's literally sprinting through the forest after her. After about thirty or so yards, he gains on her and is able to tackle her to the ground. She immediately starts squirming, fighting him and cursing.

"Let me go!" she yells at him from her face down position.

Cory flips her over easily enough. She's scrawny, so it's not hard to do. Her hands lash out, slapping at him with lightning speed. When that proves ineffectual, she tries clawing at his face. She manages to lash him with one full slash across his right cheek. She's drawn blood. He can tell by the stinging pain.

"Get off, asshole!" she screams.

4

She wriggles her skinny arm free of his grasp and goes for the pistol on her hip. Cory grabs her wrist and painfully bangs it on the ground until she releases her gun.

"Let me go!" she yells in a rage. "They'll kill you. They'll kill you for this, you son of a bitch!"

She pulls her tiny wrist free and punches him in the side of the head. He knows that it hurt her knuckles. It certainly didn't hurt his hard head. Cory manages to capture both of her free hands and pin them above her head.

"Who are you?" he yells at her.

"Fuck you!"

Nice. Her hair is as colorful as her language.

"Who are you, woman?" he demands.

"Get off me!"

"What are you doing here? What are you doing out here in these woods?"

She whips her head to the side and won't look at him. Cory simply grasps both of her thin wrists in his one palm and turns her stubborn jaw with his other. He's hit with a pair of light grayish blue eyes that are on fire with anger and fear. Pale red eyebrows frame her light eyes.

"Fuck you, asshole," she says in a quieter tone. "If you're gonna rape me, then just do it, you prick."

"I ain't gonna rape you, ya' bony bitch," Cory tells her angrily. Why the hell would he rape her? Well, in her defense, he is laying on her, one leg in between hers. "What are you doing on this property? Who's gonna kill me? You with people?"

"Oh, you have no idea what kind of people I'm with, asshole," she promises.

A sprinkle of tiny brown freckles litter her nose and the apples of her tanned cheeks. Her cheekbones are high and hollow beneath. Her jawline is delicate, however, and feminine. Her mouth is almost the color of cherry juice and is a stark contrast to the pale blue of her fiery eyes. Her blue bandana is askew on her head. Her bright red hair is splayed out on a bed of green ferns and forestry. She looks like something from a medieval painting. Except for the

5

fact that she could be a murderous, thieving bitch with a group of like-minded men who have taken over the farm.

She's still rambling and threatening him with her men.

"Yeah?" he growls. "Well, they haven't dealt with me yet, bitch."

"Fuck you, asshole," she swears again, her cheeks reddening with anger and exertion. "They'll tear your ass up for this."

"Oh, really?" he taunts with a smug confidence that is born of months of stalking and killing men with an ease and finesse that he's acquired while staying alive.

She wiggles beneath him, which oddly begins to stir a lust in his groin. What the fuck? That wasn't the reaction he was expecting from his body. What's going on here?

Cory leans farther back from her. It is then that he notices her t-shirt. It's a black concert tee. There is dirt on it here and there as if she's been working outside all day laboring away. There are the faded yellowy letters for the rock band Metallica scrolled across the front. There is a faint, telling bleach mark at the left shoulder. He's staring down at his own shirt.

"Where'd you get this shirt?" he demands, his ire rising to new levels.

She doesn't answer but shoves upward. His lust is forgotten. Cory presses upward. He stretches to his side, probably smashing her as he reaches for the pistol he'd knocked out of her hand.

"What the hell?" he nearly whispers with disbelief as he holds the pistol for her to see. "Where'd you get this?"

"Get off!" she yelps.

"I'll kill you, you stupid bitch. Where'd you get this gun?" he shouts in her face, not caring that spittle hits her cheek from him.

"From my friend, asshole," she argues. "Now get off."

"You think I won't kill you? You think I won't rape you? You'd better start answering some questions," he threatens.

The woman beneath him screeches, lurches upward and manages to get slightly free. It's all the encouragement she needs. She grabs a handful of dirt and leaves and smashes it into Cory's face. Then she scoots out and crawls away. He grabs her foot. She kicks his shoulder. A moment later they are both to their feet. She tries to run again, but Cory grabs her from behind. She lets out a blood-curdling scream, so he covers her mouth with his hand. She bites him hard. Cory whips her around to face him. It's a huge mistake. She knees him in the balls. He doubles over and howls in pain and anger. She's a damn, dirty fighter.

The last thing he sees of her is the red of her hair flashing against the green of the forest as she sprints away.

"You'd better run, you red-haired witch! I'll find you!" he shouts in anger.

He takes a knee until the need to vomit passes. Using the butt of his rifle, he finally shoves up and goes for his horse. She can't outrun his horse. She can't run forever. If she's heading toward the farm, which it looked like she was, then he'll catch her there. He'll also kill every one of her group that took over the farm. She'd been wearing his shirt. Cory knows it because it had the bleach stain on the shoulder. When he'd left, he'd not had that shirt with him because it was winter. She's gotten it from him and Simon's cabin. He worries for his friend. If anything has happened to Simon, he'll kill the people who did it. Killing is what he's become rather proficient at during these last eight months. He has no fear left inside of him. He barely has any kindness, either. And he sure as shit doesn't have any goodness.

He makes it back to his pack and mounts up. He tries the radio again and gets nothing. His family isn't answering and now he understands why they hadn't earlier, either. He takes a second to catch his breath, bring his rifle around in front of him and whistle to his dog. He's going to go clean house on the fuckers that are at his farm. He's going to find that red-haired witch who had his brother's gun.

7

Chapter Two
Paige

"Help!" she screams repeatedly at the top of her lungs as she flies past the horse barn. She trips, goes down, scraping her palms, but gets back up again. "Help! There's someone in the woods!"

The men come filing out of the different buildings and barns, all on high alert. Her brother runs toward her, too. Hannah, Doc and Sue come onto the back porch. They all meet near the front of the horse barn. John grabs his rifle which was leaning against the hay wagon.

"Paige, what is it? What's wrong?" her brother asks as he grabs her by the shoulders.

She points toward the woods, trying to catch her breath from the run and blurts so quickly that some of her words jumble. The two dogs start barking, which adds to the overall chaos of the scene. "There's a man. A man in the woods. He attacked me. He has a gun."

"Slow down," Derek orders. "Calm down. Tell us what happened. Why were you in the woods alone?"

"I asked Simon if I could stay and pick herbs, but I... I think I wandered too far," she answers Derek.

"Who was in the woods with you? Are you sure it wasn't one of the family you saw?" John asks patiently, although Paige can see a vein working in his forehead.

"Yes, I'm positive! He grabbed me. Pinned me down. He was a big man. Huge. Like a dirty, hairy Viking. He's huge. Like Kelly big. He had a gun. He was threatening me!"

"Where at in the woods?" John asks in a deadly tone as he discharges the magazine from his rifle, checks it and slams it back in with force. "How far from here?"

"Not far. Out where we were picking herbs, maybe a little farther."

"Did he hurt you?" Simon asks with deadly intent.

"No, not really. He tackled me to the ground and was asking me all sorts of weird questions. But he has a gun, maybe one on his hip, too. Don't go out there!" she cries hysterically and grabs her brother's arm before he can turn away to leave.

"What kind of questions?" Kelly asks.

Grandpa, Sue and Hannah have joined them. He's carrying his old shotgun, but he seems calm. Paige doesn't feel calm. That creep in the woods could have friends.

"Maybe he's one of those men that got away," she suggests.

"What kind of questions did he ask? Questions about the family, about the farm? About us soldiers?" Derek repeats Kelly's line of questioning.

"Yeah, sort of. I don't know. It all happened so fast. He wanted to know where I got this shirt," she tells them. John and Derek give each other a puzzled look.

"What? Why would he want to know that?" Kelly asks.

Hannah has come to stand directly beside him and has slipped her hand into the crook of his arm. Paige can tell that she is afraid. They should all be afraid. That guy in the woods was a dangerous, huge Neanderthal. The look in his dark eyes was crazed and malevolent.

"I don't know!" Paige shouts with impatience.

"Let's go," John says firmly.

She notices that Reagan flinches and touches his arm. He nods down at his wife and turns to go. So does Kelly. They aren't three steps into their mission when the thundering of a horse's hooves comes from the area near the cattle barn. The rider is still a good distance away, but John lifts his rifle to take aim.

9

"That looks like him!" Paige cries frantically. "He didn't have a horse, though."

Kelly and Derek mimic John with their own rifles. Kelly's has a scope, but Derek will use the front sights of his. The rider approaches fast and hard as if he is one of the four horsemen of the apocalypse coming at them. Paige firmly believes that he might just be. Reagan also has her rifle.

"Hold on, guys," Reagan calls out from the porch where she has taken up position.

She's looking through her scope.

"Wait a minute," she yells and even holds up her hand to the men. "Don't shoot. I don't know…"

"Hold your fire!" Kelly calls loudly and steps forward to John. "Don't shoot, John."

"Who is it, Kelly? One of them?" Doc asks.

"No, I think…." He pauses a moment before saying, "I think it's Cory? It is! It's Cory."

"Damn, I could've shot him," Derek remarks as if sick to his stomach and expels a deep breath.

Reagan hops down from the porch and confirms it loudly.

"Cory?" some of the other family members call out with excitement. Paige does not mirror their joy. As the rider approaches closer, he swings down before the horse even comes to a full stop. It *is* him, the Viking from the woods who had just threatened to kill her.

He looks around as if confused for a moment. His rifle is still out in front of him as if he'd expected an all-out battle when he'd leaped from that wild looking beast. He stops moving forward and just stands there in surprise. His long, wavy black hair hits right at his shoulders and covers half of his face. His beard isn't a whole lot shorter. He looks like some sort of insane caveman. His crazed eyes scan the crowd.

"Cory!" Kelly calls out to him.

His eyes dart to Kelly and he steps hesitantly forward. Kelly rushes to him and grabs him in a bear hug.

"Man, little brother, it's been too long," Kelly remarks and finally releases the other man.

Sam rushes forward next and nearly vaults into Cory's arms. He returns her hug with one arm, suspending her a good foot off the ground. He is as huge as Paige had assessed. When he'd been lying on top of her, pinning her painfully to the ground, he'd felt like he weighed three hundred pounds. Now that she has a chance to see him while not running away in a blurry flash, he's not at all fat or heavy from weight. He's just big. His shoulders are wide, as wide as Kelly's. His biceps are the size of hams. His dirty shirt stretches tightly across his thickly muscled chest. None of these quick assessments make her feel any better about him.

Hannah finds her way to him and reaches out. He steps forward and takes her slim hand.

"Cory, I'm so glad you're home, honey," she says. Then with a fierce intensity in her voice, she orders, "Don't ever leave like that again."

"Sorry, Hannie," he mumbles.

One by one, different family members, even the children, hug and kiss this man who is obviously Kelly's brother who's been gone for nearly a year. For some reason, Paige had thought he would be younger, scrawnier like a teenager by the way that Simon talked about him. They step back to give him room to breathe. His brown eyes scan the group again and land directly on her.

"Red-haired witch!" he hisses and steps toward her with aggressive intentions.

Kelly and John jump forward to hold him back.

"Whoa, whoa, whoa, little brother," Kelly says with a chuckle. "She's with us."

"She had your gun," Cory says. "I saw her in the woods."

Paige would like to scoff. Out of fear of this maniac, she holds her tongue. He'd assaulted her in the woods. That would've been a more accurate description than 'saw her in the woods.'

"She had my shirt and your gun," he explains.

"You shoved me to the ground, asshole!" Paige shouts.

He looks at his brother and then John and calmly replies with a shrug, "Reaction. She had your gun, Kel."

11

Kelly tells him, "Yeah, I lent it to her."

"I'm just glad you're both ok. That could've gone a lot worse," Reagan interjects, breaking up a potential argument.

"Who the hell is she?" he asks as he returns Kelly's pistol to its rightful owner.

Paige watches as he indicates with his long finger toward her. Naturally she inches closer to Simon. Cory looks her up and down, his eyes settling on her shirt for a long time. At least she hopes he's just looking at her shirt and not contemplating what's beneath it. There is a heat in his unguarded gaze, however, that warns her that he might not be looking at the shirt alone. She interlaces her fingers with her brother's.

"That's Paige," Kelly offers, getting a frown from the psychotic Viking.

Simon steps forward with her, although she literally digs her heels into the soft ground and leans back. He doesn't seem to notice or care but continues dragging her toward her enemy.

"Cory," Simon greets the other man. "This is my sister, Paige. Remember I told you all about her? She made it here, man. She was alive all this time."

Cory is now within two feet of her. She doesn't like it and won't meet his gaze. Instead, she stares at the chicken coop off to their immediate left. She doesn't notice her social gaffe until Simon nudges her. He nudges her kind of hard. When she glances up, Cory has his hand extended toward her in greeting and has obviously been holding it there a long time.

"Hi," he says with a cocky smirk as if he hadn't just been lying on top of her in the woods and threatening to kill or rape her to get her to give up information.

She gives him a sidelong glare and shakes his hand quickly. When she tries to pull back, he holds on a moment longer until her eyes meet his. The smirk has turned sensual. Paige snatches her hand back in irritation.

"It's nice to meet you, Paige," he says, revealing his white teeth.

Her eyes just widen. She wants to curse him out in front of his family. She gives him her best sneer and doesn't answer. She literally locks her teeth together to stymie her need to curse.

"Like your shirt," he remarks smugly.

Nobody comments because they probably don't understand their strange interaction. She still doesn't answer him but stands close to her brother. Simon had told her that she could borrow Cory's t-shirts or hoodies, whatever she needed since he was gone. They weren't sure he was ever going to come back. She wishes Simon hadn't made that offer. Now she wants to burn this damn shirt. He seems like a real dick, and Paige sorely wishes he hadn't come back.

"What'd I miss while I was gone?" he asks like a smartass and gets an uproarious bunch of laughter from all of the men.

"Quite a lot, Death Stalker, quite a lot," Kelly remarks.

Paige doesn't find the humor in any of it. And she doesn't like his nickname. He'd stalked her in the woods just a few minutes ago. He'd threatened to kill her. She'd like to tell the family that part, but they seem so happy to have him home. Everyone's faces have smiles of pure joy plastered to them. Even Doc, who is usually calm and reserved, is exuding happiness. She doesn't want to spoil this family reunion for them. But that doesn't mean she has to like this dick, either. Nor does she trust him.

"Well, I figured I should bring the stallion back to get those mares bred again," he tells them.

"So you're telling us that you came back to offer your stud services?" John jokes.

Everyone laughs again. They are all elated to have this jerk back. Not her. She'd like to tell him to go back to wherever the hell he's been. They've been just fine without him.

"You're just in time for your favorite time of day, brother," Kelly remarks.

"Dinner?" he asks with a grin, his beard unkempt and disgusting.

"No, chores!" John jokes and gets more laughter from the crowd.

"Bummer," Cory says with good humor.

13

"Yep, let's get you settled in," Kelly answers. "We might give you a pass on chores tonight. And dinner will probably be ready soon."

"You've got a friend there," Reagan observes his dog.

The little kids have already been petting his dog and loving on her. She looks as mean and mangy as her owner, but the kids know no fear when it comes to animals. The German shepherd is a puddle of goo in their hands.

"Yeah, couldn't shake her," he says.

"Real lady's man, huh?" John jokes.

"Yeah, I guess so," Cory says with another grin that exposes two deep dimples this time near the edge of his scraggly, black beard.

"What's her name, Uncle Cory?" Arianna inquires.

Why is she calling him uncle? He's not her uncle at all. Paige has some suggestions on what they could call him.

"Damn... well, she doesn't really have a name," he stutters as if he is covering up something. "Why don't you guys give her a name? I never got around to it."

He picks up the reins of his stallion, a brutal looking beast who is stomping and snorting ferociously.

"Let's get your gear and we'll take care of chores before dinner," John suggests. "Guess we can let you off the hook for milking the cows for just one night, right?"

"Sure, cool," Cory murmurs.

This soft, quiet tone of his is nothing like the roaring monster he'd been in the forest. They unload three big bags, cargo style military bags, from his horse. Kelly takes his rifle.

"Army issue? Where you been, little bro?" Kelly asks, observing one of the bags.

Cory's eyes take on a haunted look for the barest of seconds but quickly change back. "A little bit of everywhere."

Reagan jumps in to relieve him of the big interrogation that was brewing, "Great. You can tell us all about it later."

"Thought maybe you guys got overrun or something," he tells Kelly. "I ran into her in the woods with your pistol and... man, I couldn't get you on the radio, either."

He's thumbing his finger at her. She squints her eyes at him. He just smirks again. Creep.

"Oh, yeah, sorry, man," Simon offers. "We had to switch channels. Had some problems. I'll fill you in. Let's get him turned out to pasture. Come on."

"Hurry up, boys," Hannah calls out jovially. "Dinner will be ready in less than an hour and then you all have a meeting in town tonight, don't forget."

"Meeting? What's that all about?" Cory asks.

"There's a lot to fill you in on," Simon tells him.

The men split up to take care of chores. Paige and Sam follow along with her brother and the creep to the barn where he hooks his horse to a tie ring. It's preferable to stay near her brother than to let this psycho out of her sight. His equipment is dusty and rough looking, just like him.

"Glad to have you back, brother," Simon tells him a moment later.

Traitor, Paige thinks to herself. She doesn't think her brother would like how this Cory jerk had treated her out in the woods if he knew the truth of it.

He even turns his back to her and hugs Cory. She stares down Kelly's brother who returns Simon's hug. He's taller than Simon, which enables her to clearly see Cory's face. His eyes look troubled. When he catches her staring at him, though, the smugness returns. She wishes she'd kicked him in the balls harder.

"Good to be back," he tells Simon. "Things sure changed around here."

"You have no idea," Simon says. "Paige came here with her two friends and a little girl. Her friend now lives over at the Reynolds. She's gonna marry Chet if you can believe that."

"Really?" Cory asks as if in disbelief. "Where's the other friend?"

His question is guarded as if he is wary of new people being on the farm. Screw him. He's been gone for a long time. He doesn't exactly have a weighty opinion right now on who does and does not get to live here.

"He was killed a while back," Simon answers quietly.

15

Paige lowers her gaze. Sam puts a comforting arm around her waist. She leans down and gently presses her head against the other woman's.

Cory doesn't even flinch or show an ounce of emotion before asking, "Killed how? On a run or something?"

"No, the farm was attacked, Cor," Simon tells him as he removes the stallion's bridle for Cory.

"What?" Cory asks in genuine shock. "What the fuck happened? Oh, sorry, Sam."

Is he apologizing for swearing? If so, she'd like to remind him that he owes her about a hundred apologies. Of course, she hadn't been in her best form, either, just a short bit ago.

"It's ok, Cory," Sam says and goes to him.

She places her hand on Cory's arm to reassure him.

"We're just glad you're home," she says kindly and hugs him around his middle.

Apparently she really likes this asshole. Paige doesn't get it. Just because someone is family doesn't mean you have to like them. She'd like to enlighten them all to this concept. Sam steps away again.

"We'll let you two get caught up while we get the chores done. See you in the house," Sam says.

She doesn't have to tell her twice. Paige is glad to get out of the barn and away from that creep. As they are leaving the barn, Paige glances over her shoulder. Her brother has his back to her. He's squatting down and checking the horse's front hoof. Cory is staring right at her. Right at her butt. She glares at him until he grins and turns away as if he wasn't doing anything wrong. Super creep. She can't wait to get her brother alone later to tell him what went down in the woods. Her palms itch, the hair on the back of her neck stands up and her flight instincts are kicking into high gear.

Sam says as they walk toward the yard, "Let's collect the eggs first. Then we'll head over and help with the cows."

"Sure. Sounds good to me," Paige answers and follows along.

They each pick up a wicker basket hanging on the side of the coop and go inside the small building to collect the little brown eggs from their cozy boxes bedded down in straw.

"I wanted to let Cory and Simon talk by themselves," Sam says.

"Oh, ok," Paige says. She wants Cory to get kicked by that big horse of his.

"They have some things they need to work out," Sam tells her.

Paige realizes that Sam has stopped collecting eggs and is looking at her.

"I mean, don't get me wrong, I don't think they're going to work out everything right this second, but I also didn't want to crowd them, either," Sam says quietly as if she is conveying a secret.

"What do you mean?"

"You know, because of what happened to Em?"

Paige shakes her head and furrows her brow. Cory and Kelly's little sister was murdered by some bad men like the ones who'd raided this farm. "I don't understand. Wasn't she killed by some guy when they were on a raid or something?"

"Yes, technically," Sam says and looks around Paige as if she is making sure they are still alone. "But Simon told me he feels really guilty for it. He said that Em nagged him to tag along instead of waiting for them at the cabin and kind of persuaded him to side against Cory with her. Cory never would've let her go with them. He was way overprotective of her. She sneaked out of here and caught up to them in the first place."

"I knew that part, but I didn't know that Simon talked Cory into anything," Paige admits, finds another egg and tucks it into her basket with at least a dozen others. Almost every morning the family eats eggs for breakfast, a lot of eggs. She'd been a vegan before the fall of the country. That hadn't lasted long. Now she's a carnivore like the rest of them. She hadn't had much of a choice in the matter. It was either eat wild game that they'd catch or go hungry. It wasn't like she had a fresh garden before she came to the farm. She had to eat meat and eggs when they could find them. The other option was to go out and chomp on grass like a cow. She could've converted back, but the apocalypse has changed her viewpoint on many of her former ideals. Now she's pretty sure she'd eat a baby seal if she had to. The world has changed. The people in it have changed, as well. Those who couldn't adapt are probably dead.

Sam nods sadly and says, "Yes, he did. I know he feels terribly guilty over it, too. He won't talk to me about it anymore, though. I've tried. Maybe he'll talk to you?"

Paige shrugs and replies, "I doubt that. He's not a kid anymore that needs my help. He is more independent than I am now. I really don't think he'd discuss it with me. Hell, Sam, he'd probably talk to you before me."

Sam frowns hard and shakes her head.

"You don't understand how close Cory was with his little sister. They were tight. He kept her alive when they were younger for four days before Kelly got to them in Arkansas. Their parents were both killed. I guess Cory's the one that found them. Then he had to hide with Em until Kelly got to them. I can't imagine. He was only like sixteen or seventeen. He's so loyal. And he was crazy about her."

Paige says, "Well, it's not really anybody's fault. It wasn't like they meant for her to get killed. It just happens. I mean, look at Gavin. He came here. We made it all the way here only to have him be shot and killed so soon after. This is the safest place that I've been since the fall. Nothing really ever makes sense anymore. I doubt if there's anyone in the country still alive that hasn't lost someone."

Sam's eyes tear up and she bites her lower lip.

"I'm sure they'll work it out," Paige offers optimistically. "Men have a very different way of communicating than we do, but I'm sure they'll talk it out some day."

Sam nods and says, "Yes, I don't know how men communicate. You're right. It's not anything like the way that we do, though."

The younger woman rolls her eyes as if she's frustrated and goes back to plucking eggs from nests. Sam passes her basket of eggs to Paige to carry to the house while she plans on heading out to the horse barn to help with the evening feeding. Paige surely won't argue with that decision. She'd rather do anything than be around the horses. Or the newly arrived family member.

A few hours later, the family is gathering together in a loud flurry of movement and chaos. People are carrying trays of food. Others are collecting kids and coercing them into washing their hands in the mudroom. Others are just missing.

"Paige?" Hannah calls over to her.

"Yes, I'm here," Paige answers her and goes toward the stove where Hannah is lifting a heavy pan.

"Of course you're here, silly, or I wouldn't have asked for you," Hannah says on a sassy laugh. "Why don't you go up and get Sam for me? I called her some time ago, but she must be drawing in her room again. That girl, I swear."

"You're gonna swear?" Reagan asks jokingly. "If you are, hold on a minute so I can write this down."

She and Kelly laugh and bump fists, conspiring against Hannah.

"Oh, no! I don't think I need to really swear. You two heathens do enough of that for the lot of us!" Hannah jabs with impatience.

"I'll get Sam," Paige tells her and flees the room. That is only bound to get worse. They've vexed Hannie and when she gets mad, she can really lay on the guilt. She's a funny little person. Sometimes Paige thinks she runs the whole family.

She takes the stairs two stairs at a time and starts down the long hall toward Sam's room. The bathroom door opens, and she expects Sam to come out. It turns out to be Derek with his head down.

Paige tries to pass him, but his hand lashes out and clamps down onto her upper arm. What the hell? When she glances up, it isn't Derek at all but her arch nemesis. Her heart skips a beat, or twenty. She hadn't recognized the dirty Viking because he's shaved his beard and mustache clean off. His face is chiseled and angular and smooth and clean.

He's wearing a towel around his waist and nothing else. The skin on his torso is still damp. Beads of water trickle over the grooved planes of his pectorals and down over the waves of his stomach muscles. She feels even more out of sorts now. The hallway, although easily six to eight feet wide, feels too small and claustrophobic. He looks even bigger when he's nearly naked. She backs up a step, still in his grasp.

"Hey there," he says as if she's startled him, as well.

She jerks free and glares at him.

"I actually wanted to get you alone..." he starts.

She interrupts him, "Why? So you can finish the job you started in the woods?" She tries to keep her voice low so that the rest of the family doesn't hear her.

"No, if I'd wanted to finish the job, I would have. Trust me that wouldn't have been very difficult," he brags.

"You say that, but I got away from you," she returns with a haughty attitude.

He chuffs through his nose and grins as if she is being humorous. His dark hair is still uncut and skims his shoulders.

"Yeah, ok," he replies with an enormous amount of sarcasm. "Look, I just wanted to say that I'm sorry. I thought you were trespassing on our property. I saw the gun and knew it was my brother's. I saw the shirt, which I notice you've changed, and knew that it was mine."

His eyes skim the front of her, lingering on her chest. Of course she'd changed out of his dumb shirt. She wears one of her long-sleeved tees borrowed from Reagan. So, naturally, it is plain and black. At least it isn't his. Paige folds her arms self-consciously over her front. His keen brown eyes meet hers again and there's that lust again before they travel south once more. She's not some sort of naïve young girl. She knows that look.

"Hey, eyes up here, asshole. You stay away from me," she interjects and points to her own blue eyes and then at him. "I don't care who you're related to on this farm. Stay away from me. I don't like you, and I sure as hell don't trust you."

Cory just grins down at her again. This pisses her off more. She's always been tall for a woman and relished this fact. At five-nine and a half, she's the tallest woman on this farm. This guy makes her feel very dwarfed by his height and width.

"Don't like me, huh?" he asks dryly. "You're kinda' spunky, aren't you?"

"Go to hell," she hisses and spins on the ball of her foot to the stairs. Screw Sam. She doesn't want to have to pass that asshole again to get down the stairs. Someone else can go back up and fetch Sam for dinner.

She nearly runs Kelly down on the first floor near the staircase.

"I think your brother needs clothes," she says in a rush. "And can you get Sam for dinner while you're up there?"

He looks confused and surprised but answers amiably, "Oh, sure, Paige. No problem."

God, how can Kelly be so nice and kind and sweet and be related to that jerk on the top floor?

She keeps right on going until she reaches the music room. This farm is big enough that she can avoid that creep. She's starting to wonder if maybe she and Simon shouldn't leave, after all.

Ten minutes later, they are finally all assembled in the dining room. Cory sits across from her. Small miracles. At least he is clean enough to come into the house finally. His filthy dog is sitting on the back porch waiting for him. The dog obviously isn't too smart if it aligned itself with the likes of him.

Doc leads off with a long prayer of how thankful they are to have Cory home. Paige doesn't even close her eyes but stares across the table at him. She notices that he is the only other person who doesn't bow his head and pray. He doesn't notice her watching him, but he also doesn't join in with the family's prayer.

"Pass the mashed potatoes, Sam," Simon requests beside her when the prayer is finished and the noise starts.

Sam sits right beside her brother. She always has. The table is crowded, so the children eat in the kitchen and in the music room. Hannah and Sue had discussed it during the final food preparations before everyone had come in that they need to come up with a new dining room plan. Most days in good weather seasons Sue and her family eat in the big house. Snowy or stormy days they'll stay out in their log cabin and Sue will prepare food from her pantry storage of canned goods. Today they've made roasted pork, gravy and mashed potatoes. The children picked sweet corn from the garden to go with it along with the homemade rolls Sue and Hannah made. Paige

21

weighed herself the other day and wasn't at all surprised to find that she's gained three pounds in the last few months. She was more surprised that it wasn't a bigger gain.

Helping herself to an ear of corn and some of the pork, she passes dishes along to Derek, who sits next to her.

"Eat more than that, son," Doc says to Cory.

"I'm fine, sir," he replies. "Haven't had anything this good for a while. Or hot and filling."

"What have you been eating?" Reagan asks.

"Mostly meat and vegetables," he answers honestly. "Wild game, turkey, deer."

"Where'd you get vegetables, Cory?" Kelly asks next.

He sighs before answering, "Well, you see, that's the thing I wanted to talk to everyone about. In the next day or so," he pauses and shakes his head. "...or hell, maybe a week as slow as they are, I have a small group of people coming this way. Not to the farm. I'd never do that. But they're coming to town in Pleasant View."

"Oh yeah?" Derek asks.

"Where are they from? How'd you meet them?" John asks.

"Ohio. Went up north for a while. Met them at an old, closed down ammo depot up there. They're good people. I felt bad when I told them I was leaving. I felt... I don't know. I guess I felt obligated to help them. Mostly it'll be women and kids, a few older people. That's all they had in their group. Probably why I felt like I couldn't just ditch them."

"I think that's a very noble thing to do, Cory," Sue comments.

"Yes, I agree, Sue," Doc adds. "It's the right thing to do. Grams would be proud of you, son."

Cory looks like he'd prefer to die on the spot under such praise. Paige hates this Saint Cory shit. He wasn't so saintly in the woods. At least he has on clothing again. He wears black cargo pants and a white t-shirt that has seen better days.

"Where all have you been? You said Ohio," Reagan asks.

Cory pauses in between mammoth bites and says, "Yeah, Ohio for a while. Pennsylvania. Kentucky. Just kind of moved around. Went through your old college town, Reagan."

"Yeah? What was it like? It was going to hell pretty damn fast when I was hightailing it outta' there," she says.

"Reagan," Hannah scolds for the swearing.

"Pretty messed up. In the city center area, it was fried. On the outskirts of the cities, it was better. Jet was shot there."

Reagan says, "I thought I saw a stitch scar on his shoulder."

"Yeah, you can check it out. I'm not a doc like you, so it's probably not the best," Cory admits.

"What's it like everywhere else? Any better than here?" Kelly interrupts. "Paige told us how rough some of the places were out there. I'm just wondering if you went to different areas if it was any better."

He sighs and takes a moment before answering, "Not really. Some places are worse. Some about the same, but I don't think I'd say that anyone is doing better. There was a group in Columbus, Ohio, that had natural gas running in their town. That was good. They had shut-off valves tied in everywhere so that they could cut it and restart it. It was a pretty good system if it lasts."

"That's great," Derek remarks.

He looks to his wife and she nods in agreement.

"Brought back a bag of medical supplies, bunch of bottles of antibiotics for you from a couple zoos up there in Ohio," he tells Reagan.

John remarks, "Zoos. Smart. We never thought about zoos for a source of medicines. We'll have to look into going on some runs to zoos soon."

"Yeah, that is a good idea," Reagan replies. "We're really low on some meds. Thanks, Cory."

He nods in her direction, catches Paige's gaze and winks. What the hell? She'd like to throw her ear of corn at him. Creep.

"Damn, we really shoulda' thought of that," Reagan says. "We should hit up all zoos and vet clinics and forage for antibiotics and meds."

John smiles at her.

23

"You said that a group had natural gas going. So people are working together like here in Pleasant View?" Doc asks with hope in his voice.

"Some are. Well, you know how that goes," Cory tells them. He takes a bite of potatoes before continuing with his explanation. "There are bands of good people working together, but then there are bands that are scum who want to rob and kill. And those are the ones that need dealt with."

Paige notices that his eyes radiate such a cold intensity that she flinches. Reagan had told her a few months ago that Cory was going on a killing spree when they'd left him in that cabin in the woods after his sister had died. She hadn't really believed Reagan. Either that or she hadn't really wanted to believe her. She's leaning toward believing her now after looking into his vacant eyes.

"We're just glad you're home safe and sound," Hannah says, trying to lighten the mood.

"What did the big cities look like if you went through any? When we did coming home, you remember, they were congested and a mess," Kelly asks, going back to their conversation about the state of the country.

"Worse," Cory replies and stuffs a piece of bread into his mouth.

He's avoiding this question, it seems to Paige. He's not telling them a lot of details about his adventures. Perhaps that's for the best. He also doesn't know about the radio transmission that Sam had heard in Doc's office a few weeks ago. She wonders if the family will tell him. He seems like sort of a loose cannon.

John presses him, though, "Were they trying to work together in the big cities?"

Cory shakes his head and says, "Not in Cleveland, Louisville, or Pittsburgh. There aren't a lot of people left there, either. There's definitely no congestion anymore. The ones that are still living in the big cities are the ones you have to watch out for. They've formed groups that are a lot like the ones I heard about from Simon that attacked the farm."

"At least people are starting to pull together in the smaller towns," Sue says.

"There were the usual rumors about different cities having power and being back on the grid, but I never saw any of that. Mostly people were using oil lamps, gennies, or solar. One woman I stayed the night with had a wind turbine on top of her house," he explains.

"That's all we can do until full power gets restored someday, if it ever does," Sam says.

"Don't get your hopes up too high, Sam," Cory tells her. "There were also a lot of rumors about people migrating to the South or to the West to warmer climates. Who knows? They're probably just dead."

Nobody picks up that circle of conversation again. They would all like to hold onto a little hope, even if that is all it ends up being.

"We need to wrap up soon, everyone," Doc says, cutting in on the gloom. "Need to head into town for that meeting."

"Yeah, Simon told me what's going on," Cory says. "I'll go with you."

"Why don't you just hang out here with the women and keep an eye on the farm while we're gone. Get some rest, too," Kelly suggests.

"Yeah, man, me and Derek, Kelly and Doc are going in," John says. "Just stay with Simon and rest up."

Cory nods, but Paige can tell that he'd like to go with them. She wasn't planning on going tonight. She'd offered to stay behind.

"I'm going!" Reagan says as if she and her husband have argued about it.

"Don't remind me," John says sarcastically.

Reagan smiles widely, messing with him. He leans over and kisses her right in front of everyone.

"Zip it, boss," he chides and gets a cocky grin from her.

A short time later the men leave in Doc's pick-up truck. Paige and the rest of the women have helped to clean up after dinner and are readying the children for bed. She misses Maddie and wishes she could walk over to the Reynolds' farm to visit her. Talia likely has her

25

in bed by now. Plus, they are under strict orders to stay close to the farm when the men go to town like this. They don't need her help tonight with drawings of the wall. They are going to town to try to settle a dispute.

She's sitting on the step of the front porch watching the new dog co-mingle with the two existing ones when her brother comes around the corner of the house. The mangy mutt keeps pestering her for attention. Growing up in Arizona, they'd only ever had little yippie dogs like Yorkies and Pomeranians. She's never been particularly comfortable around large breeds.

It doesn't take long for the three dogs to break through their awkward sniffing and unsure behavior. They play together in the yard, spinning and chasing one another around in circles. If only people were as simple as dogs, life would be so much easier. People are much more complex and difficult to understand.

"I'm heading out to the cabin," Simon tells her. "What're you doing?"

"Nothing. Just hanging out watching these mutts," she replies and stands.

"Wanna' come with me?" he asks.

"Yeah, sure. Think I'm gonna turn in soon. I'm beat," Paige confesses. It's been a long, exhausting day. She'd helped with getting the kids ready for bed and had even tucked two in for the night.

"Crazy day, huh?" he asks rhetorically.

Paige is about to tell him what a creep Cory had been to her in the woods when he adds, "Good day, though. Cory finally came home."

"Uh huh," she answers noncommittally. Maybe now isn't the time. Her brother seems so happy that she hates the idea of ruining it for him.

They walk together to their cabin in the woods. What she hadn't anticipated seeing upon their arrival is Cory already there. He's unpacking the rest of his gear as if he's just settling in.

"I feel like one of the bears in the Goldilocks story, only this one should be called the Redilocks story," Cory says to them as they enter the small cabin.

"What?" Simon asks him.

"Somebody's been wearing my clothes. Someone's been sleeping in my bed," he answers, gesturing toward Paige.

Simon laughs. Cory grins slightly, showing his dimples a lot more this time since his shaggy beard is gone. He swipes a hand through his wild hair and looks at her.

"I sleep here with Simon," she explains, although she isn't quite sure why she feels the need to do so.

"In my bed I see," Cory points out and turns his back to her.

"You weren't here. Maybe you can sleep in the house," Paige suggests tightly.

Cory turns back to her, dangling one of her lacy white bras from his index finger, "This definitely isn't mine."

Paige glares at him and in haste snatches her bra from his finger.

"No, it's cool, sis," Simon offers, oblivious to their interaction with his back turned. "We don't want to kick Cory out. We can all stay out here. There's plenty of room. I'll just go get one of the twin mattresses from the basement for you. We'll set you up in here with us."

"I won't necessarily be here a lot at night anyway, so it won't matter much," Cory says, drawing their confused stares.

"What do you mean? Why not?" Simon asks.

"I'll be gone a lot. Working," he replies.

This makes no sense to her, but she doesn't care. Good. She's glad he won't be around much. She wonders if she should suggest right now that he be gone a lot during the day, too. Or perhaps she should wait a while to share that idea.

"Doing patrols? Yeah, we still do those. Gotta keep a good watch on the place," Simon concludes. "I'll just run up to the house and grab that mattress. Be right back."

Her brother blasts back through the door with more energy than she feels tonight.

"Not patrols," Cory mumbles after Simon is gone.

Paige is leery of him, to say the least. She goes to the far corner of the cabin and sits on Simon's bed.

"I'm not leaving this cabin, asshole," Paige starts angrily and crosses her arms over her chest. "I'm never leaving Simon again."

"I didn't say you had to, sass-mouth," he retorts and barely looks over his shoulder at her.

It's like he doesn't care enough to even look at her when he speaks, as if she is insignificant. She watches warily as he crosses to the dinner table, which is only big enough to hold four chairs. He picks up an empty gun clip and starts jamming ammo into it.

"Why are you loading that clip?" she asks hesitantly.

"Not a clip. This is a magazine," he answers.

Paige would like to club him over the head with whatever gun it came out of. She still hasn't learned much about guns and shooting them or self-defense. The men have been too busy to work with her and Talia.

"So? Why are you loading it full? Did you load those other three, too?"

"Yep," he answers, still not looking in her direction.

He screws a silencer onto the end of it.

"Why? Are you expecting company?" she asks, her impatience at his noncommittal answers growing. The sun will set soon, which causes a dull amber glow to filter into the room through the two west-facing windows.

"Look, beanpole, if I wanted to play twenty questions, I'd ask Ari to come out here and bug me," he retorts.

He slings his rifle over his shoulder. What an ass! She doesn't think any of the men would find his crass behavior and name calling funny. He grabs his backpack next. Then he pulls on a pair of leather boots. These ones look different than the scroungy shoes he had on earlier. They look like the military boots that the Rangers wear. He must've retrieved them from under his bed where she'd seen boxes of his belongings stored there. She hadn't snooped. She hadn't felt the need. Now her curiosity is slightly heightened at this strange, aloof man, this dangerous man. He goes to the door and opens it, but her next sentence halts him. He doesn't turn around to look at her, though.

"Where are you going?" she asks and approaches him.

"To work," he answers. Then he peers over his shoulder at her. "Don't wait up, witch."

Paige is left standing there staring hard at that door. Simon returns shortly with her new mattress. He tries to place it in her own corner which would be closer to Cory than him. She insists he put it right directly beside his own bed on the floor. That spot suits her just fine until she can get rid of that creep who has gone "to work."

Chapter Three
Reagan

"Why didn't you want Cory to come?" Reagan asks her husband who sits beside her in the back seat of SUV.

"He's not ready to be around the people in town yet, honey," he explains gently.

John takes her hand in his and rubs his thumb gently over her knuckles. Kelly is driving while Derek rides shotgun, and they are discussing the local political situation. Grandpa sits on her other side in the back seat smoking his pipe, of which he thankfully blows the gray plumes out the open window.

"What do you mean? He got a shower," she quips.

John chuckles and replies, "Yes, that would've helped immeasurably. But he just needs to settle down a little first."

"Get some rest and settle in?"

Grandpa says, "No, honey. John means settle down that demon inside of him. He's not there yet. It may have helped him to be alone for a while, but he's still restless. Didn't you see it in his eyes?"

"I don't know," she admits with a shrug. "I guess so."

"We need to give him some time, babe," John tells her. "If things get heated in town, he's not likely to have much patience with pettiness and local politics. He has a short fuse right now."

Reagan doesn't comment further. They are probably right. She's sure as hell not good at reading people, not like John.

"With the problems in town, the missing thugs still out there, and everyone going into fall harvest panic mode, it's better to just keep him at home for a few days at least. Maybe a few weeks," John says and kisses the top of her head. "He's a little too intense. He needs some decompression time."

Derek must've picked up on some of their conversation and comments, "Yeah, it's a big enough pain in the ass in town right now. We don't need to unleash Cory on them, especially not on Mr. Hernandez."

"It would make the meetings shorter," Reagan suggests and gets a lot of male laughter in return.

Everyone nods or agrees out loud with Derek. Jay Hernandez has supposedly taken a vote within his small district, and they are announcing their decision tonight at the town meeting. This situation with the people in town is becoming frustrating for Reagan. She'd like to tell them to just go to Hell and fend for themselves. The McClane family doesn't really need to be involved with the town people. They'd lived for over a year on the farm in total seclusion with the exception of their two neighbors and Condo Paul's small community. Unfortunately, she also knows that none of the people there, and more importantly, none of the children would have medical care if her family went back into seclusion. That part would not sit well on her conscience. Without her little Jacob in her life, she's not sure how she'd go on. Even though she hadn't wanted to be a mother, he'd been tossed into her lap. He's the best thing that's ever happened to her. But she doesn't have a single relative that lives in town. She just doesn't want to see any of them die from sickness or injury. She blames John for that. Before he'd stumbled into her life, she was content to stay a hermit for the rest of her days. Now she feels an obligation, just like her grandfather does, to the people in their community.

When they arrive near the town hall, Kelly cuts the engine and they disembark. John helps her down. He really just wants to pull her up against him, Reagan knows. She obliges by kissing his bare neck.

"Hm, you're behaving awfully naughty beings we're going into a meeting," he teases.

"We could sneak off for a little bit before we go in," she suggests as she hooks her finger into the waistband of his jeans.

For a moment, John looks like he's going to agree with her plan, but then he just grins, as usual.

"The good thing is that when we get back, your sisters should already have Jacob put to bed," he hints.

Reagan stretches up onto her tiptoes and presses another kiss to his mouth. "Let's hope," she says haughtily.

He shuts the car door, takes her hand in his and pulls her along.

"You're a bad influence, Mrs. Harrison," he jokes as they climb the stairs of the town hall.

"That's your fault," she gives it right back.

He laughs, "Nothing new there."

Her sexy as hell husband holds open the door for her. Then he swats her derriere when she passes through.

"Think this is gonna go well?" she asks quietly.

John frowns hard, "No, I don't think so, babe."

Reagan shoots him a cocky grin and says, "Try to not shoot anybody, Dr. Death."

He gives her a harder frown before tugging her close and wrapping an arm around her waist. This is where she feels safest, when John is embracing her this way.

Arguing in the meeting room at the end of the second-floor hallway draws her attention. Apparently this isn't going to go well at all. They take their seats in the room as men and women continue to complain at one another. Reagan wishes she had a cup of coffee. This would all go down so much easier with some caffeine. That well dried up long ago, though, and she's just left with a slow, oncoming headache.

Roy, a good man from town of whom she'd had the honor of sewing up this summer after the Target raid, announces the official beginning of the meeting. People are slightly subdued. She keeps her hand on John's thigh. She can never be too sure of how he'll react. And she likes his muscular thigh. That helps, too.

It doesn't take long to figure out why the people are upset. Jay Hernandez and his small sector of families in the new development part of town are seceding from the rest of the town. They are starting their own town and don't want anything more to do with Pleasant View.

"Mr. Hernandez..." Grandpa starts but is interrupted by Jay.

"Sheriff Hernandez now, Mr. McClane," Jay corrects her grandfather.

What the hell? This guy has already made himself the sheriff of his small quadrant? This is progressing decidedly fast. Interesting.

Grandpa doesn't miss a beat and says, "Jay, look, I think you need to take some time and think about it. That could be a dangerous decision. You won't have the protection of the security force we're building."

"Right, man," Roy says. "How you gonna protect yourselves against an attack? You don't have enough people over there."

"We'll get by," Jay answers. "Don't worry about us, not that any of you did before."

"That's not fair, Jay!" one of the women in the crowd calls out.

Another man says, "Yeah, we have to get the wall around town built before we start out your way. You know that. It wasn't like we had a choice. We had to protect the assets here in town like the medical clinic and the food pantry and the older folks that can't protect themselves."

"Well, now you can," he answers dramatically. "We've made a decision, took a vote and that's the way it's gonna be."

"You didn't include any of us in this vote that you took, Mr. Hernandez," Grandpa observes. "How can that be a vote of the town?"

"It wasn't. It was a vote within our community. They want me to be the sheriff, too. We don't need your help anymore," he answers.

Reagan watches her grandfather's expression turn from cool to irritated. He's hiding it well, but she can recognize it. This guy is a fool if he thinks that his small community, some of which are women and children, will make it through the winter without their aid. She's also not sure if the voting system in their community was fair. Jay Hernandez is a very loud and boisterous man. He could've intimidated people into this. None of the people from his area who are present say anything. They don't appear to be cowed, but she's not sure since she doesn't know most of them all that well.

"We will get to expanding the wall in the spring, Jay," Grandpa adds. "You are over a mile outside of the city limits. It's just going to take some time."

"No thanks, McClane," he answers rudely.

Reagan doesn't think his disrespect for her grandfather, which is clearly increasing, is going to go over well with the men. John's thigh muscle tenses under her palm. Grandpa is certainly not the leader of their town. The sheriff is the acting authority. And in the spring they've talked about adding a new city council staff and a mayor, which will likely be whoever wants to volunteer. But most everyone in town looks up to her grandfather. He'd been their town doctor for over thirty years. He was considered a pillar of their small community. Jay Hernandez does not share this esteem of him obviously.

"We're on our own. We don't want anything to do with the town," Jay repeats.

Condo Paul says, "Why not? We didn't have a wall, either. We had to build our own. We're too far out to be a part of the town's wall, but that doesn't mean that we don't want to do business with the town or be a part of it anymore."

Jay keeps going, pissing off Reagan and the rest of the people, "We're busy working on building our own wall. It'll go up faster if we don't have to come over here and work on town stuff and harvest with the farmers."

Paul shakes his head and looks at John who mirrors his action. This makes no sense. Helping each other is the only way to survive.

"Wait a minute," Mr. Henderson breaks in.

Reagan knows that he owns one of the last chicken and hog farms in the county. Many of the big business grocery store chain farms had squeezed out people like Mr. Henderson. She thanks God that he never gave up. Those big farms are gone, abandoned by the employees who'd been poorly paid to work them. Mr. Henderson's meat chickens and pork feed nearly half of the community. She also knows that Jay's group is supposed to be helping him harvest his grain later this month. Without the grain, his livestock won't survive the winter. And if the coming winter proves to be like the last one, they are in for a long, hard season of cold and snow.

Mr. Henderson continues, "You mean to tell me that your group isn't going to help me bring in my crop?"

"No, we're not," Jay answers with a confident attitude.

"But I've been giving your people, Jay, food for the last two years. What do you think you're going to do for food all winter?"

Jay says, "We'll be fine. We have some new people living in our community now, and they've assured us that we won't starve."

John jumps in on this one, "Hold on! Who are these new people?"

"They're some men I trust, who our community trusts to help us make it through the winter and get our wall built."

"Who are they?" John presses. "We don't just allow people into the community, Jay. You know that. They have to be agreed upon."

"I'm one of 'em," a man says and stands.

He'd been sitting a few rows back from Jay, quietly taking in the discussion until now. The man is of average size and build and wears his hair in a short buzz cut.

"And you are?" Condo Paul asks.

"Greg, my name's Greg," he answers.

Some of the people who live in their town are not actually from their town, but transplants from other areas or extended family of people who used to be from their town. Usually, the men or Condo Paul or Roy will vet the newcomers to make sure they seem peaceful and able to contribute to their community. They don't need people like the visitor's group settling in their town.

Reagan looks to Grandpa, who seems to be trying to place this man's face. He gives her a nearly imperceptible shake of his head. She doesn't recognize Greg, either.

"Where you from, Greg?" Derek asks.

He's a master interrogator. Many times, Reagan just hangs back and watches him do his magic. All three of the Rangers are good at getting information from people. Derek had sniffed out a small group of people who'd come last year that he hadn't trusted. And it was a good thing. They'd robbed one of the local farmers before coming to their town. Kelly had found out about it from the farmer when he'd delivered a load of potato starts to them a week later. They'd gone on a mission looking for the thieves, but they were long gone by then. Fortunate for them.

"From Kentucky, up above Louisville," Greg answers.

"Where specifically above Louisville? What town?" Derek asks.

"What's it matter?" Greg asks.

"It actually matters quite a lot. We have a lot of people who have family up near Louisville," Derek says. "Perhaps you know some of them."

"Who are you? The new police around here?" Greg asks as if he's affronted by the questioning.

"Something like that," John says and stands. "Why don't you want to answer any of his questions?"

"I don't think I actually need to answer a bunch of questions. This is kind of bullshit. I'm not asking to live in your town. I'm going with Jay," Greg says with a touch of antagonism.

"We just try to ensure that we're keeping out the kind of people who would mean the town harm," Derek explains. "We've had problems with that. It doesn't usually end well for the people who come here looking for trouble."

Kelly laughs once and says, "No, it doesn't."

Greg's eyes dart to Kelly. He calms down considerably.

"So maybe some of the folks in this town know some of your people from Louisville," Derek returns to that line of questioning.

"I doubt it. I wasn't a real social kinda' guy back then."

"Ok, that's fine. How did you end up down here in Pleasant View?" Derek asks.

"Just movin' around, man. That's all," he answers.

"Why are you with Mr. Hernandez now?" Derek asks.

"Just thought I'd help him out. Stick around. Be a part of his new town. Like I said, this is new for me, too. I didn't use to be real social."

"Mm-hm, and you are now? You want to help Mr. Hernandez's community?" Derek presses.

"Sure. Sounds like a good place to set down some roots," Greg says.

"Do you have family or is it just you?" Derek asks.

Reagan watches her brother-in-law's face take on a tenseness. She doesn't think Derek is buying this guy's story.

"Nope, just me and a few of my friends," Greg says.

"A few?" John asks.

"Sure. I've got a few friends who are staying," Greg adds. "We'll get our wall done fast."

His accent sounds farther south than just Kentucky. He almost drawls out some of his vowels like Talia, and she's from New Orleans.

John jumps right back on the friend question, "How many men are staying with you?"

"Five. If you have to know," Jay answers for his new friend of whom none of them are familiar.

"And you mentioned food supplies. How are you going to keep the group in enough food for the winter?" Derek inquires.

"Look, we came to deliver our decision and we have done just that. This meeting is over, McClane," Jay says to Grandpa. "We don't answer to the town anymore. We don't interact with you all anymore. We're on our own and so are you."

"I wish it didn't have to be that way, Mr. Hernandez," Grandpa says.

Jay and Greg and the handful of people from their sector don't reply but simply leave without another word. Then a hundred questions get tossed around the room all at once.

Reagan has an uneasy feeling about the new situation with Jay's group. It doesn't make sense. They should want to stick with the town. This will be like starting over again. Why would they want to? She also doesn't understand why he is being disrespectful of her

37

grandfather. He seems angry, which is ridiculous since everyone has been helpful with this man and his group.

"That could've gone better," Derek says to their small circle that includes Roy and Paul once they have sequestered on the front steps of the town hall after the meeting adjourned.

"Seems fishy," Paul remarks.

John chuckles uneasily and says, "Yeah, man, no kidding. I don't think we've got the full picture of what's going on over there."

Kelly nods in agreement and says, "It feels like they are hiding something. None of that even made any sense. And who was that dick? He's a little cocky for just rolling into town, isn't he?"

Roy interjects, "He acts like he's callin' the shots over there."

John and Derek both nod. Grandpa does, as well.

"Something about it stinks. I hope we don't have problems with Jay's group," Reagan admits what she's been pondering.

"You mean Sheriff Jay?" John jokes.

As usual everyone chuckles at her nutty husband. Leave it to him to lighten the situation slightly. She wraps an arm around his waist as Roy leaves.

"Want to walk me down to the clinic? I want to check out our antibiotic supplies and add the ones that Cory brought home," she asks her handsome husband.

One of the teenagers in their town, Mark, jogs over to them. He came here with his family last year from Buffalo. His parents are Caucasian, but he and his younger brother are African American. They were orphaned when the first tsunami hit New York and were taken in by new people who assumed responsibility for them. The wife had led the family to find her grandmother here in Pleasant View, but the grandmother passed away shortly after they arrived.

Mark asks John, "Hey, Mr. Harrison, my dad wants to know if you could help him with his rifle. It jammed twice on him hunting turkeys the other day, and he just isn't able to get it unjammed and fixed, sir."

John looks at her and she smiles, "Go. I'll just run over to the clinic real quick and meet you back here."

"That wall isn't built yet, babe," John tells her. "You aren't going over there alone."

He calls over to Kelly, who is still shooting the crap with Condo Paul. Her brother-in-law agrees to babysit her. Reagan rolls her eyes at both of them.

"Glad to have your brother back?" she asks him as they start the half mile trek to the clinic.

Kelly actually smiles widely and says, "Hell yeah. He needs to keep his little ass home for good."

Reagan laughs at his crass language. "Little? He's damn near as big as you, Hulk. Do you think he'll leave again?"

"I sure as hell hope not, little Doc. He needs to get re-connected to the farm and to us. That'll hold him here. Wish he had a woman here. That would help."

"Maybe we should get Hannie on finding him one. She sure hooked you," Reagan jokes.

"No kidding," he says. "I had one damn foot out the door, but she reeled me in."

Reagan changes the tenor of their conversation because she is curious to get Kelly's opinion, "Think he'll be ok?"

Kelly pauses a long while as they continue their walk before answering, "I think so. It's hard to tell."

"Did you guys ever know anyone who was messed up like Cory?" she asks.

"Oh yeah, little Doc," he says sadly and lays a hand on her shoulder. "Yeah, we knew people like Cory. Sometimes they work it out. Others don't, not really. A lot of vets committed suicide for the very same reason, Reagan. They lose someone close to them, lost their buddies or friends in combat, and they can't get over it. I just pray that Cory has the strength to come out of it."

"Do you think he's been gone killing people, Kelly?" she asks as the clinic comes into view.

He sighs on a hard frown and nods.

"Yeah, I think so, too," she agrees.

Kelly unlocks the chain on the clinic door, and they enter the empty building.

39

"It might help him to be around the other young people on the farm that are close to his age," Reagan adds as she scans her inventory list. Some of the supplies that they normally keep at the farm have been moved to the clinic since the town is now doing twenty-four hour a day patrols. She and Grandpa still keep quite a lot out at the farm since they don't want to take any chances of a raid. "I'm just gonna leave a few bottles of this antibiotic he found and take the rest back home."

"Sounds good. Paul's been on patrol with the newbs training people this week in town. But I still think it's probably a pretty good idea not to leave everything here. Ya' never know," he foretells.

"Back to the subject of Cory, do you think it will be helpful to be around the other kids at the farm like Paige and Simon?" she asks.

Kelly purses his lips and thinks a moment before replying, "Maybe. He's always been close with Simon and Sam, but it doesn't sound like him and Paige got off to a good start. So, maybe."

Reagan laughs as they close up the clinic again. "No shit. She didn't look too fond of him. Of course, I wouldn't be either if he tackled me and scared the shit out of me in the woods like that."

Kelly laughs, too. "Yes, I can see how that might cause some tension."

"He's not exactly tiny, Kelly," Reagan says with a chuckle. "That would've been like a bulldozer hitting poor Paige, she's so frail."

"I don't think I'd call her frail," he corrects. "She's a tough cookie. I mean, hell Reagan, that kid lived over three years mostly on the road trying to get to Simon. She's one tenacious badass chic if you ask me."

"Yeah, no shit," Reagan agrees. "Lot tougher than me."

"I don't know about that, little Doc," he says and playfully bumps his shoulder against hers.

They head back toward the town hall to meet up with the rest of their group. The sun has set completely, which gives the town a spooky feeling. She's always on edge when they are in town after dark. There aren't street lamps anymore lighting the sidewalks and roads. No phosphorescent glow comes from the windows of the stores on the main drag. No traffic lights work. The only light in town is from the sparse illumination from inside homes. Most of the families in town are hooked up to solar power, thanks to the instructions of the men in her family and Paul, who'd helped them. But solar is not as strong or consistent as electricity, so most homes use it sparingly at night. Thus the limited lighting in the streets.

"Think Jay's gonna be a problem?" she asks as they draw near their destination.

He doesn't answer her, so Reagan looks up at him. When he stares directly down at her, she wishes he would stop. The honesty in his eyes is hard to bear.

Kelly foretells, "Yeah. Yeah, little Doc, they're gonna be a problem."

Chapter Four
Simon

A week later, Cory's friends from the armory in Ohio finally arrive in Pleasant View. The new sheriff of their town calls over the radio to let them know of the arrival. Since Simon doesn't have a patient, he and Cory jog over to the new entrance gate to greet his friends from up north. This is Cory's first trip to town since coming home, and they've been working all day on the wall. He and Cory had gone across town to check Paige's drawing to study an area that could be a potential breach spot for intruders. Before they even got to Simon's sister, they were interrupted by the new guests. Paige and Sam also follow along with them.

An older man standing near the big Army truck extends his hand to Simon in greeting. A young, attractive blonde comes forward and hugs Cory. He returns the greeting but stands back immediately after. A few of the children run over and hug his thick leg. Apparently these people really like his best friend. Simon sure does, and he's glad to have him home.

Cory introduces them to everyone in the vicinity, which is mostly McClane family representatives and a couple of the men from town. The family had informed the town of Cory's impending arrival of friends. For the past two days, he'd been getting increasingly anxious about whether or not they'd make it. He was planning on going out tomorrow to look for them. Now he doesn't have to.

"We have two empty homes a couple streets over ready for you guys," Cory informs the blonde.

She smiles widely at him before saying, "Sounds great, Cory. Lead the way!"

They will have roughly four adults in each home with a small number of children, too. They don't seem to care. As a matter of fact, they seem in awe of the small, efficient town and the minor amount of improvements that they've been able to make. Simon, on the other hand, is highly frustrated at the slow pace of progress they've made. There are simply just not enough hours in the day to get it all done. He has so many ideas for even more projects and improvements they could be doing. But before long, winter will be upon them again, which will make getting projects done more difficult.

They get the group settled in, introduced to their new neighbors and leave them to do their unpacking. They didn't have much, Simon noticed. It hadn't taken long to haul their meager possessions into the furnished homes. The one house belonged to the local butcher, a single man who'd been killed right at the beginning of the apocalypse. The other home belonged to a retired school teacher in her eighties who'd passed away less than a year ago. The people in town left the former owners' belongings and furnishings in the homes. Simon's glad that someone will be occupying the lonely, desolate homes. They have quite a few others in this town.

The remaining residents of Pleasant View, especially the new sheriff, hadn't been very open to the idea of having new people coming into their tiny town. Once they'd heard about the ammo and guns they were bringing, it had gone more smoothly, the medicine easier to swallow.

"I almost didn't recognize you, Cory," the blonde, Jackie, comments as the five of them including her young son walk to the clinic.

Cory chuffs through his nose, "Well, had to clean up. The family doesn't like it when I go full-on caveman."

She giggles, a light, high-pitched sound. This woman seems awfully fond of Cory. Simon takes a second to look at her more closely. She's very pretty, not very old, but likely older than Cory. She also walks closely next to Cory instead of walking ahead of them with Paige and Sam.

Simon says, "Yeah, we thought maybe a Cro-Magnon man was comin' out of the woods."

Jackie giggles again. She's a short, thin woman, her hair a pale blonde with matching eyebrows. Her brown eyes are warm with longing as she regards Cory.

"I like this look on you," she says. "You look rather handsome."

Up ahead of them, Paige snorts rather rudely. She has talked to him repeatedly about how much she doesn't like Cory and would like it if he moved back to the big house and out of "their" cabin. Simon has had to explain many times that the cabin belongs to him and Cory. He hates to hurt her feelings, but Cory was at the farm before her. It's not really a seniority thing, but Cory and the rest of them built the cabin by hand. It would be like evicting him out of his own house. Simon can't ask that of him. She will just have to get used to Cory living with them.

"Yeah, he just about killed Paige when he first got here!" Sam tosses over her shoulder.

Simon frowns unhappily.

"Well, I don't know if I'd put it that way, Sam," Simon tries to correct her.

Paige, of course, jumps in, "Yes, he did!"

"Beanpole doesn't like me too well," Cory says with a cocky smirk to his friend, Jackie. "In case you couldn't tell."

To prove his point, Paige sneers over her shoulder at them. Simon doesn't really like it when Cory calls his sister a beanpole. In Cory's defense, Simon's heard Paige call him far worse. They clearly don't like each other, which makes it difficult for him. He'd definitely called that one wrong. He'd thought many times that those two would get along and that he couldn't wait for Cory to come home and meet her. He always assumed they'd be fast friends.

"Cory, don't call her that," Simon tells him

"Sorry, bro," Cory says, although he doesn't say it with any truly genuine feeling. "It's true, though. She hates my guts!"

"And don't forget it, either," Paige says without turning around.

"Ok, you two," Sam scolds.

"Let it go already, beanpole," Cory remarks with sarcasm.

"You threatened to kill me!" she hisses angrily.

"Oh, my!" Jackie remarks with unconcealed surprise.

"Minor misunderstanding," Cory antagonizes with a nonchalant shrug and waves his hand, dismissing the charge.

"Misunderstanding my ass! You tried to kill me," Paige continues her argument.

Luckily Jackie's son has skipped ahead and is running and chasing Cory's dog. The kids at the farm finally named her Shadow. It was better than Damn Dog, which is what Cory had confided to Simon was her real name. She sleeps most nights out in their cabin.

"What ass?" Cory asks. "You don't have an ass, ya' skinny beanpole."

"Cory," Simon warns. He hardly means it, though. Policing these two could be a full-time job if he wanted it, which he does not.

"Well, she doesn't," Cory remarks on a smart-aleck smirk.

Great, now Simon is looking at his own sister's butt. Gross. He groans. Her butt is narrow and lean just like the rest of her. His sister is built like a lithe gazelle, all long limbs and sleek muscle tone. Her body is completely different from Sam's. She is short and curvy and soft. Everything about her is petite, including her delicate bone structure and tiny face.

He has tuned out the usual jabbing by his sister and Cory and is instead staring at Sam in front of him. Her black ponytail swishes back and forth in time with her hips. She's still in her beige riding pants from their morning patrol at the farm. He wishes she wouldn't wear those when they come to town. They are way too snug and outline her every curve. Luckily her t-shirt is too big on her and is baggy and shapeless. He believes that her shirt used to belong to her older brother. It has the name of some church youth group she'd mentioned to him once. She has a few of her brother's shirts that she likes to wear to keep her dead family fresher in her memory. He knows what lies under that shirt that is too big. They've been swimming in the lake at the farm quite a few times over the last four years. He'd walked in on her when she was changing. She'd been pressed up against him in the hayloft when they'd slept there after the Target group's attack on the farm. He knows what hides under there, and the image of her burns behind his closed eyelids at night when he crashes at the end of the day.

Sam glances over her shoulder at him and smiles, rolls her bright blue eyes and turns back. He doesn't return it but scowls instead. He knows she is only smiling conspiratorially at him over the two combatants in their group, but he can't even manage a grin. His thoughts about her have turned lewd and inappropriate on every level. He can't afford to have these thoughts about her. It's not right.

They arrive at the clinic where Cory introduces Jackie to Reagan and Doc. She is amiable and sweet. She's also incredibly grateful to have been invited into their small community. She chats with Doc about her background as a dental hygienist, offering her services. They are none too happy to take her up on her offer since they have not been able to provide dental services yet. With the winter season fast approaching, it's hard telling what they'll see this year as far as sickness goes and adding to that is the lack of dental care people are receiving which isn't going to help. He's just glad he got his braces removed a few months before the fall. Pulling those suckers off with a pair of pliers would've been painful.

"Hey, Simon," Reagan says, taking him to the side. "Will you and Sam clean up the last two exam rooms and pack up our gear? I still have one more patient and so does Grandpa. Paige can help, too, if you want. You don't mind, do you?"

"No, that's no problem, Reagan," he tells her. "I don't need help, though. I can probably do it myself."

"I can help!" Sam offers with a bright smile.

She's obviously overheard their conversation, as usual. He should've known. She's never far from him. Simon grimaces and walks away.

"I'm going over to the wall where John and Kelly are working. I want to check on an area where I think we can make an improvement," Paige says.

"Ok, well, you guys work it out," Reagan says. "I'm headed back in to get my last patient."

Doc also leaves, Jackie hangs around with Cory, and Simon prepares to clean rooms.

"I'll walk you over to the build site," Cory says to Paige.

She retorts with, "No thanks."

Simon barks testily, "Paige! Just let him. Good grief, we don't have the wall done yet. You know the rules. None of the women in our group just go bee-bopping around town without one of us. You don't even have a weapon today."

His sister looks offended, which makes Simon feel like crap. He's not as frustrated with her as he is with himself.

"Fine," she mumbles.

"Can you guys drop me back at my new house?" Jackie asks kindly.

"Sure thing," Cory says to her, grinning down into her brown eyes. "Then I'll escort the beanpole over to the work site."

"Ugh," Paige complains and storms out the front door.

Cory and Jackie follow after her, also taking her son and Damn Dog.

"I'll take room three. You can have room two," he grumbles.

"Ok," Sam perks up and bounces off to clean the exam room.

As he sanitizes and re-organizes the room, stacking equipment and storing things away, he has time to reflect on his friend. Cory has been leaving every night after dark and not returning until nearly dawn each morning. When he'd questioned him, Cory had told him not to worry about it. He doesn't know where his friend is going at night when he leaves, but soon he plans to follow him and find out for himself.

"Need help? I'm all done," Sam offers from the open door a short while later. She's usually faster than him at sanitizing the rooms.

"No, I've got this," Simon tells her.

She ignores him, comes into the small exam room and helps anyway. When they finish, they go to the storage room to collect the basketsful of items that get taken back to the farm for safe keeping.

47

The light is the dimmest back in this space, and they usually need to use flashlights to better see. The solar power at the clinic is not as powerful as the system that fuels the big house back at the farm.

Sam bumps into him occasionally, which does nothing to calm his nerves around her. He reaches over her head to a shelf above her and pulls down a basket of syringes.

"Excuse me," he tells her cordially. Simon has been trying his best to keep things light and emotionless around Sam ever since she'd drawn that picture of him in the woods. That had been too intimate, too much of a personal examination of him. He has no idea why Sam would draw pictures like that of him, but he hopes it doesn't happen again.

She just chuckles at him, "No problem, Dr. Murphy."

Sam uses his last name and this ridiculous title when she's behaving impertinently. She knows that it irritates him.

"Sam," he reproaches. "You know I'm not a doctor. Don't call me that."

"Close enough," she argues and tugs her ponytail free of its rubber band. "Phew, that was giving me a headache. I try to wear my hair pulled back when we're at the clinic, but it makes my head sore after a while, ya' know?"

Simon just shakes his head at her with the usual amount of confusion and frustration he has where she is concerned. Her head gets sore because she has a thin little neck and too much hair. No wonder she gets headaches. Her thick, lush locks have grown completely out again after the butchering she'd given herself four years ago to make herself unattractive. She could shave her head bald and she'd still be just as demure and appealing although she doesn't know it. He places the emptied basket back above her head on a shelf and tries not to think of her soft hair that had brushed against his bare bicep when she'd pulled it free of its snare.

"Simon's new friends seem nice, especially Jackie," Sam remarks.

"Yeah, sure," Simon agrees.

"Where are the trays?" she asks, mostly of herself. "Oh, found them."

"They don't have very many young people with them, though," Sam says as she places sterilized surgical instruments back into the metal tray.

"Why would you care about that?"

She shrugs and says, "I don't know. Maybe I was hoping they would've brought a truck full of cute boys!"

Simon stops dead in his tracks.

"What? Is that supposed to be funny?" he demands.

Sam chuckles at him arrogantly.

"Why would you care?" she asks as she stacks more items on the shelf beside them.

"Stop trying to antagonize me, Samantha," he reprimands.

Sam just laughs at him again.

He's moved to the shelving unit behind them and is taking gauze and bottles of herbs and placing them in the basket at his feet. Sam scoots around him and drops more bandaging and syringes into it. They both reach for a package of sterilized instruments at the same time. Her small hand lands on top of his. Her soft touch leaves a burning sensation on the back of his hand. He can't believe she would actually want a truck full of cute boys to come to their town. That's not like her at all. She's afraid of most men. But something about her saucy attitude and insinuation grinds at his nerves.

"Oh, you've got that one? Sorry," she needlessly apologizes.

Before she can remove her hand, Simon flips his over and holds onto her fragile wrist. The intensely sweet smell of her rushes at him in a wave. It is likely from her recently freed hair that is perfumed with the scent of the clean, herb-tinged soap from the farm. Maybe it's the poor lighting or the contrast of her black hair and pale skin, but when her eyes meet his, they seem on fire. The bright blue color of her eyes positively glows in the dark, bleak room. Long strands of her black hair have fallen forward and cover her shoulder and hang down almost to her breast.

Simon takes a deep breath and tries to keep himself in check. It doesn't help when she's staring at him with that puzzled, innocent look and parted, dewy lips.

"What is it?" she inquires so unknowingly.

49

He swallows hard and shakes his head. His resolve is gone, long gone. The beating of his heart is as loud as a group of tribal drummers on a deserted island. Very slowly, very calmly, Simon releases her hand, placing it for some absurd reason back down at her side as if she couldn't have managed to do so on her own.

"Simon?" Sam asks.

Then she wets her bottom lip with her tongue, not suggestively, not in a way that would be lascivious because he knows that she does not think that way. But it's more than he can take because he *does* think that way. He thinks that way about Sam all the time. Lately, that's all he does. He thinks about Sam when he's studying medical journals. He ponders her soft curves when he's supposed to be on patrol in the middle of the night at the farm. He examines the soft shapes of her delicate face while he's milking a cow and she's yammering away beside him about who knows what. When they ride together, he finds himself staring at her thighs gripping the horse's sides or her small hands that are so soft yet firm on the reins. He can't even let himself think about the flirty arch of her black eyebrows or the dark pink of her small mouth.

"What is it, Simon? Is something wrong?" she asks again and bites her lower lip.

"Damn it," he swears under his breath, earning a startled expression from Sam.

Simon sinks his hands into the hair at either side of her face and snatches her to him. Her surprised yelp gets smothered as his mouth covers hers in a kiss that nearly buckles his knees. Hers do, though, and he has to hold her up. He's not sure if he's frightened her, but he also doesn't know if he could've stopped himself from doing this, either. He's wanted to kiss her for so long, since the first day he'd found her hiding on the floor of her closet. Her fragile, doll face has beckoned him ever since.

He staggers forward, bumping them both into the shelving unit. His dirty leather work-boots scuff against the tile floor. Not wanting her to get hurt by the steel shelf behind her head, or at least that's what he tells himself, Simon removes his hands from her face and wraps them around her middle. He lifts her clean off the ground and up close to his front, up against his chest like she'd fallen asleep that night in the barn. Her stifled squeal of surprise is brief as his mouth covers hers again. He kisses her thoroughly, letting the need for her that has grown for so long explode from him. His tongue slips past her teeth as he ravages her tiny, Cupid's bow mouth.

Her arms wrap around his neck, fingers sliding into his hair, which causes him to groan. His hands slide down and cover the tops of her thighs, then under her bottom, that same bottom he'd been staring at during the walk to the clinic. The perfect, heart-shaped bottom that he's caught himself staring at many, many times in these same stretchy tight riding pants.

"Oh, fuck!" Reagan yells from the door. "Shit! Sorry!"

Simon immediately drops Samantha to the ground, and they separate as fast as humanly possible. Reagan spins and flees from the storage room as if she has spied a snake on the floor. Simon is left standing awkwardly with Sam, but the mood is gone as if a bucket of ice water has been sloshed over his head. And his hormones.

"I'm sorry," he stutters. "That was a mistake."

"It was?" Sam asks and touches her fingertips to her reddened lips.

Simon rakes a hand through his red hair, tousling it and probably making it stand on end. He is the most disgusting, amoral man alive. He feels like he might vomit.

"I…we should never… I'm…that was disgusting," he blurts on a single, held breath. He actually meant to say that *he* is disgusting, but so many thoughts had popped into his idiotic brain at the same time that it came out wrong.

"That was dis…. What?" Sam asks brokenly with tears in her eyes and also flees the room.

Simon can't respond. It is like his mouth is filled with dried bread crumbs. He feels like either punching something, someone or doing something violent. Crap. He's a total scumbag, no better than the Target men. No better than… him. He's no better than him, Bobby, his cousin who'd stolen her youth and so much more. He'd promised himself that he'd always take care of her, protect Sam from men that would hurt her again. And here he is behaving just like those men.

Reagan reappears at the door to the storage room where he is still rooted to the same spot, his muscles shaking with an unrequited need for Sam and an anger and an untapped rage at himself.

"Hey, sorry about that," Reagan apologizes. "I didn't know that you…"

"It's fine," Simon tells her. "That won't ever happen again. I'm gonna move into town, leave the farm."

Simon moves to squeeze past her, but Reagan snatches his arm. Her small hand on his bicep is nothing like what Sam had made him feel with her hand on his. Reagan is like his foul-mouthed, yet intelligent older sister. He loves her like crazy, nearly as much as he loves Paige. He loves all the McClane girls, but Reagan even more because they've worked so closely over the years as she'd patiently taught him medicine and anatomy and physiology and about diseases. He can barely even look her in the eye. His guilt is at an all-time high.

"The hell you are," she argues. "Don't even say shit like that, Simon. We need you on the farm. You know that. You know better than to even suggest leaving."

"I can't be around her," he confesses. He still feels like he might vomit. His face and neck and chest feel flush and hot. He wishes Reagan would move out of his way.

"Why not, Simon? You obviously care about her."

"It's wrong. It's sick. I'm a disgusting pig," he says and looks at the doorframe.

"What are you talking about? Why would you say such a thing? I mean, I'm not good with relationship shit and all, but that certainly doesn't make any sense. You're a really good person, Simon."

He shakes his head, "Please, don't say that."

"Why not? Hey, talk to me. What's going on here?"

"Just don't tell anybody you saw me doing that. They'd all be so disappointed in me, especially your grandfather. I don't think I could bear it."

"Why would anybody be disappointed in you? Sam's eighteen. It's not like you're trying to sleep with a married woman or molest a kid, Simon. Sam is an adult and so are you."

He flinches. Sometimes he wishes Reagan was just a bit less blunt. Or crude.

"Just don't tell anyone. Please," he begs.

"Sure, I won't say anything. But I still don't understand," she confides.

"Sam… she… she's a good girl, ya' know?"

"Duh, of course she is. So are you, idiot. You're a good man," Reagan says impatiently.

"You don't understand, Reagan," he returns with a touch of frustration. "I have to take care of her, look out for her."

"We all do, Simon," she tells him. "It's not like that's your job alone. We all look out for each other. That's how this works, dummy."

He grimaces at her insult but is more than used to it.

"I failed her before. I can't ever do that again. I have to keep her safe, even if that means keeping her safe from me," he answers, his hands shaking and notices the surprised expression on Reagan's face.

Simon squeezes past her and rushes from the clinic. He doesn't know where Sam went, but he jogs down to the wall building site. He knows that he owes her an explanation, but he can't face her just yet. It doesn't take long to find Cory at the build. Some hard work alongside his best friend should help to quell his roller coaster emotions. Then he remembers that Sam always calls *him* her best friend. The vomit feeling comes back.

Chapter Five
Cory

A few days after his armory friends arrive in town, Cory and the men spend a long day working on the farm bringing in the final cutting of hay for the summer. He's stacking the last dozen bales for the horses up in the hay loft as the others put away and clean the equipment.

"Hey, Cory," Sam says from the ladder, her head poking up through the hole in the floor to the loft.

"Hey, kid," he calls over to her. "Watcha' up to?"

She shrugs and climbs the rest of the way up to stand near him. She's carrying her sketchpad and a little pouch full of pencils and erasers.

She rushes over and attempts to lift a heavy, oblong bale, "Here, I can help!"

Cory just smiles and takes her by the elbow, leading her to a bale where he places her on her bottom.

"Just sit and keep me company, little sister," he instructs.

"I wish I was bigger or stronger like you… or taller," she says on a frown.

Cory laughs and replies, "No, you're just fine the way you are, Sam. You don't change a hair on your head, kiddo. You do stuff around here that I wouldn't have a clue how to do like making soap or beeswax or biscuits or taking care of the chickens with Hannie.

You do help out. You also help out a lot with the little kids. You don't need to be anything but what you are."

She smiles under his warm praise. Her bright blue eyes twinkle. Sam still looks like a kid to him, even though she's an adult now. There is a youthful innocence about her that makes him feel fiercely protective of her, makes everyone in the family feel protective of her. He knows his best friend feels especially protective of Sam. He also knows that her innocence was taken from her by that son of a bitch, Bobby, who'd nearly destroyed her. But there is still something innocent, childlike even, about Sam. Each of them carries a lot of baggage around with them. Some of it is so heavy that it causes a crippling, permanent damage. Sam is just better at hiding hers.

"Thanks, Cory," she says.

"Drawing anything cool?" he asks. Her art is insanely good. She could've had a successful career as an artist in some capacity if the world hadn't fallen apart, even though he knows her passion was for horses.

She extends her pad, showing her current drawing which is of the men in town building the wall around it. The detail with which she has captured the different materials used to build the wall is crazy. Every rivet in the steel sheeting, the grain in the wood they've used, the men who are contributing to the build, down to the clothing they all wear are all there in every minute detail. He and Simon are even in the drawing. It's literally like looking at a black and white photograph of the build site.

"This is amazing, kiddo," he tells her. She just gives her usual modest shrug.

"Thanks," she replies.

She tucks her sketch into her backpack, stores the rest of her supplies and waits patiently while he finishes stacking the hay.

"Are you and Paige getting along any better?" she asks him while fiddling with twigs of hay sticking out of the bale on which she sits.

He smirks and say, "Yeah, sure. We're best friends now, didn't you hear? We're probably gonna braid each other's hair later."

Samantha laughs gaily at this and shakes her head, sending her black ponytail swishing back and forth.

"Cory!" she chastises half-heartedly. "She's really sweet."

Cory chuffs and says, "Mm-hm. I'll take your word for it."

"She is. She's really nice and kind and so pretty. Gosh, she's like some sort of tall, graceful supermodel. I feel like a dwarf around her… or a hobbit."

Her joking makes him laugh. She's always been able to make him laugh. He stops quickly, though. It feels wrong to laugh. He hasn't laughed since his sister was killed. Laughter in a world without Em feels so wrong. She was the one who brought laughter and smiles and joy to this sickening, ugly world. Without her in it, Cory just doesn't feel right about doing it.

"You're not a hobbit, Samantha," he says. "You are way prettier than that beanpole. She's a hag."

"Cory," she scolds with sincerity. "That was just plain mean. Give her a chance. You know she's not a hag. She's gorgeous."

Cory gives a good snort of derision and says, "If you say so. Might wanna' get your eyes checked, kiddo. Maybe Simon can examine them."

"Here, look at this," she says, removing her drawing tablet again.

She flips to a page and leans it toward him. There is a black and white charcoal of Paige there. Cory is astonished by the degree with which Sam has captured her. A soft wave of her hair is covering part of her face. The sprinkling of freckles covers the bridge of her nose and crests of her cheeks. The fiery light of her eyes comes through the shadows.

"That's a heck of a picture, Sam," Cory says, impressed.

"I'm not showing it to brag, I'm showing it so that you can see how magnificent she is, Cory," Sam corrects him with a chuckle.

"You'd be better off drawing the horses instead of wasting your time on this red-haired witch," Cory remarks with sarcasm, trying to deflect her praise of Paige.

"Cory!" Sam shouts with a laugh. "You're so mean."

He's saying this, but he has looked at Simon's sister and found something other than haggard looks and a beanpole body. She is tall, admittedly so. But Paige is also supermodel good-looking as Sam had described her. Her face is very different than any other woman's. It's odd and unusual, but that's what makes her beautiful. Her mouth is too full. Her eyebrows are too fair. Her cheekbones are too high. Plus, she has a set of long, lean gams on her that could stop traffic. However, he's not interested in her because she's also a mega-bitch and, more importantly, his best friend's sister. There are certain boundaries that even an apocalypse can't tear down. Bro's before ho's and all. He's not interested in a serious relationship with anyone, so he'd only be looking for a purely non-platonic, solely sexual release with her which he's not too sure Simon would appreciate. He's bigger than Simon, but his friend is a pretty good shot so Cory won't go sniffing for trouble where he doesn't need to. He does like messing with her, though. She's got a bad temper to match her hair, so it's a fun past-time pissing her off. She's still got a bug up her butt about his death threat in the woods. He'd like to tell her to lighten up, but he's not sure if her gun skills match her brother's.

"Ready, kid?" he asks and pulls Sam to her feet again. She's wearing riding boots, but Cory doesn't remember seeing her out riding this morning. "Going riding later?"

"Reagan and I were going to, but she ended up having to work on canning with Sue and Hannah instead," she answers.

"She ought to be in a good mood," he jokes, getting a chuckle from Sam.

"I know, right?" she answers. "We can't ride today because I'm watching the little ones later after dinner. Don't forget. We're supposed to be having a meeting tonight. Lots to go over."

"There is always a lot to go over," he replies sarcastically as they leave the barn and walk toward the house. "Catch ya' later."

"Ok, Cory," she says over her shoulder and disappears into the kitchen.

Cory pulls off his t-shirt and tries to wipe most of the hay from his sticky, sweaty chest and stomach while standing at the bottom of the porch stairs. He doesn't want to drag half the barn's hay in onto Hannah's clean floors. His arms come next. Removing the tiny, annoying pieces of hay from his body and mostly from his shirt will make it easier for the women to do his laundry. The laundry usually gets done two days a week. Everything is brought to the big house and whoever is available to help Hannah and Sue pitches in. It's a laborious job with so many people living on the farm. Cory and Simon usually carry all of the soiled and then laundered and folded baskets full of laundry back to each person's room or cabin for them. It's easier for them to be the runners than to have the women carry armloads and basketsful of clean laundry. The work they do on the farm is exhausting enough without hiking out to the cabins and up and down the four stories of the big house. Whichever men are around the house always chip in and help. Most of the time, however, they are out in the fields or working on equipment or lately in town working on the wall. But the hauling job always goes to them.

Paige and Kelly come around the corner. She's toting a rolled up paper, like an architect would carry, as she walks beside his brother. She has an unfeminine manner of walking like a tomboy.

Kelly starts in with, "Grow out of that shirt, too, little brother?"

He chuckles and shakes his head. "Nah, I think I'm done growing."

Kelly quips before he goes inside, "Let's hope, man. Let's hope."

"What are you doing?" Paige asks hesitantly.

Cory notices that she doesn't come closer to him but keeps her distance.

"Trying to get most of the hay out of my shirt. Helps the girls when they do the washing," he answers as he continues to rub and pick at the bits of hay stuck to his sweaty stomach. And because he can't resist, "Wanna' help?"

Her top lip actually curls on one side with disgust, "Pass."

"You sure?" he teases. "Probably haven't seen anything that looks like this in a while." Cory indicates toward his stomach muscles and even flexes to expose more ridges. His body has literally been transformed in the last four years from the hard work, military workouts, and running. Gone is the lean and lanky teen body that he used to own. When he was gone, he kept up on his workouts, doing sit-ups, chin-ups and push-ups along with running- not counting the running he did in stalking mode and then skirmishes.

"I see it every night when I take my shower, you fool," she comes back at him and lifts her t-shirt to show off her own toned stomach.

Then she snatches the hem of her shirt back down and stalks irately into the house. Cory is left standing there looking like the fool she'd called him. That wasn't the answer he'd been expecting. He thought she'd either cower or be impressed by his physique. Other women were. He also hadn't suspected that she was quite that toned out underneath her clothing. He's never seen her working out or doing much of the work at all on the farm other than getting in the way of everyone else who is working. She's mostly a pain in the ass, truth be told. But Simon told him that she used to like running and that she'd done so in school. She actually had a small six pack. Impressive. Small, but impressive, nonetheless. It was also sexy, but he's not going to tell her that. She's still a mean, pain in his ass bitch.

He heads straight to the mudroom to scrub up, ends up waiting in line for the sink behind the chattering kids and grabs a t-shirt from the clean laundry pile in the cabinet when he's done. He's not sure which person the shirt belongs to. It is probably something that was brought back on a raid, since he seriously doubts that any of the family used to be NY Giants fans. It's a tad too tight, but he's not changing again. The women keep a stash of shirts in the old maple cabinet in the mudroom for the men to change into without going to their rooms or out to the cabins for fresh shirts. Jackets and shirts are what get the dirtiest with jeans following at a close second. Reagan also borrows from this pile sometimes. She's not exactly a fashion diva, so she couldn't care less if she's wearing one of the men's t-shirts. As usual, Cory is the last one to the dinner table, and he tries to ignore the stern expression Hannah is shooting in his direction. He loves his dainty sister-in-law, but she can be rather terrifying.

The seating arrangements have been set up to make better use of space, but it's still crowded. He'd rather just go eat in the kitchen or on the back porch or out in his cabin, but he knows that it

59

would break Hannah's heart. Hurting her would be too much. Pissing her off could be detrimental to his health.

Reagan had told him that Hannah took the loss of Em very hard and has been depressed for months. She also said that since he's been home, she's seen a slight improvement in Hannah's attitude. He'd lob off his left arm to take away her grief if it would work.

"Paige has an idea for the wall," Derek says when the prayer wraps.

Cory helps himself to roasted chicken baked with fresh herbs from the garden. He grabs a roll, too, before the bread basket gets passed by him. He missed the home-cooking when he was gone. This is so much better than a rabbit on a spit over an open fire. Damn Dog also appreciates the table scraps more than she did his crispy, charred fire pit disasters.

"Go ahead, Paige," Doc encourages.

"Well, I'm thinking that we have a good amount of reinforcement going on inside with the support braces, but what if we used cement barriers on the outside?" she suggests.

"Where would we get something like that?" John asks.

"Out by the freeway. There have to be some still out there that we could move into town," Kelly says.

"Either that," she says, "or we could cut telephone poles and bury them about three feet, leaving three to four feet or more sticking out of the ground. That would stop a vehicle from even getting close."

"Right," Cory jumps in as he helps himself to roasted potatoes and carrots. "Stagger them, too, to create an even wider margin of intimidation."

"Exactly!" Paige says. "We also need to discuss what we're going to do on the south side project."

She certainly does chirp up when she's talking about construction projects, Cory's noticed. He hates to admit it, he really hates to admit it, but her drawings of the wall build have helped immensely. It helps them stay on track and avoid errors. They can't afford setbacks or wasted materials. She's a very talented architect.

He's never telling her this. Hell freezing over wouldn't even get it out of him.

The south side is the other end of town where they are having more difficulty with the wall because of the terrain. He's still thinking about her flat stomach and couldn't give a hoot about the wall.

"We need a bulldozer or a tractor with a loader," John says.

"I know, but that's probably not gonna happen. We need to conserve gas," Derek corrects.

Kelly adds, "We may just have to do the best we can over there. The wall just might not be as strong on that end of town."

"What are some of our alternatives?" Doc throws out.

Paige jumps in, "If we cut off three streets, then we could shorten the distance of the build and not need to go that far."

"That would likely eliminate a good ten homes full of families," Doc says.

"Right, they'd just have to condense into other houses in the enclosed sector or bunk up with other families," she adds.

Doc shakes his head. "I don't think they will go for that. I know at least two of those families out there. They've been living in Pleasant View for decades. We'd be asking them to leave their homes unattended, which would likely also leave them open to being raided and looted."

"We need a different solution," Derek says.

Cory is remembering Paige's smooth skin on her stomach and wondering what it would feel like under his hands.

"Cory!" Kelly grumbles as if he's said his name ten times.

"What? What'd I miss?" he asks.

"Did you see anything that people were using in any of the walled-up cities out there that could help?" his brother asks with a deep scowl of impatience.

"I don't know," he admits but then adds, "Why don't we just put up chain link fencing or whatever we can find and then top it off with razor wire? I mean, if it's good enough for a prison, it's good enough for our town."

"Would that work?" John asks almost rhetorically.

Doc purses his lips in contemplation. Kelly and Derek look to one another.

"I think it would," Paige answers. "It's a high spot, high on that hill with the drop-off on the other side which is what's making it so difficult to work around. So it's not likely that someone could ram through it in vehicles. Of course, unless they have a tank or something. But the problem is the fencing structure itself. It wasn't ever going to be as stable as the heavy duty materials we're using everywhere else in the town because we can't get a good support system to hold it up. So, maybe your chain link idea would work, knuckle-dragger. It's not going to stop bullets, but it should prevent humans from walking right through down on the south side."

"It also wouldn't stop sniper fire," Cory says as he stuffs bread into his mouth to stop himself from returning her insult. He stares openly at Paige, thinking about her face, criticizing the angles and arches. Ok, so Sam is right. She is rather beautiful. Her eyes dart around nervously seeking approval from the family. She clearly doesn't feel like she fits in with everyone yet.

"No, but hopefully the people doing patrols would be alerted to something like that before it ever happened and can sound the alarm to people in town," Reagan says.

Jacob is at her side begging to be excused from his dinner in the other room so that he can go outside with the other kids to play. She kisses his cheek and sends him on his way.

"A wire fence is going to be easy to cut with the right tools or equipment," Kelly says. "It's not the same as trying to come through a solid sheet of steel or plywood like we're using elsewhere."

"We'll just have to make sure that we brief the people doing the patrols in town that the south side area will need to be covered more frequently than the more secure areas," John offers.

"Ok, great," Reagan says. "Now where the hell are we gonna get razor wire and chain link fencing?"

The men look to one another.

"We're gonna have to hit building supply centers," Cory offers. "See if they have anything left like that. If not, then we could get it from a prison or military installation. When I was at the armory, it was acres upon acres of fencing. We could yank it out of the ground and take it."

Hannah pipes in, "That could be dangerous. I don't think you should go as far as that would take to gather those kinds of supplies."

Kelly quickly grasps her free hand, since Mary had insisted on sitting on her mother's lap and is being held back from grabbing everything in sight by Hannah's other hand. She's a handful already. Cory is mad about his tiny niece. She's a feisty, adorable runt.

John adds, "We could hit Fort Campbell for chain-link fencing and supplies if it hasn't been looted or taken over. As long as it's still abandoned."

"Where's that?" Hannah asks nervously.

"Not far, Hannie. Just up the road in Kentucky," John answers.

"It'll be ok, baby," Kelly consoles Hannah gently. "We've gone there before. It was empty."

"Right, Hannie," Reagan says. "These guys will be just fine. They've done runs enough damn times over the years. They've got it down to a fine art."

"I don't know," Hannah says weakly. "And stop cursing at the dinner table like a heathen," she adds not so weakly.

"I can go, too," Paige offers.

Cory chokes on his drink of water. Then he laughs obnoxiously. It can't be helped. "Yeah, right! Like we'd take you with us."

"What?" she counters defensively. "I'm good at sneaking around. Gavin and I did that all the time. How do you think we got our own supplies?"

"Sneaking around?" John asks.

She replies, "Yes, sneaking, being stealthy. That's what we did. That way we didn't have to fight it out with people because we didn't always have ammo or even a gun, let alone a bunch of them as you all have."

"Well, we don't worry so much about being stealthy, so you can stay here," Cory chides.

"You aren't really trained, either, sis," Simon adds, getting a glare from his sister. "We don't let anyone go with us that hasn't been trained. You know that. We've just been very busy, but we'll get you trained."

"I'm sneaky, though. I've survived almost four years on my own with my two friends and a toddler!"

"You need training," Reagan says. "Trust me, I've seen you shoot." She laughs bawdily.

Paige grins, exposing dimples in her cheeks and says, "Ok, so I'm not the greatest with the guns, but I can help."

"Cory and Simon can work with you on shooting and learning our operating procedures," John says. "I wouldn't have a problem with you going if you are trained by them."

"This isn't going to be something that we can haul back in one load," Kelly adds. "That is a vast amount of square footage that we have to cover on that side of town. It's going to take multiple runs. If you do the proper training, then maybe you'll get to go on one of them. Plus, we should have townspeople going on runs for it without us, too."

"All right," Paige agrees with a nod. "I want the training anyway. I don't want to be the only loser on the farm who can't protect it."

"I don't know about that!" Sue says. "You did pretty well the night it was attacked by the Target freaks."

"I got taken for hostage!"

Doc quips, "Minor detail."

Everyone laughs, and the family moves on to a more uplifting topic. Cory doesn't like the fact that Paige was taken hostage by anyone, that any man had felt brave enough to grab her. He would feel the same about anyone on the farm, but Simon's sister had been assaulted. Nobody should have the balls to even step foot onto McClane land, let alone man-handle his best friend's sister. She's a skinny twerp. It's bullshit that she was hurt. The escapees have a bounty on their heads, a bounty set there by him. Revenge is the payment on this bounty. And he'll have his.

Hannah eventually says, "Your friend stopped by yesterday when you were in town."

"Talia? How is she? How's Maddie?" Paige asks.

"They're doing great. She is getting along quite well with Bertie, and Maddie is adjusting to living over there. Chet's crazy about her, about them both," Hannah relays.

"We should have their wedding next weekend as we originally planned," Doc says. "No sense in delaying it just because of the wall build. If they are going to live together over there, then they ought to be married. It's only right."

And for this reason alone, Cory doesn't tell anyone about his situation with Evie Johnson, their neighbor's widowed daughter. He also won't mention his relationship with Jackie from the armory. Doc would flip his lid. Cory has visited Evie once since he's been home but hasn't met with Jackie. She's living in a house full of people and her small son. He thinks that breaking it off with her soon would be for the best. It should go well since they hadn't made a commitment to their relationship being serious or long-term. At least he thinks it should go well. Women are mostly a mystery to him and highly illogical.

"I guess we better get it figured out and planned then," Sue says. "Some of us women can go over tomorrow to talk with Bertie and Talia."

The conversation finishes and so does their dinner. The table cleared and the rush to complete whatever chores didn't get done yet ensues. Cory moves his stallion to the second horse pasture since Reagan told him that there is a mare in season over there. Keeping the herd going is imperative. It's also important to breed the horses for use in trade. His stud blasts through the gate, spotting his mate waiting for him. Soon the screaming and fighting and eventual mating will happen. They don't need an audience.

On his way back, he spots Paige trying to open the gate to the horse pasture closer to the barn. She's attempting to turn out a mare that was locked in the barn recovering from a cut on her hip. The woman is having zero luck. The other horses have bunched up at the gate on the other side. It happens. They just want to see what the other mare is up to and greet their friend.

"Get back, you stupid pricks," Paige hisses under her breath at the horses.

She apparently thinks nobody is around to hear her expletives. Cory chuckles and steps into her line of sight, startling her. She's barely got the mellow old mare she's handling under control. Good thing she doesn't have Jet. He'd literally give her a run for her money.

"Need some help?" he offers.

"Hell yes, I need help! What's it look like?"

He snatches the lead line out of her hand and gives it a sharp snap with his wrist near the horse's jaw. It's enough to settle the mare right down.

"Back, back, good girl," he urges the mare a few steps away from the gate and then unlatches it. "Just show them who is the boss. That should be easy for you. They were probably pissed at you for calling them pricks. These *are* mares, after all."

"Well, they're all stupid!" she scoffs irritably. "I don't care what the hell sex they are."

"My stallion would beg to differ," he jokes as he shows her how to shoo away the horses on the other side of the gate. He breezes right through with the mare, careful not to let the gate hit the horse in the rump, which is a good way to startle them and get run over in the process.

After he releases her, they go back out where he refastens the lock on the gate.

"That sure as hell was easier when you did it," she complains.

Cory chuckles, "Not bad for a knuckle-dragger, huh?"

She tries to suppress a smile. Cory looks over at her frequently as they walk to the cattle barn further along on the path. She has a smudge of dirt on her cheek and a big gray smear on the shoulder area of her shirt as if the mare had rubbed her forehead there. They like to do that, use humans as scratching posts.

"You'll get it," he reassures her, even though he's not sure why he's doing it. "Just takes practice."

"I don't know about that," she says. "I've been here for the whole spring and summer. I'm not getting it yet, and I hate those dumb horses."

"See there? That's your problem. They know you don't like them," he tells her.

"They aren't the only ones around here I don't like," she replies with a sassy attitude and shoots him any icy blue squint.

"You are feisty," he accords and follows after her. "I'll give you that much."

He admires her slim hips swaying in front of him as she heads into the barn. He's starting to wish she wasn't related to Simon at all. He's going to need a visit to Evie Johnson soon.

"Are those a pair of full-length jeans you're wearing, you big Amazon?" he taunts because he has nothing to better to do as they shovel silage to the pregnant cows in the back of the barn. She's wearing thigh-skimming blue-jean shorts. Her bare legs go on forever, right down to her dirty, worn out, black leather ankle boots.

She snorts indignantly at him and replies, "Are you going for that whole Amish look again or are you going to shave?"

He laughs loudly, frightening one of the dairy cows. He hasn't shaved in a few days, and it's obviously showing.

"It's my high levels of testosterone. That's why I grow a beard so quickly," he teases and blocks her from getting another heavy shovelful. "Guess it means I'm virile and all."

She stops, looks up at him in shock and her mouth falls open.

"Yeah, right," she remarks snidely.

Cork smirks and runs a hand through his sweaty hair. She's in his way more than he is in hers. She's slowing him down. He could do this a hell of a lot faster if she'd just go to the house. Of course, this is more entertaining than just shoveling silage by himself to a bunch of dumb, lazy cows.

He sidesteps in the narrow space between the long wooden trough and the grain container made of stainless steel. "Care to find out just how virile?"

Instead of running from him or shrinking back, Paige puffs up her chest in a show of force- which really isn't the smartest idea on her part- and juts out her stubborn jaw.

67

"You don't scare me. I got away from you once, caveman. I can do it again," she says forcefully, her light eyes flashing with anger and bold defiance. "I'm not afraid of you."

Cory looks her up and down, notices how when he lingers on her chest that she doesn't huff and puff quite as much, and finally lets his gaze fall onto hers.

"You should be," he says with more huskiness than he means to.

She still doesn't shrink back or run away in fear, but her eyes register his intention. He can see it there that she understands the implication. Paige shoves the handle of her shovel into his hand and spins on her foot.

When she is halfway down the aisle away from him, Cory calls out, "Good riddance, witch! You were just in my way."

He finishes his chores and is joined a few minutes later by Simon, who keeps hounding him about where he is going at night.

"Come on, man," Simon gripes. "Just tell me. I'll go with you."

"No thanks," he tells his best friend. "I don't need help. Besides, I'm just visiting the Johnson's daughter again. No big deal. And I don't need your help with that." This is a blatant lie, but Cory isn't about to tell Simon that he's tracking the three to five fuckers who are still out there somewhere. The scumbag bastards who thought they could attack the McClane farm this summer while he was gone and get away with it.

Simon doesn't look like he buys into this falsehood, but he also doesn't comment again. They finish up and head for the big house. Hopefully, the kids are done in the bathrooms, or more likely that their parents have forced them to wash up and are done. Sue and Derek have running water and a full bathroom in their cabin care of stolen and looted plumbing supplies and a hot water tank from the Lowes store in Clarksville. They took four hot water tanks instead of just the one they needed for Derek's cabin. Even though they shower and bathe in their own cabin at night, along with their three kids, there are still a lot of people using the main house facilities. He and Simon are supposed to be adding a full bathroom to the cabin so that they'll have their own shower system, but they are simply too busy working on the wall build in town. If his annoying sister is going to insist on staying out there with them, then she's probably going to want a full, working bathroom of their own. They have a sink and toilet, but nothing fancy like a shower or tub or even a door yet. He wishes she'd go back to the house. And take her silky, lacy bras and undies with her that she leaves scattered around in the cabin.

Some of the family is gathered in the music room for family music night, which is not his cup of tea. He's also skipping the meeting. He ducks out the back door quickly and jogs to the cabin in his dirty clothing. His hair is still wet from his shower and drips onto his bare shoulders. He's forgotten once again to take clean clothing to the big house.

When he gets to the cabin, he expels a groan of irritation because Paige is sitting at the table sipping hot tea and going over her plans on the wall. She whips her head around and mimics his groan with one of her own. His traitorous dog is lying at her feet.

"I see you've been using your witchy ways on my dog again," he remarks with feigned anger. Damn Dog has been sleeping at the foot of Paige's mattress on the floor. Sometimes she even crawls onto the bed and sleeps on Paige's feet. She may be a damn good guard dog and had his back in the field many times, but she also loves women and children.

"Your mangy mutt and you should both sleep in the barn," she says with a glare and pushes his dog with her bare foot. She's way too heavy to be shoved. She doesn't even budge but stands instead.

Damn Dog whines softly and places her big head in Paige's lap. Paige sighs and rolls her eyes at the German shepherd. Then she reluctantly reaches down and pets her. The tail wagging commences.

"Defector," Cory calls Damn Dog, who just looks briefly at him before grinning, drooling and going back to lying her head on Paige's knees.

"You're as annoying as your owner," Paige scolds, although she is still petting his dog.

Cory ignores her, starts stripping out of his soiled clothing and changing his dirty socks. He glances over his shoulder. Paige is staring at him. She averts her eyes but not before sending a nasty expression in his direction.

"Get a good look, Princess," he remarks, indicating with a hand to his torso. "You can look all you want, but this temple isn't for you."

"Damn, and there you go ruining my dream," she says with fire.

Cory chuckles at her as he pulls on a clean black shirt, matching pants and his boots.

"Where are you going? Where do you go every night?" she asks.

Paige joins him at his bed where he is jamming items into his backpack and checking the extra magazines for his rifle. He taps one firmly against the sole of his boot.

"Got a date," he lies and looks directly down at her. She is clearly scrutinizing his answer.

"Sure you do," she quips and picks up a map from his bed. She points to the red pen marks, "What's this about?"

Cory snatches it from her and shoves it into his sack. He hits her with a look of impatience.

"Those are all the hot babes I've banged in this county," he lies again just to get her goat.

"You couldn't get laid carrying a bag of gold in a whore house, Neanderthal," she insults.

"Bet I could get laid in this cabin, maybe even tonight," he taunts and leans toward her.

"I sleep beside my brother *and* his big rifle. I also have a knife of my own," she returns.

Cory admires the grayish-blue of her eyes set against her tan, freckled skin and the shocking red of her bright hair. It's pulled back into a long braid that hangs to the middle of her back. She smells pretty damn good, too. She should be using the same soap as he does since everyone on the farm uses the same soaps, but it sure smells better on her skin. He may just actually have to go visit Evie Johnson, after all, tonight.

"Your little dagger would be like a pin prick," he jests and slides the rest of his gear into his pack, slings it over his shoulder and grabs his rifle.

"You'd know all about pricks," she insults as he goes to the door.

"You could, too, if you weren't such a red-haired witch," he reports and slams the cabin door.

It'll be good to get away from her for the rest of the night. He can't decide if he wants to throw her on his bed and make love to her or club her over the head. She's one, big-mouthed, pain in the ass, tall wench. She does have a nicely toned ass, though.

Cory shakes his head as he retrieves one of the geldings and saddles him as fast as possible before anyone discovers his stealthy exit from the farm. He has work to do. Dirtbags need to be killed, and he needs to visit Evie sometime late tonight, too.

Chapter Six
Sam

"Don't let me fall off this damn thing, Sam," Paige complains from behind Sam on the back of the mare.

Sam just chuckles and replies, "You won't. I promise. She's a gentle old lady, aren't you?"

She reaches down and strokes and then pats the mare's thick neck.

"I hate these things," Paige says, apparently referring to the horses. "I don't trust them."

"Just don't do anything crazy around them and you won't have anything to fear," Sam tells her.

"Crazy, like what?"

"Sudden movements toward their heads can scare them. Getting off on the wrong side can sometimes spook them. Little things. Trust me, most of the time, the horses are more afraid of us."

Paige snorts. "Not likely."

"She has no capacity for vengeance, so you don't have to worry about her holding a grudge if you mistreat her or make a mistake. They forgive rather easily," she says.

"Wish people were that easy," Paige observes.

"I know, right? Me, too," Sam concurs. "Just relax. She won't hurt us. Also, relax your grip on my waist. I can't hardly breathe."

Paige says, "Oh, sorry."

They are riding alongside Reagan and Hannah, who rides behind her sister. They are all four heading over to the Reynolds farm to meet up with Talia to plan her wedding. Sam is so happy for

Chet. She doesn't know Talia all that well, but Chet has been like a brother to her for the last four years. And Talia seems like a good person. She's been nothing but honest and kind to her. Sam thinks they will have a happy marriage. She hopes they will have a good life, a peaceful one.

They ride past the Reynolds family burial grounds, something of which everyone seems to have on their properties.

"Are those relatives?" Paige inquires about the small wooden crosses staked into the ground.

"Yes, their family," Sam explains as Reagan pulls ahead of them. "Mr. and Mrs. Reynolds and the youngest brother, Billy. I guess they were all just as nice as Chet and Wayne, but I never met any of them. They were killed when their home was attacked."

"Yeah, I think Reagan told me about that. And the other one?"

"Their cousin. His name was Lenny. He died from pneumonia about a year after he arrived on their farm."

"Wow, everyone has lost people, family," Paige reflects morosely.

"Yes, they have. Even if you can stay alive and not be killed by someone, there is always still that threat of illness that can take your life."

"I suppose you're right," Paige agrees.

They pass the graveyard and continue on up to the house where they hitch their horses to the posts of the front porch and dismount. Talia immediately comes bounding out the front door, followed by little Maddie.

"You're here!" she exclaims and hugs Paige tightly.

"Hey, baby girl," Paige says to Maddie and swoops her into her arms after she and Talia have parted.

Sam notices that Paige's eyes tear up at their reunion. Every time her friend has come over for a visit during the past few weeks, Paige has been in town working on the wall.

They go into the house where they meet up with Bertie and Vickie, the lady that's been staying on their farm who was severely abused by men that were friends with the Target group and was held captive in a cabin in the woods. There are signs of wedding planning going on by the looks of the dried flowers and patches of lace on the kitchen table.

Reagan leads Hannah to the table where she takes a seat and immediately starts reaching for things.

"Talia's going to wear my wedding dress," Bertie announces with a smile.

"Oh, that's wonderful," Hannah exclaims. "I brought you our grandmother's pearls to borrow for the wedding if you'd like, Talia."

"Really?" Talia asks. "I mean, that's generous of you but are you sure?"

Reagan interjects with, "Absolutely. She would've wanted you to use them. Sue wore them on her wedding day, too. And so did Hannah."

"Didn't you, when you married John?" Paige asks of Reagan.

Hannah snorts and answers for her, "We were lucky just to get her into a dress. Are you kidding?"

Everyone laughs at Reagan's expense, and she grins.

"Sue said she'll come over tomorrow morning to go over the meal plans again with you, Bertie," Hannah says.

"Oh, good. I need all the help I can get."

"We're bringing sweet corn enough for an army, and Hannah and Sue are making cheese and breads, too," Reagan tells her.

Hannah offers a demure smile. Sam has noticed that her dark depression over the loss of Grams and Em has lifted just slightly since Cory returned. She is glad for it, too. They all love Hannah. Nobody wants her to be sad all the time. Grams especially wouldn't want that for her.

"The men are working on butchering one of the steers because we're almost out of freezer beef and have a lot of people to feed this coming weekend," Bertie tells them.

Sam doesn't miss the grimace on Paige's face, but she also doesn't laugh at her friend. Since Paige used to be a vegan, perhaps she doesn't find the idea of slaughtering a cow too delightful.

"Yeah, the Johnsons are coming and so are a few of the families from town, I hear," Hannah says.

"Yep, it's going to be great," Bertie says. "A lot of bad things have been happening this summer and we need a day to just celebrate being together and joining up with our families and friends. *And* to celebrate my new sister."

Talia smiles and loops her arm through Bertie's. Sam is so happy that Bertie finally has a few women living on their farm. For too long she was alone with just Chet and Wayne as her companions. She needed women for company. It's also been good for her little daughter to have Maddie to play with, as well.

A few hours later after they've helped them with some decorating projects and have stowed it all away to be brought out in two days for the wedding, Sam and her group leave their farm. Paige hugged Talia for an extra long time before they departed.

"I'm so happy for Talia," Sam observes. "Chet's such a nice man. He'll be a great husband and father."

"Yeah, he seems cool," Paige says as they ride back to the farm.

The four of them chat about the wedding and the happy couple and how lucky little Maddie is to be adapting well to the Reynolds family. When they reach the barns again, Hannah and Paige dismount first.

"Hey, Paige," Reagan says, "will you see Hannie back to the house? Sam and I are going for a quick ride."

"What do you mean you're going for a ride? That was a quick ride. Why would you want to prolong the torture? Are you a secret sadist, Reagan?" Paige jokingly asks.

"Well, I did get married, so…"

"Maybe John is the sadist," Hannah remarks coyly.

Reagan laughs bawdily, and Sam joins in. Hannah simply smiles tolerantly at their humor.

Paige says, "I told Simon that I'd help him anyway. You guys have fun… if that's possible."

Hannah loops her arm through Paige's. Sam watches the other two women head toward the back of the house before shooting an inquiring gaze to Reagan.

"Let's go for a ride, kid," she says to her. "It's been awhile since we had time for it."

"Ok," Sam agrees but with a certain amount of suspicion at Reagan's motive.

They ride past the horse barn and take a familiar route into the woods and up into the deeper forest. The shade provided by the thick foliage and leaves won't last much longer. They trot through an especially sparse area and canter across the top field. Nothing in the world could be more joyful to Sam than a warm fall day racing across an open pasture. Her mind frees itself from the entanglements of her dark past, the ever-dangerous present, and her uncertain future. It is just her and the beat of the horse's hooves, the rhythm of their bodies moving as one graceful unit, and the wind whipping through her loose hair.

They slow down once again as they enter the top pasture's wooded section. A short distance to their east, the men have run fencing so that the cattle can graze throughout the woods now, too. She even hears one mooing, probably frightened by the noise the horses are making as they pick their way through the forestry. They ride for a while discussing the farm and the clinic in town. Then Reagan gets quiet for a few moments.

"I want to know what you know," Reagan states and pulls her horse to a complete stop.

Sam circles around and reins in beside her.

"What... what do you mean, Reagan?" she asks nervously.

"The radio. I know you heard something. Spill it," Reagan orders bluntly.

"Um... I don't know," Sam says, biting her lower lip.

"I'm not asking, Sam. I need to know. And I've been watching you. You're walking around this farm with this big secret. Just tell me."

"I don't want everyone else to know, Reagan," she admits. "I'm afraid. I don't want anything to split up our family."

"Me neither. And I can help if you tell me."

Sam sighs and furrows her brow. Her mare sidesteps, and she reins her back under control.

She begins slowly, "I was tidying up Grandpa's room for him. You know, like Grams used to?"

Reagan nods and urges her to continue.

"The radio was already on. I went over to change it to a music cd when the static just stopped and an actual voice started. He said that he was the President. He said some political stuff I didn't understand. Then he started talking about the military. He barked off orders."

"Like what?"

Sam recalls, "He said that all military men, former and active duty when the country fell apart and are of the age of less than forty-five should head to one of the three states where they were re-establishing the military."

"I remember part of that came through," Reagan says. "It was Iowa and Oklahoma. Where else?"

"Colorado," Sam tells her.

"Did they say why?"

"He said that the acting President had basically gone insane and that the soldiers were to report in to the commanders that the Vice President had set in place in those states."

"Bullshit, it is a coup," Reagan snarls. "He's trying to overthrow the old President with force. They're going to have a damn civil war. What else?"

"He said any member of the military who doesn't report in shall be hanged," Sam says, feeling the color drain from her face.

"How the hell would they even know that?"

"I don't know. He said that his troops will be traveling the country rounding up men to join his army and will also be searching for men and women with military experience."

"Fuck him," Reagan states simply.

"What if they find our family members? What if they take John and Kelly and... all the guys because they are of the right age?"

Reagan snorts, "Do you really think that's gonna play, Sam? Our guys wouldn't leave the farm to join this jackass's fight just because he says to."

"Right," Sam says with a worrisome frown.

"The game has changed. The country fell apart. They can't just decide to call up the military for their little pissing contest."

"There was more, but it was pretty sketchy. He said something about an EMP. I don't know if one was used or not. John and Derek said that we weren't nuked, so I don't even know if that part's true."

"We weren't nuked, but something could've happened since. Hell, if these two dudes are going at it like this, then maybe an EMP was used. I don't know."

"He even said stuff about politics and the suspected locations of the camps of soldiers working with the old President."

"Way to be a rat," Reagan says with disgust about the message. "What about the attack, the sickness you said he spoke of that hit a few years ago? Did you really not remember what he said or were you just saying that?"

"I don't remember the name of the disease, but it was terrible. It wasn't the pneumonic plague, but I can't recall the name. He said hundreds of thousands of people, maybe millions worldwide were wiped out by it and that the CDC doctors were taken to some research facility in a bunker to work on it. The way he was talking made it seem like it was a biological weapon, like someone released this disease. I'm not sure I understood that part, though. Then it got fuzzy again, so I don't know if it was ever resolved."

Reagan nods thoughtfully before contemplating.

"A lot of different countries in the Middle East had weapons like that. I don't know how the hell they'd release one over here, though. What'd they hop on United Airlines to get here? I don't think so! We also had weapons like that, not that our government would've ever admitted to it. We kept a lot of dangerous diseases and cured sicknesses at research facilities, too. But anyone wanting to hit us with bio warfare would've had to get it overseas to the U.S., and I don't know how they could have unless they had a badass rowboat. Still interesting, though."

Sam nods thoughtfully, considering her big sister's words.

"It sounded like variance or something. Sorry," Sam says, trying her best to recall the disease.

"Variola Major?" Reagan asks with a sharp glance her way.

"Hm, maybe," Sam says. "That sounds like it."

"That's fucking great," Reagan swears.

"What?"

"Variola is smallpox. It has killed millions and millions of people since the beginning of recorded time. It's highly contagious and very deadly. It was wiped out with a preventative vaccine, but not anymore. If people haven't been vac'd, and they haven't been since the fall, then there's definitely a possibility of it making an appearance."

"That's so terrible. Have we been vaccinated?" Sam asks with definite concern.

Reagan bumps her gelding forward and they begin moving again.

"All of us adults would've been, but not the kids. Many doctors weren't even recommending vaccinating children for it anymore because there was such a small risk of it popping up in the United States."

"When I went to Nashville with my mom when the fall first started, my Uncle Scott vaccinated me and my siblings for just about everything."

"Oh, I'm sure he vac'd you for pox if you weren't already," Reagan reassures her.

"Do you think the men would leave if we told them about all this?" Sam asks, trying to hide her fear.

"I'm not sure," Reagan says.

They ride for a distance in silence. Sam doesn't even take in the beautiful views around her.

"Don't tell anyone else, Sam," Reagan orders.

"Oh, um…"

Reagan stops her horse again and turns in the saddle to face her. "I mean it. Do not tell anyone, not even Simon. Never tell any of the family what you know, what you heard. The men could decide to leave. They feel such a fierce loyalty to our country. We have to protect them from making a wrong decision, Sam. Tell no one."

Sam nods vehemently. Reagan reaches over and takes her hand, squeezing it to give her strength. This is a big move for her older sister. She doesn't typically initiate touching. Reagan doesn't flinch as badly as she used to, but she doesn't enjoy her space being crowded or people needlessly touching her.

They continue their ride, talking about other subjects like the kids, the animals, the harvest and their town.

Reagan reins in beside her and says, "So, do you wanna' talk about it?"

Sam tries to play dumb about that fateful day at the clinic and replies, "What do you…"

"Get real, Sam. You're about as good at lying as me."

Sam smiles with embarrassment and shrugs, trying not to show her coloring cheeks. "I don't know."

"What's happened since? Anything else?" Reagan inquires after the incident at the clinic when she'd caught her and Simon kissing in the stock room.

"No, nothing. He hasn't even talked to me. At all! He is avoiding me even more now than ever."

"Maybe he just hasn't had a chance," Reagan offers with a grim smile. "It's kind of hard to be alone with so many people living on this farm."

79

Sam chuckles and nods. "Did you tell everyone… or anyone?"

"No, your secret's safe with me. Besides, Simon asked me not to tell anyone, so I'm bound," Reagan tells her, a frizzy blonde curl blowing into her face.

Sam exhales with relief. She's glad nobody else knows. It's embarrassing enough having Simon think she's disgusting without the whole family knowing. They would probably think she threw herself at him. He's too good and kind to do or even think anything of a deviant nature.

"Ok, good. I don't want anyone to be mad at me," Sam admits guiltily.

"Why would anyone be mad?" Reagan asks with a degree of confusion.

"Because Simon's…. Simon is," she states but cannot finish.

"Too young? I sort of agree. You're both young, Sam. Hell, what do I know? Maybe you aren't. People grow up a lot faster now, I suppose."

"I didn't mean young," Sam says and lowers her eyes.

"What did you mean, kid?" Reagan asks as they come down the back hill that will lead to the hog barn.

"Nothing," Sam deflects and steers her horse a few feet away from Reagan's. She doesn't want to reveal too much to her older adopted sister. It's not that she doesn't trust Reagan because she does. It's that her feelings are too humiliating to voice.

"It looks like you might get your chance to talk to him," Reagan says and points to their south.

Simon and his sister are collecting herbs again in the denser part of the forest. Paige is becoming quite the helper to her brother with herb collection. He tosses back his head and laughs heartily at something his sister has said to him. Sam frowns. He never laughs around her anymore. He won't even look at her most of the time.

"No, I'd rather not. I'm just going to head back with you, Reagan," Sam says quickly, tightening her grip on the reins nervously.

"Hey, guys!" Reagan calls loudly. "What's going on?"

Sam would like to shrivel up and die. She'd also like to knock Reagan over the head. Simon's head snaps up. When he sees that she's with Reagan, Sam notices that he turns away with a frown. His sister waves jovially to them as they draw near.

"Tractor's broke," she calls out.

"Really? Again?" Reagan asks her.

"Yeah, something's wrong with the... I don't remember what," Paige answers with a scowl.

"The hydraulic hose and also a part for the thresher snapped," Simon informs her impatiently without turning back to face them.

"Oh yeah," Paige says with a grin. "Hydraulic hose. Excuse me, Mr. Perfectionist."

Simon doesn't answer but just grunts at his sister instead.

"What are the guys doing about it?" Reagan asks.

Paige replies, "I think they're going on a run for a few parts. John said something about not having another one on the farm."

"We used the last hose and patched it a couple times," Simon interjects over his shoulder. "We need to have three or four. Plus we have some other parts- like for the thresher- on the list that we should try to find. Stuff that's going to go bad soon."

"Who's going?" Sam asks.

Simon doesn't answer her but turns away again. Paige shoots a confused look at her brother but takes up the conversation for Simon.

"Kelly and Cory are going tonight, I guess," she answers.

Reagan frowns and bumps her horse a few feet forward. "I'm going back. I need to talk to John. Sam's gonna stick around and help you guys. You kids behave now."

Paige laughs and nods. Sam would like to follow her mentor but knows that Reagan will just reject the offer. Instead, she dismounts and ties her mare's reins loosely to a thin branch. The horse tosses her head angrily, wanting to return to the barn with Reagan's gelding. Sam just pats her neck and rubs her velvety muzzle once. She cautiously approaches the others and decides to stick by Paige.

"I hope they're careful," she comments quietly, averting her eyes from Simon who has finally turned to face them.

"They will be," he says to her. "Don't worry, Sam."

She nods grimly but can't help the concern she feels every time any of the family leaves the farm for a supply run. Simon turns quickly away with a pained grin.

"Right," Paige adds. "The psycho's going, so Kelly will be safe."

81

"Paige," Simon warns.

Of course she's referring to Cory as a psycho. She really, really doesn't like him. So much for Simon's assessment that they'd get along great if Cory ever came home. He's been home for weeks and they still hate each other.

"Cory's really sweet," Sam tells her friend. Paige's light eyes jump to hers. "You two just got off on the wrong foot is all. He's a good guy."

This just gets a snort from Paige before she pushes her wavy, loose red hair behind her shoulder. The leaves on the trees are starting to turn out their fall colors with a flair that catches Sam's artistic eye. Some of the hues match the light to dark red strands of Paige's locks.

"Yeah, he's a real charmer," Paige remarks with sarcasm. "When can you start working with me, Simon, so that I can go on runs, too?"

"What's your hurry?" he asks impatiently.

"I want to contribute more, help more. I used to do runs for my group all the time. Sometimes I'd go with Gavin, but other times I'd go alone…"

Simon interrupts her with a groan of misery. "That's great. I really don't like thinking of you out there by yourself. You could've been killed, you know."

"I know, but I wasn't. I'm a lot more stealthy than you're giving me credit for," Paige says proudly.

"No way, beanpole," Cory's deep voice from the woods startles them as he enters their relaxing, peaceful scene of herb procuring.

"Damn it, Cory!" Simon curses as he swings around to face their intruder. "I could've shot you, bro."

"Missed opportunity," Paige says gaily.

"There's no way in hell you're stealthy, ya' big Amazon," Cory jibes, ignoring Simon's reprimand.

Sam jumps in to defend her new friend, "Hey, that's not nice, Cory! Paige isn't an Amazon. She's beautiful."

Paige grunts and exclaims, "Good grief, Sam. I don't know about that."

"Me neither," Cory interrupts on an obnoxious chortle, earning another glare from Paige.

"Shut up," she grinds through her teeth.

Sam just smiles gently at their heated exchange. She catches Simon staring at her. When she tries to offer a smile his way, he turns his back to them again.

"C'mon, beanpole," Cory says directly to Paige, who looks just as startled as the rest of them. He rolls his eyes impatiently, extends his hand, which gets ignored, and says, "Reagan said she needs your help with something back at the barn. That's why I came out here."

"Why would she need my help?" Paige asks confusedly.

"Who knows?" Cory answers and then adds because he can't seem to not antagonize her, "I personally think we should start your training, too. First up would be staying out of the rest of our ways."

Paige scowls at him but takes her brother's help in getting up from her squatted position. They leave a moment later; Paige still glaring, Cory still smirking.

Simon is clearly not happy to be left alone with her. Sam's quite sure that Reagan doesn't need Paige's help with anything in the barns, either. She's cooked this up to have her be alone with Simon. Sam would rather shrivel up and die on the spot. He looks like he'd prefer to do the same. He even glances not once but twice toward the path on which his sister and Cory just departed as if he'd like to follow.

Sam clears her throat and says, "Have any luck? Finding any useful herbs, I mean."

His eyes jump furtively to hers before glancing away. "Um, yeah sure. Found some goldenseal. That'll be helpful."

"Oh... good," she mumbles uncomfortably. Why do things have to be strained between them? It's killing her, this separation.

Simon glances at her and shakes his head with a frown, "We should head back."

He turns to go, but Sam grasps his arm quickly. "Simon, wait. We... we need to talk."

A wind gust spirits through the forest, flipping her dark hair into her face. Simon reaches out and tucks a handful behind her ear for her.

"Let's go," he says firmly and takes her hand into his and the reins of her mare into his other.

Sam doesn't pull away. After they begin walking, he attempts to dislodge his hand from hers, but Sam holds fast. She notices the tight line of his mouth pinch even tighter.

"Will you not talk to me?" she asks in a soft tone.

"There really isn't anything to say," he states firmly and shakes free of her grasp.

He walks faster than her, but Sam trots to catch up.

"I think there is, Simon. You kissed me. Don't you remember?"

He halts, causing her to bump into his shoulder. Her mare even tosses her head indignantly.

In a clipped, angry tone he says, "Of course I remember. How can I not?"

He looks grossed out or severely distressed by this conversation. It only makes Sam more confused and disheartened.

"What's wrong? Why have you been avoiding me? Do you… do you think I'm… disgusting?" Sam asks hesitantly, afraid of his response.

Simon shakes his head and looks to the tree tops before answering, "No, Samantha. I didn't mean it like that. I shouldn't have said that."

Sam frowns and stares at her feet covered in dusty, black riding boots that come to her knees. Simon's long, tanned index finger hooks under her chin, forcing her to look up at him.

"You aren't disgusting. I'm a stupid idiot for saying that. I just blurted. You're," he pauses for a long time, "not disgusting."

"Then why won't you talk to me? I don't understand. Are you mad at me? Is that it? Do you hate me now? I couldn't bear it if I thought you hated me, Simon," Sam babbles because she can't seem to stop. "You can't be mad at me, ok? Please say you aren't. I'm sorry. I can't take this. You're my best friend."

"I'm not your best friend, Sam," Simon retorts on a hiss, then rakes a hand through his auburn hair.

"Please don't say that, Simon," Sam says softly, near to tears. "Please don't. You *are* my best friend. I understand if you don't have feelings for me. Heck, who would? I just couldn't bear it if you weren't my friend anymore."

"What the hell's that supposed to mean?" he asks angrily, a line pinching between his brows.

"I need you to be my friend. I can't go through this life without you. I'll back off. I'll give you space. But please don't shut me out, not completely," Sam begs brokenly as a tear slips down her cheek.

"Why would you think that nobody would have feelings for you? That's what I wanted to know," Simon demands with an edge of hostility.

Sam doesn't understand why he's so angry. She bites her lower lip instead of answering.

"I'm sorry," she repeats.

"That kiss wasn't your fault, Sam. It was my fault, so stop apologizing. It'll never happen again, ok?" he says.

His dark blue eyes are serious and steady. Sam nods.

"I understand," she responds while swallowing the hard lump of rejection in her throat.

"I'm sorry I'm such a pig. It won't happen ever again," he says with defeat and brushes her hair behind her ear again. "I'm considering moving into town anyways. I'd be closer to the practice if there's an emergency."

Sam furrows her brow with confusion. Why does he think his behavior was piggish? She opens her mouth to ask him, but Simon turns and walks further along their path with her horse. She jogs in front of him and places her hand on his chest.

"What do you mean, Simon?" she demands. "You can't leave the farm! Please! I'll do whatever you say, Simon. I won't bug you anymore. I'll give you more space. I'll stop pestering you! I'll stop asking you to hang out. You can't leave."

"Sam, stop it," Simon demands.

He is speaking to her as if she is being hysterical. She is being hysterical. How can he even think about moving off of the farm? Her hands begin to shake, and she is helpless to stop it.

"No, Simon!" she says in a rush of breath. "You can't leave here. I'd die without you."

"Stop being dramatic. You'd be a hell of a lot better off without me pawing at you," he says angrily.

"What?"

"Come on. Let's just go back, ok?" he says as he takes her hand and pulls her along with the horse. "There's work to do. We don't have time to be out here screwing around and arguing."

85

Sam scowls hard up at him, but he refuses to look down at her again. He tugs her, forcing her to follow after him on the narrow path. He gives her the reins to her horse. As the barns come into view, Simon picks up the pace until he's dropped her hand and is pulling away from her.

"Simon, wait," Sam calls weakly.

"I have stuff I need to do," he barks in a clipped tone over his shoulder.

He jogs away as if he can't stand to be near her a second longer. Sam slumps against the back wall of the horse barn, far away from the eyes and ears of the family. There she slides to the ground, ignoring her horse who is impatient to be returned to her friends. With the reins still in her hands, Sam draws up her knees and presses her fists to her eyes and cries in earnest. Simon's rejection hurts more than she wants to admit. She thought just perhaps he might have feelings for her like she has for him and has kept hidden so well all these years. Apparently the kiss at the clinic had been nothing more than boredom or the idle experimentation of a young man who has nobody else with whom to practice. She can handle just about anything that happens to her. She's proven that to herself many times over. But the idea of him leaving the farm is enough to break her.

Chapter Seven
Simon

As usual, the plans change and Simon ends up going on a quick run for the hydraulic hoses with Cory instead of with his brother. Derek needs Kelly's help in the cattle barn. Last week's rains had flooded a section in the far west corner and left the foundation unstable in that area. Erosion can ruin an old barn like the cattle barn, and Simon knows that Derek and John will need Kelly's strength to help dig out the mud and dirt by hand and reset those barn stones. They'll likely work on that project well into the late evening hours.

And so, he and his friend are moving around the town in the near dark looking for supplies, anything worth taking, and fuel and tractor parts to finish the harvest. They've raided abandoned homes, garages, sheds and barns many times over the years, as well. They are usually hunting for any supplies that can be taken back to the farm or to the town. They've found medical supplies, ammo, sometimes weapons, helpful books, canned goods, bedding, clothing- especially for the growing kids- and on the rare occasion, coffee for Doc. Unfortunately, they've also seen a lot of dead bodies in those homes, which are always images that Simon wishes he could forget. They'll also scout out for fencing materials. They've been to this city a few times before. Ashland City is or was a small town, but at one time they did have restaurants, a grocery store, a few pharmacies, and several car repair shops. Sam went with them the last time, but that was during the day. For some strange reason, the cities are usually more dangerous at night. Naturally, they've left her at the farm for this one, and Simon's glad for it because she doesn't need to be in danger. And he doesn't need to be around her.

Her confrontation in the woods had left him unsettled. He was glad that he didn't have to stay at the farm tonight because some of the family was going to meet in the music room to discuss Jay Hernandez's group, who have segregated from their town. Then it was family time. Simon doesn't want to be forced into family time with Sam in the same room. He's a rat bastard who doesn't deserve to be in her presence. When he'd gone to town the other day to work at the clinic, he'd taken some time and searched out a place to live. Even though Reagan had gone off the deep end at the idea of him moving out and so had Sam, Simon feels like it might become necessary. He'd found a small one-bedroom apartment that didn't appear to have been damaged by flooded pipes back when the first winter after the apocalypse occurred. So many homes and structures were destroyed by water lines. It would be nothing like living on the McClane farmstead in that small apartment, but at least he wouldn't have to be around Sam on a daily basis and worry about losing his self-control again.

"Up ahead," Cory's voice breaks into his thoughts.

They are moving on foot through a once industrialized section of the town where a large shopping center complete with a small, three screen movie theater and shops had encroached on the commercial industry there. Simon immediately spies what Cory has also seen. There is a faint, glowing light, likely from a fire, coming from a building near the end of the short street. Even though it's still early fall, the weather has been chilly for the past few nights. It appears that someone is using fire as a source of heat if he were to guess. The last time they came to this particular city, they didn't have a whole lot of trouble. Simon's hoping for the same again.

"Check it out?" Cory asks.

Simon wavers just a moment before answering with a nod. He'd rather they just get the supplies they need and head back to the farm, but there could be people up ahead who may need their help. They aren't the saviors of the world, but they try to help when and where they can.

"I'll flank," Simon offers, gets a nod from his friend, and starts out at a slow jog toward the rear of the building with dim interior illumination. They both wear headsets with throat mics so they can communicate if and when they separate. This sort of communication with the other members of their team in the field is essential. It prevents confusion and errors.

Simon creeps to the rear entrance, peeks through a broken window there and doesn't come up with much. He tries the door. Locked. Damn. That would've made it easier. Now he'll need another source of ingress. He may be able to use this locked door once he's inside as a point of egress if he needs to get the hell out quickly.

He checks around the corner and finds the alleyway empty. A long row of windows, some broken, line the side of the brick building. It appears to have been an indoor storage facility of some sort. After trying a few windows, he finally finds one that has broken panes and is unlocked. Cory should be making progress in the front, as well.

Simon climbs through the window and moves silently around in the old building, careful not to knock into the debris on the floor and the left-behind articles scattered nearly everywhere. He comes to a storage locker where bunk beds and cots are lined against the interior walls. As they'd suspected, people are living in this building. A little girl is dead out asleep on the bottom bunk of one bed. She is perhaps seven or eight years old. Under her bent arm is a threadbare stuffed rabbit. Nobody else resides in the room, but all of the occupants' items are in crates and boxes stacked against the wall. Two picture frames sit near the bed on the floor and contain photographs of a family obviously taken before the apocalypse. There is a father, mother and three young kids in the photo, and they seem genuinely happy posing for the professionally-snapped and edited picture. It was apparently taken before the apocalypse because they are clean and neat in appearance and not haggard and tired and dirty like so many people that he's come across during the past four years, especially those who come to the clinic for help and have had a rough go of it. He wonders if the other members of this family are still alive or if this child is an orphan like Jacob and being raised by other people.

Simon sneaks down the hallway as quietly as possible, not running into anyone as he goes. Another locker provides a view of the same, minus a sleeping child. Personal belongings and items are being kept in plastic storage containers, and there are two twin-sized beds inside. Tattered blankets and quilts lay on the beds, and only one bed has a pillow. He quietly backs out of the room again.

"All clear," Cory says across the air. "Families."

"Got it," Simon answers in a whisper and backs slowly down the hall and right out the same window.

They don't bother with families, especially ones who seem to be doing fine on their own. There is no sense going in guns blazing when they are obviously self-sufficient and trying to establish a community. Even if it is in a formerly climate-controlled storage unit facility.

He makes it to the other end of the alley again and meets up with Cory.

"Run into anyone?" Simon asks of his friend.

"I saw three adults talking in a big room where the fire was going. Looks like they're all living there together. Saw a couple kids sleeping."

"Yeah, that's what I found, too," Simon tells him. "I think there are probably a bunch of families in there. There were emptied out storage units being used as mini apartments or something."

"Cool," Cory says as they walk away. "Whatever works, bro. In Cleveland there was a group of people living on the second floor of a hospital. It was huge. That hospital was like city blocks big, man. But they were pretty smart if you ask me. They had beds, towels, maybe even some water or power or medicine if any was left."

Simon nods. Then they slow jog toward a more densely congested area of stores, gas stations and restaurants. They already know that the big places like Walmart have already been stripped clean in most cities. They need gas for their vehicles, parts for the farm equipment and anything else they deem as usable. The family relies on them for these types of missions, and Simon would hate to let them down.

They've left the Hummer outside of town, near a park with a copse of tall, dense trees to keep it concealed. Whatever items they do find, they'll need to haul them back to the vehicle to then be transported home. They won't, however, be spending the night in the area. They are needed back home as soon as they can get there. The last time they came to this city with Sam, they'd ridden horses since it's so close to home. Simon's glad that Kelly approved the use of the Hum-Vee.

"You know, I was thinkin' why couldn't we just use hooch for the vehicles?" Cory asks as they slow to a walk and head toward Main Street.

"What do you mean? What the heck is hooch?" Simon asks, crossing the street with him.

There are absolutely no lights on anywhere else in this town. It is for all intents and purposes, a ghost town with the exception of the occupied indoor storage units. It was the same the last time they came. He doesn't even remember seeing the fire in the storage units building then, but they hadn't gone to that section before. Simon's not sure where the residents have disappeared to, but they are mostly all long gone. They hadn't run into one single living person or animal when they came before. This town is only a few miles down the road from the farm, and therefore, a good place to try to salvage supplies. Unless, of course, the people that were living in the storage lockers turn out to be dangerous and hunt them down and kill them when their backs are turned. He glances a few times over his shoulder to make sure they aren't being followed.

"Hooch, moonshine. That's the jars of stuff I brought back. It's liquor. I was thinking since it's mostly pure alcohol that we could distill our own and make enough to fuel the vehicles," Cory suggests.

"I don't know. Maybe we could talk to Derek. He seems to be good at figuring that stuff out."

"Or we could ask K-Dog," Cory adds.

Simon knows he is referring to the Navy Seal living at the condo community. He was a dog trainer with the Seals and thus the nickname. His real name is Keith, but nobody calls him that. Except maybe his wife, Anita. Mostly the men call him K-Dog. He brought his dog with him when he flew home from the Middle East and ended up back in Little Creek, Virginia, where he was part of Seal Team Four. And his Navy dog, Tracker, lives at the condo community with him and his new family. Keith says that she is an invaluable member of the security team there and walks the night beat with him when he's on duty. K-Dog is great with figuring things out and finding a solution to problems that come up. And he and Derek tend to pow-wow on issues when their respective groups become stuck on some dilemma or another.

"Yeah, he'd probably know if we can use it," Simon agrees.

Cory points to their west, indicating they should move in that direction. He's spotted a mom-and-pop auto repair shop. It could be

91

a fortuitous find. They haven't been to this particular mechanic's shop before, so hopefully nobody else has found it either.

Simon flanks, ascertains nobody is in the building and meets back up with Cory in the front before they go in together. They search shelves, tool boxes and the storage area in the back of the small building but don't come up with any parts that can help for the farm equipment. Cory grabs a set of brakes that he says they can use on Doc's old pick-up truck when the current ones wear out. Simon finds a set of socket wrenches, but they don't find a part for the thresher.

Doc told them to check out the antique tractor museum on the far edge of town for the thresher parts. Simon knows they definitely need a new belt and possibly a new cylinder. Last year they used the Johnson's combine thresher, but it has hit the skids and seems to be completely unrepairable unless John Deere is going back into business soon. They also can't afford the fuel to run it anymore. He's glad they have the antique version, but it is about a million times more work. And now it is broken down, too. The last resort option is to bring in and harvest the wheat by hand, which can be done but would take so much more time and back-breaking work.

They continue their search of the repair shop, and Cory finds a few more parts they can use on the farm vehicles.

"Look," Simon calls over to his friend, who joins him a moment later. "Gas cans."

He points to the red plastic jugs against the wall in a dark corner. They pick them up and give them a jiggle. Two are full, the third one is about half to three-quarters full. This is a good find. This will provide them with at least four or five trips to the clinic from the farm. Simon hopes the gas is still useable. It could be four years old or it could've been found and stored here more recently by someone. Cory shows him that he also found a container of bar oil for the chainsaws and some axle grease, which they use all the time on the equipment. Simon finds two unopened jugs of car oil, another lucky find.

"Good job," Cory says as they leave the building.

"Thanks, Dad," Simon harasses his friend, earning a punch to his shoulder. He just chuckles at Cory.

They fast walk back to the vehicle to stow away their booty before heading out again. This time they take the Hummer because they are moving to the other side of town where the antique museum and other businesses are located.

Out of the blue, Cory asks, "So what's going on with you and Sam? Are you two fightin' or something?"

Simon tries at nonchalance and shrugs. "I don't know what you mean."

"You suck even more at lying than you do at pickin' up chics," Cory jeers as he drives around a torched school bus. Neither of them comment on it.

Simon frowns and says, "You pick up enough women for the both of us."

Cory laughs with good humor and replies, "Yeah, you're probably right about that. Maybe someday yours will drop, and you'll give me a run for my money in the hottie picking up department."

Simon smirks at the ball-dropping comment and adds, "Or maybe you're just picking up girls with no sense of smell, and I'm waiting for someone a little more discerning. Or just one whose olfactory senses still work."

Cory laughs loudly this time, not worried too much about the noise he creates. Simon knows that his friend has killed many people while he was gone; he can see the change in him, the ruthless, confident, predatory manner he carries now as if he is the greatest threat to the territory and not distressed about being the prey anymore.

"Don't go using big words on me, Professor," Cory warns with a grin. "I'd hate to return you to your crazy sister with a black eye."

Simon chuckles. "Calling my sister crazy is a little bit pot calling the kettle black don't ya' think?"

Cory purses his lips, pauses a moment and then says, "Yeah, I guess you're right. But at least I'm nice. She's crazy *and* mean."

"Define nice," Simon air quotes before returning his grip to his 30-06 rifle. "Because I think there might be some people in Ohio, Pennsylvania and wherever the hell else you went that might not agree with your self-assessment of being nice," Simon informs him as they turn down the next street, drive to the end and hide the vehicle behind the farm implement museum.

"Hey, you know, I didn't kill everyone I ran into. Give me some credit," Cory says as if he's slightly affronted.

"Right. I'm sure that you let a lot of them go and then banged all their women," Simon jokes about his friend's man-whore status. "Are we gonna' have a bunch of women showing up claiming you're their baby daddy?"

Cory laughs loudly again, followed by Simon's quieter chuckle.

"Not only did I not kill everyone I ran into, I didn't bang every chic, either."

"Yeah, sure," Simon mocks.

"Well, not *every* one," Cory teases with a wink.

"Keep in mind our shortage of antibiotics, Clap Master," Simon jokes further.

"The clap?" Cory says on an obnoxious shout of laughter. "I didn't tell the world to go to shit right when I got old enough to sew my oats," Cory says as they both pull down their night-vision gear.

"Sewing your oats would be an improvement. You're pulverizing them."

"Wow, that was almost crude, Professor," Cory jokes. "I'm impressed. I thought you mighta' turned half girl while I was gone. You've been hangin' out with a lot of women."

They silently shut the SUV's doors and move toward the rear entrance to the building.

"I've been hangin' out with Derek and your brother, too, so…"

Cory nods and says, "Yeah, like I said, you've been hanging out with women."

Simon chuckles. As they approach the building full of antique farm equipment on display, the joking and talking ceases. They use hand signals to communicate. Simon tries the door, which doesn't seem to be made of steel or anything heavy-duty. It's locked. Cory nods and steps toward the center of it while Simon covers him. Cory gives it two solid kicks with his booted foot, and the door bangs inward smacking against the wall. There is a small storage area with metal wall units of shelves, likely where they will find the parts they need. They sweep inside, doing checks and clearing one section at a time.

It's mostly a wide pole-barn style building with a cemented floor and tall display windows at the front. Old tractors and farm machinery are spread out around the building. A small office, probably not much larger than a ten-by-ten space is off to their right. All areas are cleared before they spread out. Simon finds an antique thresher almost identical to Doc's, other than the fact that it looks like it's brand new and never used; the restoration of it is that precise. And it's just sitting undisturbed like the rest of the farm implements in the building. Cory comes over to him with hydraulic hoses and a cardboard box full of other parts he's salvaged somewhere.

"You know what I'm thinking?" Simon asks his friend as he considers the parts they need for the thresher. He notes that a belt for it is sticking out of Cory's box.

"Why you can't just tell Sam how you feel about her?" Cory asks and raises his night-vision gear. He's holding a small flashlight.

Simon sighs, frowns hard at his best friend and answers, "No. And don't be an asshole."

"It's kind of my specialty, according to you. Definitely according to your sister…"

"We should just take this," Simon interrupts and points to the thresher.

"Take the whole thresher?"

"Yes, why not?" Simon asks rhetorically. "We should hitch the Hum-V to that trailer out back and take this. It'll last for years. It's like brand new. I've been looking it over, and it seems like it's in good working condition. Then we'd have two of them. If one breaks, we can use the other until we find parts. Matter of fact, I think we should tell the guys and come back for a lot of this equipment. If we can't use it, then there will be others who could."

Cory considers this for a moment before answering, "Yeah, maybe. How the hell do we get it out of here?"

"I think there's a sliding garage door over there on the south wall," Simon tells him. "We could hook the trailer up to the hitch on the Hum-Vee."

"Let me find a winch. We're gonna' need one to pull it onto the trailer."

"And some straps or chains to hold it down."

"Right," Cory says before they split up to find the items they need.

It takes them a lot longer to find everything they require for the thresher theft project, but a few hours later, they have the equipment on the trailer that they've hitched to the Hummer. It took a lot of straining, swearing on Cory's part, and self-doubt on Simon's, but they got it done. They'll not stay longer in the town, not with heavy equipment, fuel and parts on the trailer. They can't make a quick get-away if they need to now. They'll drive slowly and carefully the few short miles back to the farm.

Cory hops in the driver's seat, which is how it usually goes since Simon is better with sniper style shooting from a moving vehicle should a situation arise. His friend plugs his stolen iPod into the outlet on the dashboard. Reagan brought it home for Cory a few years ago. Later, they figured it out that it belonged to Sam's older brother. Then he'd felt like shit for using it. But Samantha, being her kind self, had insisted that Cory keep it. She said it made her happy knowing that Cory would get some use out of something that belonged to her brother.

Before long, rock music pumps at a low decibel through the vehicle, but not loudly enough to interfere with surveillance of their surroundings. There are even tracks on it from Samantha's dead brother's band. They aren't too bad, or weren't. Maybe he would've been some big rock star someday if the world hadn't gone to hell and he hadn't been murdered by the men in Simon's traveling group. Listening to her dead brother's tracks usually makes Simon feel even guiltier and eventually sick to his stomach at the fate of her family, the fate he was helpless to stop.

"Deer in the road up ahead," Simon alerts Cory as he spies through his scope.

"I miss the good old days when I actually hunted them with my dad. It's not that hard gettin' one anymore. Not much of a hunt."

"No kidding," Simon agrees as his friend slows the vehicle while they wait for probably twenty white-tails to cross the road. They can't afford a busted grille and radiator. It happened one time a few years ago when Kelly had been driving to Nashville on a run. He'd hit a buffalo in the road. It had caused quite a lot of damage to the Hum-Vee, which had been difficult to repair. Simon had been on that trip with Kelly and Derek. Luckily, though, Derek's a hell of a mechanic when the situation calls for it. He'd been able to repair their vehicle enough to get the rest of the way to Nashville and back home. They'd found a lot of parts for the Hummer at an Army base up north. He, John and Cory had gone on that run. They'd brought back a veritable bounty that time. Simon knows that John had been hoping to run into old friends, but the base had been deserted. It's the same place John suggested they steal fencing. K-Dog is going with a group of men from town next week to dig up a massive amount of chain-link fencing from that base if it's still abandoned.

They pull onto the oil well road near the Johnson's farm and move at a snail's pace to avoid destroying the trailer or losing the thresher in the deep ruts of the dirt road. It's nearly midnight when they make it to the barn. Derek and Kelly, both on watch, immediately come out to greet them. Doc even comes over to join them. They are genuinely excited about the thresher and some of the other finds they've brought back. Doc, on the other hand, is concerned about stealing the thresher. He explains that the former owner of the antique farm museum was a friend of his. It is very likely that the man is dead. And in no uncertain terms, Kelly tries to let Doc down gently. The Rangers agree that the other equipment should be commandeered, if for no other reason than to offer some of it to neighbors and friends who might have a need.

They decide to call it a night and unload everything in the morning when there is more light. He and Cory head out to the cabin, where Paige should already be asleep. They try to move around quietly in the cabin so as not to awaken her.

"I'm not asleep," she whispers to him.

"Oh, sorry," Simon apologizes. "Hope we didn't wake you."

"Nope," she replies. "I can't sleep when you aren't here."

She's lying on her simple mattress beside his bed.

"What about me?" Cory asks, stirring Paige's ire. "Have a hard time sleeping without me here, too?"

She snorts in the dark, barely visible by the dying fire in the wood-burning stove.

"Hardly," she answers. "It's just too bad you came back."

"Aw, now you know you'd miss me," Cory teases.

"Tomorrow I'm going to haul your mattress to the hog barn," Paige threatens.

Cory crashes loudly onto his bed and laughs. Simon climbs over his sister and lies on top of the blankets in his own bed. She has the cabin a little too warm for his taste.

Simon reaches down and ruffles her messy hair, "You don't need to worry when I'm not here, sis. We take a lot of precautions. We don't make mistakes."

"Everyone makes a mistake at some point, Simon," she says quietly. "Even when they're careful. Even when they take precautions."

It sounds as if Cory is already asleep on the other side of the room. He's breathing loudly, steadily.

Paige adds, "Trust me."

Her tone is serious and melancholy. Simon's not sure if she's just tired or if she's genuinely upset about something.

"What do you mean?" he asks.

"Nothing," she evades.

Simon rolls over so that he can face her. He can just barely make out the soft lines of her face and the curve of her slim hip. Her red hair, in contrast to the darkness, nearly glows from the dwindling flames on the other side of the room. His sister just has a warmth about her, or like Samantha likes to say, an earthiness.

"What is it? Something that happened with your friends while you were on your own?"

She squeaks out a barely audible, "Yes."

"Mistakes were made," Simon speculates.

"Yes, big mistakes," she says and then frowns hard.

"Tell me," Simon demands gently. He prods a few more times until she relents.

"We...we were on our own, just the four of us," she says and then pauses for a long time.

"Go on," he urges.

"I don't really wanna' talk about it, Simon," she says.

Paige tries to turn away from him, but Simon holds her shoulder so that she cannot.

"Maybe you should," Simon suggests.

"We were on our own," she starts again. "After we left the third FEMA camp, we tried going it alone for a while. We were north of Atlanta. This was before we hitched a ride to Jersey with those Army guys- or Marines I guess is what they were. We found a big warehouse. Thought it was empty. We were camped out there for about a week. Gavin went out one night looking for more baby food and formula for Maddie."

She doesn't continue but sighs hard. Simon gives her shoulder a gentle squeeze of encouragement.

Paige clears her voice before continuing, "So he was gone and it was just me and Talia and Maddie. The baby was asleep on a dirty old crib mattress we'd found and dragged in there. It was the middle of the night, like right now. I'd been out running around and looting already that day. It seemed like I walked the city for miles with Gavin that morning and afternoon looking for food and water. We were exhausted, but he volunteered to go back out alone so I could get some rest. I was sound asleep. I woke up when someone grabbed my foot through my sleeping bag. I thought it was just Gavin."

Simon grimaces. He's not sure he wants to know what happened. He wishes he could tell her to stop, but at his damn insistence she feels compelled to recount her story. Instead of making her stop, Simon clenches his jaw to brace for what's coming.

"It was a man. He looked hungry… and dirty. Wild even, like he was even more desperate than us. He was maybe thirty years old or so. I figured he was robbing us for our food, which wasn't much. I don't even remember what he said. I was still in my sleeping bag. He tried to grab me, pull me up. I kicked him. Then I realized he wasn't there to rob us. I heard Talia crying out for help. She was only about twenty or so feet from me, but I was too busy fighting with that man. Maddie was on the little mattress over against the wall in a corner thankfully still sleeping. I didn't want him to notice her."

Simon swallows hard and listens.

"I could just barely see my friend. I was struggling against the guy who was on top of me trying to get me out of the sleeping bag. There was another man. He was already on Talia. She wasn't fighting him or crying out for help anymore, though. He had a knife to her throat. I just remember the hopelessness in her eyes as he raped her. She was just lying there looking at me. Tears were streaming down her face, but she wasn't making any sounds. I figured it was up to me to do something. I had to stop the man who was hurting her and the man who was going to rape me. I had to save her and save myself, too. The man ripped open my sleeping bag, broke the zipper. I had a knife in my pillow case. It wasn't much of anything. It wasn't like the daggers you guys all carry or the one that Sam carries. It was pathetic. I didn't really know how to use it. It wasn't like you and I grew up hunting and fishing. I managed to slip it out. I tried to stab him. I don't even know where. I can't remember. I think I attempted to stab him in the chest, just cut him somewhere near his chest. I wasn't very

99

successful because he knocked it out of my hand. He punched me in the jaw. I tried fighting back. I punched and kicked at him. He was skinny but stronger than anything. It was like he was high on drugs or maybe just evil. I remember thinking that I'd failed my friend. I didn't know what they'd do to Maddie, either. If they'd kill her or kill us. A second later, Gavin came in and shot the man on Talia. Then he shot the man I'd tried to stab."

"Were you...?" Simon can't bring himself to finish.

"No, thank God. I was only seconds away from being raped, but he didn't get to because Gavin saved me. I had a sore jaw for a few weeks. Gavin was afraid it was broken, but I assured him that my skull was harder than it looked. He always fought so hard for me and Talia and Maddie. That's why she took his death so hard. Why we all three did. He was like our big brother."

"I'm sorry I wasn't there for you," Simon says, his stomach turning at her story.

"I know," she concedes. "After that and after Talia had a few days to heal and rest, we left that place. A few weeks later, I shot a man who'd jumped Gavin when we were on our way on foot to another FEMA camp. He'd sneaked up behind my friend and hit him with a baseball bat. Gavin found a small gun on the man who'd raped Talia and gave it to me after that bad night. I used the last bullet returning the favor for Gavin."

"Good, he deserved it," Simon tells his sister.

"Yes, he did. I didn't feel bad at all. By then, I was done feeling sorry for anyone. Not after what happened to Talia. It just became about surviving and finding you. That's the only thing that kept me going. And it's why I never slept the night through until I came here. I don't always sleep the whole night through even here, but I sleep a lot better."

Simon has to blink hard to clear his mind. "Was she all right? I mean, after the rape?"

"No, not really. She never was again. I think she's fine physically but not mentally. It wasn't until we made it here that she seemed any better at all. I'm glad she's found Chet."

"He'll always look after her and Maddie," Simon whispers in the dark. "You don't have to worry about her now. The Reynolds are good people. Chet's a tough man, able, good, kind. And hard when he needs to be."

"I'm relieved. She told me the other day when we went there to help plan the wedding that she's pregnant. Chet is over the moon about it. So is Talia, but I'm not so sure it's a great idea."

"Wow, that's some news."

"She asked me not to tell everyone, so keep it on the DL," Paige implores.

"Don't worry about her. He'll take good care of her and Maddie and their new baby," Simon assures her.

"He doesn't seem like he's too lethal, but if you say so."

"Oh, he is. Trust me, he is. She's safe now," Simon promises. She has no idea how lethal the Reynolds brothers can be when the need arises. And Chet's been shot twice, although his sister doesn't know of the first time. He's a lot tougher than his kind smile reveals.

"He seems like he really cares for her. I'm glad because I won't have to worry about her. And I'm glad they just live next door... sort of," Paige says.

They are both quiet for a few moments. "I'll never let anything like that happen to you again, sis," Simon promises. "I swear it."

"I know," Paige says solemnly. "But mistakes get made, Simon. We'll have as long as we *get* to have together. Sometimes it's out of our hands. Things happen. Mistakes."

She rolls onto her side away from him again. Simon has a difficult time going to sleep. He lies awake for hours thinking about his sister and her friends and the trying times they've had while on the road fending for themselves. Her words seemed prophetic, and he doesn't like to consider the possible truth behind them.

According to the wall clock, at a little after three a.m., Cory rises and dresses to go wherever he goes. Somehow he senses that Simon is also not asleep. He stops at the foot of Simon's bed before leaving.

"I'm glad your sister made it here safely, bro,' and that... well, she didn't suffer like her friend. If anything ever happens to you, I'll take care of her. You have my word on it. I promise."

Cory states this without asking anything in return and without conditions. His friend is a man of his word, too. Simon knows he wouldn't offer something like this without meaning it entirely. He also knows that his sister and Cory don't even get along well, but he's still putting forth a pledge to protect her above all else. Before he can even respond, Cory leaves the cabin without another comment.

101

Simon finally falls asleep a few minutes later, but his dreams are plagued with nightmarish visions of his sister coming to harm's way on his watch because he makes a mistake.

Chapter Eight
Paige

"I just don't know if this is going to be enough bread!" Hannah exclaims as she turns out the last loaf from a glass pan onto the stone surface of the island.

"Don't worry, Hannie," Reagan tells her. "They're cooking like a whole damn cow or something, so it'll be fine. Besides, men are going to concentrate on eating the meat, not bread."

Paige grins. The kitchen smells insanely good. They are all covered in flour, but it was worth it. They've made yeast rolls, biscuits, and loaves of bread to take to Talia's wedding dinner.

"Don't speak like a heathen in Grams's kitchen, Reagan Harrison!" Hannah corrects.

"Well, it's enough bread," Reagan restates.

"Right," Sue agrees. "And as soon as Paige finishes with the Caprese salad, we'll have that, too. The guys took over the roasters full of sweet corn, and I have two trays of cheeses cut up at my cabin that we're taking. I'm gonna run out to my house and see if Derek's got any of my kids ready to go yet. I seriously doubt it!"

Paige smiles and nods. Reagan snorts once and laughs at her sister's dilemma. Paige was given the task of cutting up the remainder of the summer tomatoes and mixing them with basil, oil, and chunks of mozzarella cheese that Sue and Reagan made yesterday.

"Hey, Paige, if that dress doesn't work, let me know and I'll send a few more over for you to try on," Sue says kindly, her brown hair pulled into such an elegant chignon.

"Ok, thanks, Sue," Paige calls to her before the oldest sister dashes through the back door.

They should be leaving for the Reynolds farm in a few hours, but they are still in the kitchen, which is nothing unusual. She doesn't want to be late for her friend's wedding, though. She and Sue have already been over there twice today. Once to deliver flower arrangements that Sue spent all night working on and the second time to deliver a small wedding cake and four pies that Hannah and Sam had made last night. Chet flew over on his four-wheeler a few hours ago to say that at last count around thirty people from town were already there. Fortunately, he also said that they've all brought at least one covered dish. Apparently everyone wants a day of celebration and joy and not the usual chaos of building the wall and defending their town from violent intruders. The McClane men went over last night to offer chairs, benches and tables they'd dragged out of the barns.

"This is finished," Paige announces.

"Cool, let me get a couple containers," Reagan suggests and disappears into the pantry.

Hannah is smiling ear to ear. She's in her element. Reagan was right when she said that her sister would cheer up if Cory ever came home. She has improved exponentially. He seems to bring her a lot of joy. Paige can't personally understand why being around that Neanderthal would bring anyone joy, but, nonetheless, she's glad that Hannah is happier.

Reagan returns with glass containers and lids, and they pour the tomato salad into them.

"I'd better hunt down Jacob and John," Reagan tells them. "There's no telling what those two are up to or what condition they are in. We need to get moving."

"Agreed! Me, too," Hannah exclaims as she removes her white apron and hangs it on its hook near the door while flailing her hands wildly around. "I should find Kelly. The last I talked to him he said he was going outside to feed the cows. Good grief! We're going to be late. And Grandpa's officiating!"

Paige laughs heartily at her new friends. Their sisterly affection is contagious.

"And you need to get washed up, sis," Reagan tells Hannah. "You are covered in flour. It's even in your hair, Hannie. Better grab a quick shower. I'll find the guys and get them hustling."

Paige took her shower already. She didn't want to jam up the shower time for the rest of the family. Her hair, she plaited in two long braids on either side of her head. It'll lay nicer when she unbraids it after it has thoroughly dried. But she pretty much has no idea what else she's going to do with it other than that. Sue told her this morning that she left a dress for her to borrow out at the cabin. Sue is the closest to her in height, but they are built very differently. Sue is curvy, voluptuous even. Paige is tall and thin and extremely unsure of herself because of it.

"I can help you, Reagan," Paige offers.

"Good, this isn't my specialty. Getting people anywhere on time or hustling kids is a lot harder than sewing stitches or doing a C-section," Reagan jokes and sighs with relief at the offer.

An hour later after assisting Reagan, Paige makes her way to the cabin with Cory's dumb dog following at her heels. Everywhere she goes, Shadow follows her. They pass her brother on the path. Simon barely offers a nod in greeting. He's a mess and covered in dirt, maybe even manure, and headed to the house for a shower. He's jogging very quickly with a bundle of clean clothing tucked under his arm.

When she opens the door to their cabin, her smile from running into her brother and seeing his dirty, frantic appearance falls flat. Cory is standing there in front of her in his underwear and nothing else.

"Shit," she grumbles and turns her face. She crosses quickly to her area of the cabin and tries not to think of the nearly naked man on the other side. She pulls her changing curtain closed with a brisk tug.

"You'd better get your ass ready, beanpole," he says.

She hardly needs him to tell her. She'd been detained even longer in the house helping the moms get their kids ready. Paige just grinds her teeth together. She's not going to let him ruin her day.

"Ya' think?" she mumbles as she pulls off her flour-dusted shirt and jeans. "I've been up at the house helping everyone get their kids ready."

Cory chuckles at her hardship before saying, "I know one kid you weren't getting ready. Arianna. I just threw her outta' here...again."

"Yeah, I noticed she hangs on you a lot," Paige notes with a grin. Arianna practically clings to Cory. She has a little bit of hero worshipping going on there.

"She's my shadow," Cory acknowledges.

She peeks over the curtain to make sure he isn't looking in her direction. He's not. He's tugging on black pants. His dark hair is pulled back into a low ponytail that extends about two inches below its rubber band.

The dress Sue has left for her is a pale peach hue. She barely has time to even consider it as she pulls it up over her waist. The back zipper is too deep for her to finish zipping. However, the dress falls just above her knees and swirls around her thighs with a swish of soft, silky material. She's pretty sure it's supposed to fall at mid-calf, but it won't come even close on her. It almost fits which is the best she's going to get. The dress should also cling more snugly to her waist, but it doesn't. Unfortunately, all she has to wear with it are her dirty black ankle boots. She tugs on some clean socks and pulls on the boots. She has no choice. It's entirely too chilly in the evening now to consider going barefoot, especially after the sun falls.

"Damn it," she swears as she looks down at her ridiculous outfit. This gown needs a pair of classic nude pumps, not dirty work boots that look like they were just in a barn.

"Break a nail?" Cory jabs from the other side of the curtain.

"Shut up. I wasn't talking to you."

"Sue's dress not fit? I can run over there and grab you something else real quick," he offers.

Her mouth almost falls open. That was actually a very thoughtful thing to offer. She's surprised.

Paige pushes the curtain aside and frowns. "I look freagin' stupid. I don't have any other shoes and nobody here..."

Cory steps toward her and interrupts, "You're fine. Don't worry about it. Nobody's going to care. You look... fine."

She notices as she removes her braids and fluffs her hair with her fingers that he still hasn't put on a shirt. But he does wear shoes and a belt.

"I don't want to seem disrespectful. I mean she's my best friend. I don't want to look like an idiot," Paige admits with a frown as she turns to look in the small mirror on the wall. It's the only mirror in their cabin.

She nearly jumps out of her skin when she feels his warm fingers on her back.

"Well, zipping this the rest of the way would help," he says with a smile touching his voice.

"Th...thanks," Paige stutters. His fingertip slides inside the dress near the top of the zipper when he's finished pulling it up and strokes back and forth against her skin there. She steps forward and turns to face him with a confused frown only to be met with a perplexed scowl of his own.

She is about to reprimand him for touching her that way when the black cord at his neck catches her attention. She's never noticed it before. There is a gold chain of some kind twined around it.

"What's this?" she asks and touches her index finger to it. A muscle in his neck flexes simultaneously with another one in his pectoral.

"Um, nothing," he says as he furrows his heavy, dark brows and turns away from her.

Sam blasts through the cabin door without knocking, which is how she usually moves around the farm. She is full of youthful energy and sass. Paige suspects that something is amiss between the young nymph and her brother, though. She's sure of it. Simon has even seemed a little moody lately.

"Cory!" she blurts. "Get ready. Good grief already. Everyone's up at the house loading into cars."

Samantha is wearing a dark red, tea length dress that swirls around and accentuates her petite curves. The color ignites her vivid eyes with a fire that nearly sparks against her pale skin. There is a red rose from Grams's garden artfully tucked into the thick bun of dark hair at the base of her neck. She even has on black patent flats and a matching black shawl with red roses printed on it. In Paige's mind, Sam looks like an exotic gypsy with her black hair in contrast to the black and red clothing. Other than her little doll face, of course.

"Where's my brother?" she asks of Sam.

"Up at the house. He's about ready, too. He hit the showers last, so that was probably a cold one," Sam says with a wicked smile.

"Sucker," Cory mumbles on a conspiratorial chuckle.

"Here, Paige, I brought you a cardigan to borrow," she says, extending her hand.

"Oh, thanks," Paige says and steps forward to accept the cream-colored sweater.

"Grandpa said it's probably going to get pretty cold later on, and since this is outdoors, we'd better bundle up."

107

Paige stands by the mirror and tries to make some sense of her hair. The halo of flowers tied into a ring that Sue made for her doesn't want to sit on her head correctly. Sam comes over to help.

"Too bad I can't just wear my bandana," Paige laments over the unruliness of her wavy hair.

Sam chuckles and exclaims, "Paige! That's not exactly a very feminine look. These flowers will be perfect with your dress. You have such lovely red hair, it's a shame to hide it all the time under those scarves."

Paige tries not to look at Cory in the mirror as he tugs on a button up black shirt, covering the broad expanse of his muscular, hairy chest. She's seen him many times doing push-ups and chin-ups in the barn. He runs with the men almost every morning. Every night, he disappears and doesn't return for many hours. She has no idea where he goes, but he always takes his horse and his rifle. She's not sure she wants to know.

He seems oblivious of them other than the occasional smile he cracks at Sam's babbling.

"I can't wait to see everyone. This is just like when Hannah got married to Kelly. That was so wonderful. This is going to be great, too. They are setting everything up in the top of their barn for dinner in case it rains, which Grandpa said it seems like it's going to. Chet strung some old Christmas lights up so it'll be more romantic. I think Talia will like it."

"I think so, too. I can't believe she's getting married," Paige acknowledges with a lopsided frown. "Six months ago, we were walking here on foot and trying to figure out where to camp out for the night and how *not* to get ourselves killed. And now Talia's getting married. Surreal."

"Yeah, too bad they don't have any more brothers," Cory remarks. "I could get rid of you and get you out of my cabin."

"Maybe you should be looking for a wife so that you can move," Paige suggests with a smug look in his direction.

"Cory? Get married?" Sam asks with a laugh. "Yeah, right. Only if we pay her off."

"Thanks, kid," Cory jokes with her and pinches her cheek gently.

"You know I'm only joking. A girl would be lucky to have someone like you, Cory," Sam corrects and hugs around his waist.

Paige tries not to scoff, but she does snort.

Sam ignores her and continues, "I'm so happy for them. It's been awhile since we've had a wedding, huh Cory?"

"Yep, kid. It's been a long time. Reagan and John were the last," he says as he buttons the cuffs of his shirt.

His clothing is more suited to a funeral than a wedding, but perhaps they are all he has to wear. Perhaps the clothing represents his feelings on weddings.

"Reagan and John didn't want everyone over for their wedding. Well, John probably did, but Reagan didn't. I don't even think she really wanted to get married, either. But she did. Thank goodness for that. Your friend is going to be so pretty, Paige. Someday I'll be at your wedding, too!"

Paige snorts and replies, "Don't get your hopes up, Sam."

"Maybe sooner rather than later," her friend hints, her blue eyes dancing playfully. "You and Jason have been spending a lot of time together."

Paige's eyes jump to Cory. He looks at her briefly before frowning and turning away. He behaves as if he has something to hide. He is not the kind of man to look away from someone in such a manner. He is usually very direct and sure. She is always the first one to look away. She actually hates his open stare and confidence.

"We're just friends," she mutters to Sam, who seems very disbelieving. Jason and she have been spending time together when she goes to town, but they've only known each other a very short time and she only sees him when she goes to town. He held her hand once while they walked around the town. That is hardly an engagement in anyone's opinion. He kissed her last week near the far perimeter of the wall. She'd been surprised by it but not overly moved. It had only lasted a brief second as they were come upon by one of Jason's friends. Again, hardly anything to write home about, but he seems like a good man. He's loyal to his uncle, the town veterinarian. He's kind and courteous. He has excellent manners, too. He's handsome in a clean-cut kind of way, which is very different than any of the men on the McClane farm, present male company very included.

"Better get a move on," Cory interrupts and holds open the door for them.

Paige squeezes past him, but he catches her arm at the elbow and halts her as Sam walks away oblivious.

109

"Be careful with Jason," he warns in a low tone.

Paige looks up into his dark eyes, affronted by his tone, the message and the grabbing of her arm. She tries to tug free, but he tightens his grip.

"That's none of your business," she corrects him with heightening anger. He holds onto her arm a moment longer, twists his mouth into a cocky, dubious expression and releases her. He sweeps his arm out to the side as if he's offering her safe passage.

"Whatever you say, ma'am," he concedes, tips an invisible hat and follows after her.

They walk with Sam to the truck and SUV and everyone piles in. They could walk to the Reynolds farm, but they are all dressed nicely and don't wish to look like they just came in from milking the cows.

Somehow she gets stuck sitting next to Cory in the back seat of the SUV. Kelly sits on her other side holding his wife on his lap. They are in their own world, snuggling, kissing, genuinely happy. Hannah has her nose buried in her husband's neck. Reagan rides in the rear with Sam, but Simon has hopped in the back of the pick-up truck that Derek drives. He's corralling the rambunctious children- all of whom had insisted on riding in the back of the truck- and keeping them under control while mostly failing at keeping them under control at all. Her brother looks impeccably dressed and handsome tonight in navy dress slacks and a white shirt that sets off his auburn hair and tanned skin. John is driving the SUV while Herb McClane rides shotgun and quietly reviews sections he has marked in his Bible.

"You clean up good for a young punk," Reagan jabs at Cory's shoulder from the back seat.

"You look nice too, little Doc," he offers with a bright white smile.

"Heck yeah, she does," John says from the front. "She's my little hottie."

"John!" Reagan reprimands with an ornery laugh.

Paige smiles at their playful mood and teasing. Reagan is wearing a short, emerald green dress and ballet flats. Her messy, wild curls are piled high on top of her head in an elegant fashion.

"You know I like that dress, woman," he teases right back.

"Shut it, mister," Reagan warns.

"Get a room," Herb says from the passenger seat.

"I've got one," John says with a grin. "Unfortunately, it's in your house… full of twenty other people, Herb."

Doc chuckles as he removes his glasses and slides them into the front pocket of his button up shirt.

"You've got a point there," Herb says with a nod.

They continue to razz each other. Kelly even joins in. Paige still feels self-conscious of her dirty boots. Hannah looks so clean and pretty in her long white dress and pale pink cardigan. Everyone looks great for having survived an apocalypse. Everyone except for her. She tugs down the hem of her borrowed, slightly too large gown and tries to wipe at some of the dust on her left boot. Cory reaches down and takes her hand as the chaos of teasing and laughter ensues around them.

"You look fine," he says and places her hand back in her lap.

"I…"

"For a beanpole," he adds with a smirk.

She is about to retort a response when the SUV comes to a stop at the neighbor's farm. Paige squints her eyes at Cory as he helps her down.

"Better get going. You're the maid of honor, whatever the hell that is. Seems important," he jests as he tenderly aids Hannah in climbing down next.

Hannah literally beams up at him and doesn't release his arm. He seems content to have her hold onto him as his brother exits the other side of the vehicle and helps Reagan and Sam.

"It *is* important," Hannah corrects him. "Being the maid of honor is very important, Cory."

Paige chuffs with disbelief through her nose at Hannah's hearing abilities. She doesn't seem to miss a thing. Hannah probably overheard them discussing her haphazard appearance. Paige leaves their group, finds Bertie near the front porch and is ushered inside to the upstairs bedroom where her friend awaits her.

"Oh, Talia," she exclaims as she comes through the door. "You look amazing. You're so beautiful."

Her friend's hair is pulled back into a French twist. There are tiny sprigs of white flowers arranged with care throughout her hair. Bertie's gown fits her perfectly, clinging to her curves, curves of which Paige has many times been envious. Bertie even let Talia borrow her short white veil. She is a picture to be certain. Paige's eyes fill with tears.

The other women leave the two of them alone, and Talia immediately rushes to Paige and asks, "Am I showing? Be honest. I feel like I have a bump already. Do you think anyone will be able to tell? I know it's not like before, but the Reynolds family and Dr. McClane are really religious. I would hate to upset anyone."

"Well, beings Chet knocked you up before marrying you, I'd say his conviction may have waned just a little," Paige teases and hugs her friend. "You can't tell at all. Don't even worry a second about it."

Talia sighs with relief and smooths her hands over the front of the dress again against her flat abdomen.

"Can you believe I'm doing this?"

Paige smiles gently and says, "No, not really! But I'm glad you are."

"If someone had told me five years ago that I'd be marrying some white boy redneck from Tennessee I'd have asked them what they were smoking," Talia jokes.

Paige laughs at her friend's dry humor. "No kidding. But Chet's great. I'm so happy for you, for you both."

"Yeah, me too. I'm so crazy in love with that fool," she says, her own eyes filling with tears.

"Better to be a fool in love, right?" Paige asks as she hugs her friend close.

"That's the rumor," Talia answers.

A few moments later, Bertie comes to announce that they're ready for them. Paige walks her friend down the aisle, which is nothing more than a grass path leading to a quaint, pretty spot beneath a huge hickory tree in the back yard of the Reynolds family home. There are about fifty people present, more than she'd have thought. The McClanes, the Reynolds, and the Johnsons are all present and accounted for, as well, and the wedding ceremony is intimate and personal. She's never been to a wedding, however, where nearly every guest carried a gun of some sort either on their hip or slung over their shoulder.

Chet's brother, Wayne, stands on his other side as his best man. Doc McClane reads words from his Bible. She has no idea if he is even licensed to perform a marriage in the state of Tennessee, but nobody seems to care. Tradition and ceremony seem important to him. He hadn't liked the idea of Talia moving into the Reynolds' farmhouse, especially not once her romantic feelings for Chet became apparent. Doc's old-fashioned, but it feels right to Paige that he is this way. So much of their country is different, broken and in such disrepair that she's glad that men like Herb McClane still believe in the sanctity and necessity of marriage and propriety.

Everyone claps, and a few of the men hoot and holler after they kiss. The women immediately begin setting up the dinner buffet in the hayloft area in the top of the big barn while the men bring out more chairs, carry trays of food and offer seating. They also somewhat keep the children out of the way and in control. Somewhat. Even the kids are excited. The younger generation of the Johnson family mingles with the McClane children and some others who came with their parents from town. Condo Paul and his family are present, but the Navy Seal is back in their village keeping watch. A couple of the new people from the armory that Cory invited to Pleasant View are even present. So are Jason and his drunk uncle, who actually seems sober for once. Two more trucks full of townspeople pull in a few minutes later. Everyone seems happy and glad to be gathered for this celebration, and there must be at least a hundred people present.

Paige stands back and surveys the long, very long, table of food choices that has been provided. She tries to hold back those same feelings that she had the first day on the McClane farm when she'd bawled like a baby at their dinner table. There is such an abundance and variety of food. The people from town have given generously of what they have. There are two stuffed geese, a glazed ham, jams for the breads, many trays of vegetables, some fresh and some probably from people's canning supplies and bowl after bowl of mashed potatoes. Hannah's baked goods and their contributed fresh vegetables including the tomato salad that she made is also set out. The Reynolds brothers have cooked enough roast beef for a small battalion. It smells divine. So long to her old vegan lifestyle. She'd like to jump in and swim in that vat of beef and broth. It's nearly big enough that she could.

She swallows the hard lump in her throat at the plentitude in front of her and dabs at her eyes. Simon wraps an arm around her shoulders, startling her.

"You ok?" he asks with concern.

She nods and tries not to start crying again at the sight of so much food. Paige glances up to see Cory on the other side of her brother. His expression is a puzzled frown aimed at her. He probably thinks she's insane.

They take their seats after filling their plates, and Wayne Reynolds offers up a prayer and a toast to the new couple. Conversations ebb and flow around her. The people from town discuss town events and their families. The farmers discuss the harvest, which is in full swing. She even helped process tomato sauce with Hannah and Sue the other day. They've been stockpiling fresh produce in straw-lined crates in the cold cellar. The men have been busy putting up the last of the hay and harvesting corn for the livestock.

Food gets passed around for seconds and thirds. She passes on even seconds. The meal is hearty and delicious and wonderful, better than any wedding reception food she's ever tasted. Her best friend is smiling ear to ear while talking with her new husband. Maddie sits with the children on bales of straw. Her little white dress was sewn by Bertie, who seems as proficient with a needle and thread as Sue. Her former charge giggles at something Arianna says. The children are in exceptionally high spirits. It's a good day. Paige only wishes that she could've sat next to Jason. She's wedged between Cory and Sam, who keeps talking around her to Cory. She'd like to move so they can sit together but refrains from making a scene. Jason is, unfortunately, sitting across from her next to his uncle on one side and Jackie from the armory group on his other.

She is a fair blonde who is rather pretty with big brown doe eyes. Paige has seen her hanging on Cory when they go to town. Her behavior toward Jason is the same. She's very flirty, which is probably just her personality. Jason catches Paige's eye and winks. She returns it with a grin.

Her brother nudges her arm, reaching around Cory to do so. When Paige looks at him, Simon is scowling. He has taken on the role of protective father figure which is mostly annoying. She just goes back to her meal, pushing food around, too full to eat another bite. She takes a peek at Cory beside her. He's glaring daggers at Jason, although the other man does not seem to notice his ill regard. Is he jealous of Jason talking so animatedly with Jackie? She's quite sure that Cory is sleeping with that woman. She suspects that's the reason he invited the group to their town in the first place. She wonders if he is in love with her.

As the sun is setting when the meal completes, everyone gathers dishes and utensils, taking them outdoors to the hand crank pump which is seeing plenty of action with the younger kids all on dish duty. She doesn't envy them. They have their work cut out for them. The men gather tables and chairs, lining the chairs along the stacked walls of hay. Some of the people from town bring out musical instruments. Talia smiles widely and claps. Paige hadn't known this was going to be a full evening event with music and dancing. She's tired and would rather go back to the cabin, but she also doesn't want to disappoint her friend, who seems so uncharacteristically happy. The young children, Maddie included, immediately begin twirling in circles before the last table is even removed. They know not of inhibitions or a valid reason to have any. They are just joyful and content to twirl in their fancy dresses for a change of the usual post-apocalyptic pace. Paige hangs back with Sam on a bale of hay. Sam just goes on and on about how romantic it all is and how beautiful the barn looks. Paige can still see a touch of sadness behind her blue eyes that Sam typically attempts rather successfully to hide.

It doesn't take long before the lights are dimmed, and the dance floor, which is just a dirty, straw-covered barn floor, is filled with dancing couples for the next hour. Lanterns have been attached to the big barn posts, and Sam was right because the clear Christmas lights wound around the beams of the ancient barn's interior lend a very romantic touch to the atmosphere. Mostly the music is country western ballads she recognizes from before the apocalypse that ran on the radio. This is apparently a big country music area because they don't seem to play anything else. It's still an enjoyable respite from security meetings and talk of the harvest season. John even volunteers to sing a few songs. His heated gaze never leaves his wife for more than a few seconds. He is so smitten with her. Reagan is dancing like a dork with her little son, Jacob and acting foolish and silly and motherly. She seems oblivious of anyone else in the room except her son. That little boy seems to bring this out of her. She's a fantastic mother, even though Paige understands that Jacob isn't really her son at all but an orphan that she and John took responsibility for.

115

Sam continues to chat amiably in her ear as Paige allows her eyes to drift through the crowd, sifting and searching and observing the people all having a good time. She's noticed that Cory has danced twice with Evie Johnson, one of the Johnson daughters who is a widow. The way that Evie looks up into Cory's smiling face makes Paige think that something is probably going on with them. He is apparently sewing his wild oats throughout the county. The attractive woman even laughs at something he says. Paige just scowls and returns her attention to Samantha.

"Wanna' dance, sis?" Simon comes over and asks.

Paige immediately looks to Sam, whose lovely face falls. The young woman quickly glances in another direction to hide what looks like disappointment.

"Um... wouldn't you rather...?"

Her brother doesn't give her a chance to answer but instead tugs her to her feet and drags her to the middle of the dance floor. John starts another song, but this time it is a blues tune with long guitar slides and a slow cadence. A man from town on a fiddle joins in, picking up on the pace of the song. She dances with her brother but scans the crowd.

"Who are you looking for?" Simon asks, his blue gaze intense.

"What? Oh, nothing, nobody," she deflects furtively. He must not believe her because he raises his right eyebrow sardonically. "Just admiring the decorations and...stuff."

"Yeah, they did a good job. This is almost like a real wedding reception."

"Remember some of the ones we had to go to with mom and dad?" she asks, distracting him.

He gives her a big, dramatic roll of his eyes. They'd been dragged to all types of hoity-toity engagements since their father was a senator. Mostly they were in gated community golf resorts and tropical island locations, once even in a castle in France.

"Those were the worst," he remarks.

"They probably got divorced, most of them," she agrees with a nod.

"No kidding," he says with a nod. "This is better. It's more real, ya' know?"

Paige understands what he's getting at. She nods with a smile, "Yeah, I know what you mean. I'm glad Talia found Chet. He's a good man. I think he'll take good care of her."

Cory taps Simon on the shoulder. He's dancing with Sam, who looks like a tiny kid next to Cory.

"Cut in, bro?" he suggests.

Paige would like to say, "hell no!" but refrains, barely. Simon opens his mouth to say something, but Cory gives him a deadly glare.

"Sure," Simon says tightly.

Her brother's body posture has stiffened, and he seems reluctant to leave her. They switch partners, and Paige is so distracted by watching her brother with Sam that it takes a moment to realize that Cory is leading her farther away from them.

"Hey," she objects, coming to a stop.

"Let them have some privacy," he says quietly, pulling her closer. "They've got some shit to work out."

His arm tightens around the small of her back. His right hand squeezes hers gently but firmly. Suddenly the giant barn feels like too small of a space. He leans closer, his head coming to rest near the side of hers. He actually smells good. Cory doesn't look like he ever smells good. Most of the time he's covered in grime. One time when he'd come home at dawn, she'd caught him washing what looked like blood off of his hands at the outdoor spigot at their cabin. He's usually sweaty and dirty. He isn't either now. He's freshly shaven, clean and surprisingly smells like the soap they make mixed with other scents that stir her senses.

"What...what do you mean?"

"I think they've been fighting about something. Probably nothing serious, but they need to work it out. She needs Simon, whether he wants her to or not," Cory says.

He is more perceptive than she has given him credit for being. Guttural grunts and smartass comments are what she usually gets from him. His breath tickles against her ear.

"Yeah, I think you're right," she agrees and turns her head just slightly, which stupidly causes her cheek to brush against his. She turns quickly back, staring straight ahead. God, she must be lonely as hell to find this Neanderthal attractive. Unfortunately this causes her to stare at the black cord at his neck, twined with that feminine gold chain. He's unbuttoned a few of the buttons at his neck, exposing a several inches of his thick neck and a tuft of dark hair on his chest.

117

He's also rolled up his shirt sleeves. He must be hot. She's not. She's already pulled on her borrowed cardigan sweater and until this dance was pretty chilly. "They seem to be in discord over something, but I'm not sure what's going on."

"Discord," he repeats softly, tufting her hair with his breath. "Seems to be a lot of that going around."

Paige can feel him smile against the side of her head. His hand leaves her back for just a second. Then she feels his fingers pulling gently at the tips of her hair that hang almost to her waist. She keeps meaning to have Sue help her cut it but forgets to ask because there is so much else to work on. She sucks in a breath at the strange sensation of him touching her hair. It causes a chill to ripple through her. She releases her breath slowly when he places his hot hand at her lower back again.

"Song's over," she says and steps away abruptly.

Paige blinks rapidly and looks up at Cory. He's just smirking as usual.

"Is it?"

"Yep!" she replies and spins on the ball of her foot, almost taking down a running child in the process. She skirts around the kids and makes a mad dash for the end of the barn.

What the hell was that all about? Ridiculous. She has zero or even less than zero romantic interest in Cory. He's a big, irritating pain in her ass who'd threatened to kill her when they first met. She digs her nails into the palm of her tightly fisted hand until it hurts. Get a grip!

She just needs some fresh air. Paige heads out of the barn as the first gurgle of thunder rolls through the valley. She tugs her cardigan closer against the wind gusts and plods down around to the bottom of the bank barn where huge sandstones frame up the foundation and lend support to the massive structure. The feminine giggle of coyness permeates her thoughts as Paige runs her hand over one of those giant stones. The low murmur of a husky male voice filters through the lower level of the barn next.

She tiptoes through the middle aisle, scaring two of the dairy cows in the process. More laughing following by more talking gains her attention and she turns left to follow the sounds. Perhaps it is Simon and Sam and they've mended their rift. She'd like nothing better than to hang out with them for a short time before returning to the party.

When she gets to the other end of the barn, she plasters on a happy smile of greeting and steps around the corner. What she finds there is not her small group of friends. Jason is there, and he is not alone. The feminine giggling was from Jackie. However, they are no longer laughing. His hands are under the woman's shirt, and he's kissing her neck passionately. Neither of them have spotted her. She slides back around the corner and stands there stunned for a moment.

So much for 'Jason is a good guy.' He's a rat. He's a rat like so many others she's known. Paige fast walks, rounds the corner and rams right into Cory's chest. He's with her brother and Sam.

"Hey!" he exclaims with surprise, grabbing her shoulders. "Careful. Are you ok?"

There are unshed tears in her eyes. Her hands are shaking. She feels like she might pass out from anger and betrayal and disgust.

"What are you doing down here, Paige?" Simon asks.

"Is everything all right?" Sam blurts.

Paige doesn't quite know how to answer that. She shakes her head, pulls back from Cory and replies, "I guess some things never change, not even after the world goes to hell. Excuse me."

She slides past Cory and runs from the barn. When she gets outside, it has finally started raining in earnest. The heavens have opened up and allowed the lightning, thunder and rain to free itself from their bonds of imprisonment. She doesn't rejoin the party. The rain feels refreshing, cleansing even, as if she needs it to clear her thoughts from what she's seen.

Paige lifts her face to the sky and closes her eyes, letting the rain sluice down over her features. The idea of going back inside now that she's completely soaked through, to face Jason and Jackie and their newfound love is not something she wishes to do. There is plenty enough light to make her way back to the McClane farm. She's needed a long run for some time. She takes off at a slow jog but eventually speeds up until she is sprinting, mindless of the muddy rain water splashing her bare calves. She hadn't realized how much she's missed running since she came to their farm. She has more than needed this. Running is how she used to stay in shape, fight off stress and deal with life. It's always been a cathartic form of relief. Staying in shape now seems to be a good idea anyway since she's never sure

119

what life is going to hand her. She just hadn't thought she'd be running from her problems. She thought her problems were finally over. Six months ago, her only problem was staying alive. Now she's right back in the real world where human interaction causes more problems than finding a small amount of food for the day. She'd rather be back out there worrying about her next meal.

Chapter Nine
Cory

He spends about an hour shooting the shit with his brother and Paul from the condo community about security and the new patrol teams in town before he realizes that he hasn't seen Simon's sister in a while, not since they found her in the basement of the barn. He had assumed that she returned to the party. Cory extracts himself from his group and searches out Simon.

He'd tried to warn Paige about Jason, but like the hard-head she is, she wouldn't listen. Cory knew about Jackie's attraction to Jason. He'd gone to town a few weeks ago to break it off with her, to let her down gently. Her group told him that Jackie had gone over to the home of the vet's son to help him on a project. She'd greeted him at Jason's front door with a smile and Jason's t-shirt and nothing else. He wasn't mad. They had a mutual understanding that their relationship wasn't going anywhere. He didn't and doesn't want a serious relationship with a woman. But his feelings toward the vet's son had also been cemented that afternoon. He doesn't like or trust him. He's seen him in town talking to Paige, obviously leading her on. He's seen him chatting up other women in town, too. Jason's a dick. He really should beat the tar out of him.

"Have you seen Paige?" he asks his friend when he finds Simon at a table in a far corner of the barn talking with Doc and some of the others from town. They're discussing medicinal herbs.

"No, I thought she came up here," Simon says, half rising out of his chair.

Cory stays Simon with a hand to his shoulder. "I think she was pissed because of that dick Jason. I bet she went back to the farm."

"I'll go and check," Simon adds with concern.

"Nah, I'm whooped," Cory lies smoothly. "I'll go. I was leaving anyway. You stay and talk. I'm sure she just went back. If I don't find her, I'll come right back to get you. She looked tired, so I'm positive she just went home. Sue and Derek already left, too."

Simon nods reluctantly but remains seated.

"You gonna make sure Sam gets home safe?" Cory asks and glances across the room where Samantha is sitting with Reagan and Hannie. He noticed at different times throughout the night that men from town asked her to dance. She'd declined them all with a pleasant smile, but Cory knows that her reason for rejecting them is because she carries with her a heavy distrust of men.

"Of course I will," Simon hisses through his teeth as if Cory's question has pissed him off.

"Easy, man," Cory chuckles with a grin. "I'm just double checking."

Simon scowls at him but turns back to the conversation at the table. Cory smirks. His friend's anger isn't really aimed at him. Simon is just upset over this rift between him and Samantha. Cory's not getting involved. He's not exactly great with offering advice for that sort of shit. He's heard that sex can be a useful make-up tool, but if Simon's in charge of initiating that, then they'll all die of old age waiting for those two to patch it up.

He gets detained twice while trying to leave which delays him another twenty minutes. Some of his friends from town want to know more about where he went during his travels. Finally, he makes it out of the barn and starts jogging for the cabin. It doesn't take long to make out the pale amber glow coming from there. She's obviously made it back safely, but he's still pissed at her for leaving and taking that kind of risk. Everyone went to the wedding with the understanding that no one would try to make the trek home alone. He feels slightly better knowing that Derek came back quite a while ago with his family so that they could get their three kids to bed. He knows because Ari was pissed. She had trailed him around the barn all night and had even snookered him into dancing with her four times. Then she'd informed him that she was going to marry him someday. Poor kid. He wouldn't wish that on anyone. And now he's the one who is pissed. He's angry that Simon's sister didn't at least tell someone that she was leaving.

A thin tendril of gray smoke wafts up from their narrow chimney pipe. It pushes its way heavenward through the blinding rain. She's apparently lit a fire in the wood-burning stove.

Cory blasts through the door, startling the hell out of Paige, who spins around and almost falls. She's changed out of her dress and is wearing a pair of very small pink shorts and a gray Arkansas Razorbacks sweatshirt. It's definitely another one of his articles of clothing unless, of course, she's taken a sudden interest in his home state's college football team. This is what she generally sleeps in, shorts and borrowed shirts, usually his. Her hair is still wet from rain water and has curled slightly. He rests his rifle against the door frame.

"Ever hear of knocking?" she asks haughtily.

"Ever hear of telling people that you're leaving?" he returns as he closes the cabin door.

"No," she answers quietly, still standing in the middle of the room.

"That was completely irresponsible," he reprimands with his hands on his hips. "This place was invaded a few months ago. Some of the men are still on the run. Do you think that maybe it would've been a good idea to tell one of us that you were heading home?"

She steps forward, trips over a small, braided throw-rug on the floor and says, "Maybe."

"Well, I guess everything's ok," he concedes and crosses the room to his bed. Cory begins removing his wet clothing, not caring whether or not she watches. Within a few moments, he has on a pair of black sweatpants. She has the cabin hotter than Hades with the cook-stove going. He's not even going to bother with a shirt. And if she doesn't like it, then she can go to bed. "Derek's back and probably on watch, so I guess it worked out. But it was still stupid. Next time let someone know what you're doing. It's not safe to go traipsing around in the dark alone."

"Ohhh, you don't know me, mister," she says in a funny tone. "I'm super duperty sneaky."

"What?" Cory asks and turns around. She's swaying to and fro in the middle of the room.

"Yeppers, I'm sneaky and fast like a mouse. You couldn't catch me even if you tried," she says and snaps her fingers.

"Apparently you weren't sneaky enough when the farm was attacked since you got taken hostage," Cory observes.

Her fair red brows pinch together.

123

"That's not cool to point that out," she babbles.

Her words are slurring. She's having difficulty focusing.

"Are you ok?" he asks and steps forward. He's wondering if she's sick, if he should run back and grab Simon or Doc. Cory reaches for her forehead, but she slaps at his hand and misses.

"Never been better!" she blends into one word.

"Are you... are you sick or something?" Cory inquires. He notices that she's staring at his stomach. She takes a few steps closer and reaches out. Her skinny index finger traces a small scar on the right side of his stomach. What the hell's wrong with her? She normally dashes out of whatever room he comes into with a nasty stare aimed at him.

"What's that?" she asks and purses her lips.

Then it hits him. Literally hits him. The smell of liquor is rolling off of her.

"You're drunk?"

"Jussa' little bit," she answers, showing the tiny measurement with her thin fingers.

"What the...?" he asks of nobody, especially not the drunk woman in front him. He scans around the room. There wasn't much for alcohol being served at the Johnson's reception. Most folks try to reserve any spirits they have for medical purposes. Then he spots it. One of the mason jars given to him from the hooch maker is sitting on his bedside table, the lid next to it. The jar was full. It's missing at least a quarter of its clear, liquid contents.

"I ran all the way here, and then I got thirsty," she volunteers.

"So you drank moonshine?"

"I said I was thirsty!" she explains with impatience.

Cory almost smiles. "Did you think that was going to be a good idea, getting cooked on hooch?"

"What's hooch? I thought it was water, so I took a drink," she answers. "And it turned out to be a very good idea actually. It doesn't taste very good, though."

He tries not to notice how close she's standing or how the rain water from the tips of her hair keeps plopping onto the front of her stolen sweatshirt. He also tries not to notice any section on that part of her body, either. Not noticing her long, tan legs isn't even going to happen, so he doesn't let himself look there at all. Watching her parade around the farm with her long legs and bad attitude is difficult enough on his senses. Most of the time he isn't sure if he wants to run his hand down those long legs or slap some duct tape on her mouth. He decides to concentrate on the sprinkling of freckles on her nose and cheeks. He's never really thought about them before, but they're kind of cute. Cory clears his voice and gives her an undeviating stare instead.

"I'd say you took more than one drink," he replies with an irritated smirk as he screws the lid back on the glass jar and stores it away under his bed, way out of her reach under his bed.

"Hey!" she exclaims. "Maybe I wanted another drink."

"You won't be thinking that tomorrow morning. You'll be thanking me," he tells her as he straightens again to his full height. She may be a tall woman, but he's still much taller than her.

"I'll never thank you for anything," she retorts on a pout.

"Probably not. You've got rocks for brains, obviously," he replies, indicating the booze stashed away for safe keeping. His intention was to give it to Reagan to use medicinally at the clinic. Apparently Paige's idea of medicinal use and his approach are in direct contrast.

"No, I don't," she argues and wags her finger in front of his chest. "Men are the ones who are stupid, not me."

"I did try to warn you," he reminds her.

"I should've known," she answers, her anger building.

She ignores his comment. He just furrows his brow impatiently at her and tries to move around Paige. She steps toward him, blocking his way. He has no idea what she is talking about, nor does he care to. He just wants to crash for the night and for her to do the same.

"Did I ever tell you I had a boyfriend?" she asks.

He knows her story, of how she got away from bandits in the city and met up with Talia in a rescue camp. He also knows that she was living with some guy and their friends before the fall. Simon told him last week about his sister's journey.

However, he replies with, "That doesn't seem possible, knowing your pleasant personality."

She huffs indignantly and says, "Well I did! He was just like Jason."

"Oh yeah? Was he a puss? Is that what you mean?"

She snort-laughs through her nose. "No. Well, actually yes. He was kind of a wimp, I suppose. He spent more time in the bathroom getting ready than I did. He wasn't like you or your brother."

"Oh, you mean devastatingly handsome and hung like a horse?" he inquires with a crude tease.

She doesn't laugh this time but sways on her feet. He reaches for her because he's afraid she's going to face plant on the hardwood floor. She knocks his hand away and stands there. After a few scrutinizing seconds of staring at his face, Paige's eyes dart to his crotch. Then she shakes her head.

"No," she says more seriously. "He cheated on me. That's why he was like Jeff."

"You mean Jason?"

"What?" she asks confusedly in her drunken state. "Yes... Jason. I meant Jason. What a jerk! My boyfriend cheated on me. That's how they're alike. I came home from class, got out early. He used to complain about me all the time. Said I didn't dress sexy and was too plain. I never told Simon what a dick he was to me. I didn't want him to feel even worse about not coming to Georgia to find me when it all fell apart. My boyfriend didn't like that I went to the track to run. Said I was too much of a jock. He didn't like my... wanted me to get a boob job."

Cory doesn't know this guy, other than that he is dead, but he'd like to shoot him.

"So I came home early from school that day. I thought I'd get myself all dolled up," she says dramatically, hanging on to the word 'dolled' for an inordinately long amount of time. Then she flails her hands around dramatically. "I was gonna take him out for a date night. Couples like that kind of stuff. That's what I read in a magazine."

Cory shakes his head, "I don't think they do anymore."

She doesn't laugh but keeps right on going, "I caught him and my roommate, my best friend no less, in bed together. In *my* bed!"

"Bastard," he comments and wrinkles his nose sympathetically.

"I know. Wait, are you laughing at me?"

"Never," Cory says, concealing his grin. It's not that he thinks her boyfriend cheating on her with her best friend is funny. It's just that her drunken re-telling of the events filled with lots of exaggerated motioning of her arms, slurring words, and wide eyes are kind of humorous. She's usually much more reserved around him. Actually, if he's being completely honest with himself, he's pretty sure Paige tries to avoid him. Lately, he's found himself looking for her on the farm grounds, hoping to catch a glimpse. He tells himself that he just likes to get a head count on everyone throughout the day for safety reasons.

"He was a creep, and I never saw it."

"What happened? Did you shoot him?"

This earns a small chuckle before she says, "No, I didn't shoot him… or her."

She walks over to his side of the room and picks up a notebook. Cory snatches it from her and tosses it on the bed. These are his notes on tracking the Target freaks. Then she starts poking around in his other things on the nightstand; a book, a small jar of salve he uses when his booted feet have been in water for too many hours. Reagan had made it for him. Then she'd warned him with a bawdy laugh not to use it for anything else. He'd just ruffled her hair and laughed. John's wife cracks him up. She's as ornery as the men.

He just turns Paige around and gives her a little push.

"So you didn't shoot them?" he asks, distracting her from her unusually bold snooping.

"Nope, I did what any girl would do. I called my mom. She talked me through it. I was going to move out the next weekend. She was going to put money into my bank account for me so I could get my own place. She never approved of me living with him anyways, so it pissed me off that she was right. She was always right about everything."

"Moms are good at that," he comments with a grim smile.

She steps toward him again, coming way too close for comfort. He wishes Simon would return. Paige reaches up and touches her fingers to the gold bracelet at his neck, held tightly there by the black leather cord. He snatches her hand gently and places it back at her own side, noting the black leather strings tied around her wrist. First she has him thinking about his mother and now he's remembering Em. He buries both of those thoughts and scowls down at her.

"Well, my mom was the queen of right. I was a dumbass, stupid brat who thought I knew more than her. That was the first day of the tsunamis. The first one hit about two hours after I got off the

127

phone with my mom. I never moved out. That was the last time I talked to my mom, too. I was impatient with her. I think I was even a rude jerk a few times because I was mad that she was right about my boyfriend and living together and I was wrong as usual."

Cory frowns at her distress. Why can't Sue or Hannie be here right now? He's not good with this kind of shit.

"Men are just assholes," she rants next.

Cory just smiles and says, "Yeah, pretty much."

God, where are the women when he needs them?

"Men only like blondes with big boobs," she states as if she's reading from a man-hater's manual.

"Not all men. Not me," he says quietly, admiring her red hair and figure. She doesn't have huge breasts, so she does have a point there. But what curves he can make out through his baggy sweatshirt seem just fine to him. He's noticed her in more fitted t-shirts before the weather turned chilly and had not found her at all lacking. She's easy to spot on the farm. Her red hair stands out like a sore thumb. What she lacks in breast mass she certainly makes up for with a set of long legs that go on forever.

"Men are creeps and assholes who cheat the first chance they get," she says.

"Probably," he agrees, joining her men-are-the-spawn-of-the-devil tirade. He figures it's probably easier than arguing a case for his fellow man right now.

She doesn't even acknowledge his comment. Why can't Simon be here to help her work through this? Or Sam, she's great with people. She's fantastic at the clinic. She keeps people calm with just a few soft-spoken words. Paige steps away from him, so Cory slips by her and goes toward the middle of the cabin. She spins around and tracks him down, though.

"I used to get blonde highlights put in my hair because my boyfriend didn't like the red."

"Again, more evidence that he was an idiot," Cory says, admiring her drying hair. He's trying to imagine what she'd look like with blonde hair, but it doesn't fit. Her hair is perfect the way it is. In its tousled state, it looks even better. It goes with her tiny brown freckles, even the ones on her exposed bare shoulder since his shirt is too big for her, enabling him a glimpse. She's also definitely not wearing a bra. No strap is showing where the sweatshirt has slid down her shoulder.

"What's wrong with me?" she asks.

A flash of lightning illuminates the cabin for a moment. The color reminds him of her eye color, a pale, iridescent, shimmery gray.

"You have bad decision-making abilities?" he asks.

She shakes her head and bites her lower lip. Then she steps closer to him.

"No, that's not it," she says thoughtfully, tapping her fingertip to her bottom lip.

"Of course not," he concedes because he's smart enough to know that this isn't something he can win.

She sways hard, and Cory reaches out for her. Somehow she stays upright and even waves away his offered help. She's stubborn as hell. It's probably a good thing since that likely helped keep her alive on the road for so long.

"Why am I unlovable?" she asks with sad gray eyes.

Cory contemplates her for a moment before replying.

"I can't see that you are. Don't be so hard on yourself," he says softly, his gaze dropping to her full lower lip. Her cheeks are rosy with high color either from the alcohol or the heat of the fire or both. She looks completely lovable in this moment. Maybe not lovable exactly but sexy would probably better describe his arch nemesis. He rarely looks at her for any extended amount of time. She's his best friend's sister. She's off-limits on every possible level. Plus, most of the time she's railing at him like a super bitch.

"I am unlovable. Trust me."

A frown line mars the smooth skin between her pale brows.

"Jason's an idiot," Cory tells her on a nod.

"That was it. My one chance to find someone," she states emphatically and waves her hand in the air as if swatting at bugs.

"I think you have more choices than you know," Cory informs her quietly.

"Nope. That was it. The well's gone dry."

"You don't notice the guys looking at you when we go to town. I have. Your brother for damn sure has. I think that poor guy's gonna need blood pressure meds one of these days."

"They're probably just thinking about cheating on me, too," she says as if it is a statement of fact and not a ridiculously silly comment.

129

"I don't think so. More likely they're thinking about not letting you out of bed long enough to cheat on you," he states and places his hands on his hips. Paige steps toward him. Cory's eyes narrow suspiciously. Her eyes slide slowly from his stomach, which causes the muscles there to involuntarily flex under her scrutiny, up to his chest and then his face. "I think you should go to bed."

Cory half turns to move away when Paige flings herself at him. Her arms link around his neck, and she presses herself against his chest. Her mouth smashes against his. His eyes widen, and he holds perfectly still. She doesn't do either. Her eyes are tightly closed. Her mouth moves painfully against his. Her teeth even clink against his once. Her fingertips dig into the long hair at his neck and curl tightly. There is no way in hell he's touching her. He's not going to return her drunken kiss, either. It is the most unmoving, non-sexual kiss of his life. He can taste the hooch on her breath, smell it on her. She's reeking of alcohol, but under the scent of liquor there is a tint of rainwater and something flowery. And she's never going to remember this tomorrow, so he doesn't want to take it any further with her. He really hopes she doesn't remember this.

She presses her breasts against his chest, which starts to stir something in the pit of his stomach. Then she coughs once into his mouth, stumbles back, and projectile vomits onto his bare stomach and chest.

"Oh my God!" she cries with wide, surprised eyes.

Cory scowls hard at her and says with sardonic humor, "Well, that was sexy."

She repeats her religious invective four more times.

Paige runs to the bathroom, slams the door and continues her vomit eruptions into the toilet. At least, Cory hopes she's puking in the toilet and not hitting the floor. He has to clean himself. He doesn't really have a desire to clean vomit from the bathroom floor, too.

Left with no choice, he goes outside to the hand-pump water spigot. He splashes handfuls of icy cold water onto his chest and stomach all while getting rained on again. He's pretty sure he invents a few new cuss words in the process of freezing himself. What the hell was she thinking? Homemade moonshine is a dangerous, inhibition-removing tool in the wrong hands. He knows that Simon's sister hates his guts. She basically lets him know this every possible opportunity she gets. She glares at him, insults him, threatens him every chance she gets and openly judges him. She's a royal pain in the ass most of the time.

When he goes back inside, she's still in the bathroom. Cory knocks once on the new door that Derek installed the other day and enters. She is still kneeling and praying to the porcelain gods for forgiveness and empathy that isn't likely to come. He steps into the tiny bathroom and holds her hair back. It's the least he can do. She dry heaves a few times and seems to have emptied her stomach. Lucky for him, she'd only hit him with alcohol and not the giant wedding feast they'd all consumed earlier.

Cory flushes the toilet for her and helps Paige stand by pulling her up by her slim arm. He takes the cup from the small ledge of the sink where they brush their teeth and pours some water for her. She rinses her mouth and spits. Cory rushes to the other room again and grabs a clean shirt from his pile. He passes it into the bathroom without looking in. Then he leads her from the bathroom once she's in another one of his shirts, a navy blue long-sleeved tee.

When they get to the other room, he even helps her into bed, which for her is a mattress on the floor next to her brother's bed. He pulls her blankets to her chin and squats beside Paige on his haunches.

Without meeting his gaze, she says, "Sorry. I was…"

"Nothing. It's forgotten already. Don't worry about it," he forgives her. If their roles were reversed, he highly doubts she'd so easily let him off the hook. From what little he knows of women, they can be fairly good grudge holders. Hell, Paige hates him for a threat he'd made a month ago when he thought she was with a group of criminals who'd taken over the farm. He's apologized for it, but she is reluctant to let it go. This one seems to hold the record for grudge holding.

"Simon's…" she says on a groan and doesn't complete her thought.

"Doesn't need to know. Like I said, don't worry about it," Cory tells her, trying to alleviate her embarrassment. "Just get some rest. You'll feel better tomorrow. And if you'd like, I'll go to town and beat the shit out of Jason."

Paige offers a small but still slightly inebriated grin and says, "I don't know if he'd be worth it."

"Maybe I'll just beat him up a little bit then," he jokes and brushes her hair back from her forehead.

"Yeah, just a little," she agrees with a toothy grin.

She looks young and innocent when her guard is down and she's smiling like this with her wild red hair tangled around her head on the pillow like a halo of fire. The hard lines that nearly four years on the road has etched around her lovely eyes soften and disappear.

"Get some sleep, kid," he tells her.

"I'm not a kid. I'm older than you," she corrects him on a long blink.

"I don't think so," he says with a disbelieving frown.

"I am. My birthday's before yours by like six months or something. Simon told me," she says.

Her remark is one of superiority as if she's older and wiser. Cory would like to remind her which one of them just puked the liquor they couldn't hold.

"Yeah, well I've got some city miles on me, so I think I'm still older," he says lightly.

"I have miles, too. Everyone probably does. We're all going to look like we're forty in a few more years," she says sadly and closes her eyes. "The whole world's a mess."

She doesn't open her eyes again, but zonks out like Arianna after a long day of play and tormenting the boys on the farm. Cory allows his gaze to trail down over her sleeping form, noting the indentation of her waist and the length of her legs under the blanket. Then he immediately gets to his feet and gears up. Since Simon's sister is alive and well, sort of, he's got a job to do.

He changes into dry, camouflage pants and a black shirt. Cory pulls on a black zip up hoodie and his boots. His plans of crashing for the night are forgotten.

"That it is," he says to the comatose woman. "But it's my job to put it back to order."

With this statement, Cory retrieves his rifle and leaves the cabin and his best friend's sexy sister.

Chapter Ten
Reagan

It's been nearly two weeks since Talia's wedding, and the activity on the farm has reached a fever pitch. The men are harvesting the wheat as well as working on the wall in town nearly every day. Kelly is even working with K-Dog from the condo community on training a militia to work full-time in town and on guard patrols at night. The sentry posts near the wall are almost complete, and they've even tapped into the old natural gas lines with the help of Cory since he saw how it was done up in Columbus. Now the guards will have a limited amount of light to work with at night on their patrols with the gas lines rigged up to power lanterns on a few of the lamps near their towers.

Today she's working on canning the last of the beans with Paige, Talia, who has come for a visit, and Sam. Then they're making soap since they're about out of their supply. She wants to get Samantha to talk to her about whatever it is that has her down. She's been drawing dark images lately, too. Reagan found a few moody sketches laying on her desk in her bedroom when she'd gone looking for Sam one afternoon to go for a ride with her. Sometimes they go alone, which Reagan has come to relish. Her adopted little sister means so much to her. She used to be more open with Reagan and would sometimes talk about her feelings, about what happened to her. But for the past few years, she only seems to turn to Simon.

They just about have all the jars filled with beans and ready to go into the canner. This isn't her area of expertise, but Hannie and Sue are busy outside on other projects. And since Reagan's not working at the clinic today, she thought she'd volunteer. Even though she really doesn't like being stuck in the kitchen, she's reasonably confident that she won't give anyone botulism.

Talia wants to learn more about canning and making soap, so Reagan called over on the radio to Chet this morning. He drove his new wife and little Maddie over on his four-wheeler. She and Paige were happy to be reunited for some quality girl-bonding time.

"Oops," Paige says as she drops a spoonful of beans onto the counter.

"Those can be our snack," Reagan jokes and gets an unsure smile from Simon's sister. She's also out of her element. "Right, Sam?"

"What?" the dark-haired doll answers from the pantry on a search for salt. "Oh yeah. We can eat those ones, Paige. Don't worry about it."

Sam emerges from the pantry again, carrying the crock of salt. Cory brought home a few containers of salt, which was good because they can never have enough of it. Reagan misses having salt on a buttered ear of corn. She misses a lot of the frivolous things that have been taken away. Last year, they traded salt for a side of beef with one of Grandpa's former patients from a neighboring town. He'd come with his two young sons and his wife to their clinic for medical care. They were all the family he had left. But he'd been glad to give up his salt for beef since he was down to a few backyard chickens and a dairy goat.

This is what they try to do for many items they need. They trade with those who have a need of their own for things they might have or for medical care. Mr. Peterson in town makes toothpaste powder for anyone who needs it in exchange for milk and eggs. He brings it by the clinic on occasion, and Grandpa or Simon greets him with the eggs and a few gallons of milk. So far, it's worked because none of them has had a cavity. She and Grandpa are certainly not dentists, nor does Reagan have any desire to be one anytime soon. The clinic keeps her busy enough as it is with sickness and injury. Just the other day one of the men working on the third guard tower fell and broke his collar bone. She hadn't needed an x-ray to tell it was broken.

"We have so much put up, it's crazy to think that we'll go through all of it," Paige comments.

Her light eyes squint with indecision. The kitchen is hot, causing all of them to have flushed cheeks. They've already processed three canners full of lima beans just today, and Reagan hopes that this will be the final one.

"We will," Sam tells her. "Trust me, we'll go through all of it and more. That's why we can and put up cold storage vegetables. If we didn't, then the men would be happy. They could just eat meat all winter and not be bothered with the vegetables."

"Oh, yes, Chet and Wayne are the same way," Talia says with a laugh.

Reagan smirks, "No kidding. Jacob's such a little carnivore already."

Her son is currently tagging along with his dad working on the wheat grinding process. He's John's little minion. He never minds, though and never tries to ditch Jacob. He's always attentive and giving of himself.

"Yeah, I've noticed," Paige says. "So is Maddie. I think it comes from eating wild game on the road. She still isn't used to eating carbs and flour products."

"I'm sure," Reagan agrees.

Talia scoffs and says in her thick Louisiana accent, "Chet brought home a turtle the other day. A turtle! And then he thought I'd kill it and cook it or something. I just looked at him like, 'Boy, have you lost your mind?'"

Everyone laughs at her story of woe. She keeps right on going with the head bobbing and finger wagging.

"I don't think he's used to anyone talking back to him, but let me tell you I was not butchering a turtle. I helped Paige and Gavin skin squirrels and rabbits but no turtles. No thanks. That's disgusting. What the hell?"

The word hell when Talia says it comes off more like *hail*. She keeps them laughing with her tale of turtle horror.

"What'd you do?" Paige asks.

"Chet and his brother brought in a platter of cut up and cleaned meat later on, and me and Bertie cooked it. Mostly I just watched. But it wasn't too bad. She deep fried it in lard. My nana used to cook everything in lard like that. My dad's mom. Man, she was a good cook."

Her hazel eyes take on a haunted look as she remembers family members who are probably dead.

135

"You used to be a vegetarian, right, Paige?" Reagan asks as she screws on a hot lid while trying to bring the conversation around again.

"Yeah, well, a vegan, so I didn't eat meat *or* dairy products. I was very much against killing animals and wearing leather, all that jazz," she says with a nod and wipes the sweat from her forehead with the shoulder of her shirt.

"Well, you're a meat eater now, girl," Talia teases.

She gets a big smile from Simon's sister before Paige replies, "Heck, when I get cold, I've considered wearing that gross bearskin Cory brought home and gave to your grandpa. I'd definitely eat one of the horses now. I hate those stupid things anyways."

Reagan laughs out loud, as do the other women. Talia slaps her friend on the shoulder and laughs, too. Reagan can tell how close these two women are, and she's glad they both survived together.

"Yeah, I got over my affinity for that not harming animals thing once I realized that vegan pizza and tofu weren't on the menu anymore," Paige says with a smirk.

"I'm sure you did," Reagan agrees as she lowers the last jar into the canner.

"The food at the rescue camps was the worst," she tells them. "They had some pretty nasty stuff. A lot of powdered food, water with electrolytes. But I guess when you're hungry you'll eat just about anything."

"You know it, sister," Talia says and places a protective arm around Paige's shoulders for a moment. "That was some gruel if I ever had any. Nothing like my nana's cooking. She could make something outta nothing. She'd make fried okra, French beignets, crawfish chowder. Yum. Hannah's cooking reminds me of hers. Plus, my nana always put up a garden, too."

"Our farm is a lot of work, but it keeps us alive," Reagan says in agreement.

"It's like a Shangri-La here, trust me," Paige notes.

"That's why we have to fight to preserve it," Reagan says. "Not just for us but for these kids. We don't want them to go through what you've been through, what any of us has been through."

She feels bad when Sam's face falls. Reagan knows that she doesn't like to talk about her past. She really doesn't even like to acknowledge it at all. As far as Reagan's concerned, Samantha doesn't have to utter a peep about it for the rest of her life if she doesn't want to. If it wasn't for John, Reagan's not sure she would've come through her own dark past, so she can understand not wanting to relive it with a good old-fashioned story hour session. She can't blame Sam at all.

"Even if Cory does live here," Paige mumbles.

"Oh, you'll come to love Cory, Paige!" Sam scolds. "We all do."

"Yep, he's as fucked up as the rest of us," Reagan swears.

"Reagan!" Sam says on a hiss. "If Hannah hears you talking like that, she'll flip her lid."

"Then you'd better give me a heads up if you see her coming," Reagan says with a wink. "Anyway, Cory is screwed up. Maybe a little more than most, but we still love that crazy kid."

"Hm," Paige says disbelievingly.

Talia says, "He doesn't seem that bad to me."

"He is," Paige insists through gritted teeth and a frown as if she finds something confusing.

"There are worse men out there than Cory," Sam says with melancholy.

"Let's get working on the soap now, since the beans are cooking," Reagan suggests, trying to change the topic so that Sam doesn't become depressed.

Sam takes Talia to retrieve the lye water from the mud room while she and Paige clean up the kitchen and prepare it for another project. Sam comes back with the bucket and places it on the counter. Then she disappears and comes back again with the scale and another bucket full of solid lard. Talia comes in holding two small glass containers of Sue's essential oils and a long stirring spoon. Reagan retrieves a jar of liquid animal fat from the pantry along with a glass jar of Sue's dried herbs.

"Paige, grab the soap pot from the mud room. It's up on top of the cabinet in there," Reagan orders as she comes back. "You're the only one of us tall enough to reach it."

When the ingredients are laid out on the counter, they start the soap-making process. Soon the house will smell like lavender and thyme-scented soap with undertones of lemony cleanliness. Even though it won't be ready to use for a few weeks, they needed to get a jump on it with making the soap because their supply is almost

137

depleted. Reagan knows that Sue has been drying wild mint in the barn to be placed in the next batch of soap in a month or so. That particular scent is Reagan's favorite. Or maybe it's her preference because it smells so damn sexy on John's skin.

Sam measures the liquid oils in a glass measuring cup and sets them one at a time on the small scale. Paige uses the pestle and mortar to grind the dried herbs to a super fine consistency. Talia begins scooping out the solid lard into a measuring cup for weighing. This reminds Reagan of the time she used to spend with Grams. Making soap was one of the few kitchen chores she used to do with her grandmother, and it makes Reagan pine for her companionship and guidance. She even misses being reprimanded for swearing and the occasional thump to the back of her head.

"Cory's not a bad person, Paige," Sam says, reverting back to their earlier conversation. "He's been through a lot, just like you."

"I guess he's not a total beast," Paige allows, which is a big concession for her.

Reagan's noticed that they don't get along. Actually not getting along would be an improvement in their relationship. Whatever else transpired between those two out in the woods on the day that Cory came home must've been pretty damn bad for Paige to hate him like she obviously does. Although she seems to be coming around, slightly.

They get the solid fats melting in the large, stainless steel pot while preparing other ingredients. Reagan leaves Talia at the stove to watch the thermometer for the right temperature.

"He kept his little sister alive for like four days or something when their parents were killed," Sam reveals as she wipes the counter with a wet towel.

"Really?" Paige asks. "How were they killed?"

Reagan jumps in to answer, "They were shot while they slept. Cory heard it and woke up. He found them murdered in their bed and overheard men going back downstairs. He got to Em. He hid with her somewhere in their house. Then when the men left after they were done stealing everything they could, he hid out in the woods behind their house. He called Kelly on the satellite phone."

"Oh my gosh," Paige says with surprise.

"It took John and Kelly about four days to get to them. That was one of the main reasons they left their military base. Kelly couldn't leave his kid brother and sister- even though they're only step-siblings- to fend for themselves. Plus, Derek knew he had to get home to Sue and the kids who were here on the farm. So the soldiers all left their base. Cory stayed hidden in the woods until the men got there," Reagan explains further. "It was up to him to keep her alive. John told me that when they found him, Cory had already dragged his parents' bodies into their back yard and buried them. He was just seventeen when this all happened, just a kid. And after that, he and Em were inseparable. She was glued to him all the time. She was a good-hearted little person, not a mean bone in her body. He was her big hero."

"Wow, that's so... I don't even know what to say," Paige remarks, furrowing her brow.

"We've all been through a lot to get here," Reagan tells her, hoping to soften Paige's hard edge of anger toward Cory. He's like a kid brother to Reagan, and she wants the family to live in harmony with one another. "He's a tough kid. Well, I guess he's not really a kid anymore, but he's still tough."

She even goes so far as to slide her hand onto Paige's on the counter.

"That part I already understood," Paige says with a smirk.

"But he's sweet, too," Sam says, defending her adopted big brother. "You just have to get to know him, Paige."

"I think it's probably better if we just avoid each other. I don't think we're ever gonna be besties."

Reagan laughs at this one. Paige has a sarcasm that matches her own.

"Never know," she suggests and gets a snort from Paige.

"I think I know," Paige argues. Then she interjects as if she is surprised by something, "Hey!"

"What?" Reagan asks.

Paige touches the gold bracelet on Reagan's wrist, one of the matching five bracelets on the farm that she'd stolen from the jewelry store for herself and the other women.

"This is the same as the one on Cory's necklace," Paige observes, running her fingers over the design. "It's wound around a black cord he always wears."

"It was his little sister's," Sam explains with great melancholy touching her voice. "It belonged to Emma."

Paige's eyes dart to Sam's and then Reagan's. She doesn't even verbalize, but her mouth forms a soft, "oh."

"Ok, Paige, add the liquid oils to the pan," Sam instructs, obviously not wanting to dwell on the subject of her dead friend.

Paige wears her signature blue bandana around her head to hold back her hair. Her used blue-jeans are a few inches too short and probably a size too big. She's wearing a long-sleeved t-shirt in hues of blue and green tie-dyes that she has knotted at her slim waist. She looks like some sort of sixties era flower child, but on Paige, it looks right. Sam is always saying how natural and earthy Paige looks, and Reagan couldn't agree more.

Paige says, "He was sort of a good guy the other night, after the wedding. I kind of drank some of that homemade moonshine he had out in the cabin, a little too much. I was just upset and made a stupid, rash decision. So there, I said something nice about him. I puked, and he was considerate enough to take care of me."

Talia laughs and says, "I can say something nice about him. That boy is fine. I mean *really* fine. Not as fine as my hillbilly, Chet, but he's a close second."

Reagan bursts out laughing as she stirs in the lye water and says, "Yes, he has grown into quite the handsome young man."

Talia grins, shakes her head and says, "I don't know so much about handsome. Chet's handsome. John's handsome. Cory's... I don't know. I don't think I'd call him handsome exactly. He reminds me of an Alaskan man. You know, big and brawny, kind of wild?"

"Exactly," Paige remarks and snaps her fingers. "That's precisely why he *isn't* attractive."

"It sounds like your judgment may have been impaired the other night, so maybe you don't remember what he really looks like. You were probably seeing double," Talia teases her friend.

"Shut up," Paige mumbles with embarrassment.

"That would explain why he gave me those quarts of moonshine the next day and said something about keeping it out of reach 'cuz it's dangerous. I thought he was kidding," Reagan muses.

Paige frowns hard and says, "It is dangerous. Especially if you get dumped on by a guy and start feeling pathetic."

Reagan smiles and so does Paige. "Jason's kind of a dick. We weren't too fond of him when we were young. He was always kind of cocky. I couldn't understand why John and Kelly thought he was cool, but he wasn't, not really. They didn't really know him all that well. They do now, though. Simon and Cory explained it."

Sam adds, "Oh well, you're better off."

"Yeah, maybe you ought to give a real man a chance. Like maybe a... what is it that you always call him... a Neanderthal?" Talia says as she nudges her shoulder against Paige's shoulder.

"Gimme' a break," Paige scoffs.

"Speak of the devil," Sam remarks.

Kelly, John and Cory come barging through the back door laughing at whatever those crazy men are always joking about.

Of course, John comes right over to Reagan and pulls her in for a sweat-covered kiss in front of everyone. His open regard for her used to bother Reagan, but she's grown used to it and could give a damn what anyone thinks anymore. She has no idea how long she'll be on this earth, and she's never going to waste another minute of it holding back her feelings for John.

"Where's Hannah?" Kelly inquires.

"She's out with Sue putting up herbs in the barn," Sam offers kindly.

"Simon's in town with Grandpa and Derek," Paige tells them.

"We already knew that, beanpole," Cory says snidely. "We're on security detail while they're gone."

If he wants to get along better with Simon's sister, he should learn some manners. Reagan watches the scowl that comes over Paige's face deepen into a grimace of loathing.

"Don't you ever wear a shirt?" she asks angrily. "It's fall. It's cold out today."

Cory laughs and answers, "Wonder why I don't have anything to wear? Someone's always stealing my shirts 'cuz they're always gone from my basket."

He's indicating toward Paige's shirt, which obviously must belong to him. Reagan can't imagine Cory wearing a tie-dye shirt, but perhaps it does belong to him. Paige's cheeks redden with anger, or maybe embarrassment. Reagan speculates that if the kitchen weren't full of people, Paige would just pull it off right now and throw it at him. She looks like she'd like to.

"Makin' soap, huh?" Kelly asks, distracting the two combatants.

The men are covered in wheat dust and bits of ground-up grain. Harvesting the grains on the farm is a sandy, gritty affair and one that Reagan is glad she doesn't have to be a part of anymore.

"Yep," Sam answers with a smile.

"Don't want you men to get stinkier than the livestock around here," Reagan teases.

John slips an arm around her from behind and buries his face in her neck.

"Smell like the livestock, huh?" he razzes and rubs his face against hers.

"John, quit!" she reprimands and gets a laugh from her devilish husband. She conceals her grin from the others and places a quick peck to his cheek to get rid of him.

"I'm gonna go find my woman," Kelly says as he grabs a handful of scones from under the glass pastry container. Then he snags a pitcher of milk from the fridge. "Make her take a break with me."

John, because he's John, says, "Yeah? The last time you two took a break together, Mary happened nine months later."

Kelly chuffs, winks at John and heads out the back door again.

"Gross," Cory mutters. "I really didn't want to think about that."

Cory snags a brown butter glazed cookie out of the same container his brother had raided and chomps away at it. Sam pours him a glass of milk and then one for herself. She tugs him by the hand to sit next to her at the island. He just gives his usual, patient grin to Samantha and plops down beside her.

"Whatcha' been up to, kid?" he asks cordially.

Reagan doesn't wait around to hear her answer but follows John from the room as he furtively signaled her to do. She leaves Talia and Paige to keep an eye on the soap.

"What is it?" Reagan asks

Her husband runs a hand through his hair, causing some of the dust and flecks of grain to fall out onto the hardwood floor. They have moved to the front hall near the music room and the entry door where it is private and quiet.

"We need to have a meeting tonight," he says. "We've got a fuel problem. We're not going to make it through the winter without finding gas or even diesel fuel. We're going to need it for getting back and forth to town. I don't want to ride the horses to the clinic this coming winter. That would be too hard and time-consuming, especially on your grandpa."

"Right, I agree," Reagan confirms. "What are we going to do, babe?"

John sighs long and hard, his mouth forming a worried and uncharacteristically pinched line.

"We're working on it. We're gonna need to go on some runs to forage for gas, but I'm not sure what we're going to find out there. Cory has an idea for using moonshine as fuel. I don't even know if that'd work. We'll see."

Reagan nods with a concerned frown. She doesn't like it when they leave the farm to do supply runs or to track down and hunt creeps like the Target men. She doesn't like them to leave for any reason unless they are all going together.

"This is something Simon and Cory can handle. I'm gonna get Cory on training Paige soon, too. She said she liked going on runs. We'll see if she still does."

Reagan shakes her head and says, "Wait. Why don't you just have Simon or you or someone, anyone other than Cory, work with her?"

"We talked about it," John tells her. "They have some issues they need to work out. This'll help. She needs to know that she can rely on Cory, that she can trust him just like anyone else around here."

Reagan knows that he means the men have talked about it. Derek is and always will be the head of security on the farm. It's a job that weighs on his mind every day. Kelly and John are in charge of training people. If they've decided that Cory should train Paige, then who the hell is she to argue? They've forgotten more than she'll ever know about proper procedure and how not to get one's ass shot out in the field on a run. They've passed this wisdom on to Cory and Simon. And Cory must've taken to it because he kept his own hind end alive for almost a year while he was gone from the farm.

"All right, babe," Reagan agrees with her husband. "When are you going to have them start?"

"As soon as possible," he says. "We're gonna keep working on the wall in town until the weather shuts down production, but we need that fuel. We need other supplies, too, like meds for the clinic so if they can get some of those, that would be great. They'll be fine to go without us."

"I'll let her know. Or maybe I'll let Simon tell her," she suggests on a wrinkle of her nose. "What about Sam? Is she going with them?"

John shrugs, "If she wants to. She's been trained, so I don't see why not. It's up to her. She hasn't been off the farm for a while so it might be a good idea to let her go with them to keep her fresh."

Reagan nods and leans in for a quick snuggle. "Hey, where's our kid?"

John laughs and ruffles her hair, "I didn't lose him. Yet. He's out in the hog barn with the other kids."

He pulls her up close for a fast, heated kiss before he takes off again. John heads back out through the kitchen door, taking Cory with him.

"This sure does smell good," Talia remarks as they pour the last of the soap mixture into the molds.

"We'll give you a few bars to take home, Talia," Reagan tells her just as Sue and Hannah come in through the kitchen door. They are carrying a basket of vegetables from the last row in the garden and a new jar of dried herbs.

"Oh, thanks, Reagan," Talia says. "We have soap over there, but I think it's whatever the guys have found over the years from who knows where. I miss the smells of the homemade soap when I lived here."

"Well, now you know how to make it!" Sue remarks. "And here, you can have these herbs, too. You and Bertie can make your own soaps. This is a jar of mint and thyme mixed. It'll smell great in soap."

"Wow, this is wonderful," Talia says when she unscrews the lid on the pint-sized mason jar full of herbs and takes a big whiff. "Thanks again. I can't wait to start."

"Wanna' stay for dinner?" Hannah offers.

She's clean from head to toe. Spic and span in her white dress, white ankle socks, and brown loafers paired with her pale yellow sweater. The only thing out of order is the few wisps of light blonde hair that have escaped her braid. Reagan doesn't know how she does it.

"Thanks, but I'd better radio Chet to let him know to come and pick us up. That is if I can drag Maddie home," Talia says with a laugh. "Bertie was gonna show me how to make pigs in a blanket, whatever the heck those are. Sounds like another weird Reynolds food. I hope I don't have to go out and butcher a pig or something."

She laughs and they all do. Talia's a hoot. No wonder Paige likes her so well. Other than her one friend at college and her sisters, Reagan has never been good at making friends with women. She really wasn't good at making friends with men, either. Mostly she was only good at making friends with old men who were her grandfather's medical colleagues. When Paige's group first came to the farm, Talia had been quiet and withdrawn. Reagan doesn't know what all they've been through, but it is probably a horrific story.

Reagan asks Hannah, "I thought Kelly came out to find you."

Her lovely sister laughs and says, "He sure did. And then I kindly informed him that I am just too busy to…take a break right now."

Reagan chuckles and says, "I bet that went over well."

"Not too well, no," Hannah admits with a grin. "He'll get over it. He's a big boy."

"Big? That's about an understatement," Talia jokes.

They ensue in teasing Hannah about Kelly for a few minutes before returning to the soap. Talia and Maddie leave a short while later and the women start on dinner. Unfortunately, just when they are ready to put the chicken into the oven, the gas to the stove gives out. It's happened quite a few times in the last months and is something that concerns the men. They worry that the oil well on the property is going dry. So while Kelly and Grandpa tend to the gas line, John stokes the fire-pit outside, and they cook the chicken over a grate on reddened coals and wood. Sue takes two cast-iron pots full of scalloped potatoes out to John, who is manning the whole cooking on an open fire concept. If Reagan were in charge, it would all be charcoaled to a black crisp and disgusting. Many times during the canning season they've used the fire-pit to run their canners instead of using the gas stove in the kitchen.

When it's time to assemble for dinner, Reagan notices Simon and his sister running from behind the barn area toward the house. She's said how much she used to like running, but she hasn't done so since coming to the farm. Apparently she's gone for a run with her brother. When they arrive at the back porch, her cheeks are flushed with high color and strands of her red hair have come loose of the bandana. She looks pretty and fresh and happy for a change. Unless she is hanging out with Simon, which she likely doesn't get to do much because of their demanding work schedules on the farm and at the clinic and the wall build, then she doesn't seem like a very happy person. Reagan feels sorry for her. At least she has her sisters and John and her grandfather. All that Paige has is Simon. Reagan knows that Paige used to be close with her father, but now he's gone and so is her mother.

She's laughing and shoving at her brother as they push through the back door. Reagan follows them carrying a platter of chicken.

"Here, Reagan!" Cory calls out and trots over as he rounds the corner from the front of the house. "Let me get that for you."

"Thanks," she acquiesces. The platter was heavier than she'd thought it would be.

Paige whips around, and she watches Cory warily.

"Move it, beanpole," he agitates.

Paige doesn't answer but shoots him a scowl. Reagan catches her pale eyes sliding down over the broad expanse of Cory's chest and bare stomach, though. The sun is getting low in the sky, causing a slight chill in the autumn air, but he seems oblivious. Of course, John is still shirtless, as well. Although Reagan doesn't quite mind her husband's shirtless torso. By the look in Paige's eyes, Reagan's not so sure that she also doesn't mind looking at Cory's, either. And when Paige meets Reagan's gaze, she pretends that she needs to wash up for dinner and makes a hasty exit from the kitchen. She's pretty damn sure that Paige wasn't just looking at Cory's necklace, either.

"Think I'm just gonna grab some food to go," Cory announces as he places the heavy platter on the island.

"What? Why?" Reagan asks. Her husband comes in next carrying the heavy pots of potatoes.

"I need to run out for a bit. I'll be back tomorrow…"

Hannah immediately jumps his case, "Hey! I don't think so, Mr. Cory. You will sit down with the rest of us and eat dinner with the family, your family!"

Kelly and Grandpa come in followed by noisy, bustling children and finally Derek, who has been working non-stop on construction and repair jobs around the farm.

"What's going on?" Kelly inquires.

Hannah states angrily, "Your brother just made the mistake of thinking he was going to tear off a chicken leg and take off instead of eating dinner with the family, and I was kind enough to correct his error in judgement!"

Simon laughs heartily at his friend's distress or at Hannah's reprimand. Reagan isn't sure why everyone always thinks she's the one who's bossy. It's definitely Hannah. She just smiles at her sister, who is waving a spatula around like some sort of angry Italian mother in her kitchen. Reagan wouldn't be more surprised if her sister also started spouting off in Italian and making hand gestures.

"Hm, looks like you were mistaken, bro,'" Kelly concedes, not interfering with his wife's dictate or coming to his helpless brother's aid.

"Yeah, as usual. Guess I got that wrong," Cory sulks.

However, he ruffles Hannah's hair, hugs around her slim shoulders and leaves the room. Her enchantingly beautiful sister smiles, a rare moment for her lately.

After everyone is seated at the dinner table, the prayer is given and food starts getting passed around, John breaks the news that they are running low on fuel. Then he breaks the harder news that he wants Cory to head up Paige's training and that he'd like them to make a trip with Sam and Simon to Nashville in a week or so. Reagan is surprised at the quick timeline, but she also understands the urgency with winter soon around the corner. She watches Paige's face fall dramatically when she hears the dictate of Cory being in charge of her training, but she doesn't defy the mandate. However, she is quiet for the remainder of the meal. And immediately following it, Cory takes off like he'd wanted to do before.

"What are we going to do if we can't find fuel?" Reagan asks later. She is sitting in her grandfather's office with her husband, Kelly and Grandpa.

"We'll figure it out," John assures her, taking her hand in his.

Grandpa sits behind his desk smoking his pipe while she and John share the leather sofa and Kelly sits in a plush chair nearby.

"I want to know what our contingency plan is going to be," Reagan says firmly. "Could we have people come to the med shed here on the farm for medical care?"

"Hell no," Kelly replies. "Nobody's ever coming to the farm on a regular basis, not even people from town. The fewer people who know about this place, the better. Sometimes you guys are treating people who've just heard from a friend of a friend about the clinic. We can't have strangers showing up whenever they need your help."

"We're working on a plan," John says.

"What are you expecting the kids to find in Nashville?" Grandpa asks.

"I may be going with them. Maybe Kelly, too. We might be able to find a tanker truck over there at the gas distribution center," John tells her.

"And if all else fails, we're gonna find a CNG converter compressor kit and change out the pick-up truck. We've still got plenty of natural gas around the county we can tap into," Kelly says, his large hands resting casually on his knees.

"Can we do that? Just convert a gas car to natural gas? I've never heard of it," Reagan says nervously. She's tired, exhausted really from canning and working all day. Tomorrow is a clinic day, and she'd like to sit it out. She's been unusually tired lately and worried that it is stemming from her illness in the spring still lingering in her system.

Grandpa answers, "Yes, we can. It's not as difficult as it might seem. The gas company trucks used to run on compressed natural gas."

"Whoa, wait a minute," Kelly says. "That changes things. Where are these trucks? You didn't tell me that part."

They've obviously been discussing this idea without her.

"Well," Grandpa starts in his usual, frustratingly slow way, "there were quite a few fracking sites in our county. There's the one between here and Clarksville- you and John shoulda' went past it when you traveled there a few years back."

"Yeah, we did," Reagan remembers.

"Right, we stopped at the one place to eat and give Jake a break," John says with a nod. "I don't remember any trucks up there, though."

"No, they wouldn't be there," Grandpa says. "That's a storage facility with pipelines. The frack site would've been a few miles to the east, off of the main road but with road access."

"Hm, all right," Kelly says. "We can run over there tomorrow, Doc, if you give us directions."

"Sure can," Grandpa says as he puffs at his pipe and then rests it in an ashtray. "I'll get my old maps out and see if I can't remember where the other sites are. I had them marked on a map somewhere around her."

Reagan rolls her eyes with a smile. Grandpa's organization skills are lacking at best. And now that Grams is gone, it's even worse trying to find things that he'd once deemed as important. He doesn't like anyone fussing with his things, but his filing system sure isn't something for which anyone can help him.

"There are quite a few distribution facilities that might have company trucks, as well, over closer to Nashville," Grandpa adds thoughtfully. "There might just be company trucks still sitting on the gas company lots. I think there were a few satellite offices spread around the area, too."

"This could be a crucial change if we can get our hands on those gas company trucks," John declares.

"I agree, John," Grandpa says.

"Tomorrow, Doc and I need to trek into the woods," Kelly tells them as Derek comes into the room.

"For what?" her brother-in-law asks as he takes a seat on the other sofa.

"Gotta find that main gas line and open it up," Kelly says.

Grandpa takes a sip of his coffee, found by Simon and Cory on their last trip, and explains, "I think that's why we're losing pressure here in the big house. We're going up there to take a look at the main line. Now it was about twenty years ago that I let them frack on the back forty, so I figure the line needs to be opened up. We've been getting our gas off of the well here, but the other lines will have hundreds of thousands of cubic feet just sitting in them since people aren't using it anymore and the gas companies aren't accessing it or using it, either."

"Interesting," Derek says. "I'll go, too. I know I'm supposed to go to the clinic with Simon and Reagan, but I think this is something that I can help with instead."

"Don't worry about it," John says. "I'll go to the clinic. We'll be fine. I'll have Roy come over and help out on security there, too."

"The farm will have to be covered by Cory, Sue and some of the other kids," Grandpa says.

149

"Yeah, it'll be fine then," John says with a smirk. "I'd feel worse for the people that tried to come onto it raising Cain if Cory was here unsupervised."

Derek and Grandpa chuckle, but Kelly barely manages a smile. He is clearly worried about his young brother's state of mind. But one thing is for sure, Cory will keep the farm safe while they're gone.

"When we all meet back here after the clinic day closes, some of us can take the truck and go see if we can find those gas company trucks," Kelly says, changing the direction of their conversation back to planning.

"Fill ya' in later," John tells his brother.

"If you find the trucks, we're going to need the compression system," Grandpa reminds them. "We have to compress that natural gas to run the trucks. We can rig the system up in the equipment shed. That's the closest building to the gas line from the well."

"Right, that makes sense," Kelly says. "It'll be easier to hook into the line out there."

They go on and on about the plans and talk about the harvest as Reagan's eyes get heavier and heavier. She'd already put Jacob to bed before they started their meeting. He hadn't wanted a bath and she hadn't been excited about giving him one, so she'd helped him scrub away some of the dirt and let him crash.

A nudge alerts Reagan that she'd fallen asleep while the men were still discussing whatever topic they'd moved on to. John's eyes smile into hers, and they retire to the third floor.

"You sure you want to go to the clinic tomorrow?" he asks as he pulls her close where she can lie on his chest.

"Yes, of course. I have to."

"No, you don't have to at all. Nobody's going to fire you if you take a sick day, boss," he teases.

His fingers thread through her curls and scratch at her scalp in a soothing manner.

"I'm all right," Reagan answers with a smile. "Just tired."

"I know," John tells her. "I've noticed that you've been tired a lot lately. Maybe you need a break."

"I don't need a break," she argues and gets a chuff from him in return.

Canning today had been tiring. Her feet and legs are fatigued from standing so long. Making the soap had worn her out, too. Then she'd worked with Hannah and Sue on dinner. Normally, this amount of work wouldn't tire her out like it had. Most times she would've tried to squeeze in a run or some yoga before bed, but today had been exhausting.

John continues to rub her head and then tease down her bare back. She's pretty sure he keeps harping, but Reagan drifts off again before John gets through his whole reply.

Chapter Eleven
Paige

She can barely make herself get out of bed the next morning. Simon is long gone from the cabin, having left early for the clinic because he supposedly had some research project he was working on there. Cory is also gone, probably milking a cow or something equally gross. She cannot believe that John has ordered her training to be executed by him. She would've been happy, eager even, to work with anyone else on the farm. And so her reluctance to rise is from her resistance to being forced into his company. He'd made sure to tell her that they'd start bright and early after breakfast, too. Then he'd chuckled obnoxiously and turned off the light beside his bed last evening.

With great irritation, Paige drags herself out of bed and dons a pair of jeans, her black boots and a yellow floral sweater, not something she'd have ever been caught dead in before the apocalypse. She throws on her brown canvas jacket and heads out to the chicken coop, one of her morning assignments. When she's done, she runs into Sam, also on her way to the big house for breakfast. She has obviously been with the horses because her hands have that signature gray dirt coating the palms. She also wears a big smile, which is her usual expression after a visit with those dangerous animals.

"Excited to start training today?" she asks with her dimples showing and her black ponytail swishing around.

"Sure. Ecstatic," Paige replies dryly.

"Oh, but it'll be fun!" Sam says.

"Yeah, maybe with Simon or you or one of the other guys," Paige explains patiently.

"No way," Sam says, wrinkling her nose. "Cory's the best. He's so good at teaching anyone who wants to learn. He's very patient. He taught me and... Em."

Her smile falls as she refers to her dead friend, Cory's young sister. Then, without missing a beat, she loops her arm through Paige's and keeps on going.

"He worked with Huntley and Justin last year, especially with knives. It's important for the kids to know how to defend themselves in case they ever come to harm. Hopefully, that never happens. That's why we don't take any of them to the clinic. I'm sure there're other kids in town that they could make friends with or play with, but Grandpa and Derek decided when we first started going to town that the kids should stay here. I used to be one of them, one of the kids. But now I get to go because I like helping out at the clinic."

"Yeah, I guess that would make sense. They seem pretty innocent. It's probably a good thing to keep them that way."

"Well, not Huntley. He's been through a lot. Remember? His father was one of the visitors. He was a very awful man, the worst kind possible," Sam informs her with a shiver.

"Right. I remember," Paige acknowledges.

"But you'll have fun with Cory. Plus, it's good to get to know him. You'll know more about the real Cory when you get finished. Besides, I'll be with you," Sam tells her as they drop their shoes on the back porch.

"You will?" she asks with confusion.

"Sure," Sam says. "Simon ditched me off today. He didn't want me to go to the clinic, so he purposely dragged Reagan there a lot earlier than usual to do his research."

She air quotes on 'research' and rolls her bright blue eyes with irritation.

"What do you mean? I thought he really did have to do research on something."

Paige is genuinely confused. Why would her brother tell her a lie?

"Nah, he does most of his research here on the farm. He was just avoiding me. He's been avoiding me, but I've gotten used to it. It seems it's his favorite trick lately."

With that statement, she goes inside and allows the screen door to slam, which is unusual for her. Normally she's a quiet little thing who glides around all graceful and delicate. Today, she seems feisty and genuinely pissed off, mostly at Simon.

Some of the family are absent from breakfast because they have gone with Simon and Reagan to the clinic. Seating is condensed to allow room for a few of the younger kids to sit at the adult table in the dining room. Somehow she finds herself stuck next to Cory. As if it wasn't bad enough that she has to spend part of her day training with him.

The plans for the day are reviewed during breakfast, but Paige can barely concentrate nor does she even follow what they are talking about. CNG, gas, natural gas, stealing trucks, whatever. She keeps finding herself staring down at Cory's huge thigh muscle straining against his snug jeans. At least he has on a shirt this morning. Although it seems as if the musculature beneath it is about to rip it to shreds in an attempt to be free. The veins in his thick wrists ripple under his skin as he scoops butter from the dish with his knife and slathers it on his bread. He's a big eater. As a matter of fact, she thinks he probably eats enough for four people. Of course, he is kind of large man like his big brother. And she'd puked on him, all over him to be more precise. Her cheeks flush just recalling that horrifyingly embarrassing night. Good God, what a loser!

Someone asks her a question, and she just nods. She wasn't paying attention anyway. She probably just signed on for cleaning out a horse stall or something equally hideous. Paige pushes the grits and scrambled eggs around on her plate and tries not to think about what a huge ass she'd been in front of Cory of all people when she was drunk. He was gone the next day, all day and then that night, as well. The family doesn't seem to say much about Cory disappearing when he does, which seems to be rather frequently. She's not sure if he was avoiding her or if he genuinely needed to do something that kept him away, but she heard him come into the cabin sometime in the middle of the next night. Neither of them has spoken of it since. However, it is still there hovering between them like a thick cloud of awkward smog.

There is ground-in dirt under some of his closely-clipped fingernails. He's such a heathen. His hair is pulled back into its usual short black ponytail. Reagan frequently calls him a hippy. He always grins that ridiculously charming grin of his. He doesn't seem to care at all what people think of him. His forearm nearest her glows with a sheen of perspiration even though she is chilly.

Suddenly, he bumps his thick leg against hers and says, "Right, beanpole?"

"What?" she croaks.

"We're ready to start your training. Remember?" he asks.

He's looking directly at her as if she's a loon. His brown eyes regard her keenly. Then he turns back to his brother, with whom he must've been talking.

"We're good to go," he reassures Kelly. "I'll get her started right after breakfast. Better eat up, beanpole."

"I'll go with you guys," Sam jumps in with enthusiasm.

"Sure, kid," Cory replies and gets a wide smile from Samantha. "You can show her some of your knife tricks. You're more proficient with one than me."

"Yeah, right!" Sam exclaims.

"You are," he insists and keeps teasing with Sam.

Paige blocks them out and bites her lower lip instead. She has no wish to be in his company all damn day long. Instead, she'd like to just hang out with Samantha. Or Hannah. Or Sue. Or even the wild hooligans on the farm, otherwise known as the kids. Arianna nags to tag along during the training, but her mother quickly reminds her that she is to help clean out the goat pen after breakfast. She spends the rest of her meal pouting.

The meal finishes and she tries to help with the clearing of it and the dish duties, but Hannah will have none of it. She gets tossed out the back door with Sam and him, whether she wants to go or not.

She follows dutifully after him as Cory goes to the med shed. He tells her and Sam to wait for him, but reappears a moment later with an extra rifle and what looks like two pistols of some kind.

"Let's go," he orders but not in a domineering manner.

They follow along; Sam all lightness and smiles, Paige all frowns and scowls of displeasure. When they come to the horse barn, Paige butts in.

"Hey, wait a minute," she protests. "I'm not riding one of those damn horses."

"You don't have to. You can always walk," he replies over his shoulder with a grin.

"Fine, I will," she says through gritted teeth.

155

He just laughs loudly and tells her, "You're riding behind me, bony ass."

She notices that when they aren't around the family, he takes more liberty with his choice of put-downs.

"That's not nice, Cory," Sam scolds him. "I'll get my mare."

Paige stands rooted at the entrance to the barn glaring daggers at his back.

"You're riding with me," he calls over as he sets the rifles against a stall door.

He slides open the door and leads his crazy stallion out of it. There is no way in hell that she's riding that thing. She *will* just walk.

"Come here," he demands this time with more dominance than before.

She unwillingly steps closer, but not too close. When she apparently doesn't come as close as he'd wanted, Cory motions to her with his hand before tying his stallion to the rope coming out of the wall. She plants her feet. He motions more impatiently this time, his mouth an irritated frown.

"Now," he insists and points to the ground beside him.

Paige purses her lips angrily, squints her eyes at him, and edges closer. When she's within a few feet of the big horse, Cory snatches her upper arm and pulls her right up beside him.

"He's not going to attack you," he assures her.

Paige doesn't believe him for a minute. The horse snorts through its wide nostrils as if his disdain for her is equal to her own.

Cory chuckles at her and says, "Why don't you start with just a simple pet?"

"No thanks."

He takes her hand in his, which is hot, and lays it gently against the horse's huge, muscular neck. It reminds her of Cory's neck.

"He's not that bad, right?" he asks rhetorically. "He's really a puss if you get right down to it."

"Yeah, sure," Paige scoffs. The horse's slick fur is shiny and warm against her palm. She's seen Cory working with this horse every day since he's come home. He babies it, really. The animal's grooming is meticulously maintained down to the very last, long hair of its mane.

Within a few moments, he has the beast saddled and bridled. And it must know they are leaving the farm because the animal starts prancing in place once they go outside. Samantha is already mounted up bareback. She's like a tiny, horse riding daredevil.

Cory swings into the saddle without using the stirrup and reaches down for her. She glares up at him. Her legs are quaking already.

"Come on. We're burning daylight here, woman," he chides.

Paige looks once to the house, then at her feet, and realizing she's not getting out of it, reaches up for his outstretched hand.

"Put your foot in the stirrup," he instructs.

Once she has that done, he tugs her right up behind him as if she weighs twelve ounces.

"Whoa, he's bigger than the other horses," she notes nervously and clutches onto Cory for dear life, sworn enemy or no.

"He's a stud. He's supposed to be bigger than the mares. Helps him get the job done," he says.

Paige doesn't think he's talking about his horse at all, especially not when he peers over his shoulder and grins wickedly at her.

"Just hold onto my waist," he says softly and turns back around.

As if he needed to tell her that. Get real. She'd rather just walk and catch up to wherever they are going. They start off at a slow walking gate and increase to a trot, per Sam's request. Her black hair is the same color as Cory's horse. It flows out behind her in the wind, and she looks as happy as she could be in this moment.

Once they clear the edge of the cattle pasture and get the gate opened and reclosed, Sam shouts, "Come on, Cory!"

Paige has no idea what she means, but Cory seems to because he laughs heartily.

"Hold on," he says quietly over his shoulder. "I know you don't like riding, but Sam does and she wants to run."

"What? No!" Paige barely gets out on a ragged whisper.

"So does Jet," he says with a chuckle.

"No, no, no," Paige repeats as if she has a severe stutter. His horse is prancing side to side and doing funny little moves under them that aren't funny at all to Paige.

"Just hold on," he says softly and turns to look directly into Paige's eyes. "I won't let you fall off."

157

His left hand slides from the reins, leaving only one controlling the beast. She's about to yell at him to keep both hands on the wheel, for God's sake! Unfortunately, her reply is cut off as his hand comes to rest on the top of her thigh. He squeezes tightly, his long fingers going nearly all the way around her leg. Her eyes widen, but she can't respond because he nods to Sam and lets his horse break free from his tight restraint. And then they are flying, or at least that's what it feels like to Paige. Sam is flying, however. Her horse isn't doing the cantering thing that Simon explained. It's galloping, and she's laughing with pure joy. Cory's horse is smooth and rhythmic, not like the mount she rode with her brother which seemed like it was mostly trying to bounce her off. It also covers a lot of ground without a lot of effort. His horse reminds her of one of those big, brutal battle horses that a knight would've rode into combat. The huffing and harsh snorting of his breath reaches her ears even as far back from his head as she is.

"Easy, bud," Cory talks to him.

The beast snorts softly again as if communicating with his master. And master he is. Cory controls the animal with just a single hand and probably his legs. She's never seen anyone ride like he does. There is no fear, no holding back. It's just all control.

"Take 'er easy," he coos.

His voice is deep and soothing, apparently to the horse, as well, because his pace evens out to a mellower lope. Sam races ahead, obviously knowing their destination. She even pushes her horse to jump right over a fallen log in the way. Cory just steers his stallion around it. She's thankful that he didn't try that with her on back of the tall stallion. She's not sure if he would've taken the jump if she wasn't with him. She knows nothing about horses and even less about his. Perhaps it wouldn't have jumped the log. Of course, as skillful a rider as he is, Paige is quite sure this horse would've jumped that log if it was on fire if Cory demanded it of him.

"Having fun yet?" he calls over his shoulder.

"Is it over? Then, no!"

He just laughs at her and says, "Relax. You might have fun. And you don't have to hold on so tight with your legs. You aren't going anywhere. I told you I won't let you fall off. I always keep my word. Just relax."

For some reason, his confidence in his own conviction is reassuring to Paige. It's not the most terrifying experience, either. The way he manages the giant horse makes her feel somewhat convinced that she isn't about to take a full gainer and break her neck. Or maybe it's the firm grip he has on her upper leg. She's actually starting to enjoy herself. She'd still rather be walking or jogging, but this isn't horrible. She can't believe it, but she does feel safe with him, which barely makes sense.

He and Sam rein in their mounts and slow down to a walking pace as they arrive at the Johnson farm.

"What are we doing here?" she asks Cory as he halts.

He swings his leg over the neck of his horse and reaches up to help her down. She takes the help without argument because she isn't sure she can get down without falling flat on her face and then probably also getting kicked there by the horse. His hands slide from her waist up the sides of her breasts and into her armpits as she shimmies down.

"Thanks," she mumbles and steps away from him with a blush staining her cheeks.

Cory just smirks in an arrogant way that makes Paige think he touched her inappropriately on purpose. She glares at his back as he ties the horse's reins to a fence post next to Sam's. Some of the Johnson kids are outside working, some of the littler kids are playing and one of the daughters, Evie, comes out to greet them. Paige has met her a few times and knows that she is a widow. She also knows Cory danced with her quite a few times at the wedding reception.

"What's going on, guys?" Evie asks after they all greet one another, her golden blonde hair tossing around in the wind.

"Brought the beanpole here over to plink at some groundhogs," Cory answers for them.

Paige shoots him a disgusted look. Shoot groundhogs? She hadn't known this was the plan. She wants to go back. Or throw up. That might be an option, too. She's never shot at animals like that before. Catching them in snares wasn't the same thing as sport shooting an innocent animal.

Apparently Evie doesn't feel the same way because she announces, "Oh, good!"

"Good?" Paige inquires as she re-ties her hair back with her red bandana.

"Yeah, sure," Evie explains. "We're still overrun. While my family and I were gone, the groundhogs took over in the pastures. They are bothersome little creatures. If one of the horses or cows steps in one of their burrows, then we could have to put it down if the damage is bad like a broken ankle. It's happened."

"Oh," Paige says simply. She still doesn't want to kill any of the rodents. She really hopes Cory doesn't want to cook and eat one when they've finished. Or perform some rite of passage ritual by eating the heart or something equally disgusting. That prospect is even more nauseating than killing one. She grimaces hard.

"Gonna work on sighting in and acquiring a moving target today," Cory tells the other woman.

"Sounds like fun," Evie says with a tinge of sarcasm and a smile touching her blue eyes.

"Wanna' join us?" Cory invites cordially and even raises his dark, thick brows at the woman.

Paige isn't sure how old Evie is, but she's pretty sure that this Johnson daughter is a bit older than Cory. She laughs gaily at Cory's invitation and then touches his arm with affection clearly written on her features.

"Ha, maybe another time, Cory," she replies with a smile. "I'm working on making apple cider vinegar with my sister. I'll send some over for Simon later."

"Why?" Sam asks as she takes a rifle from its scabbard on Cory's horse.

"Uh... I'm not sure actually," Evie says with another smile. "He mentioned that he'd take a quart when we made it. Something about using it for some kind of new experimental medicine something or other. I don't know. He usually loses me when he starts on those herbs and stuff."

"You aren't the only one," Cory remarks and grins.

The way these two are acting makes Paige suspicious of what could be going on between them or what could've happened in their past together. Are they a thing, a couple, or whatever people are calling it these days? She's not sure, but there is a lot of open smiling, grinning and, on Evie's part, touching. Perhaps when he leaves at night he is visiting this woman, this lovely widow.

"Catch up with me before you leave and I'll give you a quart or two, depending on what he wants. He said that you guys make apple cider vinegar, too, but he wants to try ours because our apple orchard has different trees in it," she says while shrugging her slim shoulders.

Evie is much shorter than her, probably by a good four or five inches. She is also curvy, nothing like her. Paige feels graceless suddenly and turns to retrieve her own gun from its scabbard. The three of them continue to talk for a few moments before Cory announces that they should get to it since he doesn't want to be away from the farm for long because Doc and Kelly are going somewhere to work on a gas line. Paige just offers a half grin and a wave to Evie before following Sam and Cory into the forestry of trees at the edge of the Johnson farm, which isn't much different than the McClane farm other than the house sits practically right on the road. They have rolling hills of tillable ground and a forest, but more grazing acreage than the McClane spread, according to Sam.

They hike a short distance into the woods where Cory instructs them to stop.

"Let's first see what you can do, all right?" he says.

"Not much," Paige mumbles. "Don't get your hopes up."

Cory just chuckles, "Well, we know you're good at running, but this family isn't made up of runners. And you aren't going to be able to run away from every situation."

Sam sits on a fallen log and takes out her sketch pad and art supplies. Her rifle leans against the log near her leg.

"I can't shoot well at all. I'm definitely better at evasion than sniping people. This is going to be a waste of your time," Paige adds with criticism.

"Oh, don't believe her, Cory," Sam calls over without looking up. "She's more lethal than she says. I've seen her handiwork."

Paige knows that Samantha is referring to the night the farm was attacked, but she doesn't have the heart to tell her new friend that most of her kills were likely a combination of blind luck and accidental kill shots. She knows she sucks.

"We'll see," Cory says softly as he loads the rifle for her. "You know this part, right?"

"Sort of," she replies honestly.

"See here?" he asks, pointing with his dirty index finger to a bullet like a smart aleck. "Bullet. Goes in here."

Paige has to bite back a nasty retort. Instead, she gives him a look that lets him know that he isn't funny.

161

"This is a seven by six-two Mauser. Doc's actually. He likes the old, historical rifles. When we're in the field, we'll be using the military rifles, but not your brother. He usually carries a sniper rifle. He's the best with the long range shots, so he's normally our cover. I carry an M16, John, too. Sometimes Kelly carries a Garand- that's a high power old rifle, a real shit-kicker, or an M4."

She just nods. Paige has no idea what all these numbers and letters mean anyway.

"What will I carry? I've never done that before," she tells him nervously and wipes her sweaty hands on her pants. "I usually just went with nothing."

Cory's eyes jump to hers, the brown depths express a deep concern. "Really? You didn't have a gun?"

Paige shakes her head and explains, "No, not usually. A couple times, but we didn't have any more bullet thingys, so what would've been the point? I had a knife. It broke when I was trying to cut wood with it, though. I just got really good at sneaking and avoiding people and…"

She pauses, shrugs, and bites her lower lip.

"What?" he asks.

"I just outran them if they saw me," she answers.

Cory's left eyebrow lifts with doubt. Then he frowns. He clearly doesn't like her answer, but it's the truth, nonetheless.

"That's insane," he says tersely and goes back to loading the rifle. "We won't be doing that. You'll listen to me. You'll learn from me. And when we're in the field, you will carry a weapon."

"I will have a weapon. The same one I had before, my feet," she grumbles at the rude, authoritative tone in his voice and the mandate.

Cory's gaze slides impatiently to hers and he scowls. It's enough to make Paige look away.

He says firmly, "We *won't* be running."

"Fine," she says quietly.

"Good, let's get started. I'll let you shoot a few and then you can reload it yourself," he offers.

He hands her the heavy rifle, which feels like it weighs forty pounds.

"See the bolt here? This is what will load a round into the chamber. A rifle doesn't shoot unless the bullet thingy goes into the barrel," he replies with a snarky wit.

"Ha-ha," she says and shoots him a grimace.

"Put it up to your shoulder," he says and stands behind her. "Press it snuggly to it. That's it. We're not gonna cowboy shoot this thing, you know, from the hip? That only works in movies. Don't ever do that, unless you want one of us to make fun of you. Your weapon always goes against your shoulder."

Cory helps her get it adjusted, and Paige tries not to think about him pressed against the back of her. His left arm slides to the end of her own, and he helps her to push the rifle a little higher into the air.

"This is the bolt," he says and takes her right hand into his own.

His hot breath hits her neck where the bandana has her hair concealed, exposing bare skin. His grip is sure and firm as he uses her hand to slide the bolt back and then forward again.

Cory steps back and says, "See that tree over there across the field? The one that's down partway with the red leaves?"

Paige nods and says, "Yes."

"Let's just see if you can hit the trunk, anywhere. Doesn't matter, just try to hit it."

"That's a really long way," Paige observes as she stares down the barrel of the rifle. The tree he speaks of is across a broad meadow sprinkled with white daisies.

"It's a really good gun, so you're in luck," he remarks with a smile touching his voice. "Here, wait."

He presses tiny orange sponges into her ears.

"Don't want you to lose your hearing," he says.

"What about you?"

"I'm already deaf… and mostly dumb, so we're good," he self-criticizes.

"I could've told you that," she whispers.

"Take a breath," he says behind her. "Let it half out. Squeeze gently. She'll bark, but you can handle 'er."

Paige's eyes widen. She squeezes one eye closed, tries to take aim, and squeezes. Total miss. And the gun is like a cannon going off not a bark as he'd called it.

Cory tells her to do it again and she does and misses once again. This goes on two more times before her frustration gets the best of her.

"Damn it!" she hisses as Cory takes the rifle from her.

"Houston, we've got a problem," he jokes.

Paige fails to find the humor and smashes her hands onto her hips impatiently.

"I told you I suck," she retorts.

"No, you don't. But if I'm right- and I usually am- you are left-eye dominant trying to shoot right-eye dominant."

She tries not to roll her eyes at his machismo.

"What's that mean?" she asks.

Sam, who is her normal quiet, tiny self, pipes up and says, "You're closing the wrong eye. That's why you aren't hitting anything."

Then she goes right back to whatever she's drawing. She's always in her own little world, a place she likes to escape to where the outside world can't reach her.

"Here," Cory says and takes the rifle from her and pulls out the string-attached ear plugs. "Come over here for a second, Paige."

His deep voice is commanding and the sound of her name coming from him has a strange effect on her insides. He leads her toward the edge of the woods facing the Johnson farm.

"See the rooster on that weather vane on their barn, the smaller barn?" he asks

"Yes," Paige answers with confusion as he points into the distance. Paige isn't sure how he can wear nothing but a short-sleeved shirt while she has on a long-sleeved sweater and a jacket. The fall air is crisp this morning.

"Now, I'm gonna hold my hands in a circle in front of your face."

Paige gives him a look of perplexed resistance and steps back. He grins and steps closer and holds his hands about a foot in front of her, forming his fingertips into a circle.

"Now close your right eye," he orders.

She gives him another look. Cory just raises his eyebrows with impatience, so she gives in.

"Still see it?"

"Yes," Paige answers.

"Now the left," he says.

"Wait, it moved," she exclaims with surprise.

"Do it again," he says and they perform the task once more.

"It disappeared again," Paige says with a furrow of her light brows.

"Ok, well, now we know what the problem is," he says and takes her arm, leading her back to where he rested the rifle against the tree.

"I suck? Like I tried to tell you?"

"No, you probably don't suck at all. You just didn't have the right skills to work with the equipment," he tells her.

Cory takes her back to the same spot where Samantha is still perched on her log, drawing with fervor. She puts her own set of earplugs back in and keeps on sketching away.

"Let's try this again," he tells her and presses the gun into her hand.

Paige sighs long and with great exaggeration, "You really think that eye trick is gonna make me the next Annie Oakley?"

"Yep, take aim," he orders.

Paige offers him a scowl and raises the rifle to her shoulder again.

"Nope," Cory says and takes the rifle. "Right there is the first problem."

"What do you mean?"

He places a large hand on her left shoulder and twists her body just slightly. Then he places the gun back into her hands and helps her pull it up into her left shoulder. It feels awkward. Of course, guns always feel awkward to her.

"Try it now," Cory says.

He uses both hands this time to turn her shoulders a little more. Then he goes too far, nearly causing her to jump, and places his hands on her hips and gives them a small twist.

"Breathe," he says into her ear.

"Give me some space!" she hisses.

She glares over her shoulder at him, which makes Cory grin at her in return. That elusive dimple peeks at her from his right cheek. Paige glares at it, too. Then she takes aim.

"We'll get you outfitted with a different rifle back at the farm before we go to the city, but for practice today, let's just keep with this one. Load a round into the chamber. Take your time," he instructs patiently.

His voice is actually soothing. Paige does as he says and aims at the fallen log with the red leaves. She squeezes and bam! She hits her target.

"Good. Again," he orders behind her.

Paige does it again.

"Good. Stay here," he says.

"What? Why? Where are you going?" Paige asks.

Cory takes the rifle from her, unloads it and rests it against the tree. He takes the pieces of white paper that Sam is already holding out to him. They apparently don't need a lot of words in order to communicate. Paige watches as he jogs across the pasture and tacks the papers to three different branches. Unfortunately, the branches wave around in the breeze. She's never going to hit any of those. While she waits for Cory to finish and jog back, she takes a look at what Sam has been drawing. She's not sure Sam even notices her as she hovers.

The sketch is of her and Cory standing near the copse of trees shooting. She has no idea how Sam has sketched this out so quickly. She's a little maniac. Paige isn't sure she is truly fond of the subject material, however. Cory is standing behind her, his arm under her own, assisting her. It's too personal and almost intimate as if they are friends or lovers just out enjoying the fall day shooting guns. None of that even makes sense. But it does seem too intimate. She just frowns and returns to the tree line to join her enemy.

"Ready to go again?" he asks.

Paige nods with reluctance but does as he says. She got a big lecture, thankfully in private, last night from her brother. He'd warned her to cooperate and be respectful of Cory while he's training her.

"Sure, but don't get too excited. I don't think I can hit those," she warns him.

"Have some confidence in yourself, woman," Cory says with a smile.

A few minutes later, she has obliterated her paper targets to nothingness, rendering Sam's art paper to shreds. And it feels pretty darn good not being a total loser who misses everything when everyone else in the McClane family can shoot like a professionally trained sniper.

"Clear your weapon before we move on," Cory says.

She doesn't really know what he means, so he shows her patiently. If there was one thing that the family said about Cory so far that's true, it's that he is a very patient instructor.

"Now, let's go have some fun," he prompts.

The three of them tromp farther into the forest, quite a bit farther until they come to another pasture that isn't enclosed with fencing. The field is cut as if the family has made hay in this particular pasture.

"We'll shoot prone for this. I want to see how you do with that, too, just in case you'd ever need it," Cory tells her.

Sam lies on her stomach on the soft bedding of the forest floor just inside the woods.

"Like this, Paige," she says to her.

"Oh, all right," Paige replies and mimics Samantha's movements.

"It doesn't take long to spot them," Sam tells her. "They pop out pretty quick."

"You don't mind shooting animals?"

"Nope, not groundhogs," Sam says. "I had a friend in my riding academy who almost had to put her horse down for a strained fetlock because of a stupid groundhog hole in her pasture."

No wonder, Paige thinks. Sam and her stupid horses and her unbridled love of the dumb beasts.

Cory kneels down on one knee between them and helps Paige get her own rifle set up.

"Found one," Sam says a moment later before Paige even has a chance to get a bullet in her gun.

"Fire at will, kid," Cory instructs.

A second later, Sam's rifle report cracks through the still air. Her gun doesn't seem as loud as Paige's. She wishes she could trade with Sam. This thing kicks hard. Her shoulder is surely going to be bruised.

"Got it," Sam reports.

Paige grimaces. Gross.

"Find one?" Cory prompts.

"No, I don't see anything," Paige answers, scanning the area.

"You will. Just relax. Pretend it's a creep thug out there trying to steal from you or something," he says.

His hand lands softly on her right shoulder. Then he gives a gentle squeeze. If he's trying to distract her, it's working.

"There's one," he announces.

So maybe he isn't attempting to distract her because he's obviously scanning the pasture better than her. Then she spots it.

"Fire when you're ready," he says quietly.

Paige does as he says and hits her target. Then she feels like shit. What a jerk! She's gone from being a vegan to an innocent animal slaughterer.

"Good," Cory exclaims and pats her shoulder roughly.

Paige tries to conceal her frown. It's hard to get over her distaste for shooting animals. Then again, if she and Simon ever leave the McClane farm, she knows for certain that she'll need better shooting skills. She's already been out there trying to survive and did a barely passable job of it. Her lack of skill had nearly cost her the only friends she'd had in the world. It had cost her roommate and friends from college their lives. She could never let anything happen to her brother. He's the only family she has left. He's the most important person in her life, and she needs to be able to protect him and watch his back.

They shoot for about another hour, sometimes from a one-knee position, sometimes from the prone position and a few more times from the standing position. Paige actually starts having fun. She doesn't relish the killing of the groundhogs part, but she does like shooting more than she'd thought she would. Cory lets her trade rifles with Sam to try out hers. He explains that she needs to be familiar with any and all of the different guns and their calibers on the farm. She finds out that it's called a Ruger 10/22. Then he has her shoot at small targets around the forest with the handguns he'd brought. Sam gets bored and ditches them and heads back for the Johnson farm to retrieve her horse and go home. She's safe to do so because there isn't any danger between their property and the McClane farm. Plus, Paige knows that Chet Reynolds and Kelly are on patrols until Cory returns.

"See? You don't suck at all," Cory tells her as they walk side by side back to his horse.

"It's kind of fun," Paige says reluctantly.

"Yeah, it is. I guess I don't usually see it like that," he confesses softly as the house comes into view.

He doesn't expand on that thought but looks off into the distance.

Evie Johnson is waiting for them near Cory's mammoth horse. She is tying a sack onto his saddle horn.

"Hey!" she calls over. "Have any luck?"

"Sure did," Cory tells her when they get to Evie. He replaces the rifle to its scabbard.

"Well, good," Evie says, a smile touching her mouth. "You've got a great teacher, Paige."

Paige doesn't really want to comment on that, so she gives a nod instead. Cory swipes a hand through his hair, attempting to secure it back into its ponytail. He still looks like a barbarian to her.

"I don't know about that," Cory says with a chuff.

"Oh, you are. You're awesome. You taught me a lot about shooting, more than I knew before," Evie tells them.

"You've taught me some things, too," he quips with a grin that conceals quite a lot.

Evie's cheeks redden slightly. Paige doesn't miss it. She also doesn't miss the other woman's eyes slide over Cory's body quickly.

"That's the vinegar for Simon," Evie stammers, indicating the canvas sack.

"Cool," Cory replies. "I'll make sure he gets it."

He and Evie stand uncomfortably in silence and so does Paige because she hardly knows the other woman and isn't quite sure how to go about small-talk with her. But she and Cory are certainly familiar, and Paige believes her earlier assumptions to be true, especially after the strange cavern of silence and the cryptic tone of their conversation.

"Good, thanks," Evie blurts.

"Catch ya' another time," Cory says, which comes off more as a promise.

This time, Paige's cheeks redden, or at least they feel like they do. For some reason, the thought of him sneaking off every night to meet up with Evie Johnson bothers her and she can't for the life of her fathom why. She couldn't care less with whom he's sleeping around. It just goes to show Evie's poor taste in men.

He mounts the stallion again and tugs her up behind him.

"See you later," Evie says to Cory.

"Maybe," he hints with a cocky grin.

"Bye, Paige," Evie says.

Paige just gives her a wave as he turns the horse toward the path home. They don't gallop across the pastures again. Cory steers his horse toward the forest where they take a well-trodden path. The foliage has started turning from those reds and bright yellows of early autumn to the drabber browns of dead leaves.

"You wanna' drive?" he asks jokingly.

"No way!" Paige tells him honestly. She has zero desire to be in charge of his wild horse.

"You're gonna need to get over your fear of the horses. We can't always take vehicles to get where we need to go anymore."

"Then I'll stay at home on those days. Besides, I thought we were taking the truck when we go to Nashville."

"We are, but you still need to learn how to ride," Cory says. "I'll work with you on that, too."

"No thanks," Paige mumbles. He smirks over his shoulder at her.

"I'll show you some of the basic hand signals we use. I'll go over them later in the cabin before bed," he tells her.

Paige is still contemplating whether or not Cory is having an affair with the Johnson daughter so his statement surprises her.

"Ok, fine," she says.

"Anything else you might need instruction on?" he asks, his gaze hot on hers.

"Not from you!"

Cory just chuckles and turns back around in the saddle.

"There are a lot of tactics and maneuvers we'll need to cover before I agree to take you with me. I know the guys want us to go soon, so we'll need to cram," he says before turning the horse up a short incline. "Lean forward."

She does as he orders, leaning into him. He smells like sweat and horse and gun smoke and something else that is unrecognizable but not unpleasant. The second the ground levels out again, Paige straightens back up to put some space between them.

"When we go out, you'll pair up with me," he informs her. "We've discussed it. Simon and Sam will stick together."

"Who discussed it? I wasn't in on that discussion and I don't like the result."

"Me and John," Cory says.

"I'd rather go with my brother," she says, a little miffed.

"We know. That's why you won't be."

"How's that make sense?"

"Because you need to get used to working with other people, too. And Sam is used to going with Simon. They make a good team," he says, maneuvering the horse around a fallen log that has rotted nearly through.

"Then why don't we all four stick together?"

"It doesn't work that way. We go in pairs of two. If only two of us go, then we generally stick together. That's just how it works," he says and then pauses. "Maybe we'll end up making a good team, too."

Paige snorts through her nose, causing him to laugh loudly. His laughter is infectious and she finds herself smiling.

"If you don't threaten to kill me again, then maybe," she tells him.

"I already apologized for that. Remember?" he asks. "Damn, you can hold a grudge."

"You didn't just threaten to kill me. *Remember?*" she asks, using his own words against him.

Cory sighs and says, "Yes, I remember. I wouldn't actually have raped you. You have to have figured that out by now, right?"

"You seemed pretty serious about it that day," she says.

"No, I was just bluffing," he says tightly. "I wouldn't have. Besides, you had my brother's gun and were wearing my damn shirt. What would you have thought if our roles were reversed?"

"I would've asked questions, not threatened to rape and kill you!" Paige exclaims vehemently.

"That's a relief," he says lightly.

"What is?"

"That you wouldn't have raped me… or threatened to," he jokes.

Paige pinches his side, causing him to jump slightly.

"Hey!" he barks.

"What?" she asks with a laugh. "Wait, are you ticklish?"

"No, but don't do that again or you'll find out," he warns.

"Huh, I think I've found your kryptonite," she teases.

171

"Back to our first inopportune meeting," he retorts with a touch of heat. "You need to think about how you would've reacted if you thought someone had killed your brother and taken his gun."

"Fine, so maybe I've been holding a grudge," she admits. That's all he's getting. She still doesn't trust Cory. She probably never will. He's big, imposing, caveman-like, and dangerous. No way, she'll never fully trust him.

"Maybe?"

Paige doesn't answer. Instead, she stares off to the side, ignoring him. He glances over his shoulder at her and grins smugly as if he's just won their debate. Fat chance. Not only is he untrustworthy, he's irritating and arrogant. She's going to ask her brother if she can stick with him when they go on this raid together. Sam seems to like Cory just fine. She can partner with him.

When they get back to the barn, he extends his forearm, allowing her to hold onto it to get down. Then he swings down and starts toward the barn. She follows dutifully, thinking she should help him with the dumb beast. He hooks the impatient horse to a tie and starts pulling on straps and strips of leather and buckles. She has no idea how to get all of this gear onto a horse let alone back off of one.

After a few minutes of trying to help, Cory says, "You're in the way. Just go wait over there and hold this rifle."

He shoves the heavy Mauser into her hands and then gives her a dismissive snub of his nose. She doesn't supply an argument but hits him with an angry stare.

"I have to relieve Kelly on watch duty, so you're pretty much free to go," he tells her dismissively.

Paige feels put out by his rudeness. His mood has darkened.

"Drop that rifle in the armory. Later, I'll show you how to properly clean one," he says when he turns toward her with the sweaty saddle.

"Oh, I thought you'd be busy later visiting Evie Johnson," she retorts and could kick herself for being such an idiot. She even frowns.

Cory's head jerks up and he looks surprised by her comment. He can't be any more surprised than she is that she'd blurted it.

"And why would you care about what I do with my free time, beanpole?"

Paige swallows hard, clears her voice and raises her chin defiantly, "I don't! You can plow it wherever you want."

"That's presumptuous of you," he remarks and sets the saddle against a stall door.

"Really? And you aren't sleeping with the neighbor's daughter? Probably half of the women in town, too?" she asks, although kicking herself would make more sense.

"That's none of your business, witch," he says with a smirk and crosses his arms over his chest, planting his feet wide.

Paige feels her nostrils flare. Her cheeks must be getting red. She spins on the ball of her foot and leaves the barn in a fit of anger. What the hell?

When she glances back, Cory is leaning his shoulder against the wide open barn door staring at her with deep contemplation. What an idiot! Why had she said any of that? She doesn't give one snippet who he's screwing. So why had she gone down that road? What a perfect fool she is.

Chapter Twelve
Simon

"That's it, Paige," Simon encourages his sister. A few days have passed since their last clinic day, and he actually has a minute of free time. "Hold it closer to your body, too."

He's in the side yard with Cory, his sister, and Samantha, who'd wanted to come along even though he'd tried to discourage it. They are showing Paige how to properly wield a knife, techniques so that she doesn't get it taken away from her, and how to defend herself against someone much larger. His sister may be a tall woman, but she's also very thin and frail, a person easily overwhelmed by just the average-sized man. Her opponent is Cory, someone who is much larger than the average-sized man.

She jabs forward at Cory, attempting to stab at his midsection. Of course, his friend naturally deflects her wrist easily and knocks the plastic, practice knife completely out of her hand.

"Ow!" she yells angrily and rubs at her thin wrist.

"No shit," Cory says with equal frustration. "I told you not to do that! Quit fighting like a girl."

Samantha laughs softly from her perch on the railing where she is twirling her own dagger around and spinning it on its hilt in the palm of her dainty hand. It's almost a juxtaposition of the laws of nature watching her tiny, feminine fingers manipulate a sharp, serrated dagger with such ease. She plays her violin with equal grace.

His sister shoots a nasty glare toward Sam for laughing at her and swings back to Cory with the same unpleasant attitude. He is simply grinning from ear to ear at Paige's distress. She stalks past Cory, gives him a shoulder shot, and retrieves the toy dagger from the grass.

"You may be a good shot like your brother, but your knife skills are pretty much shit," Cory remarks.

"Keep insulting me and find out if they get better," Paige threatens.

"Just watch your grip, sis," Simon says, trying to help her.

"Lock your bony ass grip, woman," Cory reprimands with his hands on his hips.

"You boys," Sam says and hops lithely to the ground, landing light as a feather. "You can only teach her the basics. She *needs* to learn to fight like a girl. She can't fight like a guy. She's not one, obviously."

She marches straight over, gives Simon a look of superiority along the way, and pushes Cory out of the way by pressing her small hand to his wide chest. His friend just laughs and backs up, his hands held up in surrender. She takes the plastic knife from Paige.

"What are we doing wrong, kid? Show us big brutes how it's done," Cory says.

His friend is always patient, kind and brotherly toward Samantha. Cory's the same with her that Simon was with Em. They just have an older, brotherly affection for them. Simon misses Em and her free-spirited youthfulness. He can't even imagine what Cory must feel when he remembers his sister.

"We can't fight like you. We don't have bulk. We don't have as much strength. But we do have some advantages that you don't," Sam explains and sends a naughty, conspiratorial look to Paige.

She spins her real knife in the air, flips it once, the hilt landing with a solid slap against her palm. Then she sheaths it on her hip. This small woman he'd spent most of the last few days avoiding is no longer avoidable. She is forcing her way into this training session and looking beautiful and petite and vulnerable in her snug, worn-out blue jeans, a dark blue sweater and her tall black riding boots. Her hair is down today. He hates it when it's down. It swings around all shiny and glossy and black, and Simon can still remember the way it had smelled that day at the clinic when he'd kissed her like a lecherous bastard.

"And that would be what?" Cory antagonizes and thumbs his finger toward Paige. "Looking cute and, in her case, getting in the way and being bitchy?"

Paige fires a nasty look in Cory's direction. Sam just chuckles at him as if he isn't being serious but just making friendly banter.

175

"No, silly," Sam tells him impudently. "We're faster, smoother. And most importantly of all, we're smaller."

"I don't see..." Cory starts.

Sam cuts him off by spinning around to face him and demonstrating her lightning movements. She has the dagger to his throat before Cory can even finish his sentence. Sam doesn't even come as high as Cory's shoulders, but it doesn't stop her from besting him. She backs away to start again. She gives him a beckoning little hand motion, taunting him. Naturally, not one to turn down a challenge, Cory steps toward her. Before he gets within a foot of her personal space, Sam has the dagger at his stomach, his side and again toward his neck. She's a tiny, dangerous nymph.

"Ok, kiddo," Cory surrenders with a smile. "I couldn't catch you if I tried. That's good. You've always been good with a knife. That's why I wanted you out here. I knew you could help me with this big, gangly Amazon."

Simon sends a warning look toward his friend who holds up his hands in front of him in concession. His sister mumbles something under her breath. Simon's pretty sure it wasn't a compliment.

"Here, Paige," Sam says without missing a beat. "Let me help you. Cory, come here."

She just orders them around, although she is nearly a foot shorter than either of them. Simon grins lopsidedly.

Sam takes Cory's thick arms and extends them toward Paige.

"See, Paige? When they come at you like this, you duck under or spin to their side. Spleen, stomach, inner thigh. All good spots to hit. If you can't get a solid stab, then slice and slice deep, 'kay?"

Simon's grin disappears and is replaced with a frown. Samantha isn't the kind of girl who should be talking about killing someone with a knife. She should be at a horse show or in college now studying art. Or going on a date with some artsy, hipster guy who likes sipping espresso and quoting Kierkegaard. That thought causes him to flinch. The idea of Sam dating anyone makes him instantly violent.

"Watch me, all right?" she says to them.

Cory and Paige stand back and off to the side. She comes straight at Simon.

"No thanks," he puts in quickly. "I'm just here to help my sister..."

"Yeah, I know," she says impatiently and jerks his flannel shirt sleeve until he moves. She throws her light and airy voice to make it sound sinister and evil. "Come over here and be my victim."

Cory and Paige both laugh at her. Simon doesn't. He just continues with the scowl.

"Cory can do this," he tries.

"Come at me, Simon," she insists.

Sam impatiently bobs her head at him to show her intolerance toward his hesitation. Simon takes a slow step toward her. She rolls her eyes at him, displaying more of her impertinence. The sunlight is absorbed and reflected back out of her bright blue eyes. She has a feisty look in those eyes today. Simon wishes she would've just stayed with Sue and worked on the beeswax as was the original plan until Cory got involved.

"Come on, Simon," Cory complains. "I have a lot to go over with your sister today. Get it on, man."

Simon's gaze slices across the yard to his best friend and offers an unspoken warning of his heightening irritation. Cory just smiles ruefully. Simon shakes his head at his friend and turns his attention back to Samantha.

He steps at her quickly; she ducks low. Simon gets a hand to her shoulder, but Sam spins and fake stabs him in the gut. She's fast and agile. He also doesn't want to hurt her. They square off again and she goes down on one knee to stab his inner thigh, which makes Simon jump. He doesn't like her in that region or in the kneeling position in front of him. He jams his hands into his blue-jean pockets and shrugs.

"See, Paige?" Sam asks. "They're bigger, but not smarter or stealthier."

"Definitely not smarter," Paige says, hinting toward Cory.

"Yeah, but the beanpole's super duperty stealthy, right? Remember? *Can* you remember is the better question?" Cory says with a chuckle and nudges Paige gently against her shoulder.

Sam and Simon regard him queerly, but Paige's mouth falls open, gaping wide and disbelieving. Simon has no idea what's going on between those two. Cory smiles broadly at Simon's sister and shrugs as if he couldn't help saying what he said, which makes absolutely no sense to Simon.

177

"I remember just fine. Shut up," Paige mumbles.

"And see here, Paige?" Sam says, changing the course of conversation back to the training. "If Simon comes at me from behind..."

She backs up to him, making Simon highly uncomfortable as her curvy figure presses against his front. He readjusts his ball cap. Sam snatches his arm and slides it around the front of her at shoulder height.

"Just stab his thigh," Sam instructs as if saying something so violent is just an ordinary topic.

"Got it," Paige says with a nod as she chews her thumbnail.

Then Samantha turns, sliding her body sensually against his, or at least it feels that way to Simon. He keeps his arm around the top of her, lest he test her temper. He tries to hold his breath and not breathe in that sweet headiness of Sam. She calls her sinister plans over her shoulder to his sister.

"Or spin and stab him in the back. But make sure it's to his right side and at an upward angle to puncture the liver. Very painful. Very nasty stuff. Very disabling."

His sister is rooted to her spot staring at Samantha as if she's just sprouted an extra head.

"Simon, you aren't even trying. Grab me!" Sam orders angrily.

Cory jumps in and says with unhidden implication, "Yeah, Simon, grab her."

He shoots an angry growl toward his friend, who only grins. Then he does as the nymph instructed and grabs her, picking her off the ground easily. She'd be so easy to overwhelm, and the thought makes him feel a tight anxiety in his chest.

"Get your arm free or if he has it trapped like Simon has mine, then stab to the liver. Unless you're ambidextrous like Reagan and me. Then you can switch hands or if you already have it in your left, just stab to the right side of his back. Good stuff over there, too, but not as good as the liver. You stab him in the liver, he's not getting up."

He sets her down with extra care. Simon steps away, wanting to put distance between them. She gives him an irritated look as if he's cut her lesson short. She even throws both hands up dramatically. Simon walks back toward the fence where he'd been leaning. He hears a sharp intake of breath from his sister and turns. But he's too late. Samantha lands on his back like some sort of psychotic ninja assassin. She's laughing gaily, however.

"Or jump on him like this and stab," she calls to his horrified and now laughing sister and Cory.

"Samantha!" he yells as Sam simulates stabbing his chest.

She laughs in his ear. Her breath hitting him in the face, her cheek smashed against his. Simon turns toward the others with Sam still attached to his back like an unshakable monkey. Her legs are wrapped tightly around his waist, her torso pressed to his back. He can feel every outline of her breasts and stomach against his back muscles through his thin shirt. Her mouth is almost pressed against his bare neck as she gives Paige instructions. Suddenly, he's wishing he'd have worn a coat or a barn jacket. His hands instantly grip her legs so that she doesn't fall. Even though it was her impulsive state of mind that got her into this position, literally, Simon still worries that she'll get hurt.

Paige laughs, and Cory shouts with laughter and claps his hands.

"See? We're more flexible, too! And we're springy!" Sam calls out.

"That'd work, too!" his betraying friend calls out.

"Samantha," he scolds loudly, "stop it. Stop it right now, young lady!"

She slides unhurriedly down his back to her feet. Simon turns to face her with clenched teeth. She just smiles up into his face with unabashed joy and a bit of defiance. If he didn't know any better, and certainly if he thought less of Sam, he'd be tempted to think that she'd pulled that stunt just to get at him. He'd also think that she'd done it to get even with him for avoiding her or perhaps rejecting her. But he can't allow himself to think of Samantha as deviant in nature. Defiant, maybe, but not deviant.

"Just keepin' you on your toes, sir," Sam goads, curtsies, and spins on her foot to go back to her railing seat.

She tosses the plastic knife to him and then resumes playing with her real dagger as if she hadn't just done something completely out of the ordinary. Her cheeks have colored slightly, so Simon wonders if she hadn't also realized the inappropriateness of her actions. She even winks at him.

179

Simon hands the plastic knife to his sister and joins Sam where he leans against a fence post and straightens his shirt and hat again. He doesn't stand too close to her. Cory and Paige start again, and it quickly becomes evident that Sam's instruction was more helpful than anything that he and Cory were attempting to show her.

"Why'd you do that?" he hisses quietly and doesn't make eye contact with her.

"No reason. Not everything needs a reason, Simon. Put your nerd brain to rest," she returns.

"I don't think you should do things like that," he tells her. Simon adds more sternly, "It's crossing a line."

Her fingers nimbly flick the knife to and fro and spin it around. He'd like to tell her to cease that activity before she cuts herself, but Simon knows that his advice will be unwelcome.

"A line you drew but I didn't agree to," Sam informs him haughtily. "You're not my boss."

Simon's lips twitch at her insubordinate attitude. What's with her lately? She's becoming downright hard to deal with anymore. Is this a hormonal thing? Is this what young women do before they turn twenty? He's not sure. Maybe he should discuss Sam's behavior with Doc. Of course, that could open up a can of questions he isn't prepared to answer.

"You don't have to agree to it. I'm doing it with your best interest in mind," he tells her.

"Hey, Hannah," Sam says, causing Simon to startle and look behind them.

Sure enough Hannah is using her cane approaching them and carrying a basket of vegetables and herbs. She has on her sunglasses to shield her delicate eyes from the bright fall sun.

"Hi, Miss Sam," she greets with a smile. "What's going on? Hi, Simon."

He still gets a chill sometimes when Hannah greets him without him saying something to her first. He has no idea how she does it. He rushes to her to offer help, which she declines with a soft smile.

"Hey, Hannie," he returns and is forced closer to Sam as he helps Hannah get lined up against the same railing where she rests her cane. "We're working with Paige. Getting her trained so we can go next week to Nashville."

"Oh, that's good," she says, setting her basket of goods on the grass near her feet.

Now Sam's leg is pressed against his shoulder. Why does she always have to sit on things like hay bales, fence rails and anything else that puts her legs at eye level for him? He can distinctly remember the feel of her muscular thighs in his hands. She's small and compact, but curvy as hell and muscular from horseback riding.

"Sometimes I wish I could go with you guys," Hannah says.

Simon's never heard her say anything like that before. He's never considered that she might want to leave the farm.

"No way, Hannie," Sam says. "It's too dangerous. And we need you here."

"I wish I could contribute more," Hannah laments.

Simon chuckles and lays a hand on her forearm through her pale blue sweater, "Are you kidding? Without you we'd all starve, the kids would be filthy little buggers, and this place would be overrun with heathens and cussers, like a bunch of pirates. And that would just be our family."

Hannah and Sam both laugh heartily at his quip. He doesn't ever want Hannah to think she isn't contributing. Heck, Hannah is probably the most important person on the farm.

"That's probably true, at least the part about the swearing," Hannah agrees. "How's it going with Paige?"

"She's catching on," Sam reports.

"Are you going with them next week, Sam?" Hannah asks.

"No," Simon jumps in to answer.

"Yes," Sam says immediately after.

"No, you're not. You're staying here," Simon informs her.

She nudges her leg against his shoulder roughly and huffs.

"I already talked to John and got it cleared. The four of us are going. John and Kelly are gonna go with us, too. They're looking for those gas company trucks. I guess they didn't find one yesterday, so the hunt's still on. They're gonna leave us in Nashville once they find a few. Then they're coming back here with the trucks- hopefully- and we're staying out. He said we're taking the Suburban so we'll all fit. Plus, that'll give us room to bring back plenty of supplies."

She just rambles on telling Hannie their plans for the trip and what they'll be doing and looking for all the while Simon grits his teeth so hard it hurts his jaw. He distinctly remembers telling John that he doesn't want her going on this trip with them.

181

"That's strange. Kelly didn't mention that he was going with you, as well," Hannah says with a frown.

"He just doesn't like you to worry, Hannie," Simon says, trying to calm her. She pushes her sunglasses to rest on top of her head. Her expressive eyes seem distressed by the news of her husband leaving the farm.

"I don't like it even more when he keeps me out of the loop," she complains delicately and twists the tie strings on the front of her white dress.

"Don't worry, Hannie," Simon tells her. "We'll be fine. He's just going for the ride. He and John are just gonna hit the oil company over there and get some trucks if they have any. If they don't, then they're dropping us off and coming back."

Hannah's hand shoots out to touch his arm, "What do you mean? If they don't find gas company trucks, they'll leave you there with no way to get back home?"

Simon chuckles softly and pats her small hand, "No. We'll be fine. They'll either come back for us after a few days or we'll... get a car."

He doesn't want to tell tender Hannah that he and Cory have stolen cars before and can simply do so again to get back to the farm. After not having success finding any of those CNG operating trucks yesterday or the day before at the frack sites, the men, Doc included, have deduced that the gas company employees either ditched the vehicles at the headquarters or stole them when the fall occurred. So John and Kelly are planning on looking for them when they tag along to Nashville. Either way it goes, Simon's not worried about getting back to the farm. At least, he wasn't until he found out that Sam is still going.

Sam keeps going on about their plans to Hannah, "We're gonna stay over there for a few days searching for stuff, but I don't know if we're staying in the cabin or somewhere in the city this time. Remember, Simon? You and Cory just stayed in the city the one time when you had to take a vehicle instead of horses."

"Yes, I remember," he answers tightly and tries to tune her out. Simon steps away from them and closes in on his sister and best friend.

"That's better," Cory says to Paige as she deflects his arm, spins and fake stabs his midsection.

Simon thinks his sister would prefer to practice with a real weapon when she's working with Cory. She's gotten slightly better about her hostility toward Cory but not much. She told him last night that she doesn't trust him, that she never will. Simon gave up trying to make her like Cory as much as he does. She'll just have to figure it out on her own, or not. He certainly can't force their personalities to meld.

"Thanks," his sister answers. "Guns, knives, what's next? A tank?"

Cory laughs and answers, "Maybe. Depends on what we find out there. If we come across a tank, I'll show you how to drive one."

Paige clucks and says, "Yeah, right. Like you know how to drive a tank."

"I've studied it and got to sit in one at a base up north. Same thing. See one, do one, teach one."

"Sitting in a tank doesn't hardly count as the 'do one' step. You didn't 'do one.' You missed that part," Paige corrects.

"Are you sure?" his friend asks with way too much sexual wordplay implication.

Cory gets a kick out of teasing Paige, Simon's noticed. She just chuffs and snorts indignantly.

"Yeah, I know. You get a lot of the '*doing* one' part done around here, don't you? Like the neighbor's daughters?"

Cory shoots her a fast look of surprise and shakes his head. He indicates with a nod toward Hannah. Simon doesn't think Hannah has overheard the accusation that Paige was clearly making about Evie Johnson because she's still discussing the Nashville trip with Sam. Paige simply raises her chin another inch in defiance of Cory. He's not sure how his sister knows about Evie, but apparently she's picked up on something. Cory is nothing if not discreet when it comes to his sexual conquests. They may be friends and he'd trust his life to Cory, but they don't ever discuss their personal affairs like that. Of course, Simon wouldn't have much to discuss.

"Now we're even," Paige tells him.

This confuses Simon even more, so he decides to call a halt to their bickering, "Hey, if you two are done, we should get to work on other things now."

"Like what?" Paige inquires as a cool breeze tufts her hair around. She isn't wearing one of her bandanas today and hasn't braided it either.

"Like discussing your affinity for moonshine?" Cory says, drawing curious stares.

Paige slugs him in the arm and nearly shouts, "Jerk! You are such a dick. Oh, Hannah…"

Cory grabs his sister and whips her around, covering her mouth with his large hand. Paige shoves away quickly enough without Simon coming to her aid.

"If you two are done behaving like lunatics, we need to work on this," Simon reminds them.

"Cory started it," Paige sulks and steps further away from Cory, who looks affronted by the accusation.

The morning chores are already done, breakfast is long over, and Derek and Kelly have gone to town to work on the wall.

"I'd like to go over contingency plans with you," he tells his sister.

"Right," Cory agrees. "We haven't covered that yet. We've gone over some of the basic hand signals. Remember them?"

Paige purses her dark lips and kicks her boot around in the dirt. "Sort of."

Cory chuckles and says, "That's fine. We can do them again tonight."

Paige makes a disgusted face and rolls her eyes. "Why don't we just do it my way and avoid people?"

Her comment angers Simon and he says, "Because, Paige, that's not always possible. We try to avoid people, but…"

"Well, I don't avoid them," Cory says with a smirk.

Paige is quick to jump in and jab with, "No, you just go around banging them."

"You've seen me without most of my clothes on. Can you blame them?" Cory jests, earning an eye roll from Paige.

Simon shoots him a look of impatience for joking around and continues, "*Sometimes* we're going to run into other people. Most of the time they are harmless, but others are dangerous. You need to be on the same page as us. You need to mimic our movements, follow the plans and also understand us if we can't talk to you."

He leads her to the picnic table in Grams's rose garden a few yards away and takes a map from his back pocket. It is wrinkled, tattered at the edges, and covered in red ink marks. It's a map of the city of Nashville, one they've used many times. She sits, and Simon goes around to the other side where he can stretch over the table to show her different places. Cory stands beside Paige, resting one foot on the seat beside her and his elbow on his bent knee. She looks like she wishes that Cory would have joined him on the other side.

"These marked areas are safe places. When we go to the bigger cities, we always try to get a map and mark very clearly the places that we've scouted and deemed as clear," Simon tells her, pointing to individual red stars.

"That could change," she says smartly and glances up at him from across the picnic table. "Just because they were safe a few months ago doesn't mean they still are."

"Yes, that very well could be the truth of it," Cory says. "But we'll check out the area when we go in. And you should, too, if you get separated from us. Don't just assume that it's safe because we've marked the map as it being a safe zone."

Paige nods with agreement before Cory continues, pointing at the map in front of them.

"See here? This is the downtown district. We'll try to stay out of there. Those are usually dangerous and still filled with people or scavengers. Some cities I was in were dangerous in the downtown districts, but some were total ghost towns. Now we know already that Nashville is populated with people here and there. That's why we have the safe zones marked. We'll stick to the outskirts and work in our two teams."

Simon tries not to flinch as he remembers that he has to take Sam with him.

"This is a pretty big city, sis," Simon tells her. "You'll have a compass like the rest of us and a map. If you, for some reason beyond what Cory and I can control, get separated from us, you'll go to the safe place depending on what section of the city you're in at the time."

"Ok, that makes sense," Paige says with a nod and studies the map. "My friends and I always had a plan like that, too."

"Good, then you're used to it. There are a few stadiums there, Vanderbilt University, some landmarks like the Parthenon…" Cory rambles.

His sister glances up at him. Cory looks directly down into her upturned face and stumbles on his words, seems to forget what he was saying. Simon regards his friend, catches his attention, scowls at him which gets returned.

185

Then Cory keeps going, turning his eyes back to the map instead of Simon's sister, "Anyway, let's go over some of the more important places, the ones where you'd meet for a rendezvous if the shit hits and we get separated."

"We won't," Paige says and looks up at Cory again.

This time, his friend frowns deeply when he looks at Paige. Even though the sun is glinting off of her red hair and high cheekbones and she looks fresh and pretty, Simon knows what his friend's frown is about. Cory's worried that she'll get separated from him or hurt or worse. He can read the hint of anxiety in Cory's dark eyes. Simon isn't too worried. She's going to be with a one-man army killing machine. He's very confident his friend will keep his sister perfectly safe. He's a heck of a lot more worried about his own role in keeping Samantha safe.

"There are gonna be situations, things we don't plan for," Cory tells her sternly. "You need to pay attention to what we're telling you and take this seriously."

"I am taking it serious, but you have to remember my past and how I got here. You aren't the only one who knows how to survive on your own. I didn't always go with my friends on runs. Sometimes we got separated. Sometimes I was alone, and I'm still alive. Making a run to one city isn't a big deal to me. I traveled all over the east coast to get here. I didn't have a gun or skills or help other than my two friends," Paige explains and turns back to the map. "Do you guys usually run into trouble?"

Simon looks at Cory, and they read each other's minds.

"Yes," they answer in unison.

Simon explains in more detail, "In the bigger cities, yes. In the small, surrounding towns, not usually. It's important for you to know where to go, what to do and how to handle yourself if you get separated from him or he gets shot."

"It was only a flesh wound," Cory mimics in a British accent.

Simon chuckles. They'd found a copy of a Monty Python movie at a video store once and brought it back to the farm. They'd asked permission to use the television and old-fashioned DVD player in the music room. Those two things never get used, especially not frivolously. Derek had insisted they watch it, though. Apparently he used to be a Monty Python fan. Simon found the dry humor mildly amusing, but Derek, Kelly and Cory had laughed their asses off. And now Cory's repeating one of the lines from the movie. His sister just looks at Cory likes he's a moron.

Then she asks, "You've been shot before? Is that what you mean?"

"Grazed. Not really shot. No big deal," Cory says.

"On their way to the farm when Kelly and John picked him up. Derek was shot, too. You're looking at Cory 2.0," Simon jokes. "Didn't you know? He's some sort of invincible badass now."

Cory just chuckles and punches Simon in the shoulder.

"How many people have you shot?" Paige asks, earning a huge grimace from Cory.

"Paige," Simon scolds, "that's an inappropriate question."

"And none of your business, as usual, you snoop," Cory adds in for good measure.

She crosses her arms over her chest and puckers her lips at Cory with distaste. His friend's gaze drops to Paige's chest, where she has inadvertently pushed the scooped neckline of her baggy, dingy brown shirt lower and her breasts higher. A sudden flair of righteous temper ignites within Simon, and he clears his voice loudly and jams his finger at the map.

"Hey, let's get this done!" he barks angrily, which shocks his sister and friend to attention. He glances over his shoulder to find Sam and Hannah regarding him strangely. He just frowns and turns back to the map. "Look here, Paige. If we're on the north side of the city, which we probably won't be too much, and you get separated, then head over here and meet us at the James K. Polk tomb. We'll probably skirt around that area because there is a small community up there trying to make it, so we don't want to seem like a threat and start a war with them. We'll come in from the northwest side and filter in from there."

Paige asks, "How will I know for sure that you guys can find me if we get separated? I don't understand."

Cory answers, "We'll come for you. If we can't because we're... dead or something, then the Rangers will come for you. If no radio calls come in to the farm at the allotted twelve hour mark, then the guys know to get the contingency plans rolling. They'll know we're in trouble. You'd be picked up within twenty-four hours. They hit each of the pick-up zones, unless we're all at the same spot. You'll carry enough in your pack to get you by for at least that amount of time. You just have to make it one day, or less."

"I can do that, no problem. It's better than three years."

Simon continues showing his sister where they should meet should a situation arise by pointing at different red stars on the map. She pays more attention this time. Cory pays less attention to his sister's body. And Simon completely ignores Sam who has come to sit by him on his side of the table. A short time later, they finish explaining other contingency plans to Paige and how to handle adverse situations. Then Simon tells his sister that he wants to show her how to make a particular tincture he's been working on. However, Cory changes his plans.

"Take Sam and show her," Cory says. "I'm gonna take Paige into the woods with me and work with her on maneuvers."

"Oh yeah? Maneuvers, huh?" Simon asks, remembering the heat of his friend's gaze on his sister.

"Just tactical maneuvers, man," Cory says apologetically and holds up one hand.

Simon isn't in a position to argue with Cory since John has put him in charge of Paige's training, which is fine. But he sends his friend a warning look anyway before they roll up the map and rise. Unfortunately, he doesn't want to hang out any longer with Sam than he has to, either. He would've preferred it if she would've followed Hannah to wherever she's gone off.

"Sounds good to me," Paige agrees, oblivious to the meaning behind their exchange, and leaves with Cory.

Without looking at Sam, he says, "You don't have to come with me to the med shed to work. You can go and do whatever."

"That's fine," she says. "I want to help. I like working in the shed with you."

"First I need to go to the barn to get some garlic," he tells her. "I think Sue said she has garlic hanging out there."

"Ok, I'll come, too," Sam volunteers.

Simon winces and tells her, "Why don't you go and get me about a dozen onions from the cold storage in the cellar?"

"Oh, sure," Sam answers so amiably and with a big smile.

Simon jogs out to the barn where he spends way more time than is necessary to look for the strands of hanging garlic. Then he grabs about six hot peppers Sue has curing in another area. They're still fairly fresh and haven't dried out yet. When he gets to the shed,

Sam is already there waiting for him and sitting on a stool at the side counter.

"So what kind of project are you working on today, Mr. Mad Scientist?" she asks with spunk.

Simon removes his hat, runs a hand through his hair and sets his produce on the counter.

"It's an herbal tincture, the antibiotic kind," he responds and takes a bucket from under the counter. "We need ginger and horseradish root, too."

"Okey-dokey, sir," she says with a salute and leaves to retrieve them from the back shelf.

He and Doc spend a lot of time grinding herbs and curing them so that they can be stored in small glass jars in the shed for this exact sort of use. The tiny sprite returns a moment later with two quart-sized jars of herbs.

"What's this?" she asks and picks up the book he'd left on the counter the other day.

"I found it the last time Cory and I went on a run to Clarksville. There was an acupuncturist's office over there that I raided. Most of the bottled pills were gone, but I found some books and a few boxes of surplus herbs in the back. Some of the books are written in Chinese, so we're not sure what they are yet. Speak Mandarin?"

"Nope, you're outta' luck," she quips. "I barely got passing grades in English class. I hated it. I hated most of school actually. I just always doodled in my classes."

Simon shoots her a smile as she checks out a book in English.

"I'd say you put your time to good use then," Simon remarks with a smile. "Your art is great."

"It was just to pass the time till the bell rang and I could get home to my horse," Sam admits with a shrug.

If the world was still normal and they'd gone to the same school, they probably wouldn't have even been friends. Sam had to have been a popular girl in school as pretty and sweet as she is. He was a comic book science nerd. Pretty girls weren't exactly slobbering over red-haired teen boys with tickets to Comic-Con. Even though the skinny teen body of his youth is long gone, replaced with a soldier's body, Simon still can't seem to shake some of his insecurities.

"Air…ay…" she attempts at pronouncing the title of the medical book.

"Close. It's pronounced, are-you-vay-dic. The word is ayruvedic. Or you can just say ayruveda. Same thing," Simon corrects her.

"What's this book about?" she inquires and takes a seat on the stool again.

Normally he's happy to have her help, appreciative of it. She's always great to work with and never bugs him when he needs space. She's wonderful at the clinic for the same reason. Samantha is patient and kind and the best lab assistant he could ask for. She sometimes asks questions that actually put him on a different path to figuring something out. Her brain works in a completely different way than his. She's thoughtful and expressive, where he is more logical and analytical.

"It's an eastern Indian tradition of healing with herbs in a more natural way and detoxifying the system. That kind of thing. It's pretty interesting actually."

"Cool," Sam says with her usual enthusiasm. "Reagan would say it's hippy-dippy stuff, huh? Can we use some of the practices at the clinic?"

She twists back and forth quarter spins on her stool as a young kid would do. It just makes her seem more child-like to Simon, which makes him feel like a bigger pervert for finding her desirable. If it weren't for her body and those bewitching blue eyes, Sam would seem like a pre-teen. Em was younger than her and still taller.

"We may need to depending on what direction and depletion of the medicine we end up getting into this winter," Simon tells her. "Doc and I have been working on some things."

"I'll help, too," she offers with hope-filled eyes.

Simon clears his voice, pushes his glasses a little higher on his nose, and reaches around her to collect more items.

"What's that?" she asks.

"This jug is full of apple cider vinegar from the Johnson farm. I wanted a jar of theirs to try since they have different breeds of apples over there. Doc and I want to have a few different varieties of this antibiotic to see if the apples make a difference in the healing process. Evie was kind enough to send a jar home with Cory the other day."

"Oh yeah, I remember them talking about it," she acknowledges.

"Did everything go all right the other day at the Johnson's?" he inquires, curious about his sister's knowledge of Cory's relationship with Evie Johnson.

"Yeah, your sister did great. She's a better shot than we thought," Sam says.

"I meant how do it go with Evie? Was anything out of the ordinary? Did she and Paige get along?"

"Of course, silly," Sam says with a confused smile. "Why wouldn't they? Evie's so sweet with everyone, and so is Paige."

"Hm," Simon murmurs. Sam wouldn't pick up on a rift between the other women if they'd start duking it out in the mud right in front of her. She doesn't have a mean bone in her body. "Let's start on this."

He wants to get the project finished and avoid lingering in the shed with her. Standing so close to her, smelling the clean freshness of her is wreaking havoc on his resistance.

"Ready?" he asks and gets a nod. She pulls out a rubber band from her jeans pocket and ties back her hair. "Want to cut those onions and three or four cloves of garlic for me? I'll start on the peppers since they might burn your skin."

She chuckles at him as they take cutting boards from the cabinet below them. Simon also snags a pair of rubber gloves to protect his skin from pepper oils.

"Simon, I help can the hot peppers with Sue. I think I'm used to it. Probably more than you!"

"Just do the onions and garlic," he says testily.

"Won't have to worry about vampires any time soon!"

Simon chuckles. He's more worried about his own restraint. It would take more than the scent of garlic to keep him from kissing her again.

They work side by side slicing and dicing all the while he tries to keep from bumping into her. She chit-chats about the new foal in the barn, and he tries not to think about the softness of her mouth when he'd kissed her.

Simon adds ground ginger and pulverized and dried horseradish root to a five-gallon bucket.

191

"I need the vinegar, Sam," he says as he places the rest of their ingredients into the bucket. She grabs the jug from the counter and squats beside him.

"This stinks," she says, wrinkling her pert nose. "I mean really bad. I think I'd rather die than have to…. drink this? Is that what you're making? Something that has to be drunk?"

"Yes, but only a very small amount at a time," he says as he measures the apple cider vinegar into the bucket with their other ingredients. "We'll cut it with honey for our patients this winter when the seasonal illnesses roll through. Or any other sicknesses that we might need antibiotics for."

A few years ago when he and Doc started compounding their own medicinal cures in bulk, they sawed an old wooden curtain rod in half, leaving the round finial attached. The bucket and rod act as an oversized mortar and pestle system. Simon now uses the fat end to smash and mince the malodorous concoction into smithereens.

"We'll cover this when I'm done and leave it for about a week to cure. Then we'll strain it through a cheesecloth," he tells Sam, who has already started cleaning up their mess.

"What if it doesn't work?" she asks.

"It will," he assures Sam, looks up, and gives her a grin. "This may be a new remedy, but it still has all of the antibiotic qualities in it that we need to cure or treat most sicknesses and wounds."

"You had me until you said the wound part," Sam says on a rotten chuckle. "Nobody's gonna want to rub this on themselves and smell like it. I'd rather get gangrene."

"We'll make it into a gel," he explains.

Sam wrinkles her nose again, wags her finger, and shakes her head. "No way, not rubbing it on any of my wounds. That stuff could scare away Dracula himself."

"Don't worry, I won't let you turn it down," Simon says jokingly. "I'll shower you in it head to toe if that's what it takes to keep you from getting sick."

"Ew, Simon. No way! No thanks," she says with a laugh.

"Yep, I sure will," he teases further, enjoying the sound of Sam's musical laughter.

"Then I'm making it my mission to look for some Tylenol or Neosporin when we get to Nashville," she jokes.

Her comment makes his jesting mood dissipate. "Sam, I really think you should stay here."

"I need to go," she says without missing a beat. "I'm your partner, and your sister is Cory's. I have to go. If I don't, then you guys won't be able to split up, and it will take way longer to get anything done."

Her no-nonsense reasoning is causing him to lose patience. He knows that without John approving a change, Samantha is going with him. He grinds his teeth and screws the plastic lid onto the top of the bucket to contain the smell. They take turns washing the stench of onions, garlic and herbs from their hands in the stainless steel sink. Sue's herbal soap has antibacterial components in it like citrus oils and lye. It's the same soap they use to scrub up before treating patients.

"Reagan could go," Simon proposes and then feels bad for even doing so.

"Simon, no way," Sam says quickly. "She has Jacob. That's not fair."

"You're right. I'm sorry I even suggested it. That was stupid of me."

Simon feels an enormous amount of guilt for considering Reagan for a run. She's a mom now. She has responsibilities, and unlike him, she's an actual doctor that the whole town relies upon for healthcare. He carries the heavy bucket to the back of the shed and stores it in a dark corner behind the shelving units. Sam follows him.

"It's ok," Sam says and lays her hand against his forearm.

This feels just like the day at the clinic when he'd kissed her. They are back in a darkened area of a medical clinic surrounded by tall shelving. This time, however, Reagan is nowhere in sight to interrupt him should he take advantage of Sam again. Simon swallows hard.

"You just have a big heart, Simon," Sam praises. "Nobody could ever fault you for that. But don't worry, 'kay? I've gone with you guys before. I went last year with Derek and then again with John and Kelly, remember? I'll be fine. Really."

Simon stares down at her hand a moment before she takes it away.

"You'll keep me safe, too," she says so easily. "I know you will. And I'll watch your back just like when you and Cory go together. I won't let anything happen to you, either."

193

Simon chuffs through his nose and squints his eyes at her. She's being so serious that he doesn't want to laugh at her. The idea of tiny, doll-like Samantha protecting him seems far-fetched. And he's hardly concerned about his own neck. Her skinny, delicate one is the bigger issue. He allows his gaze to drop from her face to her thin neck. It's an enormous mistake on his part. He watches an artery pump blood for a second before forcing his eyes away.

"We're hitting the hospital over there and some of the places where I might find medicines and supplies for the clinic," he tells her, trying to change the subject while fidgeting from foot to foot.

"Sounds good," she says, staring up into his eyes.

"Then we'll try to join back up with Cory and Paige for the night somewhere or if we can't get to them, we'll stay in separate areas of the cities until we can meet up the next day. We probably won't make the hike to the cabin since we don't have horses. We'll stash the car and move on foot," he says. Simon has no idea why he's going over any of this with her other than that talking is keeping his mind occupied. If only he could give his eyes something to look at and keep busy with instead of gawking at her lovely face, graceful neck, and slim figure. The cool air this morning has kissed her cheeks to a dark pink.

"Simon, are still mad at me?" she asks and drops her eyes to his chest.

Her question takes him by surprise, "Um..."

"I don't want you to be mad at me," she says, twisting her hands in front of her.

Her blue eyes lift to his and melt his insides, "Sam, I could never be mad at you. That would be like being mad at Arianna or Jacob."

"What?" she asks irritably, glaring at him. "I'm not a little kid, Simon. For goodness sake, I'm going on a raid to a dangerous city with you. I'd hardly say I'm like one of the kids."

"Sorry," he mumbles, wishing he could get out of the tight space and leave the shed.

"I... I kind of have a favor to ask. That's why I wanted to know if you were still mad."

"I am not now nor was I before angry with you, Samantha," Simon tells her and rests his right hand on the shelf by his head. It's better than slipping it behind her back and pulling her close.

His answer must amuse her because she chuckles at him, which makes Simon frown with the usual confusion he feels around Sam.

"I want to know if you'll... if you'd..."

"What is it? What do you want? Just ask, Sam. You know I can't usually tell you no, so whatever it is I'm sure you'll get your way," he admits, causing her to smile. With her big, expressive eyes, her pert nose and dark hair, Sam looks like a Disney princess character when she smiles.

"Good to know," she grins deviously.

"You already knew that," he teases.

Sam just smiles at him coyly. Her smile disappears quickly.

"I just... lately I've been thinking about them a lot, you know?" she regards him with expectation and rubs her forehead.

He knows exactly what she means. He's the only one in the McClane clan that she'll talk to about her family, her real family.

"Have you been drawing...?"

She cuts him off with a wave of her hand and says, "No, no, nothing dark. I've just been thinking about them. Would you take me to see them, Simon?"

He's taken her before. She won't let anyone else go with them to visit her family's gravesites behind her former home.

"Maybe, sure. I'll have to check with the family," he tells her and stashes both hands in his jeans pockets to keep from embracing her until she feels better, even if that task would take hours.

"I need to talk to my mom," she says honestly.

Her statement breaks Simon's heart. Everything about Sam breaks his heart when he actually allows himself to think about her or her past or the treatment she received from the visitors.

He flinches and answers, "Sure, I will take you."

"Thanks, Simon," she says with a sad little smile.

"No problem, but wouldn't you rather one of the women went with us like Hannah or Sue... or Reagan?" he asks, not sure on the last suggestion. Reagan isn't the touchy-feely type. He's not sure she could help Sam at all, although Sam is crazy about her and hangs on her every word. She rather worships Reagan.

"No, you know I don't want them," she says and kicks the toe of her boot gently at the floor.

"They might..."

"Just you," she interrupts and hits him with those eyes again.

195

"Ok, I will. I'll find out when we can go and I'll take you. Just us," he promises and touches her shoulder reassuringly because she seems like she's getting upset. Even in the state of sadness she's sunk into because of family memories, Simon still finds her alluring. He feels such a fierce protectiveness of Samantha that he can't explain, not even to himself. Sometimes he thinks he'd like to run away with her and hide Sam from the rest of the world and conceal her from men who would want to hurt her. He's seen the furtive glances the men from town give when she's working with him at the clinic. At first they look at her like most people do, like she's a kid. Then once they realize that she's just a petite, small-boned adult woman, their eyes change. None of them regard her with violent lust in their gazes because he would've killed them for it, but they do look at her as they would any attractive woman. He always has to suppress an urge to kill men when he catches them looking at Sam.

She lays her hand on top of his and offers a small nod.

"Thanks," she says softly, her lips parting.

Sam steps closer, possibly to hug him, so he slides past her, physically moving her out of the way at the same time so that she cannot follow through with whatever she had planned. If she's surprised by his move, she doesn't voice it. She simply follows him from the room. They leave the shed, Simon locking it on their retreat.

"I'm gonna go pick some herbs, ok?" he says.

"Want some help?"

"No, just have to find a few things. You should help Sue with the beeswax. I think she was needing your help," he lies and feels the immediate dissatisfaction of doing so. Sue doesn't need her help. He does know that she was going to render beeswax today, but she was supposed to be working with her young son and Talia on it since Talia wanted to learn. But he doesn't want Sam to tag along picking herbs with him. He needs to distance himself from her, really distance himself with many, many acres.

"Oh, all right. I'll go find her," she says dutifully and turns to leave.

Simon watches her depart, the gentle sway of her hips, the wind tossing her dark hair around as she pulls it out of the ponytail again. She spins quickly and calls back to him.

"Thanks again, Simon."

All he can afford her is a brief nod before he turns to leave and hunt down herbs he doesn't really need.

Chapter Thirteen
Cory

He rounds the corner with Damn Dog and finds the source of noise. Unfortunately, it's only a raccoon. It's nearly midnight, and he's back in Coopertown. The trail for the bastards that had the balls or stupidity or a combination of the two to attack the McClane farm has run cold again. He thought he was onto something a week ago when he'd gotten a tip from a nearby town that bandits had robbed two farmhouses and stolen everything that wasn't tied down. Cory can feel it in his gut that these men aren't gone for good, that they haven't fled the state. He knows they are still in the area.

Derek has said that they should suspend their searches because they can't afford the gasoline anymore. But little do they know that he's still going out most nights on his horse continuing the hunt. There's no way in hell that they can allow anyone to get away with what they did to the family and their friends and closest allies from town and the condo village. Last week he even ran into Condo Paul and K-Dog, as they were conducting their own manhunt up north of Pleasant View. He only wishes that he'd been home when the attack had occurred. It would've been so much easier to take off after them that same night, but he understands why they couldn't, not with so many wounded victims and people in need and frightened citizens.

"Easy, girl," he tells the dog, who enjoys a good scrap now and then with the occasional raccoon or opossum.

"Better head back," he tells her. "I'm on guard duty in four hours and Evie's waiting for me."

He was hoping to make some progress in his search before they leave for the city, but their trip is now only three days away and he is less close to finding them than before.

He and the dog jog back to Jet, who is tied to a post behind an abandoned home near the edge of town. He mounts up and begins the short trek back to the Johnson farm. He's supposed to be meeting Evie soon for a tryst in the old shed at the far perimeter of their farm. He picks up the pace.

Cory takes a short-cut, skirting Pleasant View and saving time by going through the woods. His sexual frustration is at an all-time high lately and he is loath to admit the reason.

For the last week, every day and each evening, he's been working with Paige on military tactics, weapons training, and as much as he can cram with her to keep her ass alive during the coming trip to Nashville. This means she's been in his constant company twenty-four-seven since they even sleep in the same cabin.

Yesterday he'd taken her into the woods again and practiced sneaking around, stalking and how to be as quiet as possible. He was surprised by her progress and what she already knew before they started. Apparently she'd been telling them the truth when she said that she was stealthy. For a tall woman, she is very light on her feet and graceful. Her combat moves still need a lot of work, certainly more than he's going to be able to address in the next three days, but he's fairly sure she'll be fine with him. He only wishes that Paige was shadowing Simon instead. When he'd questioned John about his decision to have her grouped together with him instead of her own brother, John had told him rather angrily that he needed to suck it up and get over it. He also said that he was worried that if Cory kept harassing Paige the way he does- the way he enjoys doing- that she may convince Simon to leave the farm because she's unhappy. Cory doesn't see how it would ever happen, but he'd conceded to John's orders, nonetheless. He'd also promised to stop giving her such a hard time. That one's proving more difficult than he'd thought it would be. She has such a pissy streak.

And so he's been stuck in her company for almost a full week. She's surprisingly a lot brighter than he'd given her credit for being. Paige catches on very fast to what he shows her with the exception of the hand signals and the fact that she still calls everything whether or not it's a shotgun shell or rifle round by the phrase: 'bullet thingys.' She also just calls all of the weapons by the

199

word: guns, not rifle, shotgun, or handgun, just gun. Cory supposes it's probably better than gun thingys.

She's also a lot more attractive than he'd like to admit. Her bad temper and bitchy attitude detracts from her nice ass and gorgeous face… slightly. He hadn't liked being in such close contact, but he also doesn't have much of a way around it. He even took her on a three mile run. She'd need a few rests, but she made it back to the farm with him. She explained that she used to like running in college but that she's out of shape since coming to the farm. He'd teased her about being lazy and getting off her ass once in a while and had received an ineffectual punch to his gut. Then he'd been stuck with thoughts of her ass on his brain all day and had caught himself inadvertently staring at it often. She's not at all his type, either, which is why it's so confusing being drawn to her. He likes blondes, preferably petite and curvy like Evie Johnson and never has he liked a woman with a nasty glare and feisty attitude.

He's also pretty sure she'll slow him down in the city, but that's fine. Keeping her alive and finding the supplies is all that matters. Her brother would like her returned to him in one piece and has made mention of it quite a few times.

The worst part of working with her all week wasn't the fact that he finds himself becoming attracted to her or even her bitchiness, it's that Cory is starting to think that maybe she is just a little bit attracted to him, as well. That's all he needs. A few times she had looked at his arms and once in the cabin at his bare stomach before quickly turning away. He'd slept on top of the covers that night with a t-shirt and sweats on instead of the usual pajamas of boxers and nothing else. He doesn't need a complication like Paige in his life. He isn't interested in her for anything other than a few fun hours in bed, and he doesn't want to destroy his relationship with Simon by seducing his sister. Besides, he'd probably have to hold his hand over her smart mouth the whole time. Of course, then he'd be staring more intently at her pale gray eyes and not at her full lips.

He arrives at the shed where a dim light slips beneath the crack of the rickety door. Evie is waiting for him. Cory knocks twice and enters, finding Evie sitting at a scarred, wooden desk in an equally old chair knitting something by the light of a lantern.

"Took you long enough," she chides.

Cory chuckles, shuts the door on Damn Dog so that she can't come in, and sets his rifle against the wall. It's probably doing more to hold up the wall than the slatted boards anyway. There are wide cracks between the barn-wood siding, allowing moonlight to filter inside the tiny cabin. A single cot that he dragged out here a few years ago rests in the corner. Evie usually sees to the bedding. It always smells clean and fresh, at least in Cory's opinion.

"Had some errands to run, dear," he jokes and gets a forgiving smile from her.

"Pick up that gallon of milk and loaf of bread for me?" she teases in return and stands.

She's wearing black pants and a heavy-duty red sweatshirt to ward off the night air. He feels sorry that he kept her waiting.

"No, but I coulda' had a raccoon for you," he says and tosses his jacket onto the bed.

"Gee, thanks," she says lightly and smiles.

Her blonde hair is pulled back into a bun tonight.

"It's fine, actually. I was late getting a shower tonight because the hot water tank gave out. My ice cold shower was unpleasant," she says with a grimace.

"Really? Do you guys need help?" he asks, concerned for their family friends.

"Nah, my brother took care of it with Dad," she explains. "We have two more heaters left in case of another emergency. That was smart when you guys told us to raid the home improvement stores for supplies like that. I would've never thought of hot water tanks. I forget that things like that don't last forever. I don't know what the kids will do someday when the final one gives out, but hopefully we'll never find out."

If there's one thing he likes about Evie it's that she's an eternal optimist. She always believes that this mess will turn around one day and the world will magically right itself again. He tries not to bring her down with too much realism.

She moves into his space and kisses the bottom of his chin. Cory snatches her to him and practically lifts her off the ground. She kisses him back with as much fervor before finally stepping back. Evie sits on the bed and pats it. He obliges and sits next to her.

"How's it going with training Paige?" she asks.

They always talk for a while, usually before and after the sex. She's a great confidant and gives even better advice. She was very angry with him for leaving the farm in the spring without telling her or coming back to explain his reason for doing so. He couldn't bring himself to say goodbye because she likely would've talked him out of it.

"Fine. She's a pain in the ass, but she's catching on," he answers.

"Good. I remember the day she came here," she tells him.

Cory's gaze jerks to her face. His curiosity is piqued. They both remove their shoes and lie down together. Once again, the sheets, blanket, and single pillow smell clean.

"I guess I never told you," she says, and he shakes his head. "I remember that day very distinctly. Her and her friends just walked right up onto the front porch and knocked on our door. Zach immediately went on the offensive."

She chuckles when she talks of her protective older brother.

"I'm sure. He was probably wondering how they got through all of our security on the road," Cory agrees.

"I know. But I guess they did," Evie says. "They explained who they were and who they were looking for. I mean, it was shocking. They were... I don't even know how to explain it. We went to live up north with my other brother, but we drove. We had provisions from home, a car, supplies. Even though it didn't work out because... well, you know why, we still made it back here in our vehicles. These three young people show up with a little girl and they were on foot, Cory. Can you imagine?"

He shakes his head and pushes a strand of loose blonde hair away from her cheek.

"Me neither," she says, widening her eyes. "We couldn't believe it. Paige was tiny. I guess Paige is still tiny, but she was skin and bones. Her friends, too. They looked like homeless people. They were dirty and skinny and about half-starved to death. Dad let them in the house while we called over to get Simon over here."

"That was pretty trusting of him. Your dad's not usually like that," Cory says, thinking of the Johnson patriarch, Ryan, who is a close friend of Doc's.

"Trust me, it only took a second to realize they weren't a threat. It was just so sad. I can't even describe it other than that. It was just sad seeing those three kids and a toddler. I can't imagine what they went through to get here."

Cory can. He knows exactly what they've seen and been through. He was on his own for almost eight months out there. He knows what's out there. None of it is good news. And he overheard Paige telling her story about Talia's rape and her near-rape. He just nods sympathetically.

"I'm glad for Simon, though," she says. "It's good that his sister made it here. She's been good for him. He seems happier having her with him on the farm. And she's really nice, too. I like her. She seems kind of shy, but she loves her brother and friends so fiercely. Kind of like someone else I know."

Cory tries not to wrinkle his nose, but it still happens.

"What?" Evie questions. "Seriously? You don't like her? Why not?"

He explains their first meeting in the woods and the hard grudge she's been holding against him for it and her nasty attitude since. Evie laughs at him. He scowls back.

"I'd probably hate you, too," Evie admits and lays a hand against his cheek. "Give her a chance. She's a good person, Cory."

He shrugs and scoffs.

"She's very pretty," Evie says as if she's trying to get him to admit it.

"She's all right," he lies.

"Yeah, right," Evie says, forcing Cory to confront his own falsehood. "She's more than pretty. She could've been a model or something. She's so tall and beautiful. I like her a lot. Guess some of the guys in town do, too."

She's hinting at what he already knows. He'd like to change the topic but can't seem to do so with any subtlety.

"Fine, she's pretty. Happy?" he asks impatiently and starts pulling her closer.

"I don't know," Evie says as he plies her neck with kisses. "I think I saw something the other day when you brought her over here."

"What do you mean?" Cory asks, not stopping with the kissing but adding a caress of her hip.

"I think I saw a mutual attraction if you ask me," she offers.

Cory wishes she'd stop talking about Paige. Now his brain is filled with images of her. It's also filled with images of her coming home skinny as a rail and hungry and tired. It bothers him to think of

203

her suffering. He tells himself that this is exactly how he ended up with Damn Dog.

"Nope, not attracted to her at all. She's probably attracted to me because, well, let's face it, who isn't?" he says, attempting a lighter banter with her.

He goes back to kissing Evie, this time behind her ear, which she usually likes. Then he strokes his hand down her back and pulls her up against him.

"Oh, your cocky attitude is gonna get you in trouble one of these days, Cory," she warns with a grin. "You're gonna get swept off your feet and you won't even know it. Boom, like a lightning bolt."

"Not likely," he says wryly.

"Maybe Paige'll be the one to do it, too," she suggests.

Damn, she's killing his boner. He wishes she'd just shut up about Simon's sister already. He and Evie don't have a flowers and poetry kind of relationship, but this isn't exactly getting it, either.

"No way. Not the beanpole," he tells Evie.

"She's not a beanpole anymore," Evie argues. "I think you are attracted to her. And I also believe it's a good thing, Cory. *And* I think we shouldn't see each other for a while. Not until you get this thing worked out with Paige."

And there it went. He rolls away from her onto his back. Evie leans up on her elbow to talk to him.

"I'm not attract..." he starts.

"Yes, you are. And now you need to decide if you have actual feelings for her or if you are just looking for... more of what we have," Evie tells him.

As usual, her wisdom goes far beyond his own. Cory just looks over at her.

"She's a beautiful woman, but you have to think about if your relationship with Simon could be damaged by pursuing his sister," Evie says.

Damn. What is she, a psychic or something? He'd just been thinking about this shit on his way over.

"I think you should allow your heart to open up to this woman," Evie counsels, whether he wants it or not.

"What?" Cory asks with disbelief.

"It wouldn't be the worst thing ever. Heck, it might be the best thing that's ever happened to you."

"No thanks," he replies smugly. "That's not a good idea at all."

"It was for me. I loved my husband very much. I think someday I may find someone else to love, but I don't know that anyone could ever replace my Richard. He knocked me off my feet. Sometimes that's ok, Cory. It might be what she needs, too. Paige has been through ten lifetimes of bad things I'm quite sure, and so have you."

"Evie," Cory warns.

She just laughs softly and touches his face with her fingertips.

"Look, I know what losing Em did to you. Trust me, I went through the same damn thing when I lost my husband. But you don't have to throw your whole life away because of it. You have to find some happiness in this world, even as messed up as it is now. And Em would want that for you. And I'm sure that Paige's family would've wanted that for her, too. Just tread lightly where Simon is concerned. Don't do anything rash or stupid."

"Stupid is my specialty," Cory says with a grin and pulls her closer so that she can rest her head in the crook of his arm. He knows that sex is off the table tonight, but she still deserves some comforting human contact from him.

"Don't I know that," she teases. "Seriously, though, don't hurt Simon by doing anything with his sister that you don't mean to take seriously or by dishonoring her. She's still his sister. Imagine if it were you in his shoes. Be careful, ok?"

"You got it," he says and kisses her forehead.

They lie together for another hour before he walks her back to the barns. He waits until she is safely inside their old farmhouse before retrieving his horse again and leaving. Her words are rattling around in his brain, irritating him and confusing him at the same time. When he arrives at his cabin, he finds Paige still awake reading and Simon gone. She has a single candle burning on top of the wood-burning stove and a low, dying fire going inside of it.

"Hot date with the farmers' daughters?" she asks snidely from her mattress on the floor.

Why couldn't she just have been asleep? He tries to suppress a groan.

"You have no idea," he says with sarcasm that she won't understand. Let her think about it. He doesn't care what she thinks

205

of him or Evie or their relationship or any other opinions she might have of him and his sexual prowess- or tonight, lack of.

"Spare me the details," she says and then snorts.

He strips out of his clothing down to his t-shirt and boxers and climbs into bed, pulling a sheet over his body to conceal it.

"Where's the professor?" he asks after his friend.

"Supposedly my brother does middle of the night emergency house calls with Dr. McClane."

"Someone's goat giving birth or something?" he jokes.

"No, I think someone's wife is giving birth or something," she says with disgust.

"What's with the tone?"

Paige lowers her book and regards him with open criticism, "Because, I've witnessed one live birth. That was about as gross as it gets."

Cory chuckles at her.

"Childbirth is supposed to be a beautiful thing," he teases.

"Whoever came up with that is a moron," she tells him. "I went with my brother and Sam when Anita gave birth. Don't get me wrong, the baby was cute but the birth of it wasn't. I'll be happy if I never see that again."

Cory laughs loudly this time. She's brutally honest; he'll give her that much. He considers her comment for a moment. She's the exact opposite of Evie, who tries to see something positive in everything, even within the apocalyptic society they all live.

"So, no babies in your near future?" he asks, grinning.

"I think between the two of us that you might be a father sooner than I'll be someone's mom," she says testily.

Cory laughs again and replies, "Nah, no baby daddy moments for me. But you might keep your options open."

"Options? What options?"

"Haven't you seen any action since you came here? There's plenty of fish in the sea, well, in our town," Cory pries. He can't help it. He wants to know if there was someone in town before Jason in that window of time when he was gone from the farm and when she arrived.

"Hardly," is all he gets from her.

"So, you're telling me that the last time you had sex was four years ago?"

"I'm not telling you anything. You don't need to know about my sex life," she remarks with fire.

He has to go about this more tactfully, "Come on. I'm taking a post-apocalyptic poll. You know, for future generations. People need to know these things. They're gonna want to know about our sex lives, not just how we survived off the grid."

She chuckles this time.

"Shut up," Paige says, but Cory can tell that a smile is touching her mouth.

"So, more recently than four years ago? Catch any action on the trip here?"

"Are you daft or something? Is that what you were doing while you were gone from this place? Hooking up, blazing a trail from here to... wherever you went? I was actually just trying to survive."

"Ok, so nothing out in the field. What about since you got here? Anyone in town? Anyone from a neighboring town?"

"Get real. No!" she blurts angrily.

Her temper sure does match her hair sometimes, most of the time, always. For some reason, her admission makes Cory grin like a fox.

"What are you reading?" he asks, changing the subject.

"I found this book on your shelf," she says before closing it and blowing out her candle.

"Shirts, bed, books, anything else I own that you want to use?" Cory asks and then has to erase the thoughts that come to mind when he considers what he just asked her and how she might take it. He definitely hadn't meant it as a crude suggestion, but after giving it some thought, Cory gets stuck dwelling on Paige using him for sex.

"It's about tank battles," she tells him, ignoring his question. "Do you like reading about stuff like that?"

"Yeah, I do. I think there's always a lot to learn from studying past battles," he explains, folding his arms behind his head.

"What did you want to do after school? College?"

"Nah, Kelly wanted me to go to college and so did my folks, but I was joining. They couldn't have stopped me."

"Joining what?" she asks.

"The Army, what else? I was following Kelly into the Army. I don't know if I wanted to go Special Forces like him, but I loved

207

tanks and choppers. I don't know. Maybe I would've went into the armored division."

He hasn't thought about this topic for a long time. There's no sense in dwelling on the past, on what could've or should've been.

"That's interesting," she notes.

"I liked drawing out schematics for new types of military vehicles. Engineering is where I probably would've ended up. I like putting shit together," he tells her. He's not sure why he's sharing so much with Paige. They don't usually talk this much or this personally or civilly.

"I could've designed new buildings, and you could've designed the tanks to blow them up," she reflects, a smile touching her voice.

"Except for assholes already beat us to it," Cory says, thinking of the war that started all of this.

"Yeah, assholes," she agrees.

Cory rolls onto his side where he can just make out the outline of her body across the room beneath her blanket.

"Remember when the farm was attacked while I was gone?" he asks.

"Of course I remember. It was scary as hell," she says dramatically.

"What do you remember exactly? Can you tell me anything about the men who did it or any details about the event?" he asks, trying to gain some sort of insight into that night.

"Not really," she starts. "It all happened so fast. Why do you want to know?"

"No reason," Cory lies smoothly. "Don't you recall anything?"

"I was taken captive and then hit over the head by one of them. It's kind of hard to remember things when you aren't conscious."

"What about the one that took you? Did he say anything that would tell you more about him? Did he have an accent?" he asks. He tries to focus on getting information from her and not allowing his mind to rest on the vision of her being clubbed over the head and man-handled.

"He didn't really have an accent. He was just super pissed off because he accused me of shooting some of his friends."

"Did you?"

"Yes, I did, and I don't care what you think of me," she says.

Cory chuckles softly and reminds her, "Hey, no judgement here. I'm not exactly in a position to judge over that."

"He whispered what he was going to do to me and the rest of the women on the farm. Then he'd shout at Doc inside the house to come out or he'd kill me. Then he'd go back to whispering and pawing at me. He was creepy. I'm glad Simon shot him."

Cory couldn't agree more. He's only sorry that it wasn't him doing the shooting instead of his friend.

"What about the others? What do you remember about them?"

"They came in trucks, like Doc's but a lot newer and nicer. I don't know where they got the gas for them, but they must've got it somewhere."

"Probably stolen. These types just take whatever they want from people," Cory explains softly. "Do you remember what any of them were wearing?"

"Wearing? No, why?"

He doesn't tell her that a football jersey or shirt with any sort of local or out of state advertising could alert him as to where they may have been from or from where they'd started out.

"No reason. Were there any women with them?"

"No, unless you count Vicky, the lady in town who was held captive by one of their friends," she says.

Cory is familiar with this woman. He already knew her story and that the men rescued her from the asshole creep in the woods. He knows she lived with the Reynolds family before moving to town recently.

"They reminded me of you actually," Paige says, causing his head to whip toward her.

"What's that supposed to mean?" he asks, slightly affronted.

"They just acted like a bunch of lawless Neanderthals."

"Lawless, huh?"

Paige rolls away, exposing her back to him. Cory can make out more of her figure in the dark beneath that light blanket. She yawns.

"Right. Lawless, like they had no respect for any laws. Like they were the types who didn't respect the law before everything fell apart. Like they weren't going to respect any new laws that a town would put forth now. Just a band of scumbags."

"So I'm a scumbag, lawless Neanderthal?"

Paige chuckles and says, "Hey, you said it, not me."

"I should come over there and show you what a lawless thug I can be," he warns with a grin.

"I'm sleeping with that knife you gave me, so bring it on, caveman," she warns on another yawn.

Cory laughs and lets it drop. It doesn't take long before she's asleep, her breathing even and deep, restful and peaceful. Cory, however, finds that sleep alludes him even though he's dead tired. He can't seem to get her words out of his mind. He feels like there is something in them that will reveal an important detail about the men who attacked the farm. Words that will help him find and ultimately kill them for what they did. The clues are there; he just has to piece it all together.

Chapter Fourteen
Sam

Paige hefts her duffle bag into the back of the Suburban while she and Simon each carry a crate full of food and supplies. Sam has never before stayed in the city on a raid. They've always stayed in the cabins in the woods. Simon takes her load from her.

"Got it, Sam," he tells her.

"Thanks," she says, allowing him to take her crate and backpack. She shoots him an uneasy smile. Today's the big day, the day the four of them, along with Kelly and John, go to Nashville. The nerves are kicking in. She always feels uneasy leaving the farm, even if it's just to go to the clinic. The farm has become her safe haven, her sanctuary against the darkness out there.

"No problem," her best friend says. "Why don't you go in and see if Cory needs help in the armory?"

"Sure," she agrees and jogs to the med shed. It only takes a second to find Cory. He's with his brother. With the two brothers in the small back room where the weapons are located, it feels cramped and crowded. "Hi, guys. Need help?"

They both turn with a smile on their faces. Kelly comes over to her and holds out a handgun.

"Here's the .38 you like, Miss Sam," he says and lays a gentle hand on her shoulder.

"Thanks, Kelly," she returns. "Is Hannah ok? She was pretty upset the other day about you going."

Kelly's dark eyes show his concern over his wife. He swallows hard and says, "Yeah, she'll be fine. Doc's gonna keep her busy while I'm gone. Hopefully, John and I will be back in just a few hours."

211

"Can I take anything else out?" she asks after she's holstered her revolver. She doesn't like the kick of the .45, so she's always tried to stick with the smaller caliber .38.

Cory steps toward her, handing over a heavy rifle.

"Sure, kid," he says. "Why don't you take Simon's rifle to him? The Professor's gonna need his sniper rifle to watch our asses at the oil well company. I've gotta get the beanpole's rifle."

Paige steps into the armory a second later, which leads Sam to believe that Cory had known she was there. Sam makes a hasty exit before they start at each other. She's pretty sure Kelly will call a halt to it, though since it's a mission day and everyone should be moving in sync and keeping their heads in the game as Derek always puts it.

When she gets back to the SUV, John is there with Simon, Grandpa and Reagan. Simon immediately takes the heavy rifle from her and nods.

"Remember, if the hospital is occupied, let it go," Doc tells them. "We don't want either of you to come to harm searching for anything. We're making strides everyday with compounding our own medicines."

"Right, we're doing ok on our own without any extra supplies. We'll keep compounding your hippy herbs. If that fails, we'll grow pot and give that out," Reagan quips.

Sam smiles but can tell that her mentor is genuinely afraid for them. Reagan has been out there, too. She knows the dangers. And she's probably worried about John most of all.

"Now, now, young lady," Grandpa warns.

Reagan adds, "Just be careful."

"Yes, ma'am," Simon answers politely.

"Don't take unnecessary risks, Simon," John says. "Especially not with Sam being with you instead of Cory."

"Yes, sir," Simon answers without pause.

A moment later, the others come out of the shed, each carrying rifles, shotguns and handguns. They are taking enough firepower with them to stay safe for a month if need be. Hannah and Sue come onto the back porch with their children. Everyone wants to send them off with well wishes. Derek has his head under the hood of the SUV doing last minute checks.

The sun is just rising when they pull away from the farm using the oil well road that will bring them out to the Johnson's path to the main road. Nashville isn't far away, but they will need to be extra cautious and go slow to ensure their safety. John is driving with Kelly sitting shotgun. Cory and Simon have the middle seats since they are both watching out their windows with their weapons drawn. The late autumn air hits Sam in the face as they pass through Pleasant View and out onto the freeway, which they don't normally take. Cory scouted it out the other day to make sure it seemed safe.

"Are you scared?" Paige asks beside her.

Sam looks at her, takes in the soft trembling of her long fingers and shakes her head to give the other woman some encouragement. "Nah, we'll be okay. Don't worry. Don't be scared. You'll be with Cory."

"Yeah, that's not gonna help me feel better," she says quietly and smiles at Sam. "I still wish I could just go with Simon."

"Don't worry about being with Cory. He's a completely different person when he's out there."

Paige doesn't answer but frowns while contemplating her comment.

"He'll keep you safe. Just listen to him," Sam suggests.

"That's easier said than done," she says with a smile.

The men are discussing the plans and going over potential dangers. John says something that makes the four of them laugh. It's not a surprise. He always helps to lessen the stress when they're going into a trouble spot.

"If we can't meet back up tonight, just take it easy on him. He'll be worried about Simon," Sam says.

"And you," Paige adds.

She smiles at her new friend.

"Cookies?" Kelly calls over his shoulder and passes a brown paper bag from the front seat.

Cory immediately grabs a few out of the bag, but Simon passes. He doesn't usually indulge in sweets. Sam doesn't know how he could possibly pass up Hannah's baking. Darling Hannah always sends them out with snacks, even when times have been hard and supplies limited. Sam's heart swells with love for her other adopted sister. She sends up a quick prayer to Grams to keep Hannie safe while they are gone.

213

Paige takes the bag, pulls one out and says, "Mm, what are these?"

Paige hands it to her and she opens the bag to find the round, over-sized cookies. "Yum, these are John's favorites. Cinnamon and honey cookies. They're more like a scone than a cookie, but it's the best we can do without sugar. Sure you don't want one, Simon?"

"No thanks, Sam," he says, intently staring out the window through his rifle scope.

"Now these are worth dyin' for," Cory says, earning laughter from the men in the front.

Kelly punches his fist to John's and extends it as far back as he can to Cory, who also bumps it.

"My Hannah can cook," Kelly says.

"Heck yeah she can," Cory agrees.

"Reagan has talents, too," John says.

Before he can add what he's thinking, Cory says, "What, like cursing and keeping your balls in her pocket?"

"Yeah, but she let me take 'em with me today," John says, always one to make fun of himself.

"Hey now," Simon warns. "We've got women in the car with us today, guys. Let's keep it clean."

The other three laugh at his distress. Simon is always the perfect gentleman. He rarely swears in front of the women or probably at all, and he doesn't approve of inappropriate discussions in front of them, either.

"Us women-folk can handle more than you think, bro," Paige informs him with sass.

"That's right," Cory says and glares over his shoulder at Paige. "Better be careful or Paige'll go into one of her man-hating rants. Then all our balls will be in trouble."

"Gonna shrivel up like little raisins," Kelly says.

"Hey," Simon warns again, this time with more ire in his voice.

After laughing again, they adhere to his wishes. Sam just grins at the back of his baseball hat covered head. She hates all the ball caps he wears. They cover his dark auburn hair. She should've put her sketch pad in her seat. Unfortunately, it's in the trunk.

John takes an off ramp to Route 41 instead of staying on the freeway the whole way, which can be dangerous coming into a big city. They will try to fly in under the radar to avoid being noticed by anyone. She only hopes that it works.

"Are you comfortable with your rifle?" Sam asks Paige about her AR-15, which Cory selected for her as being a good, lightweight rifle. It is one of the rifles that belonged to Grandpa, who had bought a few of them before the fall. He doesn't care for them as much as his historical military rifles, though. But Cory didn't want Paige carrying anything too heavy. Sam always carries an M16 and her sidearm. Simon will have his sniper rifle and a short barrel shotgun along with his sidearm.

"I think so. I know how to load it. That's the most important step, right?" she jokes.

"Yeah, that would be pretty important," Sam says with a smile.

John slows the SUV down to a crawl as they get closer to the city. When they come to the street he's looking for, John hooks a left-hand turn and pulls in behind the oil company building. Cory, John and Kelly jump out quickly and do a fast scan of the area, clearing it before any of them go any further. Simon stays in the vehicle with them keeping an eye out for dangers and covering the guys.

"All clear," Cory reports a moment later, letting Simon know it's safe to get out.

She and Paige climb out of the SUV and stay close to Simon and Cory. Kelly and John come back with a report a few minutes later.

"I think we've hit pay dirt," John says. "There are four trucks parked in front of this building. Only three of them have any gas in them. We'll be taking two."

Pointing in all directions, Kelly adds, "Watch our six, Professor, and find some high ground with Sam. Cory, you and Paige set up on the two corners of this street."

"Yes, sir," Cory and Simon say in unison.

"We're going to loot the inside first, see if we can find equipment we might need. Also, we need to take apart that compressor over there where they used to fuel up. We need that at the farm to compress the natural gas," John explains.

"Got it," Sam says.

"Stay close," Kelly warns. "Stay alert. Call it out if you see anything."

215

"Yes, sir," Simon repeats.

He tugs Sam's jacket and together they jog away. Sometimes when they are out like this with other people, she'll act as his spotter. This will be one of those times. He takes her across the street and down about a block and into a tall building. Simon sweeps his shotgun left and right, checking for potential problems. Then he gives her the hand signal to move forward. She stays tight to his back. The structure seems to have once been some sort of office building. They pass the reception area, cross the hall and Simon quietly pries open a door to a stairwell. He eases a flashlight from the cargo pocket on his left thigh and flicks it on. Stairwells always creep her out. They are dark, pitch dark and spooky. She always has a jittery feeling like something frightening is going to come running at them from above or from below, grabbing her ankles. It never fails to give her the willies. She also hates abandoned parks. It's strange, but Sam hates the public parks that she's seen since the fall. The weeds growing up around the play apparatuses always depress her. The graffiti, the unkempt nature of rusting slides, the squeaky hinges of the swings when the wind catches them, and flower beds that haven't been maintained just always come off as sinister. She wishes she would've never watched scary movies during sleepovers with her girlfriends. Although now real life has turned out to be worse than anything that came out of those Hollywood directors' brains.

She slides in behind him, closing the door with a soft click. Simon glances over his shoulder at her and nods. They ascend together, keeping close and going slow. Simon takes her up three flights before opening another door and leaving the stairwell behind. They come into a work area with cubicles and enclosed offices. It reminds her of her father's construction firm.

"Over here, Sam," he instructs.

They cross the room to a long row of windows. Simon is able to shove one open. Then he pushes hers up too because she can't manage to get it to budge. The windows haven't been opened for years and are stuck in place. They have the perfect view of the oil company and about four blocks in either direction. He pokes the barrel, equipped with a silencer, towards the window and immediately starts spying.

"Watch that way, Sam," he says, pointing to their right.

She does as he instructs, scanning the area. Apparently this district is fairly abandoned.

"Think Paige is nervous?" she asks quietly.

"I'm sure she is," he confesses. "But she'll be fine with Cory."

"I haven't been off the farm for a while. I've even missed a few clinic days lately," she hints. She's missed them because he ditched her at the farm before she could even get out of bed in time to get ready to go with them. He doesn't afford her an answer. Sam grins. He's so easy to read.

"Looks like they've just about got that system disabled," he says, changing the direction of their conversation.

He occasionally looks behind them to make sure that nobody is sneaking up on them. Sam inches closer to him and spies further down the street. It's a good thing the sun is high or they may be in a considerably darker building. She doesn't like the interior parts of the abandoned buildings that are so dark. Those are creepy, too.

"That's good," she whispers.

"We…we've got company," Simon suddenly says and then repeats it into his throat mic. "Someone coming in from the south. Maybe four blocks away."

Sam presses her earpiece closer and listens for John or Kelly to make the call. She sees the car Simon has spotted. She turns the knob on her spotting scope to bring it in more clearly.

"Single driver, no passengers," she reports into her own mic. The vehicle is an older model, turquoise mini-van. The driver is wearing a jacket that conceals their head. She doesn't see anyone else inside but continues to watch it closely. She also quickly scans around the area and down the road to make sure this van is alone.

"Cory, move in," John's voice dictates over their headsets. "We've got ya' covered."

She pans right and watches Cory move closer. John and Kelly have scattered behind vehicles and are hunched down for cover.

"Woman driver," Sam reports. "She's alone."

"Don't think it's a threat," Kelly confirms. "Take it slow just in case."

"Try not to have sex with her," Paige says into her mic.

Sam almost blurts out a loud laugh. Simon doesn't even chuckle. He obviously finds his sister's humor offensive. He probably

217

doesn't think she should be talking like that over the mic. Sam thinks it's funny.

"Got it," Cory returns with good humor. "No sex with the natives."

Sam watches as he approaches the vehicle, jogging down the middle of the road.

"Wait a minute," Cory says. "I think she might be hot. All bets are off."

John's chuckle comes over the ear piece. "Hey, get your game faces on," he reprimands.

"Wait," Sam says. "I think there's a baby's car seat in the front seat next to her."

"Sam's right," Simon confirms.

They watch in tense silence as Cory closes in on the driver's side door as the vehicle rolls to a complete stop. He has his hand on his mic to allow them privilege to the conversation.

"Ma'am," he says.

The woman doesn't answer, so Sam is left to assume that she either nods or is afraid of Cory.

"Where are you headed? That area straight ahead isn't real safe," Cory tells her.

They already know this because of their last trip to this city. About another mile down the road and she's going to be driving into a battle zone. They know from experience. The groups that have formed down in that district are all out for themselves and violent.

"I just need food for my baby," the woman finally repeats.

"Yeah?" he asks.

Sam watches as John closes in on the unsuspecting woman. Cory just keeps making small talk with her, but his eyes are scanning the vehicle and back seat.

"You need food, huh?" Cory says. "I can probably help with that. What do you need? I have a few provisions I could give you."

Sam hopes her child is old enough to take solids if she needs food for it. They don't have baby formula or even goat milk with them. Sam can't make out the child. The woman has the baby seat covered with a blanket, probably to ward off a chill.

Suddenly the woman says, "He's cool. All clear here."

"What did you just say?" Cory asks in a very guarded tone. "What the fuck? Is that a mic on you? Get outta the van!"

He backs up a step and points his weapon at the woman in the car, who has pulled down her neck scarf to reveal a throat mic similar to their own.

"Hey, hey, hey, don't shoot me, dude," the woman says. "I'm one of you guys, ok? We're on the same team. I see your buddy sneaking up behind the car. I'm Navy. I'm with men who are military, too."

She explains this in great haste so as not to be shot by Cory. She even places her hands in the air.

"Don't shoot me. My friends'll get pissed if you do," she says lightly.

"Get out," Cory orders as John makes his way to the passenger side and opens the door.

He takes the baby doll out and tosses it to the ground. Now that Sam can spy on the woman more clearly since she's standing in the road next to Cory with her hands still in the air, she can see her combat boots and olive drab camo pants. She has a handgun strapped to her thigh in the same manner that Reagan wears hers.

"I'm with the 4th Armored Division. What was left of my Navy team joined up with them," the woman explains. "We're a hodge-podge crew put together by our leader."

"And who's that?" John asks brusquely.

Sam can't make out what they are saying as clearly as before. A rumble of vehicles in the distance does reach her ears, though.

"That's my squad coming," the woman's muffled voice comes through.

"Who's your C.O.?" John asks.

"Sergeant Winters, but we call him Dave the Mechanic. What division were you with?"

She's obviously picked up on John being former military. They seem to be bloodhounds, these military people. They can literally sniff each other out in a crowd.

She doesn't hear John's response because Kelly's voice interrupts, "Simon and Sam, come in closer. Paige, stay on point."

"Yes, sir," Simon says into his mic.

They move out fast, leaving the windows open and abandoning their position. Simon takes her back the same way, but they exit to the south and come out behind the group on the street. Now they have a new position where they also can't be seen but can view the back of the woman's vehicle and whoever might be coming down the street.

A large Army truck rolls into view, not bothering to attempt silence or stealth. Kelly comes out from behind the gas company truck. John starts laughing, and they call everyone in including her and Simon. They walk cautiously closer, and Simon puts himself between her and the other men, who start hopping down from the truck.

It's like a family reunion all of a sudden. John and Kelly are bumping fists with some of the other men and laughing.

"Dave the Mechanic!" Kelly shouts at a man who has jumped out of the driver's seat. "How the hell are you, man?"

"Not bad, brother, not bad," the other man declares.

Sam inches closer to Simon, who seems fine to have her there. He holds his sniper rifle at hip height. All totaled there are seven men with this woman. Sam doesn't feel as safe and comfortable as she had a moment ago from inside the building. She notices that Cory steps close to Paige on the other side of the woman's car. The woman in the car has moved nearer to and is eyeing Cory with interest. Good grief. Everywhere he goes, women do this.

"What the hell, man? What's going on?" Kelly asks the other man.

"Just surviving, D-boy," Dave answers. "That's all us D-boys can do anymore."

"Yeah, I hear ya,'" John concurs and shakes Dave's hand. "What was with the decoy?"

Sam assumes he means that the woman in the car with the fake baby was their decoy. She also has no idea what a D-boy is. It must be one of the many military terms they use that she doesn't understand.

"It's how we root out the fuck-heads. We do it when we're moving through a city. If they try to haul her out of the car, we know we've got genuine assholes on our hands. I wasn't too sure when the big guy came up to her car."

"That's my little brother," Kelly tells him, which gets a laugh from Dave.

"Figures, Hulk," Dave says, using Kelly's nickname.

"Where you been?" Kelly asks.

"We were deployed out of fuckin' Fort Benning when we got back to the states. But that got fucked up quick. Some of us left after a couple months of that shit. Some of us wanted to find our families. Some of us wanted the fuck outta there. We weren't sure if it was gonna stand," Dave explains as his men stand back and nod. "Shit was gettin' real."

John laughs and nods.

"I got to my old lady in Philly and took her and our kid the fuck out of that rat maze, too. We kind of just went around picking up everyone's families. Then we settled in at Wright Patt with some fly boys I used to know. That ending up being the big suck, though. Fuckin' civilians were gettin' fugazi on us. We didn't wanna' end up killing a bunch of them, but what the fuck? Then we ended up goin' black on water. Don't know what the hell happened to all the water there. Had to get the fuck outta there right quick, too. Where ya' been, brothers?"

Sam finds his swearing funny, but Simon frowns. She's not sure if he's frowning over the sudden influx of strange men or the other man's love of colorful language. Simon is a lot like Grandpa in that regard. She suspects they both swear when they are around other men, but neither do so in front of the women. He's just old school.

"They sent us out West," John explains. "That fell apart fast, too. Then we came back through Arkansas to pick up Kelly's little brother and sister and then here to get Derek home to his wife and kids."

"Hey, how is your brother, man?" Dave asks.

Apparently these men have a past or were in the same unit or served together. Sam's not sure, but he is funny. Dave the Mechanic has a long, reddish brown ponytail, a matching beard, eyeglasses and a cigarette hanging out of his mouth that bobs around when he talks. There is a pair of aviator style sunglasses perched on top of his head, and he's still wearing mostly military issue clothing. He's a lean, sinewy man about the same height as Simon with intelligent blue eyes. His hands are covered in dirt or what looks like could be grease. Cory's hands look like that a lot from working on the tractors or trucks around the farm.

"He's doing good, man," John answers. "Has a bunch of kids, the wife, the whole thing."

"Yeah?" Dave asks rhetorically. "What about you, Dr. Death?"

221

"Yep, married, kid, the whole nine yards, too," John says and gets punched in the shoulder by Dave. "Kelly, too."

"What the fuck?" Dave nearly shouts with laughter. "What'd you find the last blind woman left after the apocalypse, Hulk?"

Silence ensues. A pin could be heard dropping. Kelly and John don't laugh at all. John looks at his feet with an uncomfortable frown.

"Actually, I did, dickhead," Kelly says dryly and then cracks a smile.

"Seriously? Fuck! Sorry, man," Dave apologizes quickly. "Makes sense, though. You gotta admit. It wasn't like you were ever gonna get one that could see your ugly mug."

Everyone starts laughing again, but Sam doesn't. He's her older, adopted big brother, and Kelly is hardly ugly. He's such a dashing, handsome man. Sam allows her eyes to scan the crowd of men. A few of them are looking at her, looking at her with interest. They aren't looking at her in a sinister manner, but it still makes her uncomfortable. Simon has relaxed slightly and slung his rifle over his shoulder. He takes her hand into his own in a protective way. Perhaps he is showing that Sam is his territory. She's not sure, but Sam does appreciate it. She doesn't like strange men, even ones who are ex-military and probably have good hearts. She presses against his side. He pulls her even closer. These men may be friends of John and Kelly, but that doesn't mean they are completely trustworthy, not in her eyes. Simon apparently feels the same.

"So, where are you holed up now, man?" Dave asks of John.

"Got a small farm, not far from here. It's safe, protected," her adopted big brother answers. John must trust this man implicitly if he's talking about the farm.

"Cool, bro. We're hunkered down up above Hendersonville. Got the same kind o' setup. Gunny's folks had a place there. It was too late when we got there. Somebody killed his parents, but we're set up on his farm. It's good, different."

They talk for a short while in the middle of the street, completely oblivious to danger or threats. Of course, two of the men are standing in the bed of the big truck with huge machine guns.

"There's about thirty of us up there now," Dave tells them.

"We run a medical clinic over in Pleasant View if you ever need help with that sort of thing. My wife and her grandfather are the doctors," John tells his long lost friend.

"Yeah? Married a doctor, huh? She ever figure out what the fuck's wrong with you?" Dave jokes.

Sam even smiles at this one.

"Not even close," John says. "But if you ever need help, come over. We're securing the town so it's getting safer."

"I'll keep that in mind. Never know when one of the kids in our group's gonna get sick. But at least I don't have to worry about my kids being safe; we're locked down tight over at our place. Got three of those little fuckers now. Keep me up at night with that responsibility shit, that's for sure," Dave swears, earning more laughter.

"Yeah, we hear ya,'" Kelly confirms.

"Does your wife do sterilizations? Think I need gelded. Don't need any more of those little shits to worry about," Dave asks with an ornery grin.

John laughs loudly. Kelly shakes his head and slaps Dave on the shoulder.

"That ain't right, man," Kelly says, still chuckling. "So you guys are doing all right then?"

"We've got supplies that we trade for shit when we need it," Dave offers with a friendly nod.

"Yeah? Like what?" Kelly asks.

"Ammo, drugs- not the fun kind- toilet paper," Dave says with a wink.

They all laugh again. Sam can understand why they like him so well. He has an easy, infectious way about him.

"Toilet paper?" Kelly asks. "What the hell, man? You're a bonafide pirate."

"Yeah, well, it's a good gig I guess. Better than tracking down terrorists in the Middle East sweatin' my balls off," one of the other men says.

"No shit," Kelly agrees.

"Where the heck did you guys get everything?" John asks.

"We found a tanker truck full o' gas up on the freeway 'bout ten clicks from here," Dave tells them. "Been usin' that for about a year now. We trade some off now and then for shit we need."

"Good, that's smart," John says.

223

"Found a semi full of shit laying on its side over in Virginia in this massive cluster-fuck pile-up of cars. We loaded all that shit into a deuce and a half and brought it back here," Dave explains. "It was full of meds and toilet paper, just about anything a pharmacy would have. Glad we checked it out. Lucky find."

"Yeah," John agrees, "no kidding. I don't think we've ever thought of that. We've raided about every town in this part of the state. We've been lucky, too."

"Good. We should set up trade with your town. We might have some shit you need and vicy-versy," Dave jokes and stamps out his cigarette on the pavement.

"That's a real good idea," Kelly agrees.

John adds, "We trade medical care with people sometimes if they have anything they can give. We don't enforce it. My wife's grandpa wouldn't go for that. He's too generous to enforce it. But people are pretty good about offering something."

"That's cool. Yeah, I figured you guys were still out there somewhere. Shit, what's it been since we last saw each other? Four years, five?"

"Right," Kelly says. "It was when we were last in Bragg."

"I think you're right, man. Time flies when the shit hits the fan," Dave jokes.

"Have you had trouble with people, groups?" John asks.

"Not too much anymore," Dave says. "We were gonna go after these dickheads over in Coopertown holed up in a fucking Target store of all places. One of those fuckers killed one of our guards about six months ago or so when he was watching the farm at night. Someone beat us to it, though."

John and Kelly raise their right hands with smirks.

"Guilty," John says with a full smile.

Dave laughs and slaps John on the back, "Ha! Looked like your handiwork, guys. Torched it, too, I saw."

"Yep, scores were settled," Kelly says.

"You guys went full-on fucking scorched earth on those pricks. Fuck them, man," Dave adds. "They were real shitbag turds if you ask me."

"There's still a few stragglers out there somewhere, so watch your asses," Kelly advises.

"Got it. Good to know. Haven't had any target practice in a while. Well, not the moving kind. Right, Gunny?" Dave says with a wicked grin, shouting to one of the men on the back of the truck.

The man doesn't say anything but salutes casually and gives a curt nod. He looks over at Sam and winks. She can barely manage a friendly half grin. He seems nice, but she clenches Simon's hand more firmly.

John explains why they've come to the city. He tells them about the CNG idea for the gas trucks and why the 'kids' have come with them. Dave laughs and says that Cory and Simon don't look much like kids. Then he calls them badass looking mother-hummers. Cory laughs, but Simon does not. They agree to meet again soon. Then Dave's crew leaves as noisily as they came in.

Kelly and John talk a few minutes more, reminiscing some of the fun times they've had with Dave the Mechanic. Then they all get back to work. She and Simon return to their position in the building but this time on the roof. Cory and Paige return to their street corners. The men work for nearly an hour to get two of the trucks running and the compressor system that is attached to the wall unhooked and placed in the bed of one of the trucks. They call them in again.

"Simon and Sam will take the Suburban from here," John dictates.

Simon utters a single, "Yes, sir."

"We're heading back. You kids are on your own," Kelly says. "Cory, you and Paige get your gear out of the Suburban before Simon leaves."

"Yes, sir," Cory answers. "We're on it."

A moment later they are all standing in a circle. Sam walks over to John and hugs him and then Kelly.

"Be careful, kid," Kelly tells her. "Keep an eye on the Professor for us."

"Yes, sir," Sam says and gives him a silly salute. He ruffles her hair, probably messing up her braid.

"Call if you need us," John instructs, referring to the satellite radios.

"Got it," Simon says.

"Everyone clear?" Kelly asks one last time.

"Yes, sir," Cory says in a serious tone.

225

Kelly walks over, lays a hand on his brother's shoulder and turns to leave. They don't communicate their emotions very well, or openly, or much at all. Most of the men in the family are the same. Sam, on the other hand, hugs Paige goodbye. She doesn't like to leave the people in her life without at least a hug. Tomorrow is never guaranteed. She's learned to tell her friends and loved ones farewell.

She and Simon get in the SUV. Kelly comes over to the window.

"Call if you need help. Cory's gonna be closer. Call him first. Then call us," Kelly instructs.

Simon bumps his fist to Kelly's and says, "Yes, sir."

Cory comes over next and says, "We'll meet at eight o'clock, ok?"

These plans have been gone over many times, but she knows they just want to be one hundred percent clear on them.

"See ya', kid," Cory says to her.

"Bye, Cory," Sam says. "Keep Paige safe for us."

"You got it," he says.

"We'll meet you at eight and have a nice dinner in the city together," she jokes as Simon starts the vehicle. Cory laughs.

"That's a plan, kid," he says and taps twice on the roof before stepping back.

Simon pulls away, his mind clearly occupied with the mission and not their lighthearted jesting. He's always the most serious one in their group. They will be skirting the city and heading northwest. There is a hospital and two smaller medical facilities in that area which they need to raid.

Sam stares into her rearview mirror. A cool rush of air hits her from the open window. It causes a shiver to course through her. Another one ripples down her spine as she watches her family disappear from her line of sight. She pulls the collar of her jacket closer as a feeling of impending disaster comes over her.

"Don't worry, Sam," Simon says beside her as he steers the vehicle around debris in the road.

Sam attempts to say something positive in return, but the words get stuck in her throat and all she can manage is a grim nod.

Chapter Fifteen
Paige

Once John and Kelly pull away in the gas company pick-up trucks, Paige experiences a moment of panic. She stares longingly down the street until she can no longer see their white trucks. Cory tugs her arm.

"Come on," he says. "Let's move."

She swallows hard and nods.

"It'll be ok," he assures her with confidence.

They walk down the streets together, using side roads and alleyways when they can. Suddenly, Cory grabs her arm and hauls her into the doorway of a six-story apartment building. A moment later, a man on a motorcycle speeds by.

"Did he see us?" Paige asks nervously.

"No way," he answers. "We're cool."

"Where are we going?" she asks before peeking around the corner.

"Shopping," Cory says with a grin over his shoulder at her.

He opens the door to the apartment complex, looks around before entering and ushers her inside. The building has seen better days, or in this case, years. Water lines must've burst at some point because the first floor carpeting is covered in black mold, the walls, too. He doesn't stop or turn to leave, though. Cory continues forward until he's reached the other end of the long hallway where he turns left. He keeps his rifle in front of him as he checks corners and dark areas. People have fled this building quickly because some of their dropped belongings are scattered here and there in the hallway, and many of the doors to the individual apartments are standing open. They come to an exit door where the sign overhead no longer glows. He presses on the door, but it must be locked.

"Now what?" Paige asks quietly.

"This way," he says and leaves the hall, forcing Paige to trail after him.

The first apartment door he comes to is locked. The second is unlocked, so Cory lets himself in. This makes Paige edgy. People could still be squatting somewhere in this building. He gives her the signal to stay put as he makes a fast search of the small apartment. He returns a few seconds later and motions her inside. The owner is no longer occupying the space, and neither is anyone else. Dust clings to every surface. It's as if someone has painted a still life of what the world would look like if people just suddenly disappeared from earth.

"Why are we in here?" she asks.

"Taking a different way out. Don't know who the guy on the bike was, but I don't wanna' run into him again."

He crosses the main living area to a window and pushes it up. Then he ushers her out it. Paige drops to the ground, which isn't more than five or so feet. Cory follows. He doesn't seem to mind that he makes more noise. They end up on a street filled with former restaurants and hotels.

"Stay close," he says softly.

His brown eyes are more serious than normal. A permanent line mars between his thick black brows. Paige's mouth opens to answer, but she just nods instead. His eyes fall on her mouth a moment before he turns around again. He signals over his shoulder to her to move out.

They jog slowly down the street, staying near the brick façades of apartment buildings and offices. Then they cross in the middle of the four-lane road where they come to a rather large shopping plaza. A video game store is nestled in the corner next to a sporting goods franchise and quite a few other businesses. Paige grins as she recalls what a gamer her brother used to be and how he and his few friends would stay up all night on the weekend to finish some level of whatever the latest video game was that just released.

Cory points with two fingers toward the center of the plaza where the two-story sporting goods store stands. Paige gives him another nod in accord. They travel in the direction of the store, but he doesn't immediately go inside once they get there. He squats low with her beside huge planter boxes between the video game and the sporting goods stores. She looks up at him. His keen eyes are scanning the area meticulously, searching out dangers. Paige is pretty sure that he's the most dangerous thing on this empty street.

"Let's go," he says, rising suddenly and jogging to the front of the store.

Paige follows, and they enter the front doors of Dick's Sporting Goods. Cory darts to their right and squats behind shelving units with very few camping supplies left. He half rises and moves slowly toward the far wall of the building, passing many empty shelves and display racks that used to house fishing gear. Paige follows again and mimics him, pressing her back against the wall and listening.

"Think we're alone," he says softly.

"Are we looking for guns or bullets or something like that?" she asks.

"No, that's likely all gone," he answers.

"Then what?"

He shakes his head, ignores her, and continues on again. Paige frowns with confusion. Why else would they come to a sporting goods store if not for weapons?

Cory leads her to the back of the store where it is much darker with the absence of windows.

"Find what you need. I'll be your lookout," he tells her.

He's brought her to the shoe department. Paige shoots him a surprised look.

"For me?" she asks. "Look for shoes for me?"

"Hurry up, beanpole," he answers testily and roams the empty area on guard. "We don't have all day."

She tries to conceal her smile but knows that she fails to do so. She literally runs to the women's section and starts scanning for a pair of gym shoes. Anything would be better at this point than her worn-out, distressed black ankle boots. There are hiking boots and a few men's loafers left but nothing in her size. Damn.

Cory appears next to her and says, "Let's try the stockroom."

He leads her to the swinging doors where he cautiously pushes one inward. They don't enter, but he does stand in the entryway a few moments listening.

"Let's go," he says impatiently and breaches the big stockroom with her.

229

Other people have thought to do the same because not many pairs of shoes are left, especially in the men's section. Paige crosses to the next aisle where women's shoes were stored. There are probably close to a hundred or so boxes left on the shelves. Apparently women have not thought to hit a store like this for supplies. She was with her friends on their own for a long time and never thought to do so. Cory holds a flashlight and her rifle while she digs through and checks sizes. Bingo! She finds a pair of hiking boots in a sturdy brown leather and a pair of New Balance running shoes.

"Put the gym shoes on," he orders quietly, looking over his shoulder.

"Ok," she answers, not needing any further encouragement on that subject.

Paige tugs off her black boots, leaving them on the floor and pulls the new shoes out of the box. She sits on the cement floor, running the laces through the holes as quickly as she can. Then she pulls them on, stands and sighs with relief that they fit and actually feel like they have some padding. She hasn't had new shoes for so long that they almost feel funny on her feet. Her black boots were on their last leg.

"Better?" he asks with raised eyebrows.

Paige groans with satisfaction and nods. "Yes, thank the good Lord. These are great."

"See any more that would fit you or the other women at the farm?"

"These are my size, too," she says, showing him the hiking boots.

"Good," he returns. "Put 'em in your pack."

"There are some more here that would probably fit the other women or kids," she says, waving her hand toward the other boxes. "There are enough for some of our neighbors and maybe some of the women in town."

"All right," he says. "We'll stop here on the way out of town in the Suburban and hit it. That's too much for us to carry."

"Oh, all right," Paige says, stuffing the hiking boots into her backpack. There's no way she's leaving these in the store in case someone else raids the stockroom before they come back.

"Ready?" he asks, shining his small flashlight around.

"Yes," she answers and takes her gun from him again.

Cory turns away from her to go, but Paige grabs the sleeve of his black jacket. "Cory, thanks."

He doesn't turn all the way back to her but gives a nod just the same.

"I just didn't want you slowing me down or whining 'cuz your bigass feet hurt," he remarks snidely.

Paige knows he's just trying to play tough. She smiles to herself and follows him from the room.

"Don't worry," she says with a grin. "I won't tell anyone and blow your cover as a big meanie."

Cory just snorts and keeps going. They raid the rest of the store, searching out anything that could be of use. She finds a thermal shirt and a pair of black cargo pants for herself in the correct length for a change. This could be useful later tonight when they are finished and hunkered down. She only has a pair of jeans and a t-shirt in her backpack. These are warmer clothes. She's not even sure where they are staying and whether or not there will be heat. She also grabs a brown stocking cap off the floor that has an embroidered label for "RealTree" on the front- whatever that means- and a pair of warm socks.

"We'll take whatever clothes are left, too," he says.

Paige nods and wanders farther away, Cory following in her wake. She finds a display case of lip balm also on the floor and grabs the last three tubes. He gives her a strange look.

"My lips are chapped. I thought Sam or the other girls might want one, too," she explains and gets a frown in answer from the Neanderthal.

She's surprised that he's actually wearing a jacket today. It's a black, lightweight cotton one with lots of pockets. Typically he runs around the farm in just a t-shirt or no shirt at all. He sleeps in practically nothing. Sharing the small cabin with him is sometimes torturous. She wishes he'd wear more clothing to bed. Most of the time she tries to avert her eyes, but sometimes it is more difficult than others. His dark tanned skin is oftentimes covered in a fine sheen of perspiration. And lately when he's gotten out of bed to either go on watch duty or wherever the heck he goes, Paige has lain awake thinking about him. It's very frustrating. She has no desire to be in his company, and yet, she finds herself thinking about him more often than not. She wonders what his opinion on different subjects might be and how he feels about different things.

231

Apparently she's lonelier now than ever since Jason turned out to be such a jerk.

Cory grabs a small stash of matches, a handful of fishing lures, and a rifle scope he finds on the floor behind the glass display case in the gun department that he says is a pretty good one. On the second floor, they find more clothing, a tent and a few sleeping bags that he says they can take when they return with the Suburban.

As they come around to the gift shop area of the store, she finds a leather-bound sketch pad with engraved deer on the front cover and complete with a box of artist's pencils. Sam would appreciate this. Cory places it in his pack. They leave through the side delivery exit. The place next to it has been burned almost to the ground. It looks like it used to be some sort of restaurant. He says that it looks like a gas line fire probably started in the kitchen.

Cory leads her to the back where they come to a door of a chain store pharmacy. He pushes but can't get the door to swing inward. Then he takes her upper arm and physically moves her to the side. She gives him a look of confusion. Her confusion doesn't last long though. Cory kicks violently a few times until the door finally crashes in. If she was alone, she would've never done that. He just caused a ruckus of epic decibels. Paige cringes but follows him inside.

They are in a storage room, and it is eerily dark and quiet. He sweeps his rifle left and right as they go. Paige stays close for fear of a person coming at her from the other side of the aisles of storage racks. Or a zombie. She's also fearful that one of those may lurk in this frightening, dingy space.

A section of shelving has been pushed over and rests against another. Cory bends to retrieve an item. He hands the box to her and raises his eyebrows. It is a small box of blonde hair coloring. She punches his arm and tosses the box back to the floor. He just chuckles. Paige even grins. What a smartass.

She stoops to pick up a pair of scissors. Then she snatches up his short ponytail and pretends she's going to lob it off. He laughs aloud this time. Paige tosses the rusted scissors down. Something catches her eye and she squats and then kneels. She sets her rifle on the floor and then her pack.

"What'd you find? More make-up or perfume or something important like that?" he teases.

Paige ignores him and slides forward on her stomach under the heavy shelving unit. She grabs the surplus box containing smaller packages of the product and shimmies back out like a centipede.

"What is it?" he inquires, closing in on her.

She pulls the box closer and uses the dagger Cory gave her to slice the tape. Paige holds up a small package from inside.

"Maxi pads, seriously?" he asks. "That's the big find that you had to honey-badger out of that hole?"

"Tampons, too," she says and pulls out another smaller box.

"Great, now can we go? I might have to scout out some Viagara or something equally important."

"The women on the farm will be thrilled with this," she says as she takes the products out of their packages and stuffs them all into her backpack. It's no easy feat sticking six boxes of the goods in there, but she's not leaving without them. "And I kinda' figured you didn't need Viagara to hear you brag."

He chuffs with manly offense and declares, "Oh, I don't. Trust me. But you'll never know, will you?"

Paige ignores him and zips her backpack closed. She doesn't care if she finds another item in the city, she's sick of dealing with her female issues without modern convenience, even if these won't last long. Her body fat dropped so low while on the road that she stopped having a period at all. But since she's eating healthy and has gained back a little weight, she's back to menstruating, which started again last month. She stands and takes her rifle from him, looking directly up into his brown eyes.

"All I'd have to do is ask all the neighbors' daughters, caveman," she tells him. "And probably half the townswomen."

"I'm a celibate man, beanpole," he murmurs as they draw near the store's swinging doors that lead to the main shopping floor.

"Yeah, right," Paige snorts.

"I am," he says and turns directly to her. "Evie and I broke it off."

"Really?" Paige asks more seriously. She genuinely feels bad for him if he liked Evie. It's hard enough to find someone nowadays. "I'm sorry. Why?"

"It wasn't that kind of a relationship," he says.

"What do you mean?"

"You know, romance, flowers, poetry, that kind of shit," he explains.

233

"So what was it?"

He just raises his thick brows with implication that Paige immediately understands. "Oh," she mumbles and looks at the floor, at her new shoes that he'd purposely taken time to help her find.

When Paige glances back up, Cory is still looking at her, but this time there is something behind his regard for her. Her breath hitches in her chest. His eyes fall there. Then he picks up her wrist. The feel of her whole hand in his few fingers does something to increase her breathing.

"What are these?" he asks of her leather cords tied there. "Why do you always wear these? Are they from him?

"Him?"

Cory's eyes jump to hers with a scowl, "Your boyfriend from college."

"No," she says and vehemently shakes her head. "No, not from him. I told you. It was over with him before the crap hit the fan. Very over."

"Then who gave you these?" Cory asks in a demanding manner as if he's jealous.

Paige looks down at the thin strings on her wrist and shrugs, "It's not like that. They're just mine. I learned a long time ago that a strip of leather can be helpful. It's more of a habit really. Sometimes I've needed a string or a piece of leather like these. They're good for a lot of things. You know, like patching a shoestring or tying something together. It's hard to throw simple things like this away."

When she looks up at Cory again, he's staring so intently at her, so directly at her face that she shakes her head and blushes.

"It's like they are a security blanket. I just feel safer, like I can foolishly control my environment and my future or something. I can't describe it to you. You wouldn't understand," she says and twirls one of the strips on her wrist nervously.

She looks up again, afraid that he'll laugh at her. But he doesn't. As a matter of fact, he has a deep scowl on his face and his mouth is set in an angry line.

Cory nods once and says, "Let's keep moving."

"Yeah," Paige agrees and follows him through the doors. She's not sure why he seems angry.

They don't find much in the pharmacy area worth salvaging, but Cory does come upon a trampled *Popular Science* magazine on the floor for Simon. Paige smiles at this. So far today, he's only scouted out things for other people. He's not actually being a total pig today. She's pleasantly surprised by his behavior. Then he points to a box of condoms and winks. She was pleasantly surprised. He opens the box and stuffs a handful into his pack.

"Celibate my ass," she remarks.

"Hey, ya' never know," he says with a wink of devilment.

Toward the front of the store, he finds a lighter, a few packs of bubblegum that he says he'll take back to the farm for the kids and an instamatic camera. Paige finds a book by one of her former favorite authors on the newsstand and stuffs it into the front pocket of her backpack. It's not like they can roll into the Barnes and Noble for the latest bestsellers. The newspaper next to the bookshelf reads March 4, 2031. Time has literally stood still in America. The story is still coverage of North Korea using nuclear weapons. Paige frowns with a touch melancholy. She takes the newspaper. She's not sure why, but it seems important. It's the last bit of written history. Maybe her grandchildren will look at it one day and wonder what it was like living in such a broken country. Or maybe she'll give it to Simon's grandchildren. That sounds better.

Cory takes two boxes of taper candles and a pillar candle and stashes those. They move down the medicine aisle next. There is literally nothing left there except for some boxes of eye drops and a few packages of cough drops. He shakes his head and indicates they should leave.

This time, they use the front door and walk down the street away from the shopping plaza. Not much is in this area; just residences, apartment buildings, an old pizza shop complete with a checkerboard awning, and a few gas stations. He squats behind a tall hedgerow with her.

"Take a break," he orders.

Paige doesn't need encouragement. She kneels beside him, balancing on one knee. He takes out a map and points to a red mark.

"The area up ahead was deemed as a no-go zone the last time we came. It was a little dangerous, a little too occupied. We'll avoid it, come out around here," he says, pointing northwest. "The college is over there. We can raid there and rendezvous with Simon and Sam later."

"Ok, whatever you say," she says.

235

"There's a lot between here and there, probably about three miles of ground to cover. We can hit some places on the way, too," he says, folding the map neatly and placing it in his back pocket again. "You holding up ok?"

"Yes, I'm fine," she affirms.

"Let me know if you get tired," he offers and helps her stand. "We can stop and rest whenever you need to."

"Got it," she says and steps away from him, although he keeps his hand at her elbow. He nods, and they move out again.

"I'd like to find a place to steal gas," he tells her. "Keep an eye out. If the gas station looks raided like the pumps are on the ground, that kind of thing, we'll pass. But if you see anything else, call it out."

"What about a gas distribution facility? Like the kind of place that supplied it to gas stations?"

"Maybe," he says. "Those were mostly used up at the beginning by the government and military. I've got some other ideas, though."

"Like what?" she inquires as they move through an area with expensive old homes.

"There are a couple micro-breweries in the area. I want to see if they have stills in the back of their restaurants."

"For what, beer?" she asks as they take a shortcut down an alley surrounded by tall trees and high fences to support the relationship of good neighbors.

"Sort of," he says. "We've got the CNG system and trucks now, but we didn't know that we'd find them. And it may not be the perfect solution, either. I've been working with Derek. We think we might be able to make moonshine and run Doc's old pick-up truck on it. We've definitely got the grain and the land to grow more if we need to."

"Really?" she asks, remembering that tragic night she'd imbibed his jar of the liquid fire. "That wouldn't be a surprise. That crap was like drinking battery acid."

"Exactly," he agrees on a grin. "It'd be better running our truck than your skinny body."

Paige frowns at him and looks down at herself. When he says things like that, it makes her feel self-conscious. She's going to have low self-esteem if she keeps hanging around him.

"I'm just giving you a hard time," he clarifies and bumps his shoulder against hers.

"I know I'm skinny. It's just the way I'm built. I can't help it. And no amount of Hannah trying to make me eat more is going to change it."

"You're fine. I'm just messin' with ya,'" he says.

Paige looks up at him and scowls. "Not everyone has the same body. I've always been tall for a girl. So I don't have big fake boobs and blonde hair like your girlfriend, Evie Johnson."

"Her boobs are *not* fake, let me assure you," he says with a bright smile.

For everything he's been through, he has a nice white smile and straight teeth.

"Spare me the details," Paige says, rolling her eyes. She hardly needs to hear about his sexual escapades. They don't have all day.

"You aren't fake, either. That's good. No dude wants to bump uglies with the bionic woman," he jests. "Besides, you've got a nice ass. And that goes a long way."

Paige's wide eyes dart to his, her mouth hanging open. Her cheeks instantly burn with embarrassment as he calls another halt at a corner.

"Hey, it's just a fact. I'm not hitting on you or anything," he admits with crude honesty and a nonchalant shrug as he peers intently down a long street full of homes.

She stares forward and doesn't bring up anything else that would lead to his physical assessment of her. They walk for a short while, nearly a mile in silence. This is the top end of the area Cory said can be dangerous, and he asks her to be as quiet as possible. She doesn't allow him to get too far ahead of her, but he does walk quite a bit faster. Right before they clear a group of buildings, Cory's left fist shoots up to shoulder height signaling a halt. He motions for her to come forward. His hand comes up toward her face, his index finger pointing toward an open field, a park of some kind.

Paige sees what has drawn his attention. There are tents set up there as if a group of traveling nomads is moving through the area. They even have livestock fenced off in a small corral. Cory tilts his head to their left as if to indicate they should leave by that way. She nods in return. They jog more quickly this time away from the group in the park. They could be harmless, but there's no sense in taking a chance. They don't live in a society anymore where strangers

237

meet and greet in a public park and exchange phone numbers for their kids to have play dates. Now the meet and greet is more like lead slinging and terror.

They move at a faster pace until she tugs his sleeve for a rest break. He doesn't argue or ridicule her. He just stops and leads her into the lobby of a fancy hotel.

"We're almost to the college. We'll rest a minute and keep going," he says. "The brewery is a few blocks from here, and there's supposed to be another closer to the school."

Paige nods because she's trying to catch her breath.

"Get a drink," Cory orders quietly while keeping watch.

She pulls her stainless steel container of water from her pack and gulps down a few drinks. She's out of shape for this. It's been so long since she was out making a run. She used to be able to jog for a solid hour before her college classes started for the day. And after the fall, she got used to walking for extended periods of time. She vows to get into better condition when they make it back to the farm.

"Ready? Or do you need another minute?" Cory asks with concern a few seconds later.

"I'm good," Paige answers and stands with him.

They find the brewery with no trouble at all and discover the fully intact still in the back of the restaurant. Cory says it will take some ingenuity, but he's pretty sure they can get it free. She's not sure how they're going to get it taken apart to fit into the SUV, but he says that he will figure something out. She's starting to learn that he usually doesn't mince words. If he says he can do it, then he probably can.

They leave through the rear exit where the grass grows with wild abandon up through the cracks of the blacktopped parking lot. Crude graffiti marks the façade of the shopping center across the street. The building looks like the far end of it has been torched at some point. Black soot crawls up the bricks and onto the roof. She checks her watch, one that Kelly gave her to use like the rest of them own. There are buttons and gadgets on it, and he'd showed her how to use it in case the need for setting their watches to sync should arise.

"There's a medical facility, hospital or something, and a small research building kind of thing over at the college," he informs her. "Doc said to check it out. See if they have anything we need."

238

This is the part of their mission that she is already aware of. She knew that it was supposed to be their job to raid the college hospital and then the college itself. It will be the first time she's been to a college since leaving her own.

"Ready or do you need to rest?" he asks considerately.

Paige shakes her head. She appreciates his concern. He doesn't seem like such a monster today, and his brown eyes are regarding her with warmth.

It takes a short while to get there, and she suspects that he is going slower for her. She isn't about to argue. A clearing opens up into a city green spot complete with picnic pavilions, a children's playground and tennis courts with weeds sticking up through the painted green concrete. She used to love playing tennis. Signs, most that have seen better days, litter the area with directions into Vanderbilt University. Cory crosses a street, cautious as they go and waves her forward. The school rests directly in front of them on a massive expanse of property that looks like it used to be lovely. Lots of tall oaks are scattered about. Everything has become unkempt and overgrown, though. They squeeze through chain-link fencing to gain access to the college hospital grounds. Paige has done this sort of thing many times in the last years trying to find any kind of supplies, mostly food, that she could for her and her friends.

"What was that?" Cory asks suddenly and drags her behind a medical van where they squat down low.

"What? What did you hear?" she asks in a panic. She'd been in a daze thinking about her past and not actually paying attention.

"Not hear. I saw something," he says, peering around the back of the van cautiously.

The soft jingle of his equipment and gear bring a feeling of comfort to Paige as if it's letting her know that he's fully prepared for whatever the day brings. His combat boots scuff against the pavement. He inches closer to the edge of the van and pulls a small pair of binoculars from his pocket.

"What'd you see?" she asks, her tension rising.

"Something reflected, like a mirror," he tells her honestly as he spies through the lenses.

He replaces the binoculars to his pocket and slides backward to her again.

"There's something in the fourth floor window," he declares.

"What is it?"

239

Cory looks at her directly and says, "Not sure. Could be a beacon for help. It's definitely a mirror catching the sunlight. Someone could've put it there on purpose to call for help."

"Oh," Paige says with concern.

"I should check it out. They might need help," he says.

"Ok, let's go," she says and starts to rise. Cory pulls her back down beside him.

"You should stay here or I can hide you somewhere. I don't know if you should be with me. People might've put that mirror there for help because they've been overrun or are being held against their will."

Paige's eyes jump to his with fear, "Please, don't leave me here, Cory. I don't want to stay by myself. I can help. I'll help you. I can watch your back."

He grimaces, looks out to the horizon and finally nods. "Stay very close. Watch corners. Watch dark spots. Don't wander away from me."

Paige nods and immediately starts doubting her own decision. Too late now. They rise and move out together. She's on his tail every step of the way to the side entrance of the small medical building. He pulls the door, finds it locked. It isn't a door he can simply kick in. It is solid steel and heavy. The lock on the doorknob is secured from the inside. He whips out a small tin box from his pants pocket and proceeds to pick it like some sort of sly cat burglar. It only takes about a full minute before they are granted entrance. She stays close again. The building is dark where they are. A narrow spray of light is coming from somewhere further inside the building.

Cory takes her to a stairwell, and she tries not to cringe as the sound of water dripping and pinging high above trickles down to her ears. A dark stairwell. Great. She always tried to avoid these kinds of intensely dark, dank places when she was out on the road. Cory doesn't seem to mind it, though. He pulls out a flashlight and his sidearm, which he positions over the light. They move inside, staying close to the walls and slinking slowly upward. When they come to the fourth floor, Cory halts, switches off the light and stands there a few moments listening.

"Here we go," he says quietly. "Stay with me."

"Right," she whispers.

He eases open the door as quietly as he can manage and steps through. This part of the building seems as abandoned as the areas on the first floor. She doesn't hear anyone talking or moving around. Paige looks to her right where a window at the end of the hallway is broken out, maybe from a storm or a tree branch possibly. She's not sure. Cory indicates to their left, and they slowly move that way. He's still holding his pistol, his rifle resting against his back.

A ping behind them causes her heart to nearly skip a beat. They both swing in that direction. Nothing is there, but Cory stares down the hall for nearly a full minute waiting patiently just in case. Then he looks at her and nods. His eyes seem worried.

They walk down the hall finding nothing out of the ordinary for an empty building. Cory pushes open one of the doors, and they go in. He walks straight to the broken window and finds the slice of mirror hanging there suspended by a string. He spins and looks around the long room with great interest. She's not sure what he's looking for. It seems to be some sort of former study center or miniature medical library. Bookshelves line the walls with thick, leather-bound books turning green with mold.

"The Professor would love this place," Cory remarks about her brother.

"I think you're right," Paige agrees, looking at the journals.

Several desks with chairs are scattered here and there. A few of the chairs are tipped onto their sides. It seems as if drifters have crashed here before, probably just for a night or two. The remnants of a temporary stay is still visible. A tattered pillow has been left behind. In the adjacent room, a threadbare blanket lies on top of what was probably an expensive oriental rug. The additional room is connected by an open doorway and an ornate wooden archway that connects the two spaces. Cobwebs hang down from the lovely woodwork. A few empty cans that used to contain beans or vegetables are scattered around. It doesn't seem as if anyone has been in this area for quite some time. Cory scouts out the same rooms and then checks down the hall again. He returns to the window and glances furtively without standing directly in the middle of it.

"Movement," Cory announces.

"What? Where?" Paige asks and rushes to stand next to him at the window.

"A few dudes," he informs her.

He's pointing in the distance to three men moving toward a different building than the one which they are in. They are maybe two hundred yards out, closing in on the same route that she and Cory just took. They seem to be moving with a purpose.

"I don't think they're coming here. Not sure, though," Cory tells her.

"Should we keep looking around?"

"I don't think so. It's time to get out of here," he says as he continues to look down at the other people.

"Are we going to follow them?"

"Nah, not with you hanging out with me today. Could be...crowded," he jokes and hits her with his dark gaze.

Paige isn't so sure she wants to pursue those people, either. She's relieved he doesn't want to track them down. She knows what he's been doing for the last year of his life and has no wish to join in on that sort of merriment.

"What do you want to do?"

"Not stick around to make friends, unless you're that desperate for a boyfriend, red," he says, glancing at her with a wink.

"No thanks," Paige says with a wrinkle of her nose as she watches the men pick up the pace and start jogging. She wonders if they are jogging toward something or away from someone.

"Let's move," he orders and starts toward the other room.

Apparently they are going back out of the building in a different direction than they came in it. She follows him, skirts around a knocked over table to her right, steps on the once lovely rug that has faded and molded just slightly at the edges. She goes through the floor with a scream of pure terror as the rug drops out from underneath her and her stomach plummets, as well. Paige grabs onto anything she can find. Before she plummets to her death, she panics and grasps onto a piece of cable wire hanging down.

"Paige!" she hears Cory yell in haste.

She's dropped her rifle somewhere, probably down to the next floor. When she looks down frantically, she can see that the floor below has a matching hole and the ones below it mirror them. The gaping holes are maybe eight to ten feet in diameter. Her grip slips and she squirms to find a better hold. If she lets go, she's going to fall to her death. She looks down again. There are dead bodies down at the bottom of the hole to Hell. Something about this scenario frightens her even more than the potential fall to death. How did this hole get broken all the way through to the ground level? Had something fallen through the building? Why was the rug covering it?

"Don't look down!" Cory shouts down to her. "Gimme your hand. I can reach you."

Paige doesn't even look up. She's too afraid to look up for fear of losing her grip. She's swaying back and forth in the air. Her legs are dangling, causing her trouble keeping a tight grip. Her hands are sweating. Then she starts to slip.

"Give me your hand, Paige," he calls down with panic in his voice. "Come on, kid. Give me your hand. I'll pull you up. Just look up and reach."

Tears threaten to escape her eyes. She finally glances up into Cory's face.

"I can't," she cries, squirming to hold fast. "I'm slipping."

"Trust me. You're all right. You've got it. Just reach for my hand, Paige," he says in a calmer voice. "Easy now."

His hand is only maybe two inches from hers. The fear she feels clenching her gut at the idea of tumbling to her death is outweighed by her fear of letting go of the security she feels holding onto her lifeline. But her common sense wins out. She nods and reaches for his grip. He grabs her tightly, firmly which makes her feel safer than just holding onto a wire. There is so much raw strength in his hand that she knows he can pull her up out of danger. The veins in his forehead stand out. His hair has come loose of the ponytail and hangs down partially in his face. He pulls her an inch higher. He's lying on his stomach near the edge of the hole. To Paige, he seems like he weighs a lot. She hopes the jagged edge of the floor doesn't give out and collapse the rest of the way under his weight. Cory switches hands and takes her by the wrist instead of her hand.

"That's it," he assures her, a bead of sweat running down his forehead. "I've got you."

He starts pulling her upward in a smooth motion right as she sees a man come up behind him.

Chapter Sixteen
Sam

After checking out the area from a nearby rooftop and then circling the block a few times, Simon maneuvers the Suburban into a parking deck across the street from Nashville General Hospital and parks it on the lowest level in a dark area where it won't be noticed among the other abandoned vehicles there. He pulls in beside a Mercedes S class, a sleek black coupe that likely belonged to a doctor who used to work in the hospital. Sam's mother used to have a Mercedes like that. She swallows the lump of hard memories in her throat and helps Simon look around to ensure they are alone.

On the other side of them is a rusty pick-up truck equipped with wood-slatted side rails for carrying tall items. He cuts the engine, and they wait in silence. The only movement she catches is a pigeon scurrying along a cement wall to their west backlit by the midday sun coming through. The level they are on, however, is nearly pitch dark. It's a good thing. That alone will deter people from looting for a vehicle. Everyone knows there aren't any more available, operable vehicles with gas still in them. This fact will also help to deter theft.

Sam says, "My uncle used to work here."

"Really? The uncle that made sure you and your brothers and sister got vaccines when the country collapsed?" he asks with interest.

"Yes," she replies softly. "My mom's brother. He was really sweet. Uncle Scott was his name. I liked him a lot. He wasn't married, but he had a girlfriend. He lived here in a high-rise in the city."

"What happened to him? Do you know?" Simon asks hesitantly.

"My dad came over here to get him a few weeks after the first tsunami, but he wouldn't leave his job at the hospital, even when it started getting dangerous," she says and pauses for a long moment before continuing. "My dad came back a couple months after things fell all the way. You know, when it got really bad? My mom was worried because we couldn't get in touch with him anymore. The phone lines were down at that point, no computers, no cell phones, nothing worked anymore. My dad took my brother and came over here. Uncle Scott was gone. I don't even know why or where."

"Did he leave a note or anything?"

"No, he was just gone. His stuff from his house was mostly still there, but some of the essential items like food and bottled water were missing. He just disappeared. It was really weird 'cuz him and Mom used to be so close. Kind of like you and Paige."

Simon frowns. "Maybe he tried to get to you guys."

Sam understands that he is attempting to offer hope.

She just shrugs and says, "I don't know. It wasn't long after that when Frank's group raided our house. Maybe he came to our place, but we were already...gone."

"Taken," Simon whispers and checks his handgun.

Sam has picked up on his need to move, to get out of the vehicle and away from the conversation that will lead them down into a rabbit hole of bad memories. She mimics his movements and prepares her own weapons. He gives her a nod when they are both ready. Simon gets out of the SUV without making a lot of noise, shutting the car door while also pocketing the keys. Sam goes around back to meet him at the tailgate.

"I know exactly where we need to go," Simon tells her.

"Me, too," she says as they head out.

Simon gives her an inquisitive glance.

"Reagan told me where to go and what we need to look for," she says with a confident grin.

"Oh, so you're in charge now?" Simon teases quietly.

Normally he doesn't joke around on a mission, but Sam's recounting of her likely dead uncle has probably made him feel guilty enough to want to cheer her up.

She chuckles and says, "Yep, I'm in charge. You report to me, sir."

Simon smiles at her and shakes his head. "Don't I always?"

Sam shoots him a sly grin and replies, "Yes, of course you do, silly."

He leads her to the exit, and they jog across the street to the hospital entrance. Nobody is around. This section of Nashville was vetted the last time they came. She wasn't with him and Cory on that trip. She had wanted to go, but Reagan needed her help at the clinic instead.

Simon glances around, his back pressed tightly against the wall. Sam is right beside him. Using his dagger, he pries open one of the glass sliding doors that used to slide open with a whoosh by motion sensing electronic controls. They sneak through and gain entry into the hospital's grand foyer. The Italian marble floors and two-story entryway were probably impressive at one time. Now the hospital just seems shabby and ready for a demo with a wrecking ball.

Apparently looters came through numerous times with violent abandon and ransacked many parts of this hospital. The electronics including the wall-mounted television players are gone from the waiting room. Someone has sprayed anarchy messages in red and black paint on the cream-colored walls. Wires hang down from some of the missing ceiling tiles. Simon keeps his shotgun in front of him in a two-handed grip and she does the same with her rifle. A stray cat runs in front of them, scaring the crap out of Sam.

"Stupid cat," she hisses angrily.

Simon just grimaces and gives her a quick nod of reassurance. Sam can hear birds somewhere. They must've built nests in the hospital rafters or in the elegant marble columns near the information desk. Wherever they are, they seem to be happily chirping their day away.

The last time she came on a run, she and Reagan had seen four dairy cows in the middle of an indoor shopping mall. They'd laughed heartily at that one. John and Simon had missed it, though because they'd gone around a corner to use the facilities, which meant peeing on the wall of the Abercrombie & Fitch store. She used to shop there with her girlfriends sometimes. Sam remembers that raiding day well because she'd been left with sad, remorseful feelings about whether or not her friends had survived. She's never seen any of them in Pleasant View or around the clinic. She often wonders about her two best friends and if they are alive somewhere with their families.

Simon taps her shoulder to draw her attention, pointing to a grimy door past the reception area and gift shop. She doesn't want to think about what the brownish-red stain on the faded white door could be. She also doesn't look to their right where the skeletal remains of a doctor still in his lab coat rest on the travertine floor. Her mother had wanted to remodel their kitchen right before the apocalypse hit, and Sam distinctly remembers her wanting to tear out the hardwood and replace it with a travertine floor. Her father had said no to the whole remodel. Sam knows that he would've done the remodel eventually. He wasn't very good at telling her mother no and actually sticking to it. Sam is quite sure that her father would've sent one of his crews over to do the job if the world hadn't collapsed.

They cross in unison to the emergency exit door that will hopefully lead them downstairs to the cafeteria storage rooms. This hospital raid isn't just for medicine.

Sam removes her flashlight from her backpack as Simon eases the stairwell door open. They slip inside together and start their descent. She stays right at his hip to keep the light beam ahead of them. They make it down the single flight of cement stairs to the lower level where Simon opens the door that is marked for hospital staff, ignoring the other exit door meant for the public. Moving slowly down the dark hallway, passing doors to storage areas as they go, Sam's heartbeat begins to accelerate. It's so gloomy in the basement of the hospital, no light from above allowed entry into this space that probably used to bustle with workers.

Sam tugs on the sleeve of Simon's flannel jacket and points to their left where she spies a sign for cafeteria storage. He nods and backs around the corner with her again. They pass an area that is cordoned off with chain-link fencing.

"What is all that?" Sam asks, nodding her head toward the large equipment and tanks.

"Boilers, heating and air-conditioning. This would've been the central command area for the structure. Maintenance men would've worked down here keeping things flowing smoothly," he explains patiently.

"Not anymore," Sam says as she observes the cobwebs and dust in every corner and on every surface of the massive equipment and control center.

Simon shakes his head and says, "No, not anymore. Let's keep moving. I don't think anyone's down here, but just in case, be on high alert."

"You don't have to tell me twice," Sam whispers. "This place is like the setting of a hospital massacre movie with some slasher guy with a knife and the dumb girl that runs the wrong way."

"I think we're safe," Simon assures her. "Besides, you're a smart girl. If a slasher comes at us, I'll just follow you."

"Maybe, but if a spider drops on me, I'm shooting it," she warns with serious intent.

Simon chuckles, turns around and smiles down at her. "That's justified."

Sam smiles in return, trying not to stare at his deep dimples or the divot in the middle of his strong chin. He has switched out his ball cap with a black stocking cap, not to ward off the chill in the air which is definitely present, but to cover and camouflage his auburn hair. It's such a shame when he covers his hair. It's so wavy and thick, the color so vivid. The other day she sketched a drawing of him studying a medical book while wearing his glasses. He was unaware of being her model and muse, or he likely would've complained. He was in Grandpa's office sitting in a wing-backed chair. He looked as if he'd just stepped out of another century, or right off of one of the canvasses of a Frank Dicksee painting. The way the soft, late afternoon light was filtering through the shades in the den with dust particles dancing about, Simon's dark auburn hair in contrast with his white, button-down shirt and the studious nature of his behavior, Sam couldn't resist a fast, outlined sketch that she later finished in her room with colored pencils. He has such an angular jawline and cheekbones that make him seem so classic. He's an interesting study for an artist's eye. She hid that one under her bed, too.

They come to the door marked for cafeteria personnel and allow themselves inside. She hopes a rat doesn't run across her foot. A few empty boxes are tipped over in the center aisle of shelving units which they must step around and over. Simon is busy scanning the large room for intruders while Sam starts looking for food supplies they need.

"Clear," Simon announces a few moments later after he's returned from checking the entire room.

Buildings that are occupied by humans are relatively easy to spot. Belongings and stashes of supplies are typically littered about. Sometimes tents or sleeping bags are set up. So far in this hospital, it's been the way they prefer: empty and long ago abandoned.

Sam roams around checking shelves and stainless steel cupboards and storage drawers. There are a few boxes of spices, but she doesn't think that Hannah or Sue would want those brought back to the farm. Sue makes her own spices by growing and then drying them in the barn. This stash is probably expired, and if not, then filled with preservatives.

She steps over a piece of kitchen equipment that looks like it was some sort of rotisserie style hotdog cooker. They don't eat hotdogs anymore. Nobody does. But the Reynolds brothers make really good sausage. She loves it in the fall when the hog butchering takes place. The whole valley seems like it smells of smoking meat mixed with the mouth-watering smell of bacon. They should start the process any day now. As a matter of fact, they are running late this year since tonight is technically Halloween.

Simon is making a racket in the next aisle over as he performs his own rummaging. Sam slides open a steel door under a countertop to reveal two sealed cardboard boxes. She drops to her knees and pulls one out. It lands with a heavy thud, one end squashing her foot. She's able to slip it out from underneath the box without calling for help. It's heavier than she would've thought. Using the knife from her hip, she slices the packing tape to reveal pay dirt. This is exactly what they need.

"Simon, come here!" she calls.

It only takes a moment before he appears next to her.

"Great job, Sam," he praises.

"These are heavy, gosh!" Sam exclaims as she lifts a big sack out of the box.

"That's a good thing," he says. "Here, let me get them."

Sam steps back with her heavy sack as Simon hefts the whole box onto the counter. He takes her bag and places it back inside the storage box.

"Think there are more in there, Simon," she notes, stoops low, and ends up crawling half inside the long cabinet to drag another box to the opening. "Yes, there are. I think there are four boxes in here. With eight bags of salt each, that's thirty-two bags to take back."

"Awesome," he says with excited eyes. "And your math's still good, too."

Sam chuckles, "Ha, it was never good."

Simon grins at her, hefts two more boxes onto the counter and says, "This is a priceless find. We were really low. You've got an eagle eye."

Sam ignores his praise and keeps looking for other supplies in the same cupboards. Unfortunately, the salt is the only find so far.

"How are we going to get all of this to the Suburban?" she asks with a frown as her light flickers. Sam hopes it doesn't go out all the way. A few taps to her palm seem to do the trick.

Simon sighs and says, "Can you cover me?"

"Yes, sure I can," Sam says confidently. "You know that."

"I can get one box at a time, but I can't do it while I carry both long guns."

"Simon, that box must weigh a hundred pounds," she tells him.

"I think it's only about sixty, maybe seventy-five," Simon corrects her nonchalantly.

"That's kind of a lot, Simon!"

"We heft those hundred pound sacks of grain at the farm, hunt and drag back deer and just about anything else. I'll be fine. I just need to know if you can cover us both while I'm carrying these. We're gonna need to make a few trips."

"Got it," she says. "I'll cover us. Don't worry."

"If we run into trouble, I'll drop this stuff and take back my rifle. I'm gonna leave the shotgun hidden down here somewhere," he tells her as he unslings the twelve gauge.

"Here, Simon," Sam says and pulls his arm. "We can hide it over here."

She leads him to the next aisle where the metal storage shelving is actually still intact. Sam kneels down and waves him to follow.

"Under here," Sam shows him. "Slide it under here. That'll hide it. Nobody's down here in this basement level anyway. It's not like anyone would look under this when there is so much to look at elsewhere."

Simon lays his shotgun on the floor and pushes it under the shelf. There is barely room to get it to fit under the tight space.

"That should work," Simon says as they rise again. "Let's get moving. We've got a lot to do. I found some boxes of sugar, too. This is going to take a lot of trips. We have about four hours till we need to meet up with Cory and Paige and get settled in for the night."

"Well, what are ya' waitin' for, then?" she teases, getting a slightly irritated grin from Simon. She lowers her voice and mimics the men with one of their favorite phrases, "We're burnin' daylight."

"Aren't you being a little sassy pants today?" he asks with a hand on his hip.

Sam just hits him with a brilliant smile and shrugs her shoulders. "Ready, Professor?"

"Let's start," he answers.

Sam feels an enormous amount of stress, but she tries her best to conceal it from Simon. She will need to keep both eyes open and watch for anything and everything that could be a potential danger. It's her job to keep them safe in order to get these vital supplies back to the farm.

He hands over his rifle with a forlorn expression on his face. Simon hefts the box onto his shoulder, keeping his shooting hand free for his sidearm. Sam tries not to let him know that his rifle is heavy on her back. His long-range rifle is heavier than many of the other weapons at the farm. She doesn't want him to worry about her. He has enough to be concerned about with trying to carry the heavy box of salt. The family will be ecstatic about the find. They use salt for many things like making cheese, preserving meat, and even medicinally.

This time, Sam leads the way back out of the basement. She's balancing her handgun and the flashlight as they ascend the darkened stairway. She prays that nobody comes at them from above. Unfortunately, on the second flight up, a rattling from somewhere above on another floor crashes down upon their ears through the deafening silence.

"Stop!" Simon whispers. "Kill the light."

She doesn't need told. Sam has the light turned off before he even finishes his sentence. They both press back against the wall so as not to be seen by anyone who might come into the hall above them. Simon has put the box down and drawn his pistol. Sam squats down. They wait for a long time. Just as she is about to suggest they keep moving, the rattling noise comes again. It sounds like someone is trying to open a locked door.

She whispers, "Could it be the wind?"

"No," his quiet response comes, sending a shiver down the back of her neck. She'd like to hold his hand but thinks better of it. He needs both hands on his gun if they get into trouble. She's been with him and Cory when there has been trouble. However, this time they are split up into two teams. She's not so sure she likes this plan after all. She understands the necessity of it as they would've been in the city for too many days searching out supplies if they moved in a big group of four. But it doesn't mean she has to like it.

"Animal?" she whispers, hopeful.

"Don't think so," Simon returns.

Sam hears him click off the safety on his handgun. He steps ahead of her. Simon finds her arm in the pitch dark and slides his hand down to take the flashlight from her.

"Stay here," he says quietly.

"'Kay," Sam whispers nervously.

He turns the flashlight back on, covering the illuminated end of it with his palm. It gives him just enough light to see by, but not enough to be seen. She watches with great despair as he climbs the stairs away from her. A few seconds later and he is gone and so is the light. Now she's totally creeped out. She tries to calm her breathing. A feeling comes over her as if something is going to run at her from below. Sam rubs at the gooseflesh on her calves and ankles before resting back against the wall again. She frowns at her own childishness because they already searched the lower level, and it was empty.

"What a baby," she whispers to herself.

Simon comes back down, hands her the light and says, "It's all clear. I checked the stairwell up a couple floors. There isn't anyone there. We're going to be careful, though."

"Do you think it was a person?" Sam asks as they ascend and reach the exit door they need.

"I think so," he says grimly. "Could've been an animal. Probably a dog. Whatever it was, they're gone now. We'll take this out to the SUV and rest a minute there where I can do some recon. Maybe we'll go to the top of the parking deck and check out the area again. Maybe I missed something."

"'Kay," Sam agrees with nerves that are fully rattled.

They make it back to the main floor but take a different exit to the east. It brings them out closer to the side of the parking deck entrance which will make it faster to get the supplies loaded. Sam keeps her gun trained out in front of them as they fast walk down the ramp to the lower level of the parking garage. Simon loads the salt into the back of the SUV, tossing the cardboard box aside.

The trips back and forth take them over an hour. And after five more similar and thankfully uneventful trips including for the sugar that Simon found, plus two heavy sacks of rice, three boxes of dried beans, bags of oatmeal and twelve smaller boxes of baking powder, they take a break and rest in the Suburban. Sam lights a small beeswax candle and places it on the dashboard. The darkness of the hospital basement and now the parking deck is just too much. She needs a reprieve. Apparently Simon either feels the same way or else he's just being accommodating because he says nothing about the light from the candle.

Simon crawls into the back and pulls out their packages of food from the farm. He hands her a sack and keeps one for himself. Sam takes a swig of her bottled water, not at all surprised to find the taste of mint in it. Sue's handiwork, no doubt. Fresh baked bread with soft, herbed goat cheese and a slice of smoked ham await her next. Hannie's handiwork. There is also an apple, some slices of hard cheddar cheese, a handful of green pepper strips, two hard-boiled eggs and a small baggie of dried deer jerky. She's not crazy about the deer jerky but will eat it just the same. She knows her body will need the protein for energy for the next few days. Another bottle near the bottom of the sack contains what is likely whey water. This one would be on Reagan's insistence. Sam hates the protein water. It tastes like a cow's utter. It's disgusting, but Reagan thinks it's healthy and good for them, especially out in the field. Sam will probably leave it for Simon and hope that he doesn't notice her lack of interest.

They dig in with earnest and eat in companionable silence for a short time until their hunger abates just slightly. He constantly looks at the side and rearview mirrors.

"Think we'll find anything else down there?" Sam asks, referring to the basement of the hospital.

"Maybe. We sure didn't get everything. That was just one small area of that storage room."

"Right. So are we going back in?"

253

Simon takes a huge bite of his sandwich and replies, "Yeah, I think we've got time. We should look around for medical supplies for the clinic if we can find any."

She consults her watch, borrowed from Derek, and says, "I think so, too. We're not that far from Cory and Paige at the college and where we're supposed to meet up later. We've still got some time."

"Hope our meet-up place is still empty," he observes and takes a swig of the protein water.

Good. Sam hopes he drinks the whole thing. He tilts it toward her to offer a drink, but she shakes her head with a wrinkle of her nose. He just chuffs.

"It'll put hair on your chest," he teases.

"I like my chest just fine the way it is, thank you, sir," she jokes. His eyes dart down to her chest and then away quickly.

"The... we're... the Parthenon is a good place to meet," he stutters.

Sam just stares at him with confusion. She also looks down at her jacket. Maybe she's spilled something on herself. She doesn't see anything. Maybe he wasn't looking at her shirt. However, it wouldn't be like Simon to be looking at anything else in that area.

"It was empty before," she agrees. "Let's hope it still is. I haven't been there with you guys. Remember? We just stayed in the cabin the last time we all came."

"Yes, but we didn't have the vehicle. This is different."

"I remember going on a picnic at the Parthenon once with my mom and the twins," she says, recalling the event.

"Really? I guess I forget sometimes that you were from this area."

"Yeah, born and raised. Haven't been to too many other places. We used to vacation down at Myrtle Beach with my grandparents. But my dad's business kept us from doing much. He worked a million hours a week."

"I know what that's like," Simon agrees.

"I'm sure, what with your dad being so important and all," Sam says with praise.

"I don't know how important he was. It was just his job. He took his political career very seriously."

"It used to be important being a politician," Sam comments. "They ran our country for us. I'd say that was pretty important."

"Yes, well they've done a swell job of it," Simon says with a lot more cynicism than he normally shows. "I'm sitting in the parking deck of an abandoned, post-apocalyptic hospital eating lunch with a girl who wouldn't have given me the time of day five years ago, and now it's up to me to keep her alive and forage a trashed out city like an alley rat because of the bang-up job the politicians of the world have done."

"Wait a minute!" Sam halts him angrily. "Who says I wouldn't have given you the time of day?"

He interrupts her with a chuckle and says, "That's all you got out of that?"

"Yes, it's the only part that's important because it involved me and you, Simon," Sam informs him with brewing outrage.

Simon looks directly at her and raises his eyebrows as if she is being ridiculous.

"Don't judge me like that. You didn't know me before. Hell, sometimes I don't think you know me now," she swears.

"Language, young lady," Simon corrects her.

This time Sam laughs at him before saying, "You just insulted me and you're worried because I said a swear word?"

"There's no reason to be uncivilized just because the world has become so," he lectures.

"I would've talked to you," she grumbles before taking a drink of her minty water.

"I doubt it," he argues. "I wouldn't have blamed you, either."

Sam frowns at his put-down. "I wasn't one of those girls, Simon."

"What girls?"

"Snobby, stuck on themselves, those kinds," Sam educates him.

"No, you probably weren't," he finally agrees, looking directly at her again.

"Besides, I wouldn't have noticed you unless you grew a mane and tail, silly. I wasn't into boys back then before the fall."

For some reason, this comment makes Simon scowl hard. Is he remembering their shared time with the visitors? She wasn't into boys then, either, but she learned very quickly that interest in the

255

other party doesn't need to be reciprocal. She wishes that Simon would just forget that time. She'd sure like to.

Instead, Sam reverts to their previous conversation, "Anyway, before we got off on all that. I picnicked with my mother and the twins at the Parthenon. I think the babies were maybe a year old. They were still in the giant, pain in the butt double stroller. I remember that very clearly. That thing was so heavy and cumbersome."

"I'm sure," Simon agrees.

He also seems glad to have left their other discussion behind.

"I just remember the Parthenon being really pretty inside and the grounds around it looking like some sort of fancy park. We sat on the grass near a pond," Sam tells him as she digs around in her sack and finds a caramel brownie. Hannah makes these sometimes because they don't require traditional brownie ingredients like chocolate and sugar. The sugar is replaced with creamed honey. The chocolate is swapped out with ground-up walnuts from the orchard. They are simply heavenly.

"It might not look quite the way you're remembering it, Sam," he says, stashing some of his lunch items back into his sack, as well.

"That would be a shame because the artwork and statues inside were lovely," Sam reminisces.

"It's a little rundown. Just be prepared. We'll have to be way more careful this time, too."

"Because Paige and I are with you guys?"

"Yes," Simon answers with blunt honesty.

"We'll be fine," she assures him, although she really can't be too confident because who knows what could happen. They could all die today for all she knows.

"You'll be fine because I *say* you will," Simon says almost angrily.

"What's that supposed to mean?"

She doesn't get an answer because he blows out the candle with a hasty breath of air and pushes on her shoulder.

"Get down!" he says fiercely.

"What is it?"

"Headlights," he says.

Simon pushes the lever on the side of her chair so that it instantly drops to a full reclining position and does the same on his side.

"Rifle safety off," he orders as he pulls his handgun out, flicks off the safety and readies his rifle, as well.

Sam pulls the AR up beside her and flicks off the safety.

"Shh," he whispers in the dark. "Be still, Sam. Someone's coming."

Her heart is about to hammer right out of her chest as dim headlights appear out of the dark. A vehicle descends the ramp and slinks slowly toward them.

Chapter Seventeen
Reagan

She breathes her usual sigh of relief at the sight of her husband returning safely from a trip. John and Kelly park the stolen gas company trucks near the equipment shed and get out. Derek is already up there, but she and Grandpa need to make the hike. Reagan would like to jog up the driveway to greet her husband but will walk at a much slower pace with her grandfather. Just recently, she's noticed that he doesn't get around as fast as he used to.

"They're back, Hannie!" she calls into the kitchen before leaving the house with her grandfather.

"I know," Hannah replies in her normal, strange way.

"Basset hound," Grandpa remarks as they go down the back stairs.

Reagan laughs and pulls her jacket collar higher. A wind gust whips through the valley, turning what's left of the leaves over on the big oak trees. The branches rustle and clink together like nature's wind chimes.

"It seems like we're in for a storm," she tells her grandfather.

He sighs and replies, "I think so. Looks like we'd better get the chores done early tonight. Might be a real gusher."

"I hope the kids are ok," Reagan frets.

"Reagan, they aren't kids anymore," Grandpa says with a chuckle. "I thought your grandmother and me were bad about the worrying."

"You were," she says with a smile as three of the children run past them, probably engaged in a game of tag.

"I think you might be worse," he teases.

Reagan loops her arm through her grandfather's, relieved the need to cringe from the touch of her family is nearly gone. She doesn't like touching other people, patients maybe, but not strangers. They still give her the willies and probably always will. Sam has the same issues. Hers just go much deeper than Reagan's. Samantha has a tendency to be open and kind, giving and sweet, but she sure as hell doesn't like strangers, especially men.

"Maybe," Reagan agrees. "I'm new to this parenting shit. I didn't know it came with so much stress."

"You're just getting started," Grandpa reminds her.

"Oh, I know. Trust me, John's better at this. He was meant to be a dad," Reagan says.

"Yes, I think you're right about that. But you are turning out to be a pretty damn good mother, little missy. Don't you forget it. You're even trying to parent the kids that aren't kids anymore."

"It's kind of hard to look at Sam like an adult. She still has a little girl face," she says with a roll of her eyes. Her hand naturally rises to the scar on her right cheek.

Grandpa chuckles again and says, "Yes, that's true. I'll give you that much. She is a precious little thing."

"I hope they have time to get to shelter if this storm rolls in," Reagan worries. She gets another laugh from Herb McClane.

"Don't worry so much. It's not good for you. Don't you know anything about the mind-body relationship?"

"Good grief," Reagan says with a smirk. "Here we go. Are you gonna try and sell me on some Eastern Indian or Chinese medicine hippy shit again? I get enough of that from the Professor."

"He's right, ya' know. That young man is an intelligent person. Reminds me of someone I used to know," Grandpa teases.

"And who would that be?"

"Hm, let me think. He was witty, good-looking, strong, extremely intelligent."

"Do you mean you?" Reagan asks with a wry smile.

"Oh, yes. It *was* me I was thinking of," he jokes with a chuckle.

"Oh brother," she jokes.

"Simon's going to be a brilliant doctor someday, just like you. And the two of you will help put this country back to right. You'll run the clinic together and maybe even add other doctors eventually."

She doesn't like thinking of her grandfather dying and leaving the practice to her and Simon or anyone else. It makes her instantly depressed.

"I can barely hold my own shit together. I don't think I'm ready to run your practice. Besides, you and I are doing fine there."

"Hey, Mom!" Jacob shouts as he jogs closer to them.

He's yelling in his usual blaring decibel tone. Now Reagan understands why parents cringe when their children yell so much.

"Can we have a campfire tonight?" he calls out.

He's being followed by other co-conspirators Arianna, Justin, and Huntley, who normally hangs out more with the men now than the younger kids. Reagan can't believe Huntley's almost fourteen already.

"I don't know, bud," Reagan answers. "It's going to rain. We could have a campfire in the fireplace, though."

"Ok, cool," he answers.

Reagan frowns at his choice of words as he runs away with his adopted cousins. He's growing too fast. For a five year old boy, he sure seems to be sounding more every day like the pre-teens on the farm.

They arrive at the equipment shed where Grandpa lights his pipe. The three men are already unloading oil company equipment, also looted, from the bed of the one truck.

"What is that?" Reagan asks, pointing to a metal box that her husband is unloading.

"Compressor kit," he answers as he sets it on the gravel floor.

Then John comes over directly in front of her and leans down for a quick peck on her mouth. Reagan tries not to blush in front of Kelly and Derek, who seem oblivious as they discuss the new gear.

"What's it for?" Reagan inquires when her husband pulls back. She swipes the lock of his blonde hair that has fallen across his forehead to the back again.

"It converts the natural gas for the trucks. We needed to have this thing to make the whole system work," he answers before returning to the others.

Kelly says, "We'll mount it to the inside wall over here, little Doc."

Reagan joins them near the edge of the shed where Derek has already cut a small hole in the wall earlier in anticipation of this find. Apparently he is a clairvoyant because Reagan wasn't so sure that they'd find anything. Of course, maybe John called on the radio to let his brother know of their fortuitous trip.

"Did you guys run into any trouble? Are the kids all right?" Reagan asks because she can't manage to stop herself.

"They're fine, babe," John reassures her as he works distractedly alongside his brother.

"We did run into some of our old friends from our outfit," Kelly offers amiably.

He is leaning against the new pick-up truck casually as the others work.

Grandpa asks, "Really? That's very interesting."

"Yeah, they're holed up near a town called Hendersonville. Guess they've got a similar setup."

"Good. We could always use more allies," Grandpa says.

Kelly laughs as he lights a cigarette, something he must've come across in the city.

"Oh yeah," he says. "Dave the Mechanic is quite the badass. His group is all tricked out. We'll make a trip over there soon and see if we can't set up some trade. John told him about our clinic, so don't be surprised if some hillbilly lookin' bastard carrying a military rifle comes in someday cussin' and spittin' chew."

Grandpa smiles and nods.

"Mechanic?" Reagan asks. "Was he a mechanic in your unit? You mean he was a Ranger or... you know."

She doesn't want to say Delta Force, but they know what she means just the same. They don't talk very often about their pasts. This new soldier entering the scene is unusual.

John and Kelly laugh as if they find her comment humorous.

"Nah, not a mechanic," Kelly explains as he blows cigarette smoke skyward. "Well, technically he could tear just about anything apart and fix it, which in the Army used to be a pretty handy trade to have because you never knew when some shit vehicle or something was gonna take a full-fledged dump. I guess he was in college before the shit started in the Middle East again. After the country got attacked, he joined up. Probably about the same time John and I got in. He's our age."

"Wow, he's really old then?" Reagan teases.

261

Kelly chuckles and explains, "You'd better be nice to me or I'll tell your sister."

"I'm not scared of her," Reagan lies.

Kelly looks off into the distance and doesn't laugh at her joke which is unusual for him. They normally razz each other endlessly.

"What are you thinking?" she asks as Grandpa wanders over to inspect the new compressor system. She knew it wouldn't take long. His brain doesn't stop. He's going to want to know everything there is to know about this CNG system and how it operates.

"Aw, I was just remembering some of the funny shit we got into over the years."

"Tell me," Reagan asks of him. "John never talks about any of it."

"Most of it isn't worth talkin' about, little Doc. But there were some funny moments."

Reagan nods, indicating that she'd like to hear. She climbs onto the open tailgate of the truck where she can dangle her legs.

"We were doing a raid up in Pakistan- off the record, of course."

Reagan laughs. It's not as if it matters anymore, but Kelly winks.

"This dick leader of some newly-formed radical Muslim group that was starting to stir up the shit again was holed up in the area. We found him easily enough. Weren't supposed to be in Pakistan. Didn't have the authority to be there, but that's mostly what our unit did. And we found that little turd and took him out. Then we… disabled his small following of dipshits. Dave the Mechanic hacked into the dickhead's computer. He was good at the computer stuff like I've never seen. That's how he got the nickname. It wasn't because he was a car mechanic. The shit he could do with computers made him the mechanic. He stole all the info he needed off of it, then he…well, he was pretty good at making funny videos and stuff, too. So he cropped a pic of this dickhead leader in a funny video. It was pretty inappropriate. I'll spare you the details, but there were goats involved."

Reagan laughs. She can only imagine. Kelly takes one last puff on the cigarette and stamps it out with his booted toe.

"You'd better get rid of that smell, or Hannah will know you were smoking," she warns with a grin.

"I'm not scared of her," Kelly says, using Reagan's words.

"Uh huh. Sure you aren't," she says.

"I'm not. She's a little pipsqueak," Kelly says, sniffs his shirt. "On an unrelated note, would you happen to have some cologne or air freshener spray on you?"

Reagan smiles at her friend. "Are you guys going back to Nashville?"

She's still worried about the four young people from their family being out there all night or for two nights without the rest of them.

"Nah, they got this," he reassures her. "They'll meet up at dusk. So not too long from now, they'll get together for the night and hunker down somewhere."

"It's just hard not worrying," Reagan admits and kicks a pebble off of the tailgate with her Converse.

"Well don't," Kelly tells her, laying a hand on her shoulder for just a second. "They're fine. They're trained. And Paige survived for three years with just her friends and hardly any weapons. She may have a few things that she can teach my hard-headed little bro."

"Yeah? Maybe. I don't think they get along all that great," Reagan reminds him.

"I'm not so sure about that one, little Doc," Kelly tells her.

Reagan furrows her brow and says, "What do you mean?"

Kelly shrugs and says, "I think I've seen a spark of interest in my brother where Paige is concerned."

"Really?"

"Yeah, but I don't think he'd act on it. I don't think he'd risk ruining his relationship with Simon by acting on it."

"Wow, that's… I don't know what to say about it. I didn't notice anything like that."

Kelly laughs and says, "Little Doc, you didn't even notice John's interest in you, and you were personally involved in that one. Don't feel bad, though. Cory's a pretty hard person to read."

"Most people are hard to read," Reagan admits with a frustrated frown. "What about Simon's sister? Do you think there is a mutual interest there?"

"I'm not sure. I don't know her well enough yet to tell."

Reagan chuckles and says, "I'm sure you will. Better yet, we should be asking Hannie this shit. She is the all-knowing."

Kelly laughs and nods his head in agreement.

"Hey, Kelly," Reagan says, "how is she? Is she doing any better?"

"Yeah," Kelly answers and then looks at his boots. "I think she's getting there. Having Cory home is helping. I kind of figured it would. Not sure why, but she likes that little bastard."

Reagan laughs and says, "Yeah, she does. Hell, Hannie likes everyone. It's not in her nature to dislike anyone."

"Another reason I don't ever want her going to town with us when we do the clinic days," Kelly tells her.

"Me, too. She's too trusting and kind for her own good. I'm thankful she doesn't go to town with us. She'd be bringing home strays, and I don't mean more dogs."

Kelly just chuckles and nods.

"I'm just glad that she seems to be getting better. I didn't like seeing her so depressed," Reagan confesses.

"Me either, little Doc," Kelly tells her. "I didn't know how to help her."

"Grandpa said she just needed time. Maybe he was right. Who knows? It's not like I'm a shrink. Hannah is so tender and gentle spirited. She had me worried. I didn't think she'd get over Grams, but when we lost Em, too..." Reagan pauses, aware that she's just brought up Kelly's dead sister, probably breaking his heart all over again. She knows how much Kelly loved her.

"I know," Kelly laments. "I was worried, too, but I think she's coming out of it. She seems happier lately."

"She does," Reagan agrees as cursing comes from the other side of the equipment shed, not from John, of course.

"I'd better go and help. We're losing daylight, and I think Derek's trying to get some of it hooked up tonight. No time like the present," Kelly remarks with sarcasm.

"Sure, I'm heading back down to the house to help with dinner," Reagan says and gets an incredulous look from Kelly. "Don't worry, Hulk. I'm mostly going down to raid the kitchen for sweets. I won't get too involved with the cooking process. It wouldn't matter; Hannie wouldn't stand for it. I almost burned the biscuits the other morning, so she's got me on menial tasks. To think I used to study microbes under a microscope all day long and my annoying little sister won't even let me near the stove."

"You're still needed around here, little Doc," Kelly assures her. "If one of us fucks ourselves up by getting blown up with this CNG shit, then you can sew us back together."

Reagan frowns, "Great. Just what I want to think about."

"Well, ya' see? Now you aren't worried about the kids in the city anymore," Kelly says with a slap to her back.

"Kelly," John reprimands as he comes to stand next to her. Then he helps her down from the truck and wraps an arm around her waist. "Good grief. Don't worry, babe. Nobody's getting messed up. It's safe… relatively."

"Gee, now I feel totally reassured," Reagan mocks and gets a laugh from her husband. "Do you even know what you're doing?"

"Um…" he says with a shrug.

Reagan scowls and asks, "Want to walk me back to the house?"

"You know I do, woman," John confirms with a sly grin. "Wanna' go for a walk in the woods?"

"Spare me the details," Kelly jokes and punches John's shoulder.

They both chuckle as John leads her away. He immediately snatches her hand into his own, and Reagan takes pleasure from his touch. She never flinches from John or Jacob. Sometimes, she still flinches when other people reach for her. She tries hard not to, but it still happens as a reflexive reaction.

"We have a problem in town," John tells her quietly as they get further away from the others.

"What do you mean?"

"We've noticed a few things missing at the build site. Your grandpa said that he thinks a box of our medical supplies at the clinic was stolen, too, the other day when it was just him and Simon working," he explains.

A knot tightens in the pit of her stomach. Years ago before the fall, this might be written off as nothing out of the ordinary as far as petty crime goes. But not today.

"What was taken?" Reagan asks him.

The slowly sinking sun sneaks through the dark cloud cover, kissing John's blonde hair and high cheekbones.

"We had some lumber and a few tools taken. Doc says that the box of stuff stolen from the clinic wasn't a big deal, mostly bandages and homemade salves."

265

"I guess we'll have to go back to keeping everything at the farm instead," Reagan says. "Did someone break a window or something like that to get in?"

"No, and that's the interesting thing. Nobody in town saw anything and there weren't any signs of a break-in at the clinic. Somebody knew what they were doing."

A chill runs unbidden down her spine. The idea that someone in town has stolen from them is a frightening proposition. They go to town all the time to help the people with the wall build and at the clinic. She can't believe that someone would do this.

"I don't understand. This just sucks," Reagan says. "Why would anyone do that?"

"We're not sure who did it," John admits, the line of his strong mouth tightening, his blue eyes intense. "We have sentries working the wall now and walking the beat at night. It doesn't add up. The wall is far from finished, but you'd think that someone in town would've seen something."

"What about the new people that Cory invited to our town?"

John shakes his head and says, "We considered that, but most of those people are old or just little kids with their moms. I don't see that they would have a benefit of doing it, either. They've actually been pretty helpful in town. Everyone has good things to say about their group."

"Yeah, I haven't heard anything bad about them, either," Reagan agrees with a frown.

"We'll root them out," John says.

For some reason, this statement scares Reagan. She doesn't want her husband in danger tracking down thieves in town. If someone felt brave enough to steal from them, then perhaps they may get ballsy enough to kill, as well.

"Maybe it was someone passing through the area," Reagan suggests.

John looks down at her and nods, although Reagan can tell that he doesn't believe this hypothesis. When they arrive at the back porch, John presses a reassuring kiss to her mouth and hugs her.

"Don't tell everyone else about this yet," he requests.

"Ok, why?" Reagan inquires because that kind of dictate is unlike the way they do things on the farm. Everything is shared, especially when the information could entail danger.

"We don't want Cory to go into town and take care of this on his own. He's still kind of intense," John tells her.

"Hopefully he doesn't show that intensity with Paige on this run. He might scare her," Reagan suggests, standing on the first step so that she can be eye level with her husband.

John chuckles and says, "Yeah, that might not be good. I'm sure they'll be fine. His intensity is what will keep them alive if they run into trouble, which is why we sent him."

"Do you think they will?"

"Nah, don't even worry about it. They're not in danger," John lies badly.

Reagan smirks at him and nods. He presses another kiss to her forehead, squeezes her waist, and turns to go.

A murmur of thunder off in the distance echoes down through their valley, their safe and secure little hideaway from the rest of the violent world. Reagan looks skyward at the storm moving in and sends up a quick prayer to ask for the kids' safe returns. She hopes the worst thing they run into in the city is finding shelter from this storm.

Chapter Eighteen
Cory

"Behind you!" Paige screams.

Cory barely gets a fast glance over his shoulder before some freak lands on his back. Without letting go of Paige, he elbows the guy to the chin. It's not as effective as he'd like it to be, however, because he's lying flat on his stomach trying desperately to haul Paige to safety from the wide hole she'd fallen into. He can't let her go or she'll fall to her death. There isn't anything else for her to hold onto but him. He's her only way out of the pit. A trap set there on purpose.

"Get off him, you asshole!" Paige yells angrily as she tries to grasp his hand with both of hers.

The guy has to be close to his size in weight, making it difficult to breathe. It is times like this when Cory is glad that he works out so hard in his downtime or he would've dropped her already. They are four stories up, so she'd likely die if she didn't just end up in a wheelchair for the rest of her life.

"Cory," she pleads shakily as her legs kick about below her in an attempt to find a foothold on something. Cory isn't about to tell her that it's just empty space all the way to the marble floor way below. There is nowhere to place either of her feet.

Her light eyes sear into his with fear for her life and probably his own. The man on his back wraps a sinewy forearm around Cory's neck. He's going to choke him out.

"Cory," Paige says again, tears falling from her frightened eyes.

"I've got you," Cory assures her, ignoring the beast on his back.

He tucks his chin tightly to his chest so the creep can't lock his arm and completely cut off his flow of air. With all his strength, Cory pushes upward lifting the man on his back as he goes. His muscles strain and shake with the weight he's hauling with Paige in his grip and the man on his back. She can't weigh more than a buck twenty, but the man is roughly close to one eighty. It is the equivalent of bench pressing about four hundred pounds, but there's no way in hell he's letting her go.

"When I'm done with you, I'll take your woman," the man taunts in Cory's ear.

With a roar of rage, Cory yanks her to the ledge where she grasps on firmly. One more tug and she's pulled halfway onto the edge of the broken floor and can scramble up to her knees. Cory shoves backward, elbows the man in the ribs and dislodges his attacker. He gasps a few times to gain air into his lungs again. He even stumbles once. The man is clambering noisily behind him. Cory turns to face his opponent, still seeing stars from the lack of air. The man is close to his age and clean-cut in appearance, even clean-shaven. His head is shaved, his clothing is neat, and he doesn't seem like the usual suspect he's run into over the years. Usually men like this look like homeless wretches down on their luck since the apocalypse hit and desperate enough to steal, rape, kill if need be. He almost resembles a yuppy college jock on roids. He's wearing a polo shirt and corduroy jacket. His khakis have a stain on the left knee, but other than that, he's well-groomed and relatively unsoiled.

Cory reaches for his sidearm since he'd set his rifle in the corner when Paige had gone through the hole. He barely has it unholstered when the man is on him. Unfortunately, the man shoves him again before he can even get it drawn all the way. This time the creep's wielding a knife and has knocked Cory's handgun to the ground where it skids a few feet away. He hadn't expected his foe to be so fast. He figured for more time when he'd tossed the thug off his back. Fine. This fight is going hand to hand. He has no problem with that. He'd just like to be a little less foggy-brained.

"Think you're tough, huh, punk?" Roid Rage asks. "I'm gonna gut you like a pig in front of your woman."

Cory doesn't respond but offers a sardonic, lopsided grin of defiance. In his peripheral vision, he sees Paige scrambling away on her hands and knees.

The man jabs at him as the fog clears the rest of the way from Cory's head. He sizes up his foe and slows his breathing to control the fight and his movements. Cory doesn't bother to take out his own dagger, the one he'd used quite a few times during the period when he was gone from the farm. It was not just used for skinning squirrels. He jumps deftly to the side, now that he has oxygen and his wits back. The man stabs again toward him.

"I'll show your woman what a bitch you are," the man brags.

Cory fast jabs the guy to the jaw, making direct, square contact. The yuppy staggers and lunges recklessly. Cory punches him again. He staggers but doesn't go down, which surprises Cory just a little. This foe may need a slug to go down and not from his fist. Roid Rage's pupils are dilated as if he's just been huffing something.

"That all you got, boy?" Roid Rage asks.

Cory doesn't engage with the shit talking but dodges the knife again. This time, though the man's knife is able to make contact with his stomach. It feels like a long bee sting across his middle. He's barely been nicked, but it pisses Cory off just the same. Paige screams with fear for him.

"She'll be doing a lot of that later on tonight," the man taunts with confidence. "I'll have her screamin' my name by the end of this day, asshole. She'll be screamin' all night long."

The corner of Cory's eye twitches. This bastard means to violate her if he wins this fight. The man lunges again, this time with less finesse and skill. Cory moves straight in on his opponent. Whatever the man is on has made him fast but not necessarily smarter or better-trained. They are locked up where the man can't stab at him anymore. Roid Rage tries to head-butt him, but Cory dodges the impact. The guy punches Cory in the stomach where he's been stabbed, obviously thinking the blow will incapacitate him. Roids doesn't know the conditioning that Cory and the rest of the men put themselves through. He simply tightens his stomach muscles and takes the hit easily.

He slides his arm through the other man's, effectively using an arm-bar technique to disable the man's right arm and the knife. Then he spins them both until he's behind the man. He swiftly takes the serrated dagger before his enemy even knows what's happened. He plunges the semi-dull knife into the other man's chest.

"Not with you she won't, motherfucker," Cory swears and stabs him again, this time to the heart.

He gives the bastard a good shove, sending him into the dark pit of hell that he'd likely constructed, the pit that almost took Paige's life. The man's dead body plummets to the ground with the knife still sticking out of his chest and lands with a loud thump at the bottom. Cory cocks his head to the side inspecting his work and mostly making sure that the man is indeed dead. Then he steps back. When he looks for Paige, she's still cowering over in the corner but has his rifle in her hands.

"Uh...hm...," Cory feels like he should apologize for the murder scene but awkwardly shrugs instead. What the hell can he say now anyway? He killed the dude in front of her. He'd do it again. He hadn't wanted to do something like that in front of her on this trip, but there wasn't exactly much of a choice. She knows he has a dark side. She'd witnessed it the first time they met. Cory just didn't really want to show it to her again. He's been working on being nicer to her. John is afraid that she will convince Simon to leave the farm with her if she is miserable. His mentor had basically threatened him to be nicer, and he'd taken well to the suggestion. Plus, lately he hasn't actually wanted to be mean to her. He has had a lot of other feelings that he also can't act on, though.

She's staring at the gaping hole the man disappeared into and she almost fell to her death through. Then she runs to him and flings herself against his chest. Her grip on the front of his jacket is enough to tear it to shreds. She's shaking like a leaf and breathing hard.

"Hey, it's ok," Cory tells her and pats her back uncomfortably. Where's her brother when she needs him? He wishes they would've brought Reagan with them. Of course, she's not exactly a consoling, tender woman. Plus, little Doc could've fallen through that floor and been the one killed by the trap. He takes his rifle from her, slinging it over his shoulder again.

"Are you hurt? Did you get hurt or dislocate anything? Did I hurt you when I pulled you up?" Cory asks in quick succession, concerned about his best friend's sister. "I pulled you too hard."

"I'm fine. I'm not dead, so I'd say I'm better than that guy," she says after a moment. "Jesus, you killed him. I mean... so fast... whoa."

271

"Sorry," he apologizes as she thinks about what her eyes have just witnessed. He hopes she has short-term memory loss from her traumatic near-death experience.

"Oh my God, did he stab you? It looked like he stabbed you!" Paige exclaims hysterically.

"Nah, just a scratch. I'm good," he reassures her.

"Let me see," she says, prying at the black t-shirt that is tucked into his pants.

Cory stays her hand and says, "I'm fine. We'll check it out later."

"I wanted to shoot him, to help you, but I wasn't sure if I'd hit you instead," she says with nerves in her voice.

"I didn't need your help," Cory reassures her. "If anything like that ever happens again, just stay out of my way."

She hasn't looked at him. Her face is still buried in his chest. She's scared out of her mind. He doesn't blame her. He probably would be if he'd almost fallen four stories, too. Plus the man's threats against her have likely shaken Paige. The thought of getting Simon's sister killed on his watch makes Cory feel nauseous. She could've died. She almost did. He could've been killed by Roid Rage, and she would've been taken and raped. Bile rises in his throat.

"I will," she says, interrupting his thoughts. "I'll stay out of the way. My first instinct was to run like I used to, but I didn't want to leave you behind."

Cory tries not to let her words mean too much. He's sure she just means because he's Simon's friend and that leaving him to possibly be killed would upset her brother. They stand there; her against his chest, him stroking her back more soothingly this time. His hand comes to rest on the back of her small skull. He can just imagine it cracking open if she'd fallen to the marble floor below them. She feels smaller in his arms than he would've thought.

"We should move," he says and steps away. Paige looks up at him with tears running down her cheeks and nods. "That was a trap. I don't know if he set it or if he was with a group of similar assholes, but let's not stick around and find out."

"Yes, that was a trap. Definitely," she says as she wipes at her damp cheeks with the sleeve of her jacket.

Cory retrieves his .45 from the floor, reholsters it and snaps the closure. He grabs Paige surely by the hand and leads her safely out of the room. At the end of the long hallway, he takes a moment to look out the window facing the street.

"We've got more company on the way and I don't think these fucks are comin' for tea," he informs her, pointing to the small crowd of people. "Looks like our friend had some friends of his own."

There are four men this time, all armed and coming toward the building. He's pretty sure it's the same men he spied earlier milling around the campus. They resemble their dead friend in their clean-cut appearances and manner of dress. What the fuck? Are they some sort of former college fraternity turned nefarious post-apocalyptic gang? Kappa Pi Thug? Three of them have rifles. Time to go.

"We need to get your dropped weapon," he says. "But first, we need a diversion. Wait right here."

Her eyes seem troubled, so he squeezes her shoulder firmly and says, "I'll be right back."

Cory takes a homemade smoke grenade from his pack. He and the other men make these for this exact reason. These little suckers make a great diversionary weapon. When he gets to the study room again, he ignites five books with his Zippo lighter and sets them near the broken window to ensure the smoke will plume out of it and draw the attention of the frat boys. Next, he ignites the string coming out of the smoke grenade and within a few seconds, purple smoke is also wafting in giant puffs through the window. Then he sprints back down the hall, collects Paige and makes his exit through a semi-darkened stairwell at the rear of the building. There are skylights high above them that permit a small bit of gray light into the narrow space. They move cautiously but quickly down to the first floor again. Before he opens the door, Cory waits and listens a moment.

"Here, Paige," he says and takes her pistol out of her hip holster. "Carry this. Safety's off, so finger off the trigger."

"Got it," she says firmly but quietly.

When they cross the threshold into the first floor area, Cory hooks a right which should lead them to the dead man and her rifle. He's not willing to leave it behind, even if it means they will be seen by those men. He'd hate to do it, but if need be he'll kill them all in front of her.

273

"Come," he instructs as he slinks around a corner. Paige follows softly in his wake. This time, she is much closer than before. Not having her rifle out in front of her probably isn't making her feel safe.

A shuffling of noisy people assaults his ears, causing him to stop, turn back and grab her arm to pull her around the corner with him again. She's apparently heard it, too, because she is frozen in place with fear. He presses his index finger to his lips and gets a nod of compliance from her.

A door slams at the other end of the hall, so Cory furtively pokes his head around the corner. It's all clear. Apparently they haven't seen their dead comrade in the other room. They seem panicked as if they are trying to get to the source of the smoke upstairs to inspect it. Cory steps into the corridor with Paige and crosses to the next area, which looks like a student lounge space. He presses her against the wall and sprints over to the dead man, who is lying on Paige's fallen rifle. Within a few seconds, he is able to dislodge it from underneath the man's body.

"Hey!" a shout from above rains down upon Cory. He looks up in time to see the other men glaring down through the trap hole at him. They've realized the fire was a diversion set by him. They've also seen their dead comrade on the floor where Cory stands beside him. One man manages to get off a shot from his handgun. Not needing encouragement, Cory barks off about six rounds from her rifle up at them, which causes them to jump back and scatter. He races back to Paige and smiles widely.

"It still works!" he says excitedly about her rifle.

Her answer is a disbelieving and slightly sarcastic, "Great."

She runs to the hole opening before he can stop her and rapid fires from her pistol about five times. A loud thudding sound from above followed by screams of pain rain down through the hole. Cory grasps her about the waist and hauls her away.

He's having a hard time not laughing, "I think you got one."

"Good!" Paige says testily and shrugs free of him.

He flicks her safety back on, tugs her hand gently and jogs toward another exit. They know they are down here. He can't take a risk of being caught in a firefight with her. If he was alone, he'd flank and kill them. They are the kind of men who would rape her no doubt, as their friend had implied. Since he's pretty sure she shot one of them, they'd kill her, too. Those men don't deserve to live. This time, they've gotten themselves a free pass.

"Through here," he says as he leads her down a narrower pass and into a commercial kitchen area. Through another door and they are out to the fading sun again. "We need to pick up the pace. Let me know when you need a rest."

"'Kay," she says hoarsely. "This is the part I'm usually good at. Don't worry about me."

He flashes her a grin which she returns as they fast walk and transition to jogging.

"You sure shooting people isn't the thing you're good at?"

She just shrugs and says, "They pissed me off."

They jog through the campus heading southwest, running faster from time to time and slower when she needs to. They periodically stop to listen and look for the Kappa club. Cory takes them farther away from the college and toward a more residential, smaller neighborhood. After a while it is apparent that they are no longer being followed, and he feels safe to stop with her.

He pulls her into an old stone church and says, "I know the downtown district is a no-fly zone. Same goes for anywhere near the river. We don't go there, either."

"What river? What do you mean?" she asks, her pale gray eyes still frightened. She is also panting lightly.

"The Cumberland River," he explains while looking out a few of the windows, or what's left of them, on the sly. "It's a dangerous area. Lot of tent cities set up over there. Some of the groups might not be too bad, but we've never stuck around to find out. As long as they seem harmless, we leave them alone. If they seem like they are thugs, then… well, you get the gist. When we come, we only go to the places that we know for sure are safe. This area was safe the last time we came. I don't know where those idiots came from. We've never actually raided on the campus grounds before, but the surrounding area used to be clear."

Paige inches closer to him until her arm is literally pressed against his side. Cory looks behind them deeper into the church to ascertain they are still alone. It seems to have been looted down to some of the pews. Even the holy water bowl is gone.

"The river itself is dangerous, too. It swells now without being controlled. It can get very unpredictable, but people live near it so that they have a source of water," Cory tells her.

275

Paige is standing with her back to the wall. Her posture is tense, her eyes still frightened.

Cory takes her chin in his hand and turns her head toward him, "Hey, we're fine. That was just a bump in the road. I won't let that happen again. They're long gone. All right?"

She nods her head, sending a strand of loose red hair over her right eye. Cory pushes it back behind her ear.

"I promised your brother I'd return you in one piece and I will."

A lopsided grin forms on her full mouth as a low rumble of thunder threatens to break up their sunny day.

"We didn't even get anything at the college," she says. "Should we go back and check it out?"

"No, not with just the two of us. Depending on what Simon and Sam find, we may be able to go back there tomorrow before we leave town. Unless we end up having to stay a second night. There are plenty of other places to loot around here. That was just one idea. The Kappa boys can have it."

Paige chuckles, "I never knew any fraternity kids like that."

"I think they belonged to a new kind," Cory jokes, trying to lighten her despair.

She drops to her knees in front of him and digs in her backpack.

"Let me see your knife wound from that jerk," she demands.

"I'm fine," he says.

"I'm not asking, Cory," Paige says with forceful intent.

He lets out a soft groan and untucks his shirt, pulling it up a few inches.

"Damn, Cory. This is kind of bad," she squints and bites her lower lip.

"No, it's just a scratch," he informs her and tries to lower his shirt again.

Paige's stops him, her hand closing over the back of his own. She whips out a small pink package from her bag. Then she removes the sanitary napkin from the package and presses it against him.

"I don't have anything to disinfect it, but this is sterile and should help until we meet up with Simon," Paige tells him from her squatted position.

He'd like for her to stop touching his bare stomach, even if she is trying to help. Her warm fingers against his skin is proving a bit much.

"Good enough," he says, grabbing for her thin, bony hand. "I've got a medic pack in my bag. We'll tend to this later."

Paige swats him away and continues blotting the blood with gentle dabs. He wishes she'd get to her feet. Seeing her knelt before him and the feel of her warm breath hitting his skin is entirely too much. She's about to learn just how much he really doesn't need Viagara.

"I wish Simon was here now. I don't know too much about this kind of stuff. He'd know if you need stitches," she laments.

"I don't," Cory says tightly.

"I'm not sure. I don't think so, either, but what do I know? He'd probably want to put some kind of stinky, herbal poultice on it or something. Then he'd have you drink some gross tea that tastes like the cow barn smells and you'd sleep for three days," Paige tells him with a wrinkle of her freckled nose at the mention of the cows.

He can barely even offer a pained grin and a single huff when she glances up at him. Cory jerks his bag free and unzips it, quickly finding the duct tape. He rips off a few small pieces and pats them down on the edges of the pad. Then he grabs her slim shoulders and hauls her to her feet.

"Really?" Paige asks dryly. "Duct tape?"

Cory shrugs and replies, "I am a man, aren't I. Thanks for the concern, but it'll be fine."

He's still holding her by the shoulders, and she regards him with a confused stare. Her eyes drop from his eyes to his mouth. They become hooded, her cheeks flushed. He's seen this look from women before.

"We need to go," Cory says abruptly and sets her away from him so he can tuck in his shirt again. Then he zips his black jacket.

Paige stammers, "Right, right. We should keep moving."

"There's a university hospital close by. It's small but could be useful," he tells her. "We've never raided it yet, but the area is good."

"What about those guys? Aren't they at the university?"

"It's not that close to the hospital, different campus. It's a big place. We'll be safe," Cory tries to assure her, but Paige frowns hard and looks upset enough to cry again. Cory touches her arm lightly and says, "They won't find us. It's spread out enough between the hospital grounds and the school that they won't find us."

"Ok, let's hit it," Paige says firmly, but she's still standing in front of him with a dazed expression.

"Stay close," he tells her and heads to the door.

They make it to Vanderbilt Hospital without problems. Cory avoids the front and decides to go in tactical from the side. From this angle, he can still see the tall brick buildings of Vanderbilt University, which is good because he can spy on their enemy once he takes a high position in the hospital. It seems like a safer bet in light of current events. On the hospital grounds, they wade through the tall grass, uncontrolled foliage, and the hedges which haven't been trimmed in four years. Cory finds a door on the side of the building, an emergency exit. He presses in, and the door surprisingly opens with some gentle persuasion. They creep inside, and Cory is overly cautious after their issues with the Roid Kappa Beta Gang.

The pharmacy on the first floor is completely trashed; not a trace of medicine is left. He points up, and they take the non-moving escalator. He has no idea how grass is growing here and there through the metal slats. The former hospital is so humid that it's like a damn terrarium. They move slowly, him in the lead.

Cory doesn't mention the long, black snake he saw slithering around a corner at the other end of the hall from the pharmacy. He figures that Paige isn't a fan of snakes. Most women aren't, at least not the ones he's ever known.

A high-pitched shriek rains down upon them as they ascend the escalator. They both freeze in their tracks. Cory glances around, causing Paige to bump into his back. He's not sure if it was a bird, perhaps an owl. The screeching comes again.

"What the…" Paige exclaims on a sharp inhale. "Are you freagin' kidding me?"

There is a black monkey perched on the handrail at the top of the escalator. It is nearly all black except for a small white patch on its face, and Cory thinks he saw a group of them at a zoo once with Em. It's not as big as a baboon, but the next time it screeches, there are some seriously sharp looking teeth exposed. He thinks they might be called a howler something or other.

"Careful, we'll go slowly. Let's not piss it off if we can help it," Cory says. "I don't want to have to shoot it."

278

"I don't care if you have to shoot it," Paige says softly. "That thing is freaking me out."

The animal hisses angrily. They make it up to the second floor without incident from the monkey. It jumps down and scuttles away when they get within ten stairs from it, but not before sending another blaring scream at them. It must be trying to intimidate them. Cory steps onto the second floor and ushers Paige toward a wall. The monkey is less than fifty feet away. He's not sure if it is afraid of humans. He's not even sure if it has ever seen a human before. Then Cory spots the other ones. There must be ten of them. Cory waves his rifle at them and shouts loudly. They all take off on all fours down the hall and disappear from his line of sight. Beside him, Paige shivers.

"That wins the prize for the weirdest shit I've seen since the fall," she remarks.

"Yeah, that was strange," Cory agrees. "Let's keep moving."

They begin raiding rooms and nurses' stations for anything they can salvage. He uses the butt of his rifle to break the lock on a steel door behind the third such station they come to. Once inside, he doesn't find as much as he'd hoped they would. Perhaps the nursing staff that used to work in this hospital had taken the supplies with them when they put in their two-week's apocalypse notice. They do take some bandaging, some sort of antibiotic salves in tubes, a box of needles to which Paige grimaces, some random bottles of medicines that are mostly expired, a box of plastic gloves, a couple rubber bags that look like they are used for some sort of procedure he probably doesn't want to understand, a few packages of scalpel-style tools, medical tape and a stethoscope.

In the hallway again, Cory leads Paige around a tipped over wheelchair on their way to a stairwell. He needs higher ground. He decides to take her to the top floor so that he can overlook the hospital grounds and hopefully some of the college. They cross to the farthest southwest corner on the top floor, and Cory peers through binoculars out the dirty, cloudy window.

"What are you doing?" Paige inquires quietly.

"Watching for our friends," Cory answers honestly.

"See anyone?"

"No, but it doesn't mean they aren't out there somewhere looking for us," Cory tells her as a bolt of lightning streaks across the gray, dusk sky. "Let's raid a few more floors for the same stuff and head out of here. We might not make it to the Parthenon before this storm hits. It's a little over a mile or so northwest of here, but we would need to find a way around the school so we don't run into the Roid gang. It might make the run over there a little longer, so we'll leave before dark. Looks like we're still gonna get soaked."

"Really?" Paige asks as if she's too tired to make the trek.

Cory hadn't anticipated this from her. Of course, maybe hanging on for dear life and straining her muscles and then running with him to get away from creeps has exhausted her.

"The Parthenon's close to a big park, but we'll go out around it if we can in case anyone's loitering there. It's also close to a lake, but the last time your brother and I came to this district, it was completely abandoned and safe. That's why we picked it with John and Kelly the other day as the meeting place."

"Oh, ok," she says on a fatigued sigh.

"Let's just finish here in this hospital and I'll decide what we're gonna do. Maybe if we can catch Simon and Sam before they drive over there, we'll hitch a ride. We've got some time, though so let's not waste it."

"Right," Paige agrees.

"Wait," he says, considering her. "Are you hungry or anything?"

She shakes her head with a frown, "No. Not at all. I think my stomach sank permanently when I fell in that trap. It's a little sick actually, so I'm good. No food for me for a while. Maybe for a couple days."

Cory grins at her humor, but wonders if he should call Simon now and stop for the day. Maybe this is too much for her. He scowls hard at her, thinking about stopping for the night with her now instead of a few hours from now.

"I'm all right," she says, reading his indecision. "I don't want to eat and I don't want to stop, either. We need to find more supplies for the clinic and the farm. I don't want to waste this trip."

Cory doesn't answer but gives her a simple nod. He leads Paige through the hospital and ends up on some sort of maternity ward floor. Cory is completely out of his league, so he lets her lead. He also lets her decide what to take from the nurses' station and the surgical rooms they find. He follows her slim hips down a dark hallway, trying not to stare at her figure as they go. They come to a baby birthing room, or at least that's what he figures it is by the looks of it.

"What the fuck is this thing?" Cory asks as he picks up a stainless steel device from a drawer with a look of horror on his face.

"You don't even want to know," Paige answers with a smile and shakes her head, sending her loose red waves over her shoulder. Her braid is more undone than neat and tidy.

Cory scowls and sets the instrument back down. He hopes the shoe horn mechanism was never used. He subconsciously wipes his palm on his pants, getting a chuckle from Paige. She picks up a few other items and stashes them in her pack.

"We can go to the floor where they offer proctology exams," she quips.

"No thanks," Cory jests. "I don't think I'm ready for one of those."

She chuckles, which is nice to hear from her. At least she isn't crying anymore. She seems sad a lot, even back at the farm. She doesn't mope around or feel sorry for herself, but she just seems unhappy. Perhaps it is because her friend was killed or the other one moved to the next farm over. Maybe it's because her parents are gone and she sees the McClane family and their love and joy and it's just too much for her. He's not sure. Hannah would probably know better than anyone else. He has no idea how to cheer up a woman or, more importantly, how their brains operate.

"You wanna' hop up on here for an exam?" he jokes and pats the stainless steel table. "We could play doctor."

In a strange and unexpected turn, Paige climbs onto the table and regards him with a plucky stare. The eyebrow has arched again.

"Doctor, I have this terrible ache," Paige teases with a sexy pout and drawl. She even coyly chews her thumbnail.

Cory clears his voice and grinds his teeth together. She pulls her new lip balm from her pants pocket and spreads it on her lips. Then she puckers her mouth and makes a smacking sound with her lips.

"I'm ready when you are, Doctor," she further instigates.

Cory shifts to his other foot, his grip on his rifle tightens, and he gives her a stern glare. He hadn't anticipated her calling him out. He was just trying to make her laugh and now he's chuckling nervously.

"Quit foolin' around," he reprimands in a more austere tone.

281

Paige cocks her head to the side and hits him with those gray-blue eyes of hers, "I thought you *wanted* to fool around."

She raises her pale red brows in two quick jerks to taunt him further. His patience is wearing thin. So is his resistance. He'd like to push her down on this cold table and show her how serious he really is.

"All talk and no play, huh?" she jeers and hops back down.

"Playing is for children," Cory informs her. She takes a few steps closer and raises her chin defiantly. "I wouldn't be playing."

Her chest rises and falls at a faster rate, and her full red mouth parts just slightly. Then she makes the mistake of letting her gaze fall to his mouth. Cory's no fool. He knows she wants him to kiss her. Her eyes start to fall shut, and she sways closer. Out of respect for Simon, he tugs her hand and whips around to leave the surgical suite, the place where babies were delivered. He has no desire to procreate one.

"Let's move," he orders forcefully as a bead of sweat runs down his left temple.

They take what they can from the last few floors as the rain starts coming down outside. It begins as a light sprinkle and quickly turns to a torrential downpour. They definitely aren't going to make it to the other side of the city.

Chapter Nineteen
Simon

The four-door, sleek black sedan drives slowly by, pauses for a long time at the rear of Doc's SUV. Simon slows his breathing and places his hand over Sam's to keep her still. She's afraid. He can read the fear in her eyes. He's not too thrilled with the idea of being caught like sitting ducks in the vehicle, but he's not afraid. He has enough firepower to disable anyone who wants to fight. He'd rather not do it with Sam in the car with him, but there's no helping it now. They're stuck in a bad place.

The black car keeps going past them. It stops every so often at different vehicles and pauses like it had at the rear of theirs. Simon watches from his concealed position. He can't see inside the darkly tinted windows to discern if there is just one person or five or ten crammed in there. The basement floor of the parking deck being so dark isn't helping him size up his potential competition. The car stops in the next aisle, backs up and comes toward them. Sam inhales sharply.

"Easy, Sam," he reassures her. "Don't move."

He can just barely make out her blue eyes in the dimly lit vehicle. But he can hear her fast breathing. She's scared and worried. He'd like to tell her that everything will be fine, but he can't bring himself to do so. He doesn't like this fighting position.

The car trolls past them, pausing again. Simon slides the sniper rifle up closer to his shoulder in case he needs it. Then the other car disappears from sight and progresses back up the ramp toward other floors or the exit. He's not sure where it's going, but he also doesn't care. He needs to get them out of this basement. He needs to get Samantha to safety. Simon exhales his held breath and sits up fully again, adjusting his seat lever and then Sam's.

283

"Do you think they saw us?" Sam asks with fear in her soft voice.

"I don't know, but we're not stickin' around to find out," Simon tells her and starts the vehicle.

"Who were they?" she asks as she starts packing away their gear.

"No idea. Could be looking for someone. Could be dangerous or just someone looking for gas," he estimates.

"Where are we going?"

"Let's pull around to the back of the hospital and we'll go in through there. I'll find another place over there to stash the car," he explains. "I don't want us to leave the car here in case they come back and find our stuff. They could also take it if they know how to hotwire this thing."

He puts the SUV in reverse just as the sound of squealing tires reaches his ears. Soon, the same headlights come careening back down the ramp toward them. This time they aren't trolling. They've spotted them or noticed their lights.

"It's them again!" Sam nearly yells.

"Put on your seatbelt," Simon orders as he slams the SUV into drive.

He maneuvers the vehicle out of the way just in the nick of time before the other car would've crashed into them and prevented their escape. This time as the car passes them, Simon gets a better look at the driver and his passenger. It appears to be just two people, a man and a woman. They look desperate. He's not waiting around to find out. The woman in the passenger seat had a shotgun.

He speeds out of the hospital parking deck, nearly ramps the exit onto the street. The big SUV slams into the pavement. Simon takes a hard left heading north.

"We've gotta lose them," Simon tells her.

"There they are!" Sam exclaims, looking over her seat and out the wide back window.

Simon maneuvers the cumbersome vehicle around an abandoned truck that is flipped onto its side in the middle of the road. He has to use the sidewalk to get around it. He's driving at a fast speed for all the debris that's in the way. Sam squeals as he bounces the SUV back onto the road. They both get tossed around along with the items in the trunk. He's glad she has on her seatbelt.

He hooks a right and revs the engine to pick up the pace. A trashcan in the road gets plowed through, sending old newspapers and trash into the air. Some of it lands on the car behind them.

"What do they want?" Sam cries.

Simon doesn't answer her. There's no good answer to offer if these people are in such hot pursuit of them. He just keeps going, swerving around a motorcycle on its side and then a semi-truck taking up most of the four lanes of the road.

"Sam, open your window and send a few rounds downrange. We need to scare them off," he tells her.

Before he even has the words out, Simon spies in the rearview mirror as the driver, a large man, sticks a pistol out his window and fires a shot at them first.

"Get down!" he yells and pushes her head toward her knees. Damn. The shot doesn't hit their vehicle. At least he doesn't think it did, but he can't be too sure. "Sam, I need you to drive. I'm gonna need to take them out."

Simon hates this. He hates having her in danger, and he hates hurting people. Why couldn't they have just left them alone?

"Oh goodness," his little companion frets.

"Just climb over here onto my lap and switch places, honey," he orders calmly, although he feels nothing that even comes close to calm.

"Oh goodness," she repeats but unhooks her seatbelt.

"You're fine," he reassures her as he whips a hard right and picks up speed again. He doesn't want that man shooting at them again. If he gains enough speed, he's pretty sure the distance between them will deter the other man or his partner from taking another wasteful shot.

Sam pushes up the center arm-rest and slides over closer to him. He hands her his sniper rifle, which she promptly lays on the vacant passenger seat. Then she climbs onto his lap carefully. It's a good thing she's small. Simon takes one hand off the wheel and covers her head with it. He knows it's a stupid thing, but he feels like he could stop a bullet from hitting her there if the other people shoot at them again.

"Take the wheel," he orders softly and she does. "Steady."

He scoots out from under her, peeking in the mirror as he does so. They've lost some speed during the switch and now the other people are closing in on them again.

"Make a left up ahead," he tells her.

"I'm not that good of a driver, you know," she complains at him.

Simon almost grins. John had taught her and then Huntley to drive on the farm because she'd never had the opportunity to learn before the apocalypse. His own mother had paid for him to take a driving course at an expensive school in Arizona. His father had thought it necessary for Simon to understand the concept of defensive driving being a senator's kid. His father had a few death threats against him over the years. Paige had gone through the same thing. But Sam's not exactly ready for a high-speed chase while being shot at.

"You're doing fine. Just try to keep it steady and don't jerk the wheel. I need a clean couple of shots," Simon tells her.

He climbs over the seat with his rifle and then over the second row, as well. When he gets to the back row of seats where he and Sam usually sit, he pries open the half window above the tailgate. He hopes it doesn't break from being left open while they are zigzagging around town. Something like that would not be replaceable.

Sam cries out and yells, "Oh, Simon, hold on!"

They hit something in the road, and the right side of the SUV skids against something just briefly. The sound of metal scraping against metal assaults his ears.

"Oops! Sorry," she calls back.

He has no idea what she's run into, but Simon also doesn't dwell on it. He takes a deep breath as another shot is fired from the other car. He thinks it hits the driver's side mirror because Sam screams.

"You ok?" he shouts.

"Yes, it didn't hit me. It just hit the mirror."

"Keep it steady, Sam. I'm taking aim," Simon calls out to her calmly.

He pokes the silencer-equipped barrel of his rifle through the open window and sights in on the driver of the black car. He has shot moving targets before, but the man has figured it out that he's after him and is swerving recklessly all over the road. This isn't just leading a moving target. This target is like shooting at an intoxicated person behind the wheel. Simon takes aim and squeezes, blasting through their windshield. He's missed both of them. The woman yells out her window at him. He's pretty sure it's not much more than swearing. It's certainly not a friendly greeting.

Sam swerves something in the road which throws him onto his side. He rights himself as another shot is fired from the other vehicle. This time it sounds like it has hit their bumper. The sound is different this time, too. The woman has fired the shotgun and is hanging half out of the passenger side window.

Simon pulls the rifle erect again and steadies his shot. He takes a faster aim this time and fires. He hits the driver dead center to the chest. Another quick succession shot and he's hit him in the right shoulder. Their vehicle skids, spins hard to the right and crashes into a building with a brick façade. It hits very hard because of their high rate of speed and not having time to apply the brakes.

Sam slows down to a crawl. He knows for certain that he's killed the driver, but he isn't sure if the woman survived the crash. Smoke is billowing out of the mangled hood and front end of the disabled car.

"Stop," Simon tells her.

They sit there in the middle of the road for a moment waiting for movement from the other car.

He whispers in repetition, "Don't get out."

Finally the woman stumbles from the car. And she isn't happy to have lost her partner or husband or whatever he was to her.

"Damn it," Simon swears.

She comes out cursing and shooting at them with the shotgun. Simon hates to do it, but he takes her out. These moments weigh on his conscience at night when the day is over, the work is done, and he's alone with his own thoughts. When he's not thinking about Samantha, he's thinking about murdering people and whether or not he'll ever find God's forgiveness for what he's done. He also wonders what his mother would think of the person he's become. She was a genteel, sweet woman. She was so much like Sam. They would've gotten along great. She only ever thought of others and was of a kind disposition. He's not so sure she would be proud of his latest accomplishments, of the lives he's taken, of the people he's killed in cold blood. These are the moments of his life for which he is ashamed.

He lowers the gun and signals with his hand for Sam to keep driving. After a few moments, he shuts the rear window and joins her in the front again.

"Pull over," he tells her. "Up there in that cemetery, Sam."

They are in a relatively remote area. A cemetery is always a desolate place, even after the world falls apart. However, they look differently than they used to. The grass is as high and unkempt as it is on the great plains of the West. A few of the tombstones have even fallen over. She pulls in, going quite a distance around the lot until she finds a place to park behind a long row of mausoleums, where some douchebag has thrown buckets of red and yellow paint on the sides. They even left the empty paint cans. She cuts the engine and sits back with a deep sigh.

"I'll be right back," Simon tells her and hastily exits the truck.

He darts quickly behind one of the tombs and vomits. He knows it isn't from the bumpy, fast ride through the city but from the fact that he had to shoot a woman. Again. Damn it.

Sam comes up behind him as he stands straight again and wordlessly hands him a piece of cloth. Then she hands him her bottle of water to rinse out his mouth. He swigs a few times and spits, thankful for the clean, minty taste. She rubs his back soothingly.

"I'm sorry you had to do that, Simon," she tells him with sincere sympathy.

"I was hoping she'd stop, that she'd just stay in that car," he admits with regret edging through his voice. "Why couldn't she have stayed in the car, Sam?"

"I know," she says and rubs his back some more.

The rain clouds that have been threatening to unleash a downpour final open up to replenish the earth.

"She looked like someone's grandmother," Simon confesses and turns to face her.

"She didn't look like my grandmother. My grandma wore cardigans with flamingoes on them and had white hair and smelled like cookies. That woman looked crazy, like she was on drugs or something."

"I think she was," Simon agrees. "Maybe they were cooking homemade drugs or alcohol. Her eyes were insane."

Sam's bright blue eyes stare up into his with concern, "I know. I saw her, too. I don't know why they did that. They were definitely going to kill us. Maybe for our vehicle or for our guns."

Simon interrupts her, "Or for you, Sam. And that's not going to happen. That's never going to happen again. I promise you that. I'll kill every person in this godforsaken city if I have to."

"I know," she answers simply.

The rain coming down picks up in intensity and volume. Simon rests his hand against her soft, pale cheek. He tries to focus on her wet skin and trusting eyes and not the dirt and grime and gunpowder residue on his fingers. The temperature is dropping fast.

"Don't worry. I'll keep you safe," he promises.

"I know," she repeats. She closes in on his personal space and hugs Simon. "I'll keep you safe, too."

Simon chuffs softly and nods. She leads him back to the Suburban, this time getting in on the passenger side and leaving the driver's position for him. He starts the SUV and cranks up the heat for her. The last thing he needs is Sam getting sick.

"You did pretty well, Miss Samantha Patterson, for not really knowing how to drive. Well, not in a high-speed chase around a post-apoc city," he praises as he locks the doors after they are seated. He checks the rearview mirror quite a few times.

"Thanks," she says. "I used to watch action movies with my dad, so I think it must've rubbed off. I'm probably gonna be the next Steve McQueen."

Simon laughs. She's the only person that could make him laugh after such a traumatic event. He's never seen a movie with Steve McQueen, but he knows of the actor and his reputation for being an all-around badass.

"Of course, I did run over that street sign and hit that parked car," she admits with a jaunty frown.

Simon laughs again and says, "All right, so you're not ready to be a Hollywood stunt driver any time soon, but you did all right."

She laughs at herself and says, "I hope I didn't mess up Grandpa's car. That street sign snuck up on me."

"Snuck isn't a word," he corrects and gets a wide-eyed, irritated look from her. "Sorry. You did very well."

"Do you think we should check the damage?"

289

"Not right now. It's running. That's all that matters," he says. "Let's hurry back over to the hospital and hit it again before we have to meet my sister and Cory. We've got maybe an hour or so."

"Ok, Simon," Sam says with a nod. "Let's go."

He maneuvers the giant SUV back to the hospital, after he figures out where they are on the map. It seemed like their chase scene through the streets lasted for an hour, when in fact it probably only lasted a few minutes and didn't throw them too far off their schedule.

This time, Simon parks behind the hospital under an overhang meant for an ambulance or perhaps a funeral home hearse. They sneak through the ER, find nothing there and head upstairs. Simon is more alert than he was earlier. And earlier he'd been on edge. Sam goes ahead of him down a darkened hallway. He watches their backs. Simon lets her go because the hospital is deserted. He's sure of it. The only things they've run into during their search of the basement and first two floors have been a flock of swallows like the ones that hang out in the barn rafters at the farm, and then a stray cat with a litter of kittens under an empty bed in a patient room. Sam had wanted to take them with her. Simon had put his foot down, but he'd allowed her to leave the cat the remainder of her sandwich. Then he'd felt bad and left the extra slice of ham from his own sack.

Simon takes the folded rucksack out of his bag. He predicts they'll need it for additional storage. So far, they've found some items that will be helpful at the clinic. Sam calls him over to inspect a tipped over nurse's cart that she's found.

He squats, and they rummage through it. Most of the items are still inside. They find some syringes and rubber tourniquets, three bottles of antibiotics, one bottle of painkilling medicine, a blood pressure cuff, a few bottles of liquid calcium chloride, a small glass bottle of nitrates, and a few other heart meds. This was likely a post-op ward for heart patients.

"These pills should help with some of the older patients, right? I recognize some of the names on these bottles," Sam comments as she helps him dump the contents into the sack.

"Yes, I think so," he agrees. "Let's check the other side of this floor. It may have been a post-op floor, so let's see if there are other meds or supplies in the other wing."

290

"Sounds good," Sam says, following him after they've cleaned out the nurses' stations, as well.

"Do you think those people knew we were in the hospital, Simon?"

He shakes his head and says, "No, I don't think so. I've been thinking about it."

She interrupts with a snarky, "I have no doubt."

"Anyways, I think they probably had a lot of the parking decks and lots memorized. If they noticed new cars, they probably figured they were going to yield a good find or gas or supplies."

"Maybe," Sam considers. "What do you think they wanted? Our car?"

"Could be, but their car seemed fine, nice even," he remembers. "They may have wanted to rob us for the gas or for food."

"We'll never know now," she replies. "Oh well. They were obviously bad. I mean I feel terrible and all, but they were gonna kill us for sure. If they weren't, then they would've approached us peacefully and asked for help."

"Yeah, that's what I think, too," he agrees with a nod. "I still feel like crap about it."

"Don't," she demands softly. "They were evil. It's that simple now. There's no middle. It's just bad or good. People that will kill us for our stuff or nice people who either want to join us or need our help."

"You're probably right," he says as they pass a long row of foggy glass windows that overlook a garden area on the ground level complete with a fountain. The area looks like a jungle.

"I'm always right. When are you gonna learn? For a smart guy, you sure don't seem to be getting this," Sam says with pluck.

Simon chuffs and grins down at the top of her head. She's not kidding, either. She's entirely serious, which just makes her adorably rotten.

"That fountain down there must run on solar power," he says, pointing to the garden. The water is green and likely slimy, too.

Sam grimaces and says, "Awesome, wanna' swim?"

"I don't even think the chickens would drink out of that," he says with a frown. "Come on."

They walk quickly to the other wing where it proves just as fortuitous. Most of the obvious places like the medicine supply rooms are raided, the doors crashed in and the rooms emptied. But other supplies that their clinic could use are still available. This side of the floor is also a step-down wing. They find clamps, forceps, bite blocks, Lidocaine, alcohol pads, Dopamine, Epinephrine and quite a few other medicines in cabinets and carts. He also grabs an entire box of saline flush syringes, which is an important find for the clinic. Sam finds intubation supplies in another area. Simon lastly grabs a stack of new, sterile- yet rather dusty- scrubs and surgical gowns for the clinic.

"What about one more floor?" Sam suggests.

"No, let's get moving again," he says as they walk quickly to the rear of the building, intent on using the stairs there to take them back toward the ER and the hidden and hopefully undisturbed SUV. "The sun has almost set, so we should head over to the Parthenon. I don't want Cory to worry about us. We need to be on time."

"Right, we should get going," she agrees with a grin.

"Let me see the map. I'm not entirely sure which route I want to take there. We're not far from it, maybe a few blocks or so."

They pause going down the stairs and squat to give their legs a break. They've been on the move all day.

Sam chuckles as she hands him the map from her bag and says, "Sometimes it's ok to get a little lost, Simon. Take the road less traveled and all."

"No thanks. That's not something we can afford to do anymore. The roads less traveled tend to end up being dangerous, not mystical and adventurous."

"Who knows? Maybe we'll have to explore some of those roads for ourselves someday," she says.

"Thanks, but I like the road back to the farm best," he admits.

"Yes," she says with a demure smile, "that's a good one."

Simon is taken away by her smile, as usual. Her dark hair is still slightly damp from the rain, but it does nothing to detract from her beauty. She's pulled it loose of its ponytail holder and now it hangs around her shoulders in waves of ebony disarray.

"Ok, I know which way we'll go," he tells her, folds the map and tucks it into her backpack for her.

"What if I choose another way?" she asks with a lift of her chin.

"We'll still go the way I choose," he says decisively, earning an impudent stare from her.

They both rise, but Sam just stands there with her fisted hands on her hips.

"What?" Simon asks with confusion.

"Really, Simon?" Sam say angrily. "Don't be such a dictator."

"I'm not being a dictator," he replies. "What are you talking about?"

Sam just rolls her eyes at him and says, "Never mind."

Then she brushes past him and tries to take the lead down the dark stairwell. Simon grabs her shoulder before she gets more than a few stairs ahead of him and halts her. He flicks on his dim flashlight and squeezes past her. His light jumps around as he goes, catching a dead and decayed corpse a few steps further down. Sam gasps with horror. Then she edges closer and takes his hand. Maybe she isn't so angry with the dictator, after all.

Chapter Twenty
Sam

By the time they get to the Parthenon, a light snow has mixed with the cold rain. The wind has picked up, and she hopes Cory and Paige are already there.

"Alpha Dog to PeeWee Little Fella', come in, over," Cory teases across the radio.

Simon shakes his head and scowls at his friend's humor.

"Professor here, go ahead," Simon returns, not feeling the love for the new handles that Cory has just assigned them.

"We're not gonna make the rendezvous point," Cory tells them. "Are you there yet, over?"

Sam is upset by this news. Simon also seems to be so because his jaw clenches with distress.

"We made it and are almost set," Simon says calmly.

"We're too far out, over," Cory tells them.

"We'll come to you," Simon offers. "What's your position?"

She knows he is looking for some sort of information that will let him know of their exact location in the city without forcing Cory to just blurt it over the radio. They never know if someone could be on the same channel as them. They must take precautions against unsafe radio chatter.

"Nah, too far. Don't go to the nerdville, either. Hotspot," Cory informs them.

She assumes he means Vanderbilt University. That's a shame if vandals and vagrants have taken it over. It used to be such a lovely old school full of beautiful brick buildings and landscaped lawns.

"Are you in trouble, over?" Simon asks with worry.

"Negative. We're all good. Gonna lock it down for the night somewhere else, over."

"New rendezvous point?"

There is a long pause and then static and another pause.

"We'll meet at Dick's, over," Cory suggests.

Simon looks over at Sam and shakes his head confusedly. Sam offers a shrug. They aren't sure where Cory means for the meeting place.

"Repeat," Simon tells him.

"Hunt, fish, camp, over," Cory says.

"Oh!" Sam exclaims, catching on. "He means Dick's Sporting Goods. I think there's one over east of the college, Vanderbilt where they were. He must've gone there with Paige or passed it today sometime."

"Got it," Simon says into the receiver of the walkie-talkie. "Oh-nine-hundred. We'll meet you at your namesake."

Sam's mouth falls open. She can't believe that Simon's making a joke, first of all; and two, she can't believe that he'd say something so crude.

"Later, dude," Cory says. "Don't do anything I wouldn't do."

Simon replies, "That doesn't leave much. Later."

He maneuvers the big SUV onto the overgrown lawn of the Parthenon and drives around toward the back. They've already driven by it twice to ascertain that nobody was squatting there. It seems safe, but like so many places they've been over the years, it could be a cesspool of criminals who would harm them.

"I hope they've found somewhere warm to stay tonight," Sam comments. "We've got the only heater, so I don't know what they'll do."

"They'll be fine," Simon tells her as he pulls the car close to the building and a rear exit. "I'm sure he'll build them a fire or something."

Sam sniffs hard, her nose running from the low temperature outside the vehicle and her hair being wet through. Then she sneezes.

"Great, now you're getting sick," Simon says angrily. "I knew you should've stayed home."

"I'm fine, Simon. I'm just a little chilly. We'll get warmed up soon enough," she assures him.

"You're probably gonna have pneumonia," he says with fervor and cuts the engine.

They both look around at their dark surroundings. They are late getting to the meeting spot. They were supposed to be here sooner to make sure nobody was around. She's thinking it's probably a good thing Cory and Paige didn't beat them to the Parthenon in case danger awaits them inside.

"I'm not getting sick. Stop," Sam insists. "I don't need a father, Simon."

The look he sends her lets Sam know that she has definitely irritated him and that he strongly disagrees with her.

"Let's go," she says impatiently and gets out of the vehicle.

Simon meets her around back and snatches her arm.

"Hey, I'm in charge here, young lady," he scolds. "I say when it's safe to go in. I wanted to wait out here a while longer to make sure nobody comes out."

"Too bad," Sam argues. She's watching tiny snowflakes land on his deep cheekbones and eyelashes. "And nobody told me that you're in charge anyways, so I think you're just making that up to lord it over me."

Simon frowns hard at her. "Your defiance lately is starting to wear thin, Samantha."

Sam just snorts through her nose and ignores him.

"Let's go in and check it out first. We'll come back for our gear once it's clear inside," he reluctantly agrees. "Just stay close. You never know."

"I think it's empty," Sam says. "Someone would've come out when they saw our headlights. Or shot at us. That seems to be a popular thing to do today."

Simon offers a lopsided grin and nods. "Right. Let's hope the shooting is done for the day. I just want to get you inside. Then we need to get you warmed up."

"Hm, sounds like that could be promising," Sam remarks with a sly smile, making Simon blush. "Are you gonna do it the same way you did in the back of the clinic?"

Referring to the kiss is off limits, but she can't seem to stop herself from bringing it up. She thinks about it often- his arms around her, his mouth so greedily moving on hers. These memories are all she'll ever get for intimacy between them. She knows Simon will never allow it to happen again.

"Not funny," he tells her and takes his handgun from his hip holster.

"It was kinda' funny," Sam mumbles as she trails after Simon to climb the stairs of the rear entrance to the massive structure.

They come to a long, open-air hallway of sorts with the massive pillars resembling the original Greek Parthenon. Sam was struck by their sheer size and beauty when she'd come with her mother. At night, however, they seem imposing, the dark corridor frightening. The pillars loom skyward to a thick roofline that must be fifty feet overhead. Water is puddled around some of the bases of the large structures. Vines climb around a few. Shadows bounce around as their flashlight beams aim forward and down. Anyone could be hiding behind one of the pillars or in a dark corner. This will be a tricky area to secure. They sneak around to a service entrance, but the steel door is locked.

"Hold my flashlight," Sam tells Simon.

She takes her lock picking kit from her pack and gets to work. She's usually faster than he is with breaking and entering. If only her parents could see her now. She doubts that lock picking, shooting at people, or fast car chases would impress them much with how she's turned out. A few seconds later, she has the lock disengaged, and they enter the tall building. Simon relocks the door so that nobody can sneak in behind them.

As they move forward, passing a maintenance room, Sam can hear the soft dripping of water somewhere. She wonders if the roof has a leak. The water pinging echoes eerily in the massive building.

"We'll take those with us when we leave tomorrow," Simon tells her, pointing at the shelf full of cleaning products.

"'Kay," she whispers. He's obviously not as spooked by this structure and the strange sounds.

They leave the back room and head toward the public areas of the museum. The building is rectangular and very dark, which takes them a long time to search. There are ornate castings along the ceiling, a two-story gold statue of the Greek goddess Athena on the second floor, and sculptures molded into the architecture. Their footsteps sound like those of a giant clomping around on the marble flooring, making it difficult to be sneaky. Sam feels bad that Paige wasn't able to meet up with them. She knows how much her new friend loves architecture.

Finally after every area and hidden nook and cranny are searched, Simon calls it safe to sack out. They unload their provisions for the night from the Suburban and set up in a small gallery room where paintings from some famous American artists were kept. A few even still hang on the walls. Sam knows he has chosen this room because it was one of the few with a lockable door, even if they are glass.

They quietly work together to get their temporary camp set up. Sam lights the two short beeswax candles from her sack and places one on the floor and one on a nearby bench. He lights the two from his bag and does the same. Everyone's bags are stocked with the same basic supplies and provisions in case they get separated. They have enough to survive about three days, which is also the same amount of time it would take to travel on foot back to the farm if they had to.

Simon gets the small kerosene heater ignited while she unpacks their sleeping bags and food. She's starving and knows Simon must be even more so since he retched his lunch in the cemetery after he was forced to kill that woman. She can't judge him for it. He'd done it to keep her safe. She's seen him do it before.

"Mm, Sue and Hannie packed us jars of roast pork and potatoes and carrots," she informs Simon as he shucks off his wet coat.

"Sam, you'd better change. I'll get that heating," Simon suggests. "You will get sick if you don't change out of your wet clothing."

Sam nods and rises from her knelt position near their crate of food stuff. She glances around the mostly empty room. There really isn't anywhere to change with any modicum of privacy.

"Um, I'm going to go out in the hall to change," she tells him.

"I don't think that's a good idea," Simon disagrees. "Just change over there in the corner. It's dark over there behind that half wall. I won't see you."

"No way," she argues. "I'm going out to the hall. I'll be right back."

Simon furrows his brow and gives her a disparaging look.

"I'm ignoring you and all your brooding stares tonight, Simon," Sam says as she goes out the door with one lit candle and her backpack.

She makes fast work of it, though. She'd been confident of her plan of changing in another room without him, but being out in the pitch dark hallway is about as spooky as it gets. The ancient-inspired building creaks and groans, echoes, pops and snaps, or at least those are the sounds she hears as she strips out of her cold and very damp jacket and shirt. She can barely see to find her rolled up clothing at the bottom of her pack. An icy shiver trails up her spine as she imagines someone coming upon her from behind. Sam pulls on clean undergarments, a dark blue, long-sleeved tee and tops it with a green flannel shirt. Black sweatpants follow, which are more comfortable for sleeping than jeans. She also tugs on a gray hoodie that Sue lent her. Wind whistles somewhere through one of the corridors, startling her. Sam stands still a moment, waiting and listening. Then she expels her held breath and resumes. Warm, dry socks are last. She'll need to put her shoes back on before they go to bed in case they need to get up quickly in the middle of the night, but for now it feels good to wear no shoes at all. She carries her dirty items under her arm with her shoes, slings her bag over her shoulder, and re-enters the room with no windows. She nearly runs Simon down, who'd obviously been waiting just on the other side of the door for her.

"Sorry," Simon blurts. "I just wanted to make sure you were all right."

"Yep, I'm fine. Just like I told you I would be, Mr. Worrywart," Sam chides and squeezes past him. She's not going to admit that it was eerie in the dark hall. He already thinks of her as a child.

She spreads out her damp clothing across one of the viewing benches at the other end of the room. She's not sure if they'll dry all the way, but it's better than nothing.

"The food's heating," Simon tells her.

"Good, I'm starving," Sam reveals. Her eyes follow him as he moves about the room.

"Don't get too excited," Simon informs her. "It's going to take a while to heat up."

"That's fine," Sam says as she pulls out her small, portable sketchpad and sets it on the floor beside her. "I've got stuff I can do."

Simon doesn't ask her, probably because he knows. Sam takes a candle and strolls around the gallery room looking at the artwork that has been left behind. It's a shame that Americans were worried about looting for liquor, cigarettes and electronics, but much of the lovely artwork in this museum still hangs on the walls untouched. Nobody tried to save it or preserve it. She studies the painting, *Mt. Tamalpais* by Albert Bierstadt. The soft hues nearly glow by candlelight. Perhaps when he'd painted this, he'd done so by candlelight or hoped that people would view it in such a fashion because the painting invokes such a vision of golds and yellows that she can literally feel the dawn breaking over the hillside he's painted.

Without turning to face him, Sam says, "You should change clothing, too, Simon. If you get sick, I'm getting payback on you for all the times you've made me drink some of your nasty tea or for having to take gross medicine that you and Grandpa have ground up."

She moves on to a painting by Samuel F. B. Morse and studies it a few moments, taking in the dark and light contrasts.

"I've only ever had to treat you once, if you remember correctly, young lady," Simon reprimands.

She hates it when he talks down to her like she's a child.

"It was bad enough just the one time that it seemed like more," Sam reminds him.

Simon stops unpacking his gear and grins at her. The light from the candles plays on his auburn hair, making it appear shimmery and gold streaked. A shadow of stubble has covered his chin and cheeks. Sam moves on to a painting by another man named Emanuel Gottlieb Leutze. He seems to have been a patriot painter who had a love for America. His painting depicts a battle from the Revolutionary War. Sam wonders what he'd think of their great country today. Seeing his proud painting on this lonely wall where no one will ever see it again makes her feel gloomy. These paintings will all be destroyed eventually from humidity and chemical weathering.

"You got better, right?" he continues with a cocky attitude.

"You're always hovering over me like I'm some wilting flower," Sam comments with exasperation. She barely had the sniffles last year, but he'd insisted- like the control-freak he is- that she take his tea for three days and some weird, powdered medicine that made her want to retch.

Simon chuckles and answers, "It's my job to keep everyone on the farm healthy. I mean, along with Doc and Reagan, of course."

"Yeah, but when Reagan got sick, you were checking me like four times a day for fevers. Gimme a break! You didn't check anyone else that much!"

"I have to take care of you," Simon says with an uncomfortable edge to his voice. "And all the other kids, too."

Sam scowls at how his last sentence makes her feel.

"I'm *not* one of the kids," Sam retorts angrily. She can barely concentrate on the lovely artwork because he's making her so mad. "Don't be such an ass, Simon."

She passes a painting of a shipwreck by Edwin Church and then pauses to study another by Mary Peale. The artist has captured the grief of her subject, invoking the spectator to wonder at the woman's source of heartache. Perhaps she had to deal with a difficult man like Simon.

"Hey, that's not appropriate language," Simon scolds her.

She'd like to yank this lovely Mary Peale painting from the wall and club him over the head with it.

"You aren't in charge of me, remember? I'll talk how I like," Sam tells him haughtily.

Simon says quietly, "You need to stop hanging out with Reagan so much. She's a bad influence."

"Wrong. She's a good influence. Now I just need her to tell me how to deal with my annoying best friend when he's trying to order me around like I'm one of the children on the farm."

The next painting is by Edwin Blashfield called *The New Dress*. It is just lovely, the tones so vibrant and realistic.

"You don't need advice from her. You're a big enough pain in my butt most of the time," he tells her.

"I'd like to give you a kick to the butt," Sam tells him without looking over her shoulder. Sometimes he can vex her nerves like no one else.

"You'd just hurt your foot," Simon tells her.

"It might be worth it," she grumbles and studies the painting again.

301

"This was about as good a place as we could've possibly picked for our first night in the city," he comments, changing the topic. "You get to look at art all night."

"I'm glad you guys decided on it," Sam agrees, admiring another painting.

"I thought it would be a nice change of pace for you," Simon comments, drawing her attention.

"You suggested it?"

He doesn't answer for a moment. "Yes, I did. Are you glad?"

"Oh, yes," Sam says. "That was really thoughtful, Simon. We should take some of these with us when we leave. Can we? They're just going to be ruined soon. Artwork can't stand up to humidity. We could give them to Grandpa. See what he wants to do with them."

"Sure, Sam," he says, appeasing her. "I'll see what we can fit in the SUV in the morning."

"Thanks for doing this, for choosing this place."

"No problem. I'm glad you like it. What are you looking at over there?"

"This is…" Sam says as she turns back to Simon, only to find him stripping out of his clothing in a semi-darkened corner of the room. Apparently he thought it was darker. It's not. She can see his long, lean torso and bare stomach quite clearly. "…um, really lovely."

Sam doesn't actually mean to say that. The painting is hardly pretty, and it's an insult to the artist to suggest it.

"Oh yeah?" Simon calls over to her as he tugs a fresh shirt down over his chest lightning fast.

Sam doesn't answer but goes back to the portable heater and their temporary camp site. She sits cross-legged on her sleeping bag and waits for him to finish dressing. Simon joins her a few minutes later wearing dry, clean clothing. He's also wearing his eyeglasses, which leads her to believe that he's tired from their hectic day. His black turtleneck and holey jeans are in stark contrast with one another. It's like he's going for the casual, yuppy-meets-grunge appearance. His distressed work-boots just add to his unusual manner of dress.

"That feels a lot better, huh?" he asks nonchalantly as he takes their food off of the heater.

Sam just stares at his finely hollowed out cheekbones, wishing secretly that she could sketch him in his bizarre, yet somehow distinguished clothing. She knows he'd reject the idea for something more practical like oiling down the guns that got wet.

"What does?"

"Getting dry clothes on. I can't stand running around when the weather's like this. It sucks," Simon admits.

"Yeah, I guess it does. I wonder if we're going to have an early winter. Grandpa said we might."

"Let's hope not. I'm not too fond of these snowy, cold Tennessee winters."

"Right," she says, remembering his roots as an Arizonian.

"Want some food?" Simon asks as he sets her small jar on the floor in front of her using the long sleeve of his discarded damp shirt. "It'll warm your belly."

"What?" Sam asks. She wasn't really paying attention. She'd picked up her drawing pad and started her sketch of him without showing it. "Did you just ask me something about my belly?"

Simon scowls. His blush is too hard to hide, so he averts his face completely from her view and turns his back to her. "No," he responds in a huff of contrite anger. "I said you need to eat."

"Oh," Sam says with a frown. She's not sure he said that at all. "Thanks. I could've got my own. Let me get the bread."

He sits across from her in the same manner on his own sleeping bag. By the time she passes the bread that has been wrapped in a muslin sack to Simon, he's already eagerly digging into his main dish. He must've been pretty hungry. He normally has the refined table manners of a senator's son, but tonight he's wolfing down his food, licking his fingers and slurping with unabashed enthusiasm. Sam just grins and takes a bite of her stew. She dips the bread into the glass canning jar, letting the dense texture sop up the broth.

"Where do you think Cory and your sister will stay tonight?" Sam inquires as she next bites into a tender, roasted carrot.

Simon pauses between bites and says, "Not sure. Hopefully somewhere safe."

"And out of this weather. I hope it doesn't snow enough to stick."

"Me, too," Simon agrees through a mouthful of food. "He'll make sure they find somewhere safe to stay. I doubt if they're far from here, especially if that Dick's store is on the other side of the school. It sounds like they didn't get too far."

303

"Yeah," Sam agrees. "I don't like that he called the college a hotspot. That has to mean they ran into problems."

"Maybe," Simon says, his eyes narrowing. "If they do or did, Cory will get them out of it. He's good at that."

"So are you," Sam praises and takes another bite of potato.

Simon chuckles and tells her, "You can be our designated getaway driver."

Sam smiles at him, admiring the way the candlelight is touching his hair and skin, what little is showing. He's removed his stocking cap, so at least his auburn hair is visible now.

"I'm happy with the supplies we got today, but we still need to scout out fuel," Simon tells her as she hands him the rest of her bread.

"Here, I can't eat this much," she says. "I thought with the guys finding the gas converter thing that we'd be ok for fuel now."

"Maybe," Simon says with a nod. "But if it doesn't work for some reason, I'd still like to bring some cans of gas back to the farm at the very least. I have a feeling we're going to need to think outside the box tomorrow to find fuel. Everywhere in this town has already been raided and many times."

"Not that hospital today. We had good luck there," Sam reminds him.

"That's true," he agrees. "But our day got waylaid by that Dave the Mechanic guy and his friends. That put a big delay in getting started."

Sam frowns with distaste and screws the lid back on her canning jar of food. She's lost her appetite thinking about that man and his friends.

"I'm glad that the guys met up with someone they used to know," Simon rambles, unaware of her distress. "I think that's pretty cool. Plus, they might make valuable acquaintances to have in case we ever need them."

Dave and his group seemed nice, probably very harmless, but she doesn't know him or his men. She also didn't like the way some of them looked at her, especially the man Dave kept calling Gunny. Sam is sure that if John and Kelly trust Dave, then he is a good man. And likely his group is made up of men of the same character. But she just doesn't have the ability to openly and easily trust people anymore.

"What's wrong?" Simon asks, finally picking up on her change of mood.

"Nothing," she assures him, packing away her food in the crate. She swigs from her bottle of water and places it on the floor near her backpack.

Simon quickly stows away his empty container, sets aside his pack, and comes back to kneel on one knee in front of her.

"What is it, Sam?"

She shakes her head and lowers her gaze to his boots.

"Was it those men?" he asks.

It is difficult to hide anything from Simon because he knows her so well. She just nods because he'll know if she's lying. She glances up at him to see concern written all over his handsome face.

"Hey," he says softly and tips her chin up to look at him. "They were ok, Sam. They weren't bad. I didn't get a vibe off of any of them."

"Yeah, you're probably right," she says with another nod.

Simon lays a hand against her cheek and gives it a gentle petting.

"You don't have to interact with them, though. I won't let them get around you, not even if they come to the clinic for anything. If they come and you don't want to wait on them, just give me a signal. I'll take care of them or have Doc treat them. If you run into them in town this winter, just come and get me. You don't have to be around people who make you uncomfortable anymore. I promise."

Sam nods and tries to give him a small grin.

"Nobody's ever going to get that close to you. Understand?"

"Yes," Sam says in agreement, although she knows that he can't promise against such an impossible to predict future. The world in which they currently live is full of unforeseen complications and horrifying probabilities. "It's just that I feel bad when I get unsure of people. They're probably nice. I don't even know any of them. I probably don't have any reason to fear them. They probably think I'm a freak."

"No way," Simon says tenderly and touches her arm. "They didn't even notice. Just me. I'm the only one who noticed. I knew you wouldn't like being around that many strangers. And that's all right. You don't have to feel bad. None of them has gone through

305

what you went through. You've got the green light to go a little freak now and then."

Sam chuckles and nods at his playful jesting.

"Just don't go full-blown freak. That'd be too much," he further teases.

Sam smiles at him and says, "Right. I'll keep it in check."

"They don't need to be looking at you anyways," Simon adds without any humor in his tone at all this time.

He rises from his knelt position and walks away.

"Why don't we get some sleep now, all right?" he suggests in a comforting manner without turning back to her.

"'Kay," Sam says with a nod.

Simon blows out three candles, carries one over next to their sleeping area and sets it down near the heater. She's resumes her cross-legged position and braids her hair into two plaits to keep the dampness away from her face and neck while she sleeps. Sam watches him shimmy his way into his sleeping bag. They'll both use their backpacks for pillows. She mimics his movements and crawls into her sleeping bag. She coils her two braids on the top of her head on her pack. She's opted out on the rule of sleeping with her shoes on. It's just too uncomfortable.

"Boy, is it cold! This room feels even colder and damper than it was outside tonight," Sam comments as she tries to zip her bag higher.

Simon inches closer to her and says, "It's because the ventilation system has been turned off for years. Scoot closer. My body heat should keep you warmer."

"Thanks," she replies with appreciation.

The cold, hard floor beneath her hip bone is uncomfortable. She has managed to slide closer to Simon and feels a warmth permeating from him. She can tell that it's not going to take long for sleep to come. She's more tired tonight than usual. Working around the farm or in town at the clinic is nothing like the stress of running around a city looting. Anxiety and fear take a toll on the body, she's learned.

"Let's play a game," Sam suggests as she tucks both hands under her cheek. Simon just stares at her with that patient look of his.

"Why don't you just get some sleep?"

The trace amount of light from the kerosene heater just barely gives her enough to see him.

"Let's play 'where would you be now and what food do you miss the most'?" Sam says.

"Sam," he warns with growing impatience.

"Come on, Simon," she presses. "We hardly ever have time to even talk anymore. You're always busy. Or you're busy dodging me!" Sam accuses.

"I'm not..."

"Sure, sure. Whatever you say, Mr. Bossy Pants."

She can see his profile, the roll of his eyes and huff of his breath.

"That's not very mature," he says and crosses his arms over his chest.

"I'm a kid, remember?" Sam taunts.

He actually chuckles.

"I'm not so sure you aren't some sort of mastermind manipulator," he admits and turns slightly toward her. "You would've had a great future with the CIA, Samantha Patterson."

Sam harrumphs and says, "Besides, if you want me to go to sleep, then you should talk with me. It'll help me relax. Then you can stay awake brooding all night."

"See there? Manipulating me again. And I don't brood," he retorts.

"Yeah, right," she corrects him. "Ok, I'll go first. I'd hopefully be riding on the US equestrian team and gearing up training for the Olympics."

"Where would you be? Here in Tennessee or somewhere else?" he asks, his curiosity piqued.

"Maybe for a while, but my parents had already been talking with a coach down in Georgia. They wanted me to attend college while pursuing my riding career, so I may have had to choose a school down there. Hey, maybe I would've gone to the same school as your sister. That would've been funny," Sam speculates.

"Yeah, funny," Simon reflects.

His tone is not like her own. He seems to find this information not humorous at all for some reason.

"What's wrong?" Sam asks him.

"Huh? Oh, nothing really. I was just thinking about you living in Georgia all by yourself. That could've been dangerous for someone like you."

"What's that supposed to mean?"

"You just would've been so young like you are now. I mean, I don't look at you right now in your life like you can take care of yourself, Sam."

"Why?" she asks. This is starting to feel insulting again.

"You're serious? You're lying next to me with your hair in little girl braids. You look like you're still fifteen. You wrecked Doc's SUV today because you never even had driver's education classes before the fall. You're just a kid really," Simon tells her.

"So are you then," Sam counters.

"Hardly," he murmurs. "Not after what I've done. I don't think anyone would call me a kid anymore."

"I don't think you ever were," Sam says with serious inflection.

"What do you mean?"

"You just seem like an old person, a grown-up. Even back when I first met you, you were like a thirty-year-old adult, not a seventeen-year-old boy. I just don't think I've ever seen you as a teenager or as you love to call me, a kid."

"Hm, maybe not. I guess I've never really thought about it," he says.

"Except for the comic books and video games!" Sam blurts on a laugh.

"I think all guys are into something juvenile at one time in their lives or another," he admits with a grin.

"You're just an old soul, Simon," Sam tells him. "I've heard Sue call you that, too. Reagan said you're so much like Grandpa that she thinks you're his long lost reincarnated brother."

"Oh, great. More master manipulators," he jokes.

"Back to our game. Where would you be? It's your turn," she reminds him.

He sighs and says, "Don't know for sure. I was looking into colleges. I really liked the idea of genetic research for medical purposes. I kind of thought I might want to go to Johns Hopkins."

"In Maryland?"

"Yep, that's the one," he teases with a grin. "Who knows, though? I was also looking into some other schools."

"Did you get really good grades in school or something? That's a pretty prestigious school, Simon."

"Uh, yeah. I did all right," he says with modesty. "Don't misinterpret me, though. I'm no Doc or Reagan on the academic level."

She's quite sure that he did more than all right if he was looking into going to a medical college like Johns Hopkins. Strangely, Sam feels proud of him.

"I don't know about that. Moving on," she announces before he can argue. "Food you miss the most."

He chuckles and says, "My mom's homemade mac n' cheese. Man, that was some good stuff. Sometimes, she'd make a big tray of it and a bunch of burgers on the grill for me and my friends on her days off from the hospital."

"That's right. She worked as a nurse. I forgot," Sam tells him.

"Yes, she was very smart. Smarter than me, that's for sure."

Sam chuckles and remarks, "I doubt that. Besides, you had to get it from someone, right?"

"I suppose so," he agrees. "I looked more like my dad, though. That's where Paige and I get the red hair. It runs on my dad's side."

"I saw the picture of her you carry in your wallet," Sam tells him.

"Right. And you definitely look like your mother. You were her twin," Simon tells her.

"I suppose so. I'm glad really because I can carry that with me, that piece of her," Sam admits.

"I'll take you there when we get back, all right? I didn't forget. We've just been busy finishing the harvest and getting ready for winter," he promises.

"I think winter's just about here," Sam says, remembering the light snowfall outside.

"No doubt," Simon agrees. "Now what food do you miss? We need to wrap this up so that you can get some sleep."

Sam smiles at him, even though she isn't sure if he can see her well because of the dim lighting.

"My mom's sugar cookies. They were so good," Sam says, drawing out the word 'so.' "She'd make them at Christmas, and we'd

309

eat so many she'd have to hide them just so she'd have a few to set out for guests. She made them for my dad's workers, too. She used to put them in little Chinese take-out containers all stacked inside so cute and pretty. She was a really good cook, but her frosted sugar cookies were the best."

"All right, this game needs to end. I'm getting hungry thinking about all this food," Simon jests with a grin.

"Me, too," Sam says with a wide yawn. "Maybe Hannah will make sweet rolls for breakfast when we get back in a few days."

"Great, now I'm thinking about those, too," Simon jests again on a groan.

At least Sam thinks he's kidding around. He sounds somewhat serious. She just chuckles at his hardship, causing him to frown.

He asks, "Are you warm enough?"

"Not really," Sam sort of fibs. "Can I snuggle closer?"

Simon's dark blue gaze jumps to hers. She can see his eyes clearly, even with the faint light from the heater.

"Uh, sure," he stammers.

Sam closes in on him, pressing herself against his side. She tries not to hear his huff of indignant protestation.

"This is better," she confesses gaily. "I think I can finally sleep now."

"That makes one of us," Simon mumbles.

Sam chuckles at him. She leans up and says in an austere voice, "Don't try any funny business, Mister."

He physically startles and says as if affronted by the insinuation, "I wouldn't, Sam!"

Sam laughs loudly this time, without worrying about anyone hearing her. "I know, silly. Trust me. I know."

"Oh, I thought you were serious."

"No, of course I wasn't. If I was being serious, I would've warned you against *me* making a move."

"Wh…what?" he croaks, his voice a little higher in pitch.

Sam chuckles again and says, "Goodnight, Simon."

Chapter Twenty-One
Paige

She is following right on Cory's heels as they weave through buildings and come to a garden area complete with brick patios, a fountain, marble statues- two of which have been knocked over- multiple gazebos, and sidewalks. He approaches an ornate old mansion cautiously, going slowly and checking every dark passageway. Paige hasn't seen a single light on anywhere in the city since the sun fell over an hour ago. She's froze to the bone. The rain from earlier turned to freezing rain and now snow. God, she misses Arizona something fierce.

"We'll stay here tonight. There are bound to be fireplaces with chimneys. We'll have heat soon. Stay with me," he orders quietly.

Paige might just follow him through the gates of Hell if there is heat waiting there. They passed a lumber yard about three blocks earlier, which they'd scoped out. He'd located quite a few bundles of chain-link fencing that he says him and Simon can soon return to the city with the truck to retrieve for use on the wall in town.

Cory steps over a plaque of some kind that has been knocked to the ground or fell on its own. It reads *Belmont Mansion,* and contains a brief description of the home and its historical roots to the city carved into the wooden face of it. The grand home is connected on either side by wings of the college that shares the same name. Intricate wrought iron works encase the second floor balconies like one would see in the architecture in the New Orleans French quarter. Carved white pillars stand before the front doors. Not bothering with any sort of sneaky tactical maneuver, Cory leads her right up the front steps of the stately home. The door is already cracked open, so they let themselves inside.

"Why don't you wait here? Guard the front door for me. I'll check it out real quick and be right back," he says.

Paige would like to argue but doesn't. Her teeth are rattling too hard to utter a protest. She closes the front door and locks it. Cory touches her arm reassuringly, nods, and disappears down the hall. Outside, the wind has turned from a soft whisper to a downright howl of anger. She tries not to shiver.

After a few moments, she can hear him moving around upstairs. She's assuming they are safe and the only occupants of the manor because nobody has shot at them. In this old place, she's more concerned about the Belmont Mansion ghosts coming at them. Also, Cory hasn't come through the floor above her having fallen into someone's devious trap. That's also a good sign. She strolls over to one of the leaded windows facing the front grounds and glances out. Paige still can't believe she almost died today. She also can't believe she was fooled by someone's amateurish trickery. Falling through that floor had to have taken years off her life. She still can't imagine how her brother would've taken the news that she'd fallen to her death. The thought sends another shiver through her.

She also can't fathom how Cory was able to pull her to safety with a man on his back and with one arm to boot. There was no way she could've pulled herself up again. Her arms were exhausted just trying to hold onto that flimsy wiring hanging down out of the ceiling. Cory's raw strength saved her. One of the things she likes to give him a hard time about is being a brute. This time, it saved her. She has no idea how he's still full of energy running around the city after pulling her to safety and then being stabbed. She's been scared in her life, terrified, especially since the fall of the country. But seeing that man slice his knife across Cory's stomach scared the shit out of her. Paige's hands begin to tremble as she thinks back on it. She braces herself against a complete meltdown by holding onto an antique sideboard.

Remembering crawling to safety only to turn around and find him engaged in a fight for his own life after saving hers was also heart-stopping. She'd scrambled to find her gun, remembered that it fell, and crawled on all fours over to collect his rifle in the corner. By the time she realized what was happening, it was over. The man had promised to rape her when he was done with Cory, and it seemed to set off a violent trigger within him. The fight had felt like it was going in the man's favor. He'd even managed to slice his knife across Cory's stomach. But when the man exposed his plan in its entirety, Cory had gone mad. She could barely even follow what was going on, it happened so fast. He'd taken the man's knife and killed him with it. Paige has never seen anything like that before. Her friend Gavin had shot the men who'd attacked her and Talia. She's shot and killed men from afar. She's seen others do it. But she's never watched the life leave their eyes up close, never seen a man stabbed to death and thrown down four flights through a hole.

He saved her life, and now she's indebted to him for it, which isn't exactly a place she wants to be. But she's still breathing because of Cory. He hadn't given up trying to save her, even when the man jumped on his back. He could've been killed. The man could've cut his throat or stabbed him in the back. Cory was barely phased by it. He'd simply kept his eyes on hers and persisted in reassuring her it would all be okay. His tenacity is like nothing she's ever witnessed. She'd completely misjudged him. He'd placed her safety and her life above his, and it says something about the kind of man he is.

Cory's deep voice startles her from her thoughts, "We're clear. There isn't anyone around."

"Good. I'm too tired to keep going," Paige admits.

The beam of his flashlight sprays around the room.

"I've locked and secured the doors and windows- what's left of them- on the first and second floors. I kind of figured you were tired. I also locked the two doors that connect to the college on either end of this floor. I don't think anyone's around over there in the school, though. School's out forever, if you know what I mean. Let's go upstairs."

He turns to ascend the grand, curved staircase coated in four years' worth of dust. The risers are covered with fading red carpeting down the center. The ancient treads groan under his weight. They hole up in a room with unbroken windows and a sizable fireplace, likely the master bedroom.

"There's another floor up, but it's just some sort of observatory or something. This is the only room left with a bed," he explains patiently.

Cory opens the chimney flue and gets to work on lighting a fire.

"I'll be back. Get our candles out and light them. We don't want our flashlight batteries to go dead," Cory instructs, busy as ever, not stopping to wait for her.

"Where are you going?" Paige asks nervously.

"To find some wood to burn," he answers at the door. "Just get changed while I'm gone. Then we'll eat and turn in for the night."

"All right," Paige answers with a frown. Even though the idea of him leaving for even a moment frightens her, she relishes the idea that she could be wearing dry clothing and eating hot food soon.

Paige drops her pack on the massive antique bed, relieved to have it off her tired back. Next, she digs out her two candles. She carefully lights them and places them on the fireplace mantle. It's just enough light to see to change out of her wet clothes. The ornate, Greek wallpapering with gods and goddesses and wildlife stares back at her. Some of it hangs in tatters. All of the remaining furniture seems heavy and older than dirt. She used to love touring historical homes like this. The trompe l'oeil faux painting where the wall meets the ceiling is lovely and typical of the Victorian period. The chocolate marble fireplace surround and mantle would've been a luxury even then. The woman who owned this mansion had good taste. Paige smiles to herself.

First she strips down to her bare skin, prays he doesn't walk in on her, and pulls on clean underclothing including a fresh t-shirt and the thermal socks she'd acquired earlier. She tugs on the rest of her new clothing from Dick's Sporting Goods. Finally she has a pair of pants that fit correctly and don't resemble dorky flood pants that barely reach her ankles. The thermal shirt over her t-shirt adds an extra layer of warmth. She places her new gym shoes, which are soaked through, near the fireplace to dry out. Then she laces her new hiking boots and sets them near the bed. She has two pairs of new shoes thanks to him. It's not something to take for granted. This is also something for which she's grateful to Cory.

Cory comes back into the room with chunks of wood, some of which looks like it came from furniture. Some of it is actual cut logs like they use on the farm. She hopes he didn't destroy any of the magnificent, historical furniture in this stately old home, even if tourists will never visit it again. He drops the wood onto the floor and yanks the ornate steel grate away from the front of the fireplace. He noisily tosses it away so that he can stack the wood inside. He's apparently not too concerned with noise. Of course, after today Paige isn't thinking there is anything more lethal, man or beast, in the entire city of Nashville than Cory.

"Should I unpack the food now?" Paige asks with uncertainty. She's never been on a run with him or even her brother. She has no idea what to expect or how they operate.

"Sure," he answers with an easy manner.

Paige watches as he ignites the dry wood with a bit of fabric and paper and his Zippo lighter. It doesn't take long before the wood is crackling softly, and the room is illuminated with a soft orange glow. She steps closer and rubs her hands together.

"I'll go get another load of wood so we make it through the night. But don't worry, I'll be back in a few minutes. See if you can get the food set on the fire to warm up while I'm gone."

She doesn't even get in an answer because he's right back out the door.

"Ok, sure," she says, being sarcastic. "No problem. I'll get right on that, dear."

She unpacks the jars and packages of food and places them on the stone hearth. Paige pushes the canning jars of food closer to the open fire, not sure what else she can do to warm them. She stands and looks around the room now that she can see better. The bedroom is relatively large in size, but everything is covered in dust. This is just like all the times she and her friends stayed in abandoned homes over the years. This one is just a bit fancier. If this were another time and the circumstances different, she would've loved going through the mansion during the day for its architectural significance. Now she's just happy to have its ancient slate roof over her head for the night.

The idea of sleeping on the bed is infinitely more appealing to sleeping on the hardwood floor. Unfortunately, their sleeping bags are in the Suburban with Simon and Sam. She crosses the room and removes the pillow cases from the pillows. Then she goes to an adjacent bedroom. There are four on this floor including the one they are going to be staying in. They all connect, as did most old homes from this time period. Paige takes the linens and a yellowing quilt from the mahogany wardrobe there. She gives them a hard shake, leaving the dust in that room. She brings them back to the room where they'll sleep and switches the dusty bedding out with the cleaner articles. It's not perfect. They aren't freshly laundered, but at

315

least they aren't coated with years of dust and dander that could make her sick with a sinus infection, which has happened in the past while on the road with her friends. She finds another room with bedding and does the same for Cory, bringing it back to their room. It's the least she can do freshening up some blankets for him.

He returns a few minutes later with another load of firewood. She has no idea where he's getting it. She also isn't going to question his source since the room has already starting warming.

"Aren't you worried that someone will see the smoke from the fireplace?" Paige asks him.

"No, are you?" he asks with a grin.

"Well, yeah. Of course I'm worried. People could see the smoke and the light in here and come after us."

Cory smirks and says, "I'm gonna hang some blankets on the windows in this room to block the light. But with this storm, I don't think anyone's coming out tonight. Besides, if they do come sniffin' around, I'll take care of them. You can be sure of that."

Paige's eyes widen, but she nods just the same. She's quite sure he'll handle anyone that comes to this mansion tonight. The thought makes her inwardly cringe.

"I believe you," she says and lowers her gaze.

He leaves again and returns with three quilts, which he arranges over the curtain rods after he has also drawn the dusty velvet draperies.

"I put the food on like you asked."

He crosses the room and locks the door.

"Great," Cory responds. "I'm going to change."

"Here? In here?" Paige asks quickly.

He unzips his jacket and tosses it to the floor. "Unless you don't want me to."

"Uh… no, what do you think I am, a prude or something? You get undressed at the cabin in front of me all the time. What's the difference?" Paige questions uncomfortably, trying desperately to seem casually nonchalant like him.

"That's kind of what I was thinking, too," he agrees but gives her a strange look.

He just continues removing clothing and dropping it. Paige turns her back and decides to set up their dinner instead of standing there gawking at him. She clears off a delicate side table with a gray marble top and carved legs, moves one of the candles to it, and starts placing the food from their packs there. She also uses a crocheted doily to remove the hot jars from the fireplace and sets them on the small table. The two rickety, feminine chairs upholstered in tufted red velvet near the window she carries over to the table. She notices in her peripheral vision that Cory has changed into dry jeans with many tatters and rips in them, no socks and no shirt. His jeans slip slightly down over one hip, exposing his bare buttock. And apparently, no boxers, either. Isn't he freezing? She still is.

"Oh my goodness," she exclaims when he turns around to face her. "You're bleeding!"

Cory just looks down at his stomach as if it's no big deal and shrugs. "It'll be fine till we get back to the farm."

"Are you crazy? We need to at least clean it, Cory! It could get infected," she cries softly and approaches him. He backs up a step.

"I don't need your mothering," he comments snidely and places his hand over his wound.

"Don't be a baby," Paige scolds. "Let me take a look at it."

She grabs his hand and, after a couple hard tugs, leads him over to the table. Paige sits and has him stand in front of her, which gives her a better close-up view of his cut. She reaches down and takes a rag out of her pack along with her bottled water.

"This isn't necessary," he says tightly.

She ignores his complaining and pries gently at the duct tape he'd slapped over the pad earlier. She tries to peel it a tiny bit at a time. This has to hurt.

"Let me," Cory says and just rips the whole strip off.

"Ouch!" she says for him. When she glances up at him, he's smirking as if he finds her funny. "All right, I'm gonna clean it now. Then we'll cover it again."

"It doesn't need to be covered. I'll just let it dry and scab up in the air."

Paige grimaces as she blots the wound with her rag. It doesn't seem as bad as she'd first thought. The blood on the padding must've been from earlier. It's not bleeding now, but it is about five inches long. Lucky for him, it's shallow and hasn't gone deep enough to damage anything. It seems superficial and likely won't need stitches. She still wishes she had some kind of disinfectant or antibacterial cream.

317

"Are you almost done? I'm kind of hungry here," he states.

Paige glares up at him, letting Cory know of her irritation. He just smirks again.

"I had to haul some bony-assed girl out of a hole today. I need food, woman," he orders, takes her hands in his and presses her gently away from him.

"See?" he asks. "Good as new."

"What's that one from?" she asks and touches a scar on his side, trying not to notice the rippling of his chiseled stomach or the way his muscles jump when she presses her cold fingers to him.

"Nothing. And don't bring it up in front of the family, either. Nobody but you has noticed it."

"If you don't want me to tattle, then you'd better fess up," Paige says with more courage than she feels as she sits dwarfed under his huge shadow. She decides standing would be better.

"Blackmail, beanpole?" he asks with a cocky grin once she's standing in front of him.

"I'm not above it, no," she admits. "I grew up with a younger brother, might I remind you."

Cory reaches toward her, which causes her to flinch. His fingers sift into the hair at her temple. He pulls a small twig the size of a match from her long strands and flicks it away.

"Same sort of situation we got ourselves into today."

Paige's mouth parts with surprise.

"Only it was three dudes that time. I didn't get as lucky, but I was able to... work it out."

"What do you mean?" she asks.

Cory smirks and says, "We came to a mutual understanding."

She frowns, her shoulders drop at his sarcasm, and she says, "You mean you killed them, don't you?"

Cory's eyebrows rise and he says with confidence, "Maybe."

Paige shakes her head in disbelief and says, "But how did you treat it? Did you give yourself stitches or duct tape it or something?"

His dark eyes regard her warily. She cocks her head slightly to the side waiting for him to respond. His gaze slips from her face to her chest and then slowly back up. She's not sure if he's doing it on purpose to put her off or if he is actually checking her out.

"Something," he answers noncommittally and says, "Let's eat. You can't afford to miss a meal, and I tend to get a little grouchy if I do."

She smiles openly at his humor, which seems to catch him off guard. He grins in return.

Cory joins her at the table and sits in one of the antique chairs. Paige is concerned that it's not going to hold his weight. It actually squeaks just like all the floors in this home. The chance of someone being able to sneak up on them is pretty slim.

She shivers after her first bite of the hot food, "Good grief, I miss Arizona. The weather on this side of the country sucks."

"Yeah, it doesn't bother me. I'm used to it," Cory tells her as he hands her a package of sliced bread.

"I've been on the east coast for a few years now, but I didn't sign on for all this. I went to Georgia Tech. At least it was warm down there. Not as nice as Arizona, mind you, but warm, very humid."

"Your dad was the governor or something, right?" Cory asks.

"No, he was a senator. But he wasn't always in government. He started out as a lawyer, then he was the public prosecutor for our county. Then it just built from there."

"Sounds like he was pretty smart," Cory remarks.

Paige tries not to stare at his bare chest. There seems to be a lot of dark hair in the center. He's still holding onto his tan from summer so his torso is a dark bronze since he never wears a shirt back at the farm when he's working outdoors. She peeks at his wound again. At least it isn't bleeding. That's a relief, but she wants Simon to look at it tomorrow since he brought his medical bag.

"Yes, he was smart. You would've liked him. When he was still just a lawyer, he liked putting away bad-guys."

"I like putting down bad-guys, too," Cory says with a grin.

Paige laughs, almost chokes on her food, and corrects him, "I didn't say putting them down like killing them. That's what you do. He put them away as in put them away in prison when he was a prosecutor."

"He sounds cool. I'm sure I would've like him. Locking them up, putting them down like rabid dogs. Same thing. Gets them off the streets. Doesn't really matter how it gets done anymore," Cory says with all seriousness as he tears a chunk of bread off of his small loaf.

319

Paige thinks about his comment for a moment before saying, "Yeah, I guess you're right. They just free roam around hurting and robbing people with no consequence now. There isn't a police force left, so the scum just do whatever they want."

"Not all of them get away with it, though," Cory reminds her.

"Not when you're in town," Paige comments. A lopsided grin spreads on his face, his big dimple peeking out of his stubble.

Cory lets go a chuckle and shakes his head, "No, not when I'm in town."

His damp hair hangs almost to his shoulders and drips tiny water droplets down his chest. He doesn't seem to notice. He hasn't been shaving lately, and his face is starting to become covered with a shadowy, short beard again.

Paige searches for the right words to express herself, but the simplest route seems to make the most sense, "Thanks for saving my life today. If you hadn't been there, I would've fallen. There's no way I was going to pull myself up. I have almost no discernable upper body strength."

Paige flexes, showing her wimpy bicep muscle. Cory reaches across the table and pinches it between two fingers.

"That is a sad little thing," he admits with a nod.

She just grins and shrugs. "I know."

"You don't have to thank me, but you're welcome," Cory says, making direct eye contact with her. "And you aren't supposed to have upper body strength to do things like that. You shouldn't have to. That's my job, taking care of you, I mean. I shouldn't have let that happen in the first place. That was a stupid mistake on my part."

Paige shakes her head and says, "No, there's no way you could've known. That guy set a trap, a sneaky one, and I fell into it-literally."

Cory manages a grin but she can tell that it still bothers him that it all happened on his watch.

"Simon will be glad that I'm returning you in one piece. I don't think I'd want to piss off the sniper in the family," Cory jokes.

"Other than the ten years it took off my life," Paige says, causing him to laugh.

Paige reaches across the table and lays her hand on top of his. What she doesn't expect is her reaction to touching him. His skin is so warm under her cold fingertips. His dark eyes dart to hers.

"Thanks again," she says softly.

Cory gives her a nod. Then, in an unexpected turn, he flips over his hand and captures hers within his own. Paige's gaze falls to their hands as he begins to stroke her fingers lightly. Then he runs his index finger over the black strings tied on her wrist. His hand is rough and calloused. She has long, thin fingers, but his wrist looks as thick as her calf muscle. His movements send a shiver up her arm. He abruptly pulls his hand away as if he found the contact unpleasant.

"No problem, beanpole," he says with a dark scowl and returns to his food.

Paige narrows her eyes at the top of his downturned head suspiciously.

After a few minutes, Cory asks, "Were you close with him?"

"Who?"

"Your old man. Did you get along?"

"Oh, yes, we were very close. He taught me to have an appreciation for things, not to take anything for granted. Of course, I did take everything for granted. I didn't think so at the time. But now that I spend most of my time thinking about where my next meal is coming from or if I'll have enough water to drink or back when feeding Maddie was the first priority for the day or how we'd give her a bath, I realize how much I took everything for granted."

"Yeah, well none of us knew it was all gonna end. That's not your fault," Cory tells her bluntly. "You've got Simon again, so that's good."

"Yes, it is," Paige says. "I just felt like this huge weight was lifted off my shoulders when I found him, like I had a reason to keep going. There were a lot of dark days for me out there on the road. Many times I wasn't sure it was worth keeping going."

"Well, he's sure as shit never gonna let you out of his sights now," Cory says with a grunt.

"No kidding!" Paige says with a laugh. "Good grief. He's the little brother. I'm the big sister. I'm older, but he acts like he's my new guardian."

321

"That's ok. Everyone needs someone to look after them," Cory tells her as he ties his shaggy hair into a short ponytail and secures it with a rubber-band from his pocket.

"Who's looking after you?" she asks in a more serious tone.

"My weapon," he says with a cocky smirk.

Paige isn't sure he means his gun. He has a very mischievous grin on his mouth.

"I'll watch your back," she volunteers, the words leaving her mouth before she can even think about them.

One dark eyebrow rises sardonically before he says, "You? All hundred pounds of ya'? You couldn't even defeat a hole in the floor."

Paige purses her mouth at him indignantly.

"Hey," she pouts softly.

Cory chuckles at her and winks. "You're fine. You don't need to save me. I'm beyond saving anyways."

His tone has become somber, as if he isn't worth saving, and this bothers Paige more than she wants to consider. Every single person at the farm would highly disagree. So would she. Paige tries to convince herself that her concern for him is because every person in the McClane family is worth saving, but it isn't quite working. Her concern for Cory seems to be coming from somewhere less superficial than that line of reasoning.

"Were you close with your dad?" Paige inquires, changing the subject. She has an unusual curiosity to know more about him all of a sudden. She hasn't wanted to know anything about him so far in their brief acquaintance. Mostly she's tried to avoid him when possible because of their first fateful meeting and, lately, for other reasons.

"Sure. He was cool. We used to work on old cars together, restoring them and droppin' motors, that kind of thing."

"That's cool," Paige says, although she really isn't sure what he means about motors.

"We'd go hunting and fishing with Kelly when he came home on leave. Kelly's only my half-brother. I don't know if you knew that or not. His mom wasn't our mom."

"Yeah, I think I knew that," Paige admits. "What about your mother? Were you close with her, as well?"

"Yeah, she was great. She worked a lot, so that kind of sucked. But she was always doing stuff for us. She always talked about Kelly like he was her son, not her step-son. She never thought of him as anything less. But Em was closest with her," Cory discloses and then clams up.

The corner of his mouth twitches when he mentions his dead, younger sister.

"Were you close with her, with Em?" Paige asks, although she already knows the answer. Perhaps he wants to talk with someone about her. Sometimes when a person loses someone close to them, people tend to skirt around the topic because of their own discomfort. She wants to open the lines of communication with him. If he wants someone to talk to, she'd like to be that person. And this thought concerns Paige that she would think of him in such a way.

Cory opens his mouth to say something, closes it again, swallows and then says, "Yeah."

"I saw a picture of her. She was very pretty," Paige offers kindly with a smile. Emma was a promising young beauty. She knows how much everyone in the McClane family loved and cherished her. She's felt their devastation of losing her, too. She understands their heartbreak. No fifteen-year-old kid deserves to be killed so violently before they even reach adulthood.

"Yeah," he answers again noncommittally.

His eyes dart around on the hardwood floor. This is not going to be the night he talks with her about his dead sister. He's highly uncomfortable.

"Sorry," Paige says softly.

Cory starts packing away his empty containers and leftover food. His chair scrapes against the floor as he stands. Paige follows suit and meets him at the center of the table. Her shoulder bumps against his arm as she reaches for the package of bread.

"Excuse me," she mumbles.

He doesn't say anything, and he's stopped packing things away. Cory is simply standing beside her stock still. When she glances up at him, he's looking down at her with a solemn expression on his face. Her breath hitches in her chest at the intensity in his eyes. A muscle flexes in his strong jaw.

"She was the best of all of us," he remarks tightly and turns his gaze to his feet.

His words bring tears to her eyes. He must feel such an incredible amount of guilt over losing her. His torment is etched all over his handsome face. A black strand of damp hair falls across his face. Paige pushes it back behind his ear. His head is hung with what she believes is shame. This is definitely not how he usually acts. There is this thick, concrete wall around him most of the time. Sure, he's a smartass and likes to razz her, but he's never hard and cynical. She's seen the violent killer in him. She's seen him joking with the guys at the farm, but she's never seen him like this. He is hiding a mountain of grief behind that broad chest.

"Cory," Paige whispers hoarsely.

She turns toward him, allowing her fingers to slide down the length of his arm to his hand. She gives it a gentle squeeze. Paige watches his eyes move slowly from their intertwined fingers all the way back up to her eyes. Then his eyes trail back down and fall on the bare skin above her cleavage. He pauses there a moment as her mouth parts. She takes a step toward him.

"We should get this cleaned up," he says as he shakes his head. "I need to do a quick patrol. Then we should get some sleep."

The spell broken, Paige steps back, drops his hand and nods up at him.

"Right, yes, we should," she stammers with embarrassment. She'd misread his eyes. She thought she saw desire there, but apparently she was wrong. Besides, she's not the kind of girl men want to be with. She's the type of girl men just want to stick on their arm and then go screw around with the busty blonde. For some reason, being rejected by Cory stings just a little bit more than anyone else. It comes from the same place as her need to save him, even if it just means saving him from himself.

"Why don't you just let me do the clean-up?" she offers and turns back to the table quickly. "Unless you need my help doing a patrol or whatever it was."

"No, I'm fine. I've got it. Just gonna take a walk through the house and make sure we're still... alone."

That sends a different kind of chill up her back. This lovely and interesting architecture that she would've enjoyed viewing when she was still in college now just seems ghostly, creepy, and very potentially dangerous if people would find them.

"Sure. I'll just stay here and pack things away then," Paige says.

When she turns back, his boots and gun are gone and so is he. For being a big man, he can move very quietly when he needs to. Paige carefully stows away their equipment, food, and dry items. Anything that's wet, she tries to spread out on chairs and the table near the fire. Then she pulls on her boots and waits for him to return. He seems to be taking an inordinately long period of time doing his check. She crosses the room and opens the door.

"Cory!" she whispers but doesn't get an answer or see his light. "Crap."

She grabs her baggie of dry rags from her pack and heads back for the door.

"Did you call me?" he asks, startling her to the point that she yelps. "Sorry. I thought I heard you."

Paige drops her hand from her pounding heart and says, "Yes, I need to go to the bathroom. I just didn't want you to shoot me."

"Oh, ok. I'll take you."

"No way. I'll find it on my own," Paige insists.

"Forget it then. You'll have to hold it till morning. You aren't going out there without me," he dictates as he points to the door with one long finger.

"Damn it. Fine. I'm not holding it until morning," she complains and follows him from the room.

"Come with me," he tells her. "There's a bathroom in the back of this place. I think someone winterized the toilets, so you can go in there. Probably a caretaker or someone did it so the pipes wouldn't freeze and burst."

He leads her by the hand downstairs again, and she can't verbalize it to him, but having her hand in his does make her feel safer in this spooky old, dark house. They go past the main tourist areas and off to the side where a small section of the home was probably used by the tour guides and employees or volunteers.

"Yeah, we saw a lot of those kinds of flooded and destroyed homes and buildings over the years," she tells him.

"Me, too," he confides.

"I always felt depressed by those places. You know someone lived in them once. They were homes to people. Someone designed and built them. Now they are just ruined, uninhabitable structures."

325

"I never thought of it like that. I just saw them as places to loot for supplies," Cory tells her as he shows her the bathroom.

She places her candle on the sink's countertop and tries to close the door. He doesn't move. As a matter of fact, his foot is stopping it from shutting.

"You aren't staying," Paige informs him and shoves gently to the center of his chest. It doesn't really do anything, but he does back up of his own volition and leave the bathroom.

When she's done, he escorts her back upstairs to their shared room. He locks the door and begins preparations for sleep. Paige removes her boots and places them right next to the bed again. Cory takes a pile of blankets and the other pillow and starts spreading them out on the floor.

"I cleaned the bed linens. What are you doing?" she asks as she pulls back the quilt and top sheet on the bed.

"Making my own bed," he says without looking at her.

"But what are you doing? Are you gonna sleep on the hard floor?"

He looks directly at her, pauses what he's doing and says very simply, "Yeah. Of course."

"You can sleep on the other side of the bed. You don't have to sleep down there."

"No, thanks."

Paige frowns with confusion as he snatches a pillow from the bed.

"I mean, if you wanted to sleep in another room, I guess that's fine. I'd prefer it if you don't, though. This place is kind of creepy," Paige admits as she looks around at the dark shadows and old furniture. "It was probably grand and beautiful at one time, but tonight it's just creepy."

"I like my balls, so I'll sleep on the floor," Cory remarks, his deep voice void of humor.

"What?" Paige screeches on a giggle.

"If I crawl into that bed with you, your brother might divest me of them," Cory jokes this time.

Paige laughs and says, "He's not really in charge of me, even though he thinks he is. I'm an adult, Cory."

"Doesn't matter. If he found out, he'd have my head on a spit."

"I didn't say to jump in and let's go at it. It's just an offer for sleep."

He mumbles something incoherently, but she can't make out what he says. He doesn't continue their conversation but goes around blowing out candles.

She decides to test the water, "Unless you were hoping for an invitation for more..."

"I think you must've bumped your head today when you fell," he remarks, confusing her.

Paige blows out the one near her and climbs into the creaky, antique bed. Even though the bedding isn't very clean, it feels luxurious compared to what she used to do for warmth and shelter on the road.

"My head is fine," she says, feeling rejected.

"Then you should know better than to joke around like that."

She sighs loudly. If only he knew she wasn't trying to be funny. She changes topic, saving face and says, "This is cozy. It's nice having a roof over my head and food in my stomach. This isn't how we used to survive."

"No? What'd you guys do?" he asks as he lies down on top of the pile of blankets.

He still hasn't put on a shirt or sweatshirt or even socks. Paige isn't sure how he's warm, but she is finally starting to thaw out.

"We slept about anywhere. And food? Don't go there. Maddie always had to come first. There were many times I didn't eat anything all day because we had to feed her. Sometimes I'd lie to my friends and tell them that I ate, but I'd already given my food to the baby. I couldn't stand the thought of her being hungry. Sometimes we'd sleep out in the woods, once in a cave, which was scary as hell. When we couldn't find an empty house, we slept in a tent in the woods or a field. But I never slept well and certainly not for very long periods at a time. I was always on edge, really afraid, ya' know?"

Cory takes a long time but finally murmurs with a lot of emotion in his voice, "Mm-hm."

"I feel like with you watching over me, Cory, I can actually sleep," she confesses softly and rolls to her side to face him. The dancing flames of the fire are touching the naked skin of his upper body, accentuating the curves and planes in a ballet of shadow and light. She jumps slightly when he speaks again because she'd been in a daze.

327

"I'm gonna go check things again," he says and hops to his feet. "Just go to sleep. I'll be right back."

Before Paige can even remind him that he just did a check, he's back out the door with his boots in his hand and his rifle slung over his shoulder. That was weird. She waits for a while for him to come back, but he doesn't. Occasionally she hears him moving about in different rooms downstairs because the hardwoods are so old and creaky, but he doesn't return. She doesn't know what she's done to scare him off, but Paige is pretty sure that he left because of her or something she said.

Sleep won't come to her. She feels bad that he's missing his own meager amount of precious sleep because of her. She tosses and turns, fluffs her pillow again, and pulls the coverlet higher around her chest. She wishes he'd come back, and not just because he makes her feel safe.

Chapter Twenty-two
Cory

He presses his back to the wall in the formal dining room, the long table still set with fine china for public display and takes a deep breath. Cory would like to go back outside and stand in the cold rain-snow mix for about an hour. It might cool his heels a little. He had to get out of there. She was pulling at his heartstrings with her sad stories and her pale eyes. She may not have meant her stories to come off as sad, but he'd felt sorry for her just listening to them. Paige very rarely opens up to him, or according to her brother she rarely opens up to anyone, so he felt privileged that she'd share anything about her struggles with him. He heard it from Sue that she had a mega meltdown at the dinner table the first night she'd come to the farm. He's seen her look at food with melancholy eyes at the farm and again at the long banquet table of food at the wedding reception of her friend. He's seen her tear up when Reagan has lent her an article of clothing to wear and again today when he'd taken her to get shoes. He needs to hit another retailer of clothing for her. He knows she only has a few things back at the farm that actually fit her tall frame. For some reason, it bothers Cory that she has so little and finds such joy in receiving a simple pair of shoes. Perhaps some of the dorm rooms here at this school still have clothing.

Her eyes are always troubled and unhappy. But tonight it had tugged at a place in his heart that he's worked very hard at keeping closed off to people. He wanted to make her feel better. Unfortunately, the only way Cory knows to make a woman feel better involves a lot of touching and cries of pleasure. He's not so sure on the psychoanalysis, sharing of feelings shit. He's a little better at a more physical sort of healing. And he sure as hell doesn't need to have those kinds of feelings for his best friend's sister.

329

Lately, though, he's been having more than just sympathy feelings for her. Especially today for some reason. Maybe it was the near-death experience they shared. Maybe it was the fact that they aren't very often alone together at the farm. Or maybe it's just because he's been having sexual fantasies about her for the last few weeks. Or basically since he first met her if he's being totally honest with himself. He has no business whatsoever having sexual thoughts about Simon's sister. Besides, most of the time she acts like he's a monster. Seeing him stab that fucker to death today probably isn't going to help her reconcile those thoughts. She probably thinks even worse of him now.

However, a couple times in the last few days and when they were practicing shooting last week, Cory has seen a look in her eyes, one that is unmistakable. Out of respect for her brother, he won't act on it even if she is attracted to him. She's probably just lonely, especially since that asshole in town is now screwing around with Jackie from the armory. For good measure, he should kick that guy's ass when he gets back home.

He passes through the first-floor main sitting area that connects the two large wings, checking rooms and window locks. He's checked them twice already. He doesn't want to go back up there. Cory rests against the window sill in the smoking parlor, looking out at the freezing rain that has turned to mostly all snow. He glances down at his watch. Damn. It's only twenty-three hundred hours. It's going to be a long night. If the bottom of the house weren't so far away from her, he'd just sack out on one of the fragile-looking settees. Still restless, Cory walks down the hall toward the back of the house to the informal dining area. He grabs a yellowed dishtowel from the cupboard and wipes down his wet rifle. The front sight on her rifle is bent from the four-floor drop, so he and Kelly will have to put it back to normal at the farm. He just needs about a million other things to do tonight to keep from going back up there to her. Hopefully, she'll fall asleep soon. She's usually asleep at the cabin by the time he comes home in the middle of the night after hunting for the creeps who'd attacked the farm. He's getting closer every time he hunts them. Leads and trails pop up. He'll eventually find and kill those bastards. He's young and has the rest of his life to find them. They are merely living on borrowed time.

Cory sets up in the fancy main sitting room again where two separate pianos are housed. He perches on the ledge of one of the unbroken, curved windows facing the rear. He almost wishes that there were creeps out there running around. At least that would give him an excuse to go out for a while. Unfortunately, the city is still, silent, and dark. He hasn't spotted light anywhere for quite some time, which is why he chose this particularly desolate spot. He didn't figure any criminal types would be interested in raiding an old mansion. Other than a few broken windows, this place is somewhat untouched because it had nothing to offer anyone.

He glances at his watch again. Shit. Only twenty minutes have passed since he last looked. He has to do something to keep her off his mind. He hadn't liked the turn of their earlier conversation when she'd brought up Em. He knows she didn't mean anything by it, but he doesn't like thinking about his little sister. It's like opening a fresh wound and rubbing acid in it. Paige understands loss, though. She's lost both parents, her boyfriend, her friends and who knows how many others. Cory scowls with distaste. Thinking of her with a boyfriend makes him sick to his stomach. Too bad her asshole ex-boyfriend wasn't still around. That thought brings a smug grin to his mouth. He wishes the dick was around tonight. Kicking his cheating ass would give him something more productive to do with his time than thinking about Paige and her fine figure and lush red hair.

He'd been teasing with her earlier when he'd pointed out the box of blonde hair coloring. He likes her hair just fine. Its fiery color matches her bold spirit. He's even come to admire her freckles. They're cute. Well, hell. This thought stream isn't helping to take his mind off of her. Cory sighs long and loud with frustration.

What he wouldn't do for a cigarette about now. He crosses back to another room that looks to have been a ladies' sitting room because of the delicate, feminine furniture. He re-checks the window locks. Then he passes a long row of family portraits that look like they were from the 1800's and heads back to the front door. The maple chair he has placed under the handle will help to deter entry from this angle. It is difficult to look out the stained glass windows in the foyer. If they get attacked, it'll be from one of the broken windows in another area. He'd gone outside on his last check to make sure that the light from their candles and the fire weren't visible on the street. Other than a very dim glow, they weren't detectable.

331

He knows for certain they're safe for the night. This pacing of the first floor is just a mental deterrent to keep him occupied.

He usually wouldn't light a fire for this amount of cold in the air, but Paige is thin and was clearly freezing her ass off. He felt bad for it, too, since they were delayed getting to the Parthenon for the meet-up with her brother. It had taken him a while to get her to the mansion with him, as well. He felt like he had to slow down for her because she seemed miserable and tired. She certainly doesn't like inclement weather. He's used to it, having been out in every possible weather condition for nearly a year by himself. The winter weather in Ohio and Pennsylvania was way worse than Tennessee. He just hopes she doesn't get sick. He should probably go back up and check on her, check her for fever. The idea of checking her for a fever, having to touch her anywhere, even just her forehead, starts Cory's blood racing. Then he'd probably just get distracted by those full lips the color of cherry juice. This avoidance thing is completely ineffective.

He still can't believe that she fell through that damn hole in the floor and was almost killed. What the hell would he have said to Simon? He knows his friend also carries a certain amount of guilt along with him over Em. Cory can't imagine what Simon would've done if he hadn't returned with his sister safe and sound. If Paige thinks that the fall took a decade off her life expectancy, then Cory lost a good fifty years off of his. She's his responsibility while they are in the city. John had made that point quite clear before they left. He knows that his friend and mentor mandated that he should be the one to train her and guard her on this mission because he wants them to get along better, get closer and learn to rely on each other. If he let John down and got Paige injured or worse on this trip, he's not sure he could ever return to the farm. He's also not sure that fooling around with Simon's sister is what John meant by getting over their differences. He definitely hadn't made mention to John or anyone else of the lustful feelings he's had for her lately. Nobody at the farm needs to know about them. It would complicate his relationship with his friend and the other men. He'll just keep it to himself until these feelings pass, which he's sure they will. Or he's fairly sure they will. Damn.

Taking a chance and hedging his bet that she is indeed attracted to him in a sexual way and then acting on those feelings would destroy his relationship with Simon. It would devastate his friend if he betrayed Simon and broke the code by which all men live. Plus, he wouldn't be pursuing Paige with any honorable intentions. He has nothing, or less than nothing, to offer a woman. It's not like he has a job or his own home, unless he counts the cabin, or security. He lives on a farm with many other people, works there with the family, and doesn't own anything other than what's in his pack. She's a former senator's daughter for shit's sake.

With little choice left, Cory drags his feet, climbing the wide staircase, passing the first landing where a tall portrait of some queen of England or another still hangs and then on to the second floor. He leans against the wall for a moment before entering, hoping beyond all hope that he'll find her asleep. He enters, shuts the door quietly, locks it and replaces the chair under the knob again. When he turns toward the room, she doesn't sit up in the bed or say anything. Good. She's out. This will make things so much easier just like when he arrives at the cabin in the middle of the night. He only has to pass her sleeping form back at the farm to make his way to his own bed. Sometimes, unfortunately, she's kicked off her covers in her sleep, and Cory is forced to look at her in short shorts and tiny t-shirts. One night when she obviously didn't have clean laundry, she was wearing one of his t-shirts and just panties. They were black. And lacy. And he'd seen them and her long tan legs when he'd passed her mattress on the floor next to her brother's bed. Luckily Simon had been gone from the cabin that night on watch duty. He'd lain awake in his bed watching her sleep for a long time, considering peeling her panties off with his teeth before succumbing to a fitful slumber.

He walks as quietly as he can to his pad on the floor and places his rifle there. Then he checks the other entry door's lock again. Next, he pulls off his boots and sets them by his rifle. His hands go to the waistband of his jeans, but he decides he'd better leave them on. Instead, he places the last two logs on the fire and returns to his makeshift bed. Right before he kneels, though, her voice interrupts him.

"You were on the right track," Paige says softly.

Cory's eyes slant in her general direction, but he refrains from looking at Paige. Avoidance is key. She's removed her thermal shirt and is only wearing a t-shirt and very obviously no bra and is sitting upright on the bed, the covers pooled around her waist.

"What do you mean?" he asks.

His eyes dart around looking for her undergarments. They lock on a pale blue satin bra lying discarded on the floor beside her. He has a hard time tearing his gaze away from it.

When he realizes that she hasn't answered, Cory forces himself to look at her. Paige does the unthinkable and allows her gray eyes to fall down over his chest to his pants. What the hell? Does she mean he should've taken off his pants? Does she want him to join her? It sure as hell seems like it. Her right eyebrow lifts jauntily, and she bites her lower lip.

He chuffs uncomfortably and points at her, "Go to sleep."

She grins lasciviously and lies back again.

"Your loss," she boldly states in the dark.

Cory lies on his padding of blankets on the hardwood floor, trying not to notice the lumps and bumps against his back or the uncomfortable ache in his pants. She sighs heavily, distracting Cory from his misery. Why the hell did she have to say something like that? Her thick hair was hanging seductively over one shoulder, her eyes playful and inviting, her mouth slightly parted. It was a definite invitation to join her, and Cory's pretty sure she doesn't just mean for sleep. She couldn't give a rat's ass about his comfort. She's wanting in his pants. He's not a young pup anymore. He knows the tell-tale signs of desire in a woman. He's seen it in her eyes for the last few weeks. It matches his own. For most of the time being an annoying, pain in his ass bitch, Paige also has a sexy as hell streak in her. And one she wants to show him a little further tonight.

He tosses and turns, checks his watch again, knows that sleep is a damn long way off. Cory can't recall a desire for a woman ever pulling this hard at him. He's slept with them but never felt an all-consuming need for one of them. His past encounters have been casual at best.

At a few minutes after midnight, Cory runs a hand through his hair and flops onto his back again, for the third time.

"Fuck it," he announces to himself and the room and her if she heard him.

He deftly rolls to his side and climbs onto the end of her bed. Then he yanks away her covers to the floor, startling the hell out of her. Paige rolls to her back, her breathing elevated probably from being stunned. Cory crawls up the bed on all fours, coming over her slowly, giving her a chance to back out. When he is eye to eye and inches from her face, his body not exactly touching down on hers yet, he waits for her to say something, to tell him to get lost or punch him or threaten him.

"Wh... what..." she stutters, although he can see it in her eyes that she knows why he's on top of her.

Her gray eyes peer closely at him, scrutinizing his actions. Cory lowers his mouth slowly toward hers. She doesn't respond. Not exactly what he was hoping for. Maybe he was misconstruing her invitation. He frowns down at her and starts to pull back.

"No," Paige cries out and wraps her long legs around his thighs. "No, don't go, Cory."

Her words are more of a weak plea. It's all the reassurance he requires tonight. He yanks her into his arms and plants a searing kiss to her full mouth, heedless of the stubble on his chin. Her fingers tangle in his hair and tug hard, pulling him impossibly tight against her. His hands start moving over her figure, that figure he's been forced to share a cabin with for way too long. He's seen more of her in the last six weeks than anyone else on the farm, and no one else on the farm has wanted to seduce her like he has. It's been torturous. His fingers dig into her slim hips and pull her up off the mattress against his throbbing erection. He holds her there with one hand rather easily because she's so slight. Cory groans into her mouth.

He's probably moving way too fast for her, but he also can't seem to slow down either. He yanks her top over her head and tosses it somewhere. For all he knows it went straight into the fireplace. Who gives a shit? He'll find her another one tomorrow in the city. He fills his palm with the fullness of her left breast which earns him a soft moan from the back of her long throat. It's almost the best thing his ears have ever heard in his entire life. She complains a lot about women with big breasts and blonde hair, but her breasts seem fine to him. More than fine. He jams his hand into her hair and pulls her head back so that he can kiss her neck and then her breast. This makes her cry out, which is even better than the soft moan a moment ago. Cory knows he's moving quicker than he normally would, which could be scaring her.

Her hands are fiddling with the waistband of his pants, trying to get the button unhooked. Apparently his frantic pace is suitable for her. She tugs hard, groans with frustration that she can't get the button free. Cory removes the condom in the front pocket and sets it on the mattress.

335

"Assuming much?" Paige jokes.

"Not at all. You just never know when you might need one. You know, for survival purposes," Cory teases. He really hadn't given any thought to the condom, certainly hadn't thought about using it with Paige. He's just learned to carry them in his pocket. He's down to his last few at the farm and doesn't have the desire to sprinkle the county full of little Corys. The box he found earlier is now stowed away in his pack, which is where this one originated.

Paige laughs and reaches for his button again. He quickly undoes it himself and pulls them down. They get tossed to the same place as her shirt. He hadn't bothered with underwear when he'd dressed a while ago. A second later he's on top of her again. In the back of his mind, in the deep dark recesses of his moral conscience, Cory's little voice of integrity is telling him to stop. He's defiling his best friend's sister. He pauses in kissing her, opens his eyes, looks down at the scene before him. She's the most alluring, on fire woman he's ever beheld. Her eyes are dazed, her body moving sensually against his, her curves soft and warm.

"Don't. Don't stop, Cory," she orders and pulls at him, her fingernails in his shoulders, her hips rising to meet his. "Don't even think about stopping."

Good enough for him. He's done listening to that inconvenient bastard of honor in his head. His mouth plunders her tender lips, taking and giving. He moves lower, kissing as he goes. His fingers work the snap and zipper on her black pants. With a quick tug, he has them whisked away. Cory leans back, kneeling between her spread thighs. He pulls down her pale purple panties one slow, painful inch at a time. He likes that it causes her to shiver. These he doesn't throw to the floor but sets on the edge of the mattress. She doesn't cower or try to cover herself. As a matter of fact, she reaches up with one hand to pull at him, but Cory snatches her wrist. Then he spreads out her long, thin fingers and flattens her palm against his stomach. His hair falls over his forehead, obscuring his view of her, so he pushes it back again. Not seeing her in all her lovely glory is not an option tonight. He slides his hand under her muscular thigh and pulls her down the bed even closer to him, against him. His fingers explore the long legs he's been ogling for so many weeks. For a redhead, she's very tan, which is probably why she has so many sprinklings of freckles on her shoulders, the top of her chest and the bridge of her small, feminine nose.

Cory catches her gaze and holds it. The gray-blue of her eye color seems silvery in the dim light. Her red hair is like a halo of fire around her on the white bedding. The feeling he has of needing to possess her on every level is nearly overwhelming. He opens the wrapper for the condom, his eyes never leaving hers. She's panting lightly and her lower lip trembles, which is exactly the response he wants from her.

Her other hand also floats to his stomach. When she tries to reach lower, Cory snatches both of her wrists in his hands and hauls her up onto his thighs. She's straddling him sensually. Paige buries her face in his neck, then presses her lips there lightly. Her fingers are digging into his back and shoulders as he pulls her head backward again. He lifts her higher, her breasts to his mouth. With one hand, he runs his fingertips down the center of her chest, around her back, and cups her ass. She starts grinding her hips into his, which causes her to rub against him most intimately. She is more than ready for him, the heat of her pressing against his shaft. He reaches down between them, touching her. This time, her head lolls back without his help. He has to place a hand against her back so that she doesn't fall to the mattress behind her. She shivers as he guides himself into her body, her thighs trembling against his.

A sharp crack of thunder explodes outside, followed by a bright streak of lightning that illuminates the room in a phosphorescent glow for a split second. The snow must be metamorphosing back to just rain. He's not even sure that Paige noticed it. She's too busy clawing at his back and pulling his hair.

"Look at me," Cory commands softly.

Her eyes pop open but have trouble focusing. Cory pushes upward, higher until he is fully embedded within her tight passage. His eyes hold hers for a few moments as he begins moving. There is no love in this act. It is carnal and necessary, fast and heated. They are both consenting adults, feeding a flame that needed to be dealt with before they ended up making a big mistake back at the farm. They are rarely ever alone together on the farm, and most of the time she gives him looks like she'd prefer to run him over with one of the tractors. He's usually too busy staring at her ass as she retreats in a fit of anger.

337

He lifts Paige higher against his chest so that he can lie her down on the mattress again. She's fairly easy to toss around at whim, which makes this infinitely more enjoyable. She's all long, lean limbs and a flat stomach. And she doesn't seem to mind him picking her up and pulling her around, either. As a matter of fact, she groans deeply as he presses her down and starts moving within her again. He creates a rhythm of pleasure that spreads throughout and between their bodies. His skin tingles wherever she presses her mouth or where her fingers tenderly land.

Her back arches, which Cory appreciates because it puts her breasts closer to his mouth. Again with the little whimpers and cries. She's more passionate than he ever would've thought. Her fingers tangle in the dark hair on his chest before she leans up and kisses him there. He's holding back, wanting to make sure she climaxes before him. But if she continues to do things like that, it'll be over soon. It's becoming difficult to control himself. He reaches down between them, manipulating and controlling her until she cries out and shivers. Cory runs a hand down her long thigh muscle, delighting in the tiny goosebumps there. Finally, he doesn't have to hold back anymore. He's careful not to be rough with her. She told him it's been since before the fall of the country that she's had sex. He likes that he's the first man she's chosen to be with in nearly four years. As beautiful and sexy as she is, men had to be after her, apocalypse or no. The thought that he is the man to be with her this way does something to him. A few more strokes and he joins her in passionate oblivion.

After a few moments and after he's caught his breath, Cory rolls gently off of her and onto his back. His heart rate begins to slow. The measure of his actions tries to creep into his thoughts, but he attempts to suppress them. Her low-throated, guttural laugh draws his attention.

"What... are you... are you laughing at me?" he asks hesitantly, his manhood beginning to feel threatened.

"No!" Paige blurts and laughs again.

She's still on her back, arms and legs-one over his thigh-splayed in carefree abandon, her eyes closed, a soft sheen of sweat on her body causing it to glow by the firelight. It's probably his sweat on her. The room was too hot for him before he added the extra wood to keep her warm throughout the night.

"What are you laughing about then?" Cory asks. He hasn't been with so many women that he feels confident enough to say that they don't sometimes laugh after sex. It seems unusual to him, but perhaps some of them do this.

"I didn't know it was supposed to be like that," she admits honestly.

Now his interest is piqued, so he rolls onto his side facing her.

"Like what?" he asks and pushes a lock of her hair from her forehead.

"Wow!" she exclaims loudly, heedless of him, their unusual, potentially dangerous surroundings and basically the whole world.

Cory likes that her hair is matted to her forehead and that the rest of it is a tangled mess all over the pillows. Her cheeks are flushed a bright pink. Her mouth is a ruddy red from his kisses. Her chin is a little red, probably from his beard. This is a good look on her. He allows his fingertips to trace her soft jaw line and down over one shoulder before taking a few red strands between his fingertips.

"Is that your seal of approval I take it?" Cory inquires with a lot of hope.

There's the guttural laugh again followed by a vigorous nod. He tries to hold back his pleased grin.

"Yes, big seal," she says with a blush blooming on her cheeks, making them even redder. Paige repeats, "Big seal."

Her arms measure something in the air above her. He's pretty sure it's not the same thing he's thinking. Even he isn't that well-endowed. Cory chuckles. She probably just can't wrap her mind around their encounter. He's having some issues, as well. He's afraid they just went from casual enemies turned one-night stand to something far more complicated.

"So I take it this wasn't how it went with your college boyfriend?" he asks because he can't seem to stop himself.

"Get real. No, I only had sex with him a few times and that was because he pressured me into it. But it wasn't anything like that."

"No?"

Paige snorts and says, "No way. He wasn't... I don't know. I guess he wasn't good at it. Not like you. Not like that. You were... your body is... whoa."

339

Cory's under no false illusions that he's a Casanova, so this is an intriguing revelation from her. Apparently her boyfriend was a selfish dick.

She still rambles on, "That was... that was... oh my God! Seriously, that was so..."

"Yeah? Having trouble describing it?" Cory reflects with a smile at her uncharacteristic failure to express herself.

She rolls toward him and announces, "But we can't ever do that again. Oh, God! I can't believe we did it in the first place. That has to be a one-time thing, 'kay?"

Reason and honesty start filtering into his brain again like unwanted stains. She's right. They can't do this. They sure as hell can't do this back at the farm. Doc would have a cow. Simon would kill him right after Kelly did. Reagan would probably get in line to murder him first. She seems very fond of Paige. He's starting to feel a little differently about Paige, too.

"Right. Of course, you're right," he agrees. "We can't ever let Simon find out. He'd lose his shit."

"Exactly," Paige agrees.

"I shouldn't have..."

Paige presses herself into his side and places a finger to his mouth, "Shh, don't say anything like that, like what you were going to say. Let's not do that."

Cory nods and captures her hand. He places a kiss to her fingertip and then sucks it into his mouth. Her sharp intake of breath makes him grin.

"You know something?" she asks.

"What's that?" Cory returns.

Paige swings a long leg over his hip and pushes him onto his back again. Then she comes up onto him, straddling his groin. Her hands rest on his chest.

"So basically the damage is already done," she leads and circles his nipple with one fingertip.

"More than done, I'd say," Cory agrees, his hands moving to her slim hips and then to her narrow waist.

"And we have quite a few hours before we have to meet... the others," she says, purposely omitting her brother's name.

"About eight or so," Cory says with a nod as he pulls her tighter and down onto his chest. Her soft breasts press deliciously there as his fingertips glide down over her back to cup her thighs.

"It was great, right?"

"Do you even have to ask?" Cory asks as his fingers wade back up and through her red locks. He can't seem to stop touching her.

"But that could've just been a fluke," she says with a grin and kisses his chest.

"Possible. Doubtful, but possible just the same," Cory goes along with her teasing, keeping his tone serious.

Her fingers thread through his chest hair to touch the little gold bracelet twined around a black leather cord. Cory snatches her hand away, kisses her palm and places it against his cheek. He doesn't really want to explain why he still wears his dead sister's bracelet at his neck. She doesn't push which he appreciates even if she is curious.

"We should probably make sure it wasn't. We wouldn't want to be left guessing, wondering, right?" she asks rhetorically as she grinds herself against him.

"Never leave anything to chance, I always say," Cory teases further as he pulls both of her hands above them against the headboard and pins them there.

"Just one last time, ok?" she asks.

"Right, one time. No more. Then we'll know, and it won't ever happen again. Agreed?" he asks, although he really doesn't want her to agree to it being their last time. Something about that seems too final for him. He's not sure two times with her will be enough. Maybe two hundred. He's not going to bring that up right now, though since she's licking his earlobe.

"Agreed," she confirms.

Cory flips her onto her back again and begins the process of performing all of the acts of debauchery and sin that he's been thinking about doing to her for weeks. Within a few short minutes, he has her writhing and squirming beneath him again.

A long time later, after she has fallen asleep, Cory reflects on what they've done. He had been so steadfast in his resolve not to have sex with her. He's not sure exactly what took place in his brain from the first floor to the second floor of this house. Downstairs, he'd convinced himself that he could resist her, resist her little hints,

341

resist himself, and hold his shit together. He hadn't wanted this to happen, to complicate their relationship, or to break faith with Simon. Now they have this gargantuan secret between them.

She brought it up again, before zonking out on his chest, that they have to keep it a secret, and that it can never happen again. As he strokes his fingers up and down her bare side and into the mass of her heavy mane, he's not so sure he's going to be able to live up to that promise.

Chapter Twenty-three
Simon

"Step away from the vehicle!" Simon shouts, frightening the two young people thinking about getting into their store of goods in the raised hatch of the Suburban. He is aiming his pistol at them.

They startle and back up. The man pushes the woman behind him and holds up a hand in surrender. He has a dagger on his hip, but Simon doesn't see a gun.

"Please don't shoot us, Mister," the young Hispanic man yells in a panic, his dark eyes darting around nervously.

They look desperate, hungry and dirty. Simon feels a little sorry for them. The woman is rail thin, and the man's not in much better shape. He's carrying a small canvas sack. Their plan was obviously to steal from them, take whatever they could from the trunk of the Suburban. Simon wonders if they just happened along and found the open hatch or if they have been watching them load the vehicle. He doesn't like the idea that someone could've been watching them and sneaked over to the vehicle while they went for more supplies inside the building.

"What were you doing? Robbing us?" Simon asks with disbelief.

"No, sir," the woman says, her eyes fearful and nervous.

"That's not what it looked like," Simon accuses.

The man fidgets, and his hand stupidly goes to the hilt of his short dagger. Simon surely hopes that it is a defense mechanism and that he isn't about to charge him. The man and his partner don't seem much older than him. If Simon were to guess, he'd say they are in their early twenties.

Sam comes out from behind one of the massive pillars of the Parthenon holding the shotgun. Now the young couple looks scared

343

out of their minds. If they thought they could take him on by himself, they are definitely out of sorts with a second gun-wielding person coming at them. The young woman tugs at the man's shirt, and they take off running. He holsters the pistol as Sam hands him his rifle she has slung over her shoulder. Simon watches them through the scope of his rifle as they run across the overgrown grounds of the park and down a hill. He watches until they are gone from view. He doesn't think they've stolen anything. Sam brushes past him and goes to the trunk of the SUV.

"They didn't get anything," she says with a soft frown.

"Good," Simon returns, still holding his rifle at his shoulder and scanning the area for possible other people who could've been with the young couple. "They're gone."

Sam chuckles and says, "Ya' think, Simon? We were holding guns on them. I would've run too!"

They've been packing away their supplies in the trunk of the SUV for the past twenty minutes. Everything is in there, but Simon had gone back to the gallery for the paintings Sam wants to preserve. He's going to strap them to the roof of the Suburban on top of the luggage rack to get them back to the farm because they simply won't fit in the hatch. He wishes they had more time. He'd pack the whole damn gallery onto the roof for her if he had the time. But, alas, they are due in ten minutes to meet his sister and Cory. He doesn't want to keep them waiting in case they run into trouble.

"I doubt it," he remarks to her. "I don't think you're a runner, Sam."

She laughs and retorts, "I don't know about that! I'm just not a very fast runner. Not like Paige. She's really fast. I went for a jog the other day with her and Cory, but those two freaks turned it into a competition and left me in the dust."

"Let's go," he says when he shuts the hatch. "Yeah? They left you? That's not cool."

Out of habit, Simon follows her to the passenger side and opens the front door for her. It's just how he was raised, to open doors for women. His father made sure he was raised with good, old-fashioned manners and courtesy toward the softer sex. She just smiles coyly up at him and gets in. Then he goes around the front of the SUV, scans the area one more time, hands his rifle in across the seat to Sam, and starts the Suburban.

"Yep, they ditched me," she continues. "But I got them back. I just ran to the horse pasture and grabbed Reagan's horse. Then I caught up to them and beat them on the high pasture."

"With no saddle again? Sam, we've talked about that. It's safer to ride with a saddle. You could…"

She laughs haughtily and answers, "Simon, please! I've been riding since I was like five years old or something. Get real. Cory thought it was funny."

"Well, I don't," he replies in a disapproving voice. Why does she take risks like that? Isn't the world dangerous enough for her? The thought of Sam falling from her horse and being injured or killed makes him instantly angry, especially at Cory. He makes a mental note to discuss her dangerous bareback riding escapade with Cory. His friend should've already reprimanded her for this, not encouraged her. Eager to change the subject, Simon asks, "So, do you think you know where this Dick's Sporting Goods is located?"

"It's on the other side of the university. We'll find it," she assures him and rolls her window down just a crack.

The weather has improved slightly, the sun is back out, and it's warm enough for jackets. Luckily, none of the snow from last night has stuck to the ground. He's not worried about himself, but he certainly doesn't want Sam to get sick. She was so cold and wet last night, he was sure she'd wake up with a fever this morning. Unfortunately, she woke him this morning because she stirred against his side. At some point in the night, she must've ditched her own sleeping bag and crawled into his, pulling her bag over them. He wasn't too keen on her doing that. He hadn't lectured her, though, because he figured it wasn't such a bad idea, that it probably kept her warmer. Luckily he was dead asleep or he could've mauled her again. Waking with her snuggled tightly against him had disturbed his senses, however.

"Turn left here, Simon," she says, disconnecting him from his thoughts.

He follows her orders, knowing that arguing won't do any good anyway. Simon tries to maneuver them down some side streets to keep away from the school that Cory had deemed as dangerous. He can still see the tall brick structures of Vanderbilt University over the trees. The peppering of stray vehicles and debris in the road makes the trip slower. A few minutes later, a shopping district comes into view and so does the sporting goods retailer. Simon pulls up near the front of the store, confident that it's safe or Cory wouldn't have them meeting at this location.

"Do you think we beat them? It's a few minutes after nine," she informs him as she consults her watch.

"Maybe," he says. "We'll wait a minute here and if they don't show up, I'll pull into that alley over there. I don't want to be sitting ducks."

"Sounds good," Sam says.

As he's getting ready to pull around to the alley, he spots Cory and his sister jogging across the parking lot. Simon puts the vehicle in park and gets out. Sam joins him on his side of the car as they wait for Cory. He's carrying a crate of goods that looks fairly heavy, and Paige is carrying a box full of things that poke out the top.

"Hey, guys!" Sam calls and waves with a smile when they are within ten yards.

When they get to them, Paige says, "Hi, Sam."

"How'd it go last night? Everything ok?" Sam asks after their well-being as she helps pack their loot into the trunk.

Cory and his sister both start stammering and mumbling at the same time with non-committal answers of "fine," "cool," and "uneventful." Simon feels an edge of angry apprehension coming on. His friend had better not have treated Paige poorly or upset her. Then his sister looks at her feet, which are clad in new shoes.

"Shoes?" Simon asks.

"Um, yeah, Cory brought me here yesterday. They still have quite a few pairs in the back. We thought maybe we could take a lot of them to the farm and then the remainder could go to people in town," Paige answers quickly.

Sam blurts before he can even answer Paige, "That's great, Paige. Wow, Cory, that was so thoughtful!"

Cory just shrugs and says, "Yeah, well, I didn't want her slowing me down. It wasn't anything."

"Seems very thoughtful to me," Sam argues. "Let's get going then. We should pull around back and get those shoes. The kids at the farm are growing like weeds. Huntley's taller than me already."

Cory adds, "That's not exactly hard to be, kiddo."

"Cory!" Sam reprimands and gets a smirk from Cory. "Two people tried to steal the Suburban this morning, so we should be careful."

"You shoot them, kiddo?" Cory asks.

"Cory! Of course we didn't. They weren't even armed," Sam tells him and gets a chuckle in return.

She scuffs the toe of her short leather boot against the ground. Her snug black riding pants cling to her curvy thighs and derriere. Simon would like to find her some baggy, oversized jeans today if possible. She's wearing his black turtleneck. He'd insisted because it was warmer than what she brought for herself. He knows she has a pink tank top on underneath it because he'd insisted that she dress in the same room instead of out in the hallway this morning. That made him nervous last night; he wasn't about to allow her to repeat it. He'd tried hard not to steal a glance as she'd changed. He hadn't really succeeded.

Cory interrupts his nefarious thoughts about Sam by asking, "What the hell happened to the Suburban? Were you playing bumper cars with someone, Professor? Try parallel parking?"

Sam laughs gaily and says, "Hey, I never said I was a good driver. It was from me, not Simon."

Cory chuckles and wraps an arm around her slim shoulders, "That's all right, little sister. We'll buff out those scratches."

She smiles up at Cory in all his scruffy, manly glory and gets a snarky grin from him in return. Simon knows that Cory is just being kind. Those scratches aren't repairable at all.

"Women drivers," Cory teases.

Sam, not one to be intimidated by Cory, slugs him in the stomach to which he laughs.

"You, hush!" she scolds with a bright smile.

"Just a small accident," Simon elucidates. "She had to drive while I... disabled another vehicle. She did well."

Paige remarks with concern, "Glad you guys didn't get hurt. That's all that matters."

"We should take anything else from here that you guys think we could use," Cory adds.

"Sure, hop in," Simon offers.

In the rearview mirror, Simon notices that Cory and Paige sit as far apart in the second seat as possible and his sister keeps looking out her window. There is something unusually suspicious about her behavior. He wonders if everything is all right with her.

"Feelin' ok, sis?" he asks.

"What?" she asks as if she is distracted. "Um, yes, I'm fine."

347

He says, "I hope you weren't in the weather too long last night. I don't want you getting sick. Were you able to get warmed up? It got so cold last night."

Her eyes widen and she looks out her window again, "Yes, fine, not sick."

Paige's mumbled response is strange. He needs to speak with her alone sometime today. He doesn't like her withdrawn manner.

"I almost fell four stories to my death," Paige adds nonchalantly as if she is making a joke.

Simon whips his head toward her with disbelief.

"Don't worry, Simon," she adds quickly. "Cory saved me."

"What was that about?" Simon asks of his friend.

Cory pauses and tells him, "Trap. Set by a bunch of creeps. She's fine."

"You take care of them?" Simon inquires.

His friend shrugs and says, "Nah, let 'em go. I didn't want to get into it with Paige tagging along with me. They were armed. We were outnumbered. We just did some E and E."

Simon nods solemnly and turns left.

"Cory got stabbed yesterday, though," Paige drops like a bomb. "You might want to look at that."

"What?" Sam screeches, nearly breaking Simon's eardrums.

"It's fine. Let's not all get dramatic about it. It's just a scratch. We'll treat it later tonight," Cory reprimands.

Unlike Paige, Cory seems in a foul mood, other than teasing with Sam. He's aloof and staring out his own window.

"Sure, no problem, bro," Simon offers. "I'll take a look at it tonight in the cabin."

"The cabin?" his friend asks.

"Yeah, I think I've found somewhere we can stash the Suburban so that we can sleep out at the cabin tonight. Kelly wants us to check on it anyway, make sure nobody's been there. I was thinking that we'd stay there for the night and kill two birds with one stone."

"That'll probably work," Cory replies. "The cabin will be a better place to sack out, safer."

Simon pulls around to the back door, and they get out. Cory shoves the employee entrance door inward since it is stuck, the hinges probably rusting from lack of use. He also volunteers to stand guard, watching the SUV, especially after the incident at the Parthenon. They make fast work of tearing shoes out of boxes and hauling them to the trunk. By the time they are done, the space starts to get cramped. Simon isn't sure how much more they are going to be able to haul. Sometimes they stack items on the roof and strap them down. However, now Sam's salvaged paintings are up there. The girls even bring armloads of clothing with yellowing price tags still hanging from them.

When they are done, Cory suggests going to a brewery to see if they can steal the alcohol-making equipment there. Simon's not sure where they're going to fit it, but they drive over there anyway. This time, they leave the girls to guard the back door and alleyway while he and Cory go into the restaurant brewery.

"See?" Cory comments with enthusiasm. "This thing'll work. We could make moonshine out of grain."

Simon looks at the monstrosity, not sure how the hell they'll ever get it back to the farm.

"What's the plan?" Simon asks his friend.

Cory smiles and says, "Not sure. Don't really have one. Too bad we don't have that trailer we stole a few weeks back. We should've brought it with us."

Simon nods and thinks about their predicament before saying, "Or one of the pick-up trucks the guys took home yesterday. It would fit in the bed of one of those."

Cory is squatted down looking at the pipework and valves. Then he sets his rifle on the floor and lies down where he can shuffle under the big tank of the still.

"Oh, yeah," he mumbles. "I think we could build one of these pretty easily. Doesn't look too hard."

"No, it doesn't, but are we going to be able to get the parts? That's the problem," Simon replies.

"I think we can do this," Cory says again. "I've got an idea."

He shimmies back out from underneath the tank and goes to the SUV again. He returns a moment later with an instamatic camera and takes three pictures of the piping and the tank.

"This is good," Cory tells him. "I think me and Derek can figure this out by these photos."

"Good," Simon confirms. "I think we should've given you the name of 'Mechanic' instead of that Dave guy."

Cory chuckles and says, "I don't think so. But those guys seemed cool."

"Yeah, I thought so, too. Sam didn't like them, though," Simon tells his friend quietly so that she doesn't overhear.

Cory glances up at him from his squatted position where he's monkeying around with the valves. "I'm sure she didn't. I don't think your sister was crazy about them, either. They just don't trust men too much. But can you blame 'em? I wouldn't either if I was a woman."

Simon jabs, "You mean more of a woman than you already are?"

Cory stands and punches his shoulder.

"How'd everything go last night with my sister?"

Cory's eyes jump quickly to Simon's. Then he turns away before saying, "Um, fine."

"Really?" Simon asks with disbelief. His friend is obviously trying to cover for whatever transpired. "You two don't exactly get along, Cor. Were you fighting or something?"

Cory grabs his rifle and says, "No, not exactly. We're trying to put it behind us and turn over a new leaf and shit."

"Well said," Simon remarks with sarcasm.

"I'm not a senator's son. I'm no great orator," he jokes.

Simon chuckles and would like to remind his friend that he really isn't the son of anyone. His parents are both dead, that part of his life long gone.

"Looks like you guys had some luck at the hospital," Paige remarks when they join up at the hatch of the SUV again. "There's a lot of stuff back here."

"Yes, it was good. Right, Simon?" Sam asks for confirmation.

He nods in agreement but says, "We need to find gas, people. We don't know how it's going to go with the CNG for those trucks, if it even works. We need fuel to continue making trips to the clinic each week. We're getting more and more patients every week who are hearing about the clinic. We have to continue our work there."

Cory snaps a picture of Paige and Sam. His sister gives an uncomfortable grin, but Sam smiles happily, of course and wraps an arm around Paige. She's always quick to offer a kind smile to Cory. Apparently the night before hadn't gone as well as Cory had said with

Paige. She seems to be keeping her distance physically from him and even walks around to the other side of the SUV to get away.

"We're gonna need to think outside the box to find somewhere with gas. Everything's already been picked," Cory remarks as they get into the SUV. "Maybe we'll find another trailer, too."

Simon notices that his sister is sitting in the back seat with Sam this time. Naturally, Sam is going on and on about the Parthenon, the architecture and the art there while Paige either nods or simply stares out her window again.

"We could head over to the river marina. Maybe steal some fuel out of boats if nobody else has thought of it," Simon suggests what he's been thinking for a few days.

"That's usually a dangerous area," Cory comments with a serious furrow of his thick brow.

"I know, but we need it," Simon argues. "Maybe we could take the girls to the cabin later and come back just me and you."

"At night," Cory suggests to which Simon nods. "Where to now?"

"Doc said to look for some new valves for the gas lines if we can find any at a home improvement store," Simon tells him. "There's a big box store, a Lowe's or something like that, to the south of us."

"Cool," Cory agrees. "Let's head there."

"Good," Sam says from the back seat. "I need to go to the bathroom."

"Me, too," Paige puts in. "Drive faster."

Simon chuckles at the girls and steps on the gas but not in an unsafe manner, of course. Plus, he has to swerve around a tipped over school bus in the middle of the road. They get lost a few times, have to backtrack, but eventually find the Lowe's store. Simon pulls around to the side, cautiously watching out for dangers.

"There, park over there, bro," Cory instructs, pointing to an area near four dumpsters.

There isn't a soul in sight, which is a good thing. Simon still can't shake his feeling of edginess. The space is perfect for hiding the vehicle, but he wonders if the store will prove abandoned or if they are walking into an inhabited village of people living in there.

"Well, I can't wait another second," Sam blurts and jumps out of the SUV.

351

Simon grits his teeth and tries not to get mad at her. He and Cory also get out, followed by Paige.

"Over there," Paige says, pointing toward a rickety wooden privacy fence. "We can go over there, Sam."

"No, that's too far," Simon counters as he slings his rifle over his shoulder.

"Too bad," Sam says. "We're going over there. Just wait for us. We could use some privacy if you don't mind!"

The fence is a good twenty to thirty yards away across a patch of overgrown grass. On the other side of it seems to be some sort of junkyard or scrap metal facility.

"Find somewhere else," Cory chirps. "That's too far, kiddo."

Sam is shoving her rifle and handgun into Simon's hands without asking.

"I gotta go!" Paige insists.

Cory sighs hard and jogs over to the area the girls want to use. He comes back a minute later and declares the area empty.

"I'm still not sure. I don't know if we'd hear you that far away," Cory announces.

"Control freaks," Sam reprimands. "Look around, Cory. There isn't a single, solitary person anywhere. Come on, Paige."

"Really, guys," Paige says, tossing her jacket into the SUV. Sam does the same with hers. "Lighten up and give us some damn privacy. We don't just whip it out anywhere and wizz. Just give us a couple minutes, ok?"

"You have two minutes and I'm comin' after you whether you're done or not," Cory says before Simon can even respond with more arguments.

He doesn't miss the sneer that Paige shoots his friend. Apparently she doesn't like him ordering her around. He's learning that most women don't appreciate that, even if the men doing the ordering only have their best interest at heart. They really are irrational sometimes. His sister is about as good as Samantha at taking orders.

Paige glances over her shoulder. She isn't looking at him, though. She's hitting Cory with a perplexed look before turning back. Sam giggles at something Paige says to her. He regards his friend, who is staring hard at the girls as they retreat. His face is concerned like Simon's right before he turns away to shove articles farther into the trunk to make room for the valves they will hopefully find. He doesn't think Cory is too thrilled with the girls' behavior today, either. At least his sister still has her gun on her hip.

Chapter Twenty-four
Paige

"I'll just go over there, Paige," Sam suggests once they round the tall, faded brown fence.

"Where? We shouldn't split up," Paige says with concern.

"Just on the other side of that shed. I don't want to pee in front of you. I have a shy bladder," Sam says with a grin before walking away.

"Um…" Paige stammers.

"It's cool," Sam reassures her. "I'll be one minute. I can go fast. Lots of people I have to share a bathroom with back at the farm has given me new skills. I've learned. Be fast or have kids banging on the door."

Her long black hair is hanging loose and free today instead of in the usual ponytail. It nearly blends seamlessly into her black turtleneck, the same one that Paige is pretty sure belongs to her brother. Sam smiles over her shoulder before disappearing to the other side of the old shed.

Paige looks around to make sure they are still alone. She quickly squats and does her business, not wanting to anger the men or have Cory come after her. The last thing she needs is to have him catch her in the middle of going to the bathroom. This morning had been unpleasant and strange enough. After a night of the best sex, the most insanely great sex of her life, she'd practically passed out from exhaustion. She'd fallen asleep on his wide, muscular chest on an antique bed in a beautiful, Victorian mansion. She's gone in a one month period from loathing to wanting him. The whole scenario had been surreal.

She's never felt like that with anyone before Cory. He played every square inch of her body like a finely tuned instrument, one that only he possessed some secret passport of information for bringing to pleasure. She is also quite sure that she doesn't really want to know where he seems to have attained such valuable insight into the female anatomy. But their second and then third time together had been even better than the first. He'd brought something out of her that she never knew she could be, could feel. She'd been uninhibited and carefree with him. Gone was her gangly, awkward ineptitude. He'd made her feel confident and beautiful, something she's never felt before. She has no idea how he feels about their sexual escapades last night because he didn't discuss it with her. His libido knew no limits. He'd initiated their third time before dawn, had awakened her from a coma. Paige hadn't felt like she'd be able to. Her poor body was exhausted, rendered weak and limp by him, but he'd somehow reawakened a desire within her. He had an insatiable appetite for touching and caressing her so softly. Paige never would've thought Cory could be gentle, either, but he was. She's under no false assumptions that he has feelings beyond anything merely sexual for her. He's certainly not in love with her. Most of the time, they can barely tolerate being in each other's company.

But this morning was the worst part. She'd awakened in a cold, empty bed. Cory was long gone. She'd slowly dragged her fatigued body from the expansive bed and found a fresh set of new clothing waiting for her beside her pack. She has no idea where he got the clothing or how he knew her sizes, but he'd gone somewhere and found her new, clean clothes. Perhaps he had gone into the dormitories of Belmont University and ransacked for items. It was greatly appreciated. He'd brought her a pale lavender, fishermen's knit, cotton sweater, a warm, sheepskin-lined denim jacket and a pair of blue jeans that fit the length of her legs correctly. He'd even found another pair of socks, pink cotton undies and a new black bra. She's pretty sure how he figured out that size. With the amount of time his hands had spent roaming freely about her body, he's probably more qualified to choose her sizes than her.

She pulled on her new clothing, tried not to wince at her aching muscles. Her inner thighs were especially sore. She'd quickly brushed out her hair and tied it in a ponytail with one of the leather strips from her wrist. His gear was gone. He was gone. The fire was out, long since gone out and only cold gray ash remained in the bottom of the fireplace instead. She hadn't been sure if he was coming back for a few panicky moments. He'd left a small brown paper sack on the stand where they'd eaten the previous evening. A bottle of water was next to it. She scarfed down the homemade scone and hardboiled egg that was tucked away in the bag, her appetite at an all-time high. Then she'd swigged some of the water, thankful he'd left sustenance for her. Paige had packed up her gear and was ready to head out and find him right as he came through the bedroom door.

It was uncomfortable. It was so way far beyond uncomfortable that Paige doesn't even have a name for it. He'd grabbed her rifle for her, announced that it was time to move, and left the room all without looking directly at her. She'd asked him to use the bathroom before they left the mansion, but that had been their only conversation. In his defense, she'd been the one to say that their sexual encounter would never be repeated.

He'd led her through the city to meet up with her brother and Sam all without speaking or looking at her. He was careful of her, helped her over some debris in the middle of a road they had to cross, looked over his shoulder frequently to make sure she was still with him, but that was it. There wasn't a big profession of love, or talk of feelings, or morning time cuddles. Just as she'd thought, he has zero feelings for her. Last night was merely another notch in the belt for Cory. It hurts a little more than she cares to admit. Mind-blowing sex is apparently the norm for him, but it certainly isn't for her. The fact that he is ignoring her tells Paige that he isn't interested in pursuing anything more serious in nature than their one-night stand. She'll just have to move on, as well, and try to put it behind her. Distancing herself from him is probably the best plan of action.

She stands and zips her pants again, readjusts her gun belt and waits for Sam. After a few seconds, she calls over to her.

"Hey, Sam, you ready?"

No answer comes. Paige gives it another few seconds, calls again, gets nothing, and decides to walk around to the other side of the shed. Perhaps she can't hear her calls over on this side. She bumps her thigh into a piece of scrap metal near the shed, curses, and rounds the building. The hedges and overgrown grasses are tall on this side, making a deep camouflage. She feels like a gazelle, as if a lion could be hidden in that thick, wheat-colored, blowing grass. It sends a chill up her back.

"Sam?" she calls quietly.

Paige creeps closer through the thick foliage. Then her heart sinks because she sees Sam's backpack on the ground. Beside it is one of Sam's short leather boots. Sam is nowhere to be seen.

She calls out but gets no response, just nothing but the deafening silence of her own voice echoing off of the buildings without a reply.

"Simon!" she screams loudly for her brother. Paige screams again and dashes back toward the guys, who both meet her in the middle. "She's gone!"

"What? Sam? Sam's gone?" Simon asks with a huge scowl.

"Yes, she went over there behind the shed to go," Paige babbles frantically as she leads them at a run toward the other side of the small building. "She wanted more privacy. I shouldn't have let her. Shit! This is my fault. This is all my fault. She's gone!"

Cory lays a hand gently on her shoulder as Simon grabs Sam's pack and shoe from the ground.

Cory questions, "It's ok. We'll find her. Did you hear anything? A scuffle? Voices?"

"No, no, nothing!" Paige exclaims with hysteria.

"They went this way. They dragged her but then it stops. I assume one of them carried her at that point. The footprints go deeper into the ground after that. Looks like two, maybe three men," Simon announces as he checks the soggy, muddy ground for footprints.

"Come on," Cory orders as he pulls her hand.

Paige follows dutifully as they sprint back to the SUV. Simon doesn't follow them. He takes off in the opposite direction.

"Where's he going?" Paige asks. She doesn't like the idea of her brother going off without them.

"He'll track. We'll follow. But we need more firepower and to lock the car," Cory explains patiently as they arrive at the Suburban.

Her hands are shaking. Cory does everything without her. She just stands there feeling useless and guilty for allowing Sam to be kidnapped in the first place. He grabs a few extra magazines for his rifle from the trunk. Then he locks the car and pockets the keys. He takes her hand again and tugs her after him.

357

"Stay close," he orders, letting go of her hand. "Don't leave my side unless I tell you to."

"What happened? How could something happen? Did someone take her?"

"Yes," he answers simply. "But they haven't gone far, especially if she's putting up a fight or if they have to carry her."

"What... where...?" Paige stutters, tears blurring her vision.

"It'll be ok. We'll find her. This isn't your fault," Cory says tightly.

"It is," Paige chokes, close to a full breakdown.

"Hold it together," Cory orders calmly. "We'll find her. They couldn't have gone far."

"Where's my brother?" Paige asks a moment later as she jogs beside Cory.

They are out of the scrap yard now and jogging down a long, narrow road, hardly wide enough for two vehicles. Industrial buildings line either side of the street. Most of them are brick, many have broken windows and wide open doors.

"He's up ahead of us. Not far. See?"

Paige squints into the distance and after a moment, spots her brother moving furtively through parked cars and trucks and then disappearing down another street. He's running very fast.

Cory picks up the pace, closing in on Simon with her. She has no idea how her brother is tracking them if that is what he's still doing. That is obviously a skill-set he's learned from the Rangers. They run for another five city blocks until they finally catch up to Simon, who has halted at the corner of a cement block building. There is an old stone church across the street, but much of the area is filled with manufacturing facilities, the grass overgrown and coming up through the cracks in the pavement, buildings looted and burned.

She stands behind Cory, who is lined up behind her brother. Paige pants lightly from their run and probably from adrenaline. She's scared to death that they will find Samantha dead, or worse yet, not find her at all, ever. Her brother uses two fingers to indicate a particular area in front of them.

"There's a man standing guard over there, Paige," Cory whispers. "We'll need to take him out. Simon will go in through the back. Looks like a warehouse or something."

"Do you think he took Sam?" she asks.

"That's them," her brother says, looking through binoculars. "Their muddy footprints lead over there. It's them. They've got her."

They haven't gone even a mile if she was to guess. Whoever took Sam didn't get far with her. They just zigzagged around the city. Perhaps she's still alive in there.

"I don't see anyone else," Simon notes.

"We'll come in through the front, brother," Cory tells her brother. "We'll cover you."

Simon's dark blue eyes are worried and impatient. They have a feral intensity in them as if he is barely containing the animal within. She is afraid for him. She doesn't want her brother to do something reckless and get himself killed because of his concern for Sam.

"Got it," Simon says as he brushes past her. "Stay with Cory, Paige. Stay together."

He grasps the back of her skull and pulls her quickly forward, kissing her forehead before taking off back down the same street. He's going to need a few minutes to circle the area to come in behind the other large building.

"We'll come in over there, see?" Cory asks, pointing toward a cluster of heavy equipment left abandoned. "You'll wait and cover me while I take out the guard. Got it?"

She nods jerkily. Her hands are shaking like crazy. She hopes nothing has happened to Sam. She's only been out of their sight for perhaps an hour. And a good portion of that time, her captors would've used up getting to the warehouse with her. Paige likes her new friend so much. She feels paralyzed by guilt. If anything happens to Sam, she'll never forgive herself.

Cory's warm hand stays her own. "Easy now. Stay calm."

He flicks the selector switch on her rifle to fire in single rounds instead of fully automatic.

"Let me lead. You're my cover. Just think about that. Remember your training. Just like plinking groundhogs. Don't let the rest of it get in your head, all right?" he asks, his dark eyes penetrating into hers.

"Yes," she answers with more courage than she feels.

"Let's move out now," he says, nods curtly to her and takes the lead.

359

They jog quietly through the area until they have come to the faded yellow bulldozer where he indicates she should squat on one knee and hide while also watching his back. Paige gives him another nod, and he leaves her. She watches in amazement as he sneaks ever so silently with his back against the wall of the building where the man is standing guard in an open doorway. The guard has a hunting rifle held in both hands out in front of him. He's smoking what looks like marijuana. He is unshaven, dirty and unkempt. Now she feels even worse that men like him would have Sam. She prays they find her unharmed.

Cory creeps along the wall until he is within fifty feet of the man but still hidden in a recess. Then he cups his hand and makes a strange sound, like that of an animal in distress. The man falls for the bait and moves toward Cory. Paige takes a deep breath and raises her rifle to offer assistance should he need it. What she doesn't expect to see is Cory sling his rifle behind his back and unsheathe his dagger. The man walks right past Cory in the dark corner and doesn't even see it coming. Her lover from the previous evening comes up behind the man and cuts his throat. Paige has to look away. The scene is gruesome. The blood sprays the brick wall of the old building. When she looks up, Cory has dragged his body into the corner and is signaling for her to come forward.

They move quickly, going inside the building and sweeping left and right. Her brother should already be to the rear and hopefully also inside. The small distinctive voice of a woman in distress assails her ears. They sprint toward the sound, coming to a wide open room with a gravel floor and an antique, rusted out pick-up truck in the corner. The room is surrounded by broken and cloudy windows. Most of the roof is just plain gone. She glances forward and sees her brother at the other end of the large space as he bursts through the other open door with his rifle raised.

What she spots in the bright mid-day sun in the middle of the room is something she would never wish upon her enemies to have to view. Samantha is sitting on a man on the gravel and dirt floor. She is straddled over him. The arc of her blade slicing through the air, the sound whishing as she stabs again and again into his chest. The soft, frantic sounds coming from Sam are frightening to Paige's ears. Sam's shirt is gone, her bra is half off, one strap hanging down her arm. Her right breast is exposed. However, it is also mostly concealed with the dead man's blood. The man is dead, long dead. She is in a rage filled state of mind, not herself.

"Sam, Samantha," Simon calls gently as he closes in on her.

Sam's eyes dart to Simon and she raises her knife at him as if she is preparing to use it on him, as well. Her lovely blue eyes aren't even seeing him. They aren't focusing correctly. The side of her face is plastered in the man's blood, and it streams down her chin and neck. It's even in her long hair. Her small, delicate hands are covered in it. Those same graceful fingers that draw such lovely art and play so nimbly on her violin are blood soaked.

"Sam, it's ok. We're here," Cory says softly and starts toward her.

Sam jumps off of the man, crouches and jabs her knife defensively toward Cory.

"Stay back," Simon warns and holds out his hand to them.

Her brother steps toward Samantha again and sets his rifle on the floor. His hands come up in front of him in a gesture of appeasement. He is able to sling his backpack to the ground next to her where he squats and pulls out a medical pack of some kind. He removes a bottle of water along with a rag. Sam allows him to take her dagger. Simon tosses it to the ground in front of Cory, who promptly picks it up, wipes it with a rag from his pocket and stashes it in his boot. Then he drags the corpse away into a far corner.

She finally speaks, softly, "He was going to…"

Paige winces. She understands what was about to happen. They all do.

"I know, honey," Simon tells her gently as he begins wiping at some of the blood on her face. "It's ok now. You're safe, Sam."

Her little hands begin shaking, and tears trickle down her pale cheeks. Paige wishes there was some way to comfort her, but she doesn't think Sam wants anyone else trying to touch or approach her. Just Simon. Paige knew all along that they share a special bond, but she had no idea it was this deep. Sam doesn't trust anyone but him.

"Was there anyone else, kiddo?" Cory asks, averting his eyes from her figure.

She watches as Cory strips out of his jacket, removes his cream-colored thermal shirt and hands it to Simon, who promptly pulls it down over Sam's head. Her eyes are showing more pupil than the beautiful blue of her irises. Paige has to look away for a moment. When she looks back, her brother is adjusting Sam's bra under her

361

shirt. Sam doesn't seem embarrassed or uncomfortable having him do so, either. She just sits there in a kneeling position.

"No, just the two men," she whispers.

Simon pulls her other boot from his backpack and puts it on for her, even tying the laces into a bow. Sam just sits there numbly, staring at nothing, wiping at the drying blood on her hands roughly against her black pants.

"There are others," her soft voice elicits.

Cory's head whips to the side as he regards Samantha, "What do you mean, kiddo? What others?"

"They were talking about taking me down by the river. They said that they were going to sell me to the boss down there. But the one, the one I... he suggested they stop here first and..."

Cory and Simon look at each other above her head as she speaks in monotones about the men.

"What do you think they meant by taking you down to the river, honey?" Simon asks as he shrugs out of his jacket and pulls it around her shaking shoulders.

"He said something about a camp down there. I think he meant there are other girls down by the river. His boss has them bring girls to the river. I think the way they were talking was that men go there and trade things for girls."

Paige feels like she's going to vomit. It sounds like a sex slave trade business has sprung up there. How could something like that have happened? Aren't people just concerned about surviving? She runs a hand over her sick stomach. Cory sees it and takes her hand into his. He squeezes it and holds onto her for a few moments, interlacing his strong fingers with hers.

"We need the truck," Simon says while still working on Sam's bloody hands.

"On it," Cory says, letting go of her.

"Should I go with Cory or stay with you?" she asks her brother.

"No, I'll go get it," Cory answers for Simon. "I'll be back in a few minutes. Keep a close watch on the doorways for Simon while he looks after Sam."

"'Kay," Paige agrees nervously.

He sprints from the building as Paige takes up a position to better see some of the entry points. Simon has a lot of the blood and mud cleaned out of Sam's hair before Cory gets back less than fifteen minutes later with the SUV. They pile in, but Sam insists that Simon sit next to her in the back seat, which leaves Paige sitting next to Cory who is still driving.

"Where are we going?" Paige asks Cory.

"Cabin," he answers.

"Really? Why? I think we should leave, go home," Paige argues softly. She doesn't want to seem impudent, but she's scared shitless of this damn city and wants to fly home to the nest, to safety and the rest of the family and the arsenal.

"You'll be safe at the cabin," he insists as he hooks a right on a road and drives at a relatively fast pace. "We have work to do now."

Paige tries not to let her mouth fall open, but it still does. Does he mean that he and Simon are going to go to the river camp to take out the bad people there? She sure as hell hopes not. They need to run. A moment later, her answer is given to her as he talks into the radio to John back at the farm. He explains the "sit rep" and then offers forth an idea to his mentor.

"We need to host a little housecleaning party on the river tonight, Doc," Cory says, using John's call sign of Doctor Death.

"We'll be there in an hour," John's answer comes promptly.

"Why don't you get ahold of your friend, the Mechanic, instead?" Cory suggests. "His group's closer and that way you guys don't have to leave the old MacDonald unattended."

Paige grimaces as she listens to this plan unfold. The silence on the radio just means the men at the farm are discussing this option.

"That would work," John says through the static.

"Have him rendezvous at the King of the Blues at twenty-three hundred hours, over," Cory says.

"Roger that," John agrees. "Call if you need reinforcements."

"Sounds like a bunch of chicken-shits," Cory says. "We've got this one, out."

John says the same, and they end their call.

"What's the king of Blues, code for someone's house or something?" Paige asks.

"BB King, the singer, the musician," Cory says as if he can't believe she doesn't know.

"I don't think I've heard of him," she admits, feeling stupid.

"He died a long time ago, but he was the best. There's a nightclub here still standing. It was his. I knew Dave the Mechanic's group would know it, especially if any of them were from around here," he tells her.

"Ok, we'll meet them at eleven o'clock, right?" she asks, still trying to catch on to the military time they all use.

"No, *we'll* meet them," he corrects her. "You'll be staying at the cabin with Samantha. You won't be going."

"But I can help," she argues.

"I'm sure you could, but we need you to stay with her," Cory says quietly.

Paige mouths the word, "oh." He's right. Samantha shouldn't be alone tonight. She's been through something horrible. Paige can't even imagine how she would've handled that situation of being kidnapped and almost raped. In her case, she probably would've been raped because she's not sure she could've stabbed that man to death. Sam is quite proficient with those knives she's always playing with, though. And now Paige understands that she is also very lethal with them, as well.

In the back seat, Simon is whispering comforting words to Sam. She isn't reciprocating the conversation. A glance over her shoulder and Paige observes Sam just staring straight forward at nothing. Simon continues to gently wipe at her hair, her hands and her face. She's in an almost fugue state. Paige realizes that staying with her little friend is not only important, it's imperative.

"Hang a left at the next street," Simon orders from the back seat.

Cory does as he says and starts heading west of the city until they are in an older residential neighborhood.

"Up ahead," Simon instructs. "There's a YMCA building. We can go around back. There's a big field there that leads to city-owned property and parks. Once we get the truck pulled into the woods out there, then it's only about a two mile hike to the cabin."

"How'd you know about this place? We don't usually leave the SUV over here," Cory remarks as he swerves around a parked, torched car.

Some of the stately homes have graffiti marring their lovely brick facades. Others have been partially or totally burned to the ground. It's a sad testament to the times in which they live when people could just go into such a nice neighborhood and spray-paint gang symbols on homes that were all protected by home security service companies. She's not sure where the residents have gone, but the neighborhood seems very empty.

"The last time I came to the city with Derek and Kelly, we found this shortcut that takes a lot of time off the trek to the cabin," her brother answers.

Cory finds the community club easily enough and pulls past the building. Chain-link fencing surrounds the property. Vines and weeds grow up through the links here and there. He actually smashes through the fence without batting an eye. Paige grabs the dashboard for support as he careens over a small hill and then into the city park. He slows down, weaves around a swingset, a slide, and a wooden play structure before stopping at the edge of the forest.

"Let me check it out," Cory says, jumps out and jogs into the woods.

He comes back a few minutes later and drives the vehicle into the forest, going slowly and steering around the thick, broken branches of trees. Cory drives as far as he can before they must stop because of a fallen, rotting tree.

"We'll hoof it from here," he announces.

Paige looks over at him and smiles complacently as he puts the vehicle in park. He glances her way, nods with a pained grin. Their uncomfortable situation this morning has been replaced with concern for their mutual friend. Knowing Cory, he's probably preoccupied with thinking about the evening's coming festivities. He hands her the keys to the vehicle.

"You'll keep them now," he says as Simon helps Sam from the SUV. "Pocket them. Keep them safe. Don't lose them. If the shit hits the fan tonight while we're gone, try to get to the Suburban. It'll get you out of the city faster. If you can't get to the vehicle, then you hide out in the woods somewhere with Sam. I'll track you down and find you."

"What about you guys?" she asks as her brother shuts his door. She is alone with Cory. "What if we take the Suburban like you're saying? What about you and Simon?"

He smirks with that usual cocky attitude he's always putting off and says, "Then we'll be hoofing it around the city and then back to the farm, too."

"Seriously?" Paige asks, thinking he's messing with her. "That's like twenty miles or so. Are you screwing with me?"

"Not yet today, but the day's still young," he replies with too much sexual implication and a wink.

Her cheeks redden and she frowns at him for the crude remark before turning away.

"I think it's actually twenty-five miles to the farm from here," he says with a sigh.

"You can't walk twenty miles back to the farm after what you're going to be doing tonight. You'll get too tired," Paige retorts and musters enough courage to look at him again. He's staring at her hair. His stare is intense and thoughtful. Then he smirks again and the humor is back.

"Well, like Kelly says, 'when you get tired of walking, you can always run'," he jokes.

Paige laughs once. "That's not nice."

Cory grins and shrugs. "Let's go. We've got to get Sam to the cabin. You'll look after her while we're gone, right?"

"Of course," Paige says vehemently.

Simon is already covering the vehicle with branches and leaves. Most of the trees have lost their leaves, but some still sport their fall colors. For the most part, their leaves are brown and dead, though. It'll help the dark tan Suburban blend right into the surroundings. Within a few minutes, the guys have the vehicle covered over. She helps some, too.

They meet Sam at the trunk and grab their extra guns and backpacks. Cory grabs the crate full of food. Without even verbalizing a plan, Simon hands his pack and Sam's to Cory along with his sniper rifle and her military rifle.

"What are you doing?" Paige stammers.

"Come, Sam," Simon says to his friend. "Up you go, kiddo."

366

"I'll walk," Samantha says weakly.

Paige notices that Simon has wrapped white gauze around her hands. Blood is seeping through. Her pants are torn at the left knee where blood stains the material. Her legs are quaking. She's barely on her feet.

Cory and Simon don't argue with her, though. Cory simply sets everything down, walks over to her, and lifts her onto Simon's back. Apparently her brother, who used to be a skinny rail, is going to hike Sam the whole two miles to the cabin on his back. She seems content to allow him. She rests her dirty cheek against his shoulder blade. Her eyes still seem unfocused.

Cory retrieves all of the items, including the crate full of their food. Then he grabs Paige's arm and pulls her forward through the woods with him. Another unspoken plan must be that he will lead and Simon will bring up the rear. It makes sense.

"Need me to get your pack for you?" he asks after ten minutes of walking.

"Are you crazy?" she asks as the sun glints through the trees onto his bare shoulders. He's removed his jacket and is only wearing a tattered wife-beater. She remembers those broad shoulders so well. The feel of them under her fingertips, his skin so silky, yet rough in places is simply too much to dwell on. There is a two-inch scratch on his right shoulder blade. She hopes it's from a branch poking him and not her fingernails last night. "You're already carrying so much. I feel like I should be offering you the help."

"Nah, I'm good. This is nothing."

She trots a few steps to catch up beside him.

"Do you think Simon's ok? I mean Sam is small, but that's still a lot to carry for two miles of hills and woods," she says with concern for her brother.

"Doesn't matter. She wasn't gonna let me touch her like that. When she gets… bad, she doesn't like being around people, especially men," Cory tells her.

"Oh," Paige says in a whisper. "That's terrible. I mean for you and her. I know how much you like her."

"Yeah, it's cool. We're all used to it. We don't bring it up or make a big deal of it. Reagan used to be worse. We just know when to back off. This is just gonna take her some time to come out of. She'll snap out of it and realize I'm still her big bro," Cory says,

367

holding a branch out of the way for her. "She just needs some space."

"Do you think she'll let me take care of her while you're gone?"

"I don't remember you having a penis last night, so, yeah, I'd say she'll let you help her," he teases quietly.

"Shh," Paige reprimands and slaps his shoulder. He just grins.

"Just be there for her. Do girl-talk or something. She'll do better with you than us anyway."

"I don't know about that. She is so close with Simon."

"True," Cory admits with a nod and brushes his long hair back. It's slick with his sweat. "Your brother is the only person she connects with when she's having a bad spell. They've been through some shit. I think it made her trust him and basically only him."

"She trusts you, too," Paige tells him.

"Not like him. She doesn't trust anyone like she does Simon," Cory says, glancing over his shoulder to ascertain that Simon's still with them. He raises his chin a notch at her brother. They have a lot of unspoken communication.

"I guess it's hard to trust anyone nowadays," Paige confides as they wade through tall weeds. The giant trees around her make her feel a little safer somehow. Walking beside Cory has the same effect.

"Do you trust me?" Cory asks, his gaze sliding onto her face.

His tone is serious, but Paige detects a certain amount of hope in it, too.

"You tried to kill me," she says with wide eyes.

"One little attempted murder..."

"And the threat of rape, don't forget!" she teases.

"Well, after the way you were last night, I should've been more worried about you raping me, woman," he jokes.

Paige's eye widen further, and she slugs him again, "Stop talking about that!"

"What? I'm just saying. You weren't exactly resisting too hard," he reminds her with a grin.

She shakes her head and glares at him. "Don't make me shoot you."

"Just pointing out some facts, ma'am," he teases.

"Stop," she warns. "You're forgetting our deal."

"Deal? Is that what the cool kids are calling it now?" he jests and bumps her shoulder.

Then she makes the mistake of looking up into his devilish brown eyes. The playfulness is gone, replaced with a hot desire, the same desire she'd seen last night. She hates the quickening of her breath and the tingling she feels in her stomach.

He leans close and whispers against her neck, "I thought it was called fucking."

"Don't be vulgar," she scolds and backs away to the sound of his soft chuckle. "And don't talk about it again."

"We don't have to talk about it. You're right. We should reenact it instead," he says huskily.

Paige stutters out, "Wh...what?"

He raises his eyebrows with two quick jerks, hinting that he is serious about his devious plan. Paige blushes and turns away again.

"Your loss," he repeats the same phrase she'd used on him last night. Paige just swallows hard and tries to concentrate on not tripping over tree roots or grabbing onto the long vines of poison ivy clinging to nearly everything.

"So, do you?" he asks a few moments later.

"Do I what?"

"Trust me?" he says barely above a whisper.

When she glances up at him, Cory is staring intently down at her. Words seem to fail Paige, so she just nods and looks at her feet. She peeks at him again to find him grinning confidently.

"Good. I trust you, too," he says.

"You do?"

Cory regards her with a smile, "Yes, and that's a lot more important to me than liking someone. I like a lot of people, but I don't trust them. I don't trust most people at all. The McClanes, your brother, that's about it. And now you."

"What about your town wenches?" she asks because she can't help the petty, female competitive bug from entering her brain.

He tosses his dark head back and laughs loudly, oblivious as usual to being quiet.

"Ha, no way. I'd never have a reason to trust them with my life. They were just... fun distractions for a while," he explains patiently. "You're one of us now, so I have to be able to entrust my life to you if something happens. It's pretty simple really."

369

"You… you'd trust me with your life? After what we've been through? I mean, we don't always get along, Cory."

"We did last night," he says with the eyebrow motioning again. "I should've just thrown you down in the forest when I first met you and seduced you into liking me. Sex seems to make you a little nicer."

Paige groans and grinds her teeth together, trying not to pay heed to his brazen comment. They come to a narrow stream that Cory makes sure everyone gets safely across. Then they pull ahead of Simon again.

"But you trust me that much?" she repeats, thankful for the new, waterproof leather boots on her feet. There isn't much worse than cold, wet feet when traveling in the middle of nowhere by foot.

He stops, grasps her chin, raising her face to his and says, "Absolutely."

Paige blinks hard. He's deadly serious. He also seems like he's about to kiss her. She hopes not. Her brother isn't far behind them. She also hopes he does.

"There's the cabin," he says, turning away and walking toward the small building she hadn't seen before. "We made it."

Simon comes up beside her and winks, still carrying Samantha with what seems is little effort.

"And so did your pussy of a brother," Cory calls over his shoulder with an obnoxious laugh.

Paige's mouth falls open at his crudeness and the insult of Simon. He truly is like being around a caveman most of the time. He's uncouth, crude and pretty much uncivilized. Last night he'd been very uncivilized, but she hadn't minded that as much. As a matter of fact, the thought of some of his more savage moments last night makes her toes curl in her boots.

She'd been worried about her brother, but he seems fine, not even winded or sweating. Sam, however, is still not talking. Simon walks past Cory and shoots him an angry look for the bad language, which just gets a laugh from Cory.

She trails after them, marveling at the concealment job the family has done on the small log cabin. Vines and overgrown shrubbery and grasses crawl up the sides of the front porch and onto the floor. It sits nestled in a small glen and would seem quaint if it wasn't for the fact this cabin isn't for a romantic, rustic getaway

370

honeymoon or family summer vacation. It's shelter from the night. It's a source of safety for a few short hours. This is her first stay in one of the family cabins. This one is supposedly larger than the other cabin that is located closer to Clarksville.

Simon lowers Sam to her feet, and she follows Cory into the cabin.

"Good," he declares. "Nobody's been here. That's a good thing."

"There isn't any electricity here, sis," Simon informs her as he leads her inside. "No gennie, either. Sorry. It's definitely what you'd call roughing it."

"This is a lot better than many of the places my friends and I stayed, so don't worry about us," Paige answers as she looks around.

"But there's water. Just pump it into the sink. Same in the bathroom. There's a toilet and sink in there. We try to keep it stocked with soap and towels. You girls can get cleaned up while we're gone," Cory offers kindly as he slings rifles and packs onto the single table.

Paige looks around the small, one room shack. A wood-burning stove, slightly smaller than the one in their cabin back at the farm, stands in the far corner. A wide, ceramic farm sink is connected to two base cupboards and a short countertop. The well pump is mounted to the top of the sink.

"I'll start a fire," Cory says and darts to the stove.

Simon calls over to him and says, "Thanks, man."

Her brother is still tending to Samantha, who he has moved to sit on one of the two beds; one of which is a small twin size and the other perhaps a queen. There is an oak nightstand separating the two beds. A lantern rests on the stand. She's thankful for the three lanterns and quite a few candles she spies spread around the small, dimly lit cabin. It's going to be dark soon. It's going to be pitch dark in this cabin without those. With her brother and Cory about to leave her, she's feeling especially on edge at the idea of being alone and being in charge. Her bravado- what little she ever had- is waning. She's never been here before, so she's not sure what to expect. Plus, she has the added responsibility of looking after Sam. It's not like she could just run if something bad happens because Sam is in no shape to run with her.

"Paige, get me some towels," Simon requests without looking up from Sam where he is knelt in front of her. "They're in the cupboard in the bathroom."

371

Paige moves quickly to the bathroom after she drops her pack on the bed. The bathroom is simple like the rest of the log cabin. A pedestal sink, a toilet and an antique claw-foot bathtub are the only fixtures other than the cupboard for linens and towels. She grabs a few of the towels, likely brought by the family from the farm or found on a run for supplies to Nashville. She rushes back to the main room and hands them to her brother.

"Grab me some cleansing fluid from my medical bag," he instructs as he unwraps the gauze from Sam's hands.

"Sure," Paige says in a rush and kneels on one knee beside him where his bag has been placed.

Cory takes one of the towels to the sink where he pumps water onto it. He wrings it out and brings it back to Simon.

"I'll fetch a bucket of water for ya, Doc," he says to her brother.

Simon sends an impatient look in Cory's direction. He hates it when anyone calls him a doctor. He turns back to Sam, who is sitting stoically while he tends to her.

"Do you want me to get some soap?" Paige asks. "You know, so that you can wash that blood off?"

"It's mostly hers, the blood on her hands," he explains as he tosses the one bandage to the floor.

"Really? What happened, Sam?" she asks her friend.

Sam just shrugs as if she doesn't know. Her shoulders slump again and she goes back to watching Simon work diligently. Cory returns a moment later with a small bucket of water.

"It's cold," he tells Simon as he places it near his knee.

Her brother looks up at her and says, "She's cut herself."

Cory touches Paige's arm and nods over his shoulder to indicate they should talk elsewhere. She follows him to the sink where he rinses the bloody rag Simon surrendered to him.

"She cut her hands when she was stabbing that guy," Cory explains.

"Really. How?"

Cory sighs softly and says, "It happens. There may have been a struggle and she was cut on her hands. Or once she stabbed him once or twice, his blood would've got on her hands. It made her hands slip on the hilt and then they would've slid forward. She probably didn't even feel it. Simon will check her cuts to see if any are deep enough for stitches."

"Oh my gosh," Paige exclaims. "I pray she's ok. I hope she isn't in pain."

"She's tougher than you think," he tells her as the blood water swirls down the drain.

"I know. It's just hard to remember because she's so tiny and sweet, too," Paige says sadly. Her heart is broken for what's happened to her friend.

Cory turns toward her and places a large hand on her shoulder. Then he says, "All women, you included, Red, are tougher than we give you credit for."

Paige grins and replies, "Wow, you sound like a feminist."

"Does that mean I like sexy, feminine women like you?" he whispers with an ornery smile.

"No, shh!" she scolds. "That's not what a feminist is."

The way he is smiling, Paige knows that he understands the meaning of the word and that he's just messing with her.

Static comes across the radio on Cory's hip. It's his brother back at the farm.

"Rendezvous with the Mechanic is a go," Kelly tells him.

She takes the wet rag from him and returns to her brother's side so that Cory can continue his conversation with Kelly.

"Here, Simon," she says, extending the cloth to her brother. "Is she ok? Does she need stitches?"

"No, the cuts are very shallow. I'll patch her up. You'll just keep an eye on her for me while I'm gone. I'll check her hands again when I get home later," he says.

She doesn't even like to think about him leaving again or the reason for their trip. She wants to go home to the farm where it's safe. Her flight or fight instincts are kicking in and telling her to fly.

"Sure, no problem," Paige tells him and sits on the bed next to Sam.

"Maybe you can get water heated on the wood-burner and help her get washed up in the tub later this evening while we're gone," Simon says, meeting her eyes for the first time. His are troubled and angry.

"Absolutely. We'll both get all dolled up and have some girl time without you lugs around," Paige declares, trying to be light and casual. She has no idea how to handle this situation with Sam. She mostly feels like breaking down and bawling like a child over what's happened to her little friend.

Simon washes away the blood splatters on Sam's hands, applies a cream and re-bandages them carefully.

"Do it just like you watched me bandage them, all right, Paige?" her brother asks.

"Yes," she says confidently, but she's not sure she can do it quite so professionally or perfectly as Simon.

"You eat some food and let Paige help you, ok, honey?" Simon says softly to Sam.

Samantha gives him a barely perceptible nod.

"I need to use the bathroom," she finally says as Simon stands.

"Sure," Paige says quickly. "Do you want me to come with you?"

Sam shakes her head and goes to the small bathroom by herself where she shuts the door quietly.

"Shit!" Paige hisses.

"She'll be ok, sis," Simon tells her gently.

"We need to roll soon, brother," Cory says as he enters the cabin again from wherever he'd gone.

"On it," Simon agrees with a nod.

Paige watches with great fascination as the men ready themselves and their weapons for the coming night assault. Simon whips off his shirt, tossing it onto the floor.

"Oh, um... should I go outside? Do you guys want some privacy?" Paige mumbles uncomfortably. It doesn't bother her that Simon is changing in front of her. He's her brother. But Cory is another thing altogether.

"You're fine, sis," Simon consoles her.

Cory laughs obnoxiously at her and says, "Really?"

She sends him a warning scowl. Simon changes without shame in front of her, pulling on black pants and a matching hoodie. Cory goes to the other side of the table where he throws down his pack and does the same. Only he doesn't pull on a hoodie or a jacket. He seems content to wear a tight black t-shirt and camouflage pants.

"Aren't you going to be cold?" Paige inquires from her spot on the bed.

He turns toward her as he buckles his belt and says, "I'm pretty hot-blooded." With his next comment, he winks. "Don't you know that by now?"

Paige blushes and turns away.

"Leave her alone, man," Simon says, falsely defending her. "Get your head in the game."

"My head's always in the game, Professor. Remember?" Cory says with a grin.

Paige doesn't want to think about that. She knows he's killed a lot of people, and she's also fairly confident he's always ready to do so again.

"Don't be foolin' around," Simon chastises like he's Cory's big brother. Cory just chuckles at him.

He loads many magazines of ammo into his cargo pockets. Her brother doesn't load as many mags but does take ammo for his sniper rifle. Then they both remove a small tub of black grease from their packs and smear the sticky contents around on their faces. Seeing them perform this final preparation makes Paige's stomach do flips. She is truly frightened she'll never see them again.

"Do you want to eat before you go?" Paige asks, preparing to dig food out of the crate and make them something.

"Nah, we'll take some stuff with us," Cory answers for them.

Sam emerges from the bathroom and just stands there staring at Cory slapping his ammo mag into the bottom of his rifle. Both men load packs onto their backs.

"I don't want you to go," she says directly to Simon as if they are the only two people in the room.

Her brother sighs, furrows his brow and crosses the room to her. He gathers tiny Sam into his arms and holds her close before kissing the top of her dark head.

"I'll bring him back in one piece, kiddo," Cory offers to give her hope.

It doesn't seem to work. Sam clings tighter.

"I'll be back soon," Simon says to her. "Stay inside with Paige. Lock the door when we leave. Keep an eye out. You'll both be safe here."

"We'll be careful, Simon," Paige says to her brother.

He dislodges himself from Sam, places her on the bed again, and leads Paige outside of the cabin where Cory is now waiting.

"Got your rifle and handgun?" Simon asks.

The setting sun behind him is spinning gold through his dark auburn hair before he pulls a black stocking cap over it. She also doesn't want him to go, but she also knows there isn't a damn thing she can do to stop them.

"Yes," she answers with a frown.

"Get her to eat something. It'll help settle her nerves. Take your time with her. She's in shock," Simon tells her.

"Oh," Paige says with surprise. "I didn't know that."

Her brother lays his hand on top of her head. Paige rushes into him, hugs him close.

"You'll be safe here. Anyone but us comes, then shoot them through the door. Don't even bother opening it. Be careful they don't flank the cabin. Then get to the Suburban with Sam and go home. We'll meet you at the farm. But I don't think anything will happen or I wouldn't leave you two here."

"When will you be back?" she asks nervously.

"Sometime in the middle of the night I suspect. It'll take us a while to run all the way to that end of the city," he says.

"Ok, I'll wait up. I'll take care of Sam. Don't worry about us. Just come back safe, Simon," she pleads softly, trying not to cry, although she feels the tears piling up and threatening to spill over.

Simon kisses her cheek, touches her shoulder again and turns to go.

"Ready?" he asks Cory, who has been standing a few yards away to give them some privacy.

"I'll catch up," he answers, earning a distrustful look from Simon.

Her brother relents and jogs away. Watching her brother disappear into the forest around them starts her heart beating too quickly for its own good. She twists her hands together nervously. Paige then presses both hands to her mouth to stop herself from calling him back.

She turns back toward the cabin, thinking Cory's forgotten something. However, he's just standing there looking at her. He's pulled his hair back into a tight ponytail. The look in his dark eyes is feral and barely controlled. He's ready for this fight. She can see it in him. He's out for blood tonight. He doesn't say anything, which makes her shift her weight uncomfortably to her other foot.

She shakes her head at him with confusion and says, "What?"

He doesn't answer but stalks forward, grabs her shoulders roughly and hauls her up against him for a searing kiss that burns her lips against his. Cory's hands move from her shoulders to sink deeply into her thick hair. His tongue plunges into her mouth, taking from her some small piece of Paige's inhibitions. His arms wrap around her and Cory lifts her clean off the ground. Her heart is pounding even harder. Her hands rest against his chest, exploring the broadness, the deep grooves of his pectoral muscles, and the hard planes. He breaks the kiss as quickly as he started it and sets her back to her feet. Then he steps away from her and chucks her under the chin with his fist.

"Don't be scared for Simon," he says firmly, his dark eyes narrowing. "I'll bring him back."

Then he jogs away without another word. So much for discretion and one-night stands. She hopes Simon didn't just witness that interaction.

Paige drags herself back inside the cabin and sets the two deadbolts which slam home with a resonating crack in the silence of the forest.

Chapter Twenty-five
Reagan

"Almost done, babe?" John asks, peeking his head through the open door of her research room at the clinic.

"Yes, give me a minute," Reagan returns with a smile as she looks up from her microscope.

Her husband ambles into the room, unaware that he could be bringing in an outside source of contamination. Reagan just smiles and goes back to the lens. She's been studying diseases a lot lately, trying to prepare for the coming cold and flu season, which has proven very deadly in the last few years. She's also been vigorously studying smallpox, but she hasn't told anyone that.

"Is Grandpa ready?" she asks him.

John slides his hands around her waist from behind before nuzzling her neck.

"That's not helping," she reprimands weakly.

John just chuckles in her ear and says, "Maybe not, but it's helping me. And, yes, he's ready. But he said to take your time because he's talking to the sheriff."

"What about?" Reagan asks as she pushes a different slide under the microscope.

"The thefts we've had in town," he tells her honestly before allowing his hands to fall away from her.

"Great," she says sarcastically. "Hope they catch whoever's doing it. I thought theft wouldn't be a problem for a while still. And here we are with some asshole running around stealing from people already. So much for our peaceful little town."

"Could just be someone too embarrassed to come forward and ask for help," John offers.

Reagan can tell that he doesn't really believe that.

"Yeah, sure," Reagan scoffs and leans back into his wide chest. He immediately starts rubbing her shoulders. "Sounds more like an asshole who's taking things that don't belong to him. Sounds like the visitors all over again. Those were some real winners."

Her husband, who smells dirty and sweaty and divinely sexy, chuckles. The deep tones of his voice draw her in like a drug.

"We don't have any leads yet," John says with a sigh and does not comment on the visitors.

"Even better," Reagan returns with sarcasm and swivels in her seat to face him.

"Don't worry," John says, laying his hand against her cheek, the scarred one. "We'll find them. It's a small town. Gossip and all."

His grin could disarm a nun. Reagan feels herself being pulled into him, into his inner warmth and comfort.

"What about Simon and the others? Any word?" she asks.

John sighs with great trouble on his mind, "No, I still think I should've gone over there. Just in case."

"But I thought you guys said that Dave the Mechanic's group could handle this with the kids... I mean Simon and Cory," she corrects. It still feels strange thinking of them as adults, especially Simon. It seems like yesterday that he was a gangly teenaged boy with freckles, glasses and tasseled loafers. He's pretty much still the same, minus the gangly part. He's filled out a bit.

"Oh, yeah. He's definitely capable of handling a small mission like this. I just don't... I don't know," John laments and tugs her lab coat until she's closer.

Reagan knows he is restless, anxious for a fight. It's not in his blood to be a farmer, a councilman of sorts of a small town, or the husband of the town doctor. He's not one to be forced onto the sidelines when a battle is looming. He's itching for this fight. She feels bad that he can't go, but they can't afford the use of the gas. They don't have the natural gas compressor up and running yet. They're close, but the system needs a few tweaks.

"I know, babe," Reagan says with sympathy, although her selfish side is glad he can't go. When John leaves her for a mission, the tightness in her chest, the shortness of breath, the heightened anxiety she feels is nothing short of a panic attack. She can't bear to be separated from her damn husband. She blames him for this, too. Before John, she didn't have to worry so much. To soothe his longing for the battle, Reagan adds, "We'll just have to find another way for you to work off all that pent-up energy."

His eyes jump to hers, instantly playful and ready for the challenge.

"Oh really?" he drawls in that sexy tone of his. "Hm, sounds promising, Doctor Harrison."

John pulls her closer, wedges between her legs dangling over the stool. He stoops over. His mouth lands on hers with a heat that is instant and consuming as usual. The hand at her waist moves within moments to cup her breast. Reagan winces and pulls back.

"Sorry," she apologizes. "Think I might be getting ready to ovulate finally. I think it's been close to three months since I last did. I'm not sure. We've been crazy around here. I lose track. But they've just been sore, so I'm assuming it's on the way. We should be more careful right now, too. Don't want to take any chances and accidentally get knocked up."

"Why not?" John asks. "Jacob could use a brother... or a little sister to look after."

Reagan snorts and replies, "No thanks. He's got enough step-siblings at the farm. I'm not a brood mare, Harrison. And don't get your hopes up like that anyway. It's not going to happen for us, John."

"Then why be careful?" he asks, brushes her hair back from her forehead and kisses the tip of her nose.

"Just in case," she says snidely and wrinkles her nose at him.

John just chuckles and pulls her down from the stool.

"Let's grab the others and head home," he suggests as they leave the lab room and he flicks off the light.

"Sounds good," she agrees and clasps his hand in hers as they check the back door and make their way to the front of the clinic.

"I'm kind of tired tonight anyway. We should get back before Hannah has dinner finished. She'll be after us if we're late. Or else she'll get the Hulk after us."

"Of the two of them," John starts, "I'm more afraid of Hannie."

Reagan laughs as he locks the front door.

"Of course you are. You're a smart man, John," Reagan says with a grin. "I wouldn't have married you if you weren't afraid of Hannie. That would've meant you were a blooming idiot."

He laughs as they meet Sue and Grandpa a few blocks down the street near the main drag where the sentries are posted.

He is speaking with the sheriff, who has turned out to be a valuable ally so far in keeping the town safe and secure, minus the random burglaries. He's a soft-spoken man with a kind disposition and an uncanny ability to talk people through their disputes and differences. He is laughing at something Grandpa had said before they arrived. Not surprising. Her grandfather is as good at making people laugh as her husband.

Static comes across the sheriff's radio, so he plucks it from his hip and speaks a few yards away from them.

"We should get going," Reagan says to her grandfather, who nods.

The sheriff grabs John's arm to halt them. He extends his index finger to indicate they should wait a moment. He ends the call to whomever it was he was speaking and turns to them again.

"Someone's at the gate for you, Doc," the sheriff says to Grandpa.

"Who is it?" John asks, the tension causing his shoulders to rise.

"Not sure. Want me to come with y'all?" the sheriff asks.

"Yeah, that'd be great," John answers for them.

They walk in a group to the wall with the sheriff. Armed sentries guard the towers as well as the entry gate.

"Open it," John calls to the guards. He has raised his rifle toward the front of his body instead of slung onto his thick shoulder.

"What's going on?" Derek asks as he jogs over.

Her brother-in-law had been working on the wall build, which seems is never going to be finished in Reagan's impatient opinion. Derek also unslings his rifle from his shoulder and holds it at a slightly more casual angle in front of him.

John explains, "Somebody wants to see Doc."

Both guards unlock the big mechanism, sliding the long bar to disengage the security system. Then they pull hard on the heavy steel doors on rollers and drag them to an open position. Reagan is surprised at what she sees. Instead of a person standing there, they are greeted by an older model white- or what was once white- short bus like the kind that retirement homes would've used to drive their residents to and from appointments.

The bus door squeals loudly as it opens and a tall man slowly comes down the three stairs, backlit by the setting sun. He takes a few cautious steps toward them.

His appearance is haggard and fatigued. He may be tall, but he's thin. His hair is nearly all white. He's wearing a military uniform that has long since seen better days and no longer fits him correctly.

"Robert?" Grandpa stutters unsurely.

Reagan can't believe her eyes as the man approaches closer. There is a fading bruise on his left cheek and one that matches under his right eye. His knuckles appear scraped and bruised, as well.

"Dad?" Sue asks incredulously.

The man holds out his hand to them.

"Dad?" Sue asks again and runs into his arms, nearly knocking him down.

"Colonel?" Reagan repeats the name he most preferred.

She doesn't join her sister in a joyful, tear-filled reunion, though.

"Robert, is it really you?" Grandpa asks.

"Yes, sir," her father answers stoically. "It's me. I'm home."

"Welcome home, son," Grandpa says and hugs her father, patting his back twice before pulling away. "Come home to the farm. We still have it in production, probably more than it ever was. You can come there with us. We were just going home for the day."

"For the day?" her father asks weakly.

"Yes, Reagan and I still run my practice here in town. Well, as best as we can," Grandpa explains.

Her father's light blue eyes dart toward her. She just inches closer to John and appoints her father a stare that does not warrant the same warmth that her sister and grandfather have offered him. She doesn't feel it, so she shouldn't fake it. This man left them years ago to be raised by his parents. He shirked his responsibilities. The apocalypse doesn't change that, doesn't give him a free pass to show up now to be father of the year.

"You've grown up so much," he remarks toward Reagan.

"Yeah, well, Grandpa and Grams fed us, so that's kind of what happens to kids," she replies with antagonism.

"Let's go home, everyone," Grandpa orders sternly.

Reagan knows he doesn't want to get into this in the middle of the street in town. He's always been a private person. Airing their dirty family laundry on Main Street isn't exactly going to please him, and he knows how she feels about the Colonel.

"I'm with some people," her father says.

"Oh?" Grandpa asks.

"They're with me," he explains.

Her father must catch the look that Derek shoots Grandpa because he quickly expands with, "They're safe. They aren't a danger."

John and Derek also exchange a look. Grandpa will have to be the one to authorize the new people onto his farm. It is, after all, his farm. And her father is obviously road wary enough to realize that they aren't going to just take in strangers without them being vetted by him.

"How many?" John asks, earning an expression of curiosity from her father as if he is wondering who John might be.

"Just three, four counting myself," the Colonel answers. "A woman and two young people."

"We'll make some room at the farm until we can figure this out. Others have stayed on the farm until we were able to find them an empty house in town. I don't see a problem," Grandpa says, looking for similar opinions from John and Derek, who both nod.

Reagan isn't as sure of this plan. For all she could care about her withered-looking old father, he could stay in town. He's obviously had a tough go of it since the country fell because he damn near looks older than Grandpa.

"Yes, sir," the Colonel answers her grandfather.

"Just follow us, Robert," Grandpa says. "We have some of the property booby-trapped, so it's dangerous unless you go in the right way. If you get lost from us, just go in behind the Johnson's farm on that oil well road. That'll bring you all the way in to the back of our farm now. The road's completely blocked. This is the only safe way in."

"Got it," he agrees and heads back to his shitty bus.

He follows them back to the clinic where they pile into the truck. Derek drives with Sue wedged between him and Grandpa in the front seat. John and she ride in the back seat together where he clasps her hand tightly. He knows she needs his strength right now. He always knows when she needs him and when she just needs him to back off.

The three in the front talk animatedly about the return of Robert. Sue seems happy. Derek is non-committal but probably happy for Sue, and Grandpa is rationing his comments with great conservative reserve.

"Hannah will be so glad," Sue says.

Reagan just rolls her eyes out of view behind her sister's head.

"You ok?" John inquires, his forehead pressing close to her ear.

Reagan nods and whispers so that the others can't hear, "It's just weird. He hasn't been home since Sue got married. He's never even seen their kids. And now what? We're just supposed to usher him and a busload of people onto the farm? Where the fuck's he been? We thought he was dead."

"Let's just hear what he has to say, babe," John says, wrapping an arm around her shoulders and squeezing gently. "It took Paige a long time to get home to Simon."

"She's a kid," Reagan hisses. "He's an adult man, a Marine, no less. And why now? Why didn't he come home sooner if he could have?"

John just frowns and shakes his head. What can he say? There isn't a good excuse for not coming home to the farm.

She glances periodically over her shoulder, spying the one working headlight of her father's bus in the foggy distance. They arrive at the farm, and everyone gets out. Kelly immediately comes off the back porch with his shotgun raised in a defensive manner. John quickly goes to him to explain as others file out of the house and barns to greet them and inspect the new vehicle. Huntley gets the scoop and runs for the house, probably to announce the newcomer to anyone still inside.

Her father comes down out of his bus again and stands there looking around at the place. Outlines of other figures are almost visible through the dark tint of the bus's windows, but nobody else comes out. Reagan notices what can only be a wide smear of blood on the side of the white bus. It's not fresh, but it's still there, nonetheless. He is still looking at the house, the barns, the back porch which no longer matches the rest of the porches because it had been burned and rebuilt. If he feels any sort of disappointment in how they have kept the farm running, then that's too damn bad. Reagan would like to point that out to him. That's when she notices the cane in his right hand that he's using for support. Grandpa must notice it at the same time because he steps forward to speak with Robert.

Hannah comes onto the back porch, allowing the screen door to slam uncharacteristically loudly. Huntley follows protectively behind her.

"Is that my Hannah?" the Colonel asks with a smile.

Kelly is at her side in a second, helping her down the porch stairs. He guides her closer until she is within a few feet of their father. She doesn't say anything or offer a hug or touch, which is strange for Hannah.

"Your traveling companions must be hungry, Robert," Grandpa says with a cordiality that the rest of them just don't feel, except maybe Sue.

"Yes, sir," he acknowledges with a nod. "We've been on the road for months."

"Yes, I would imagine," Derek says kindly.

Her father leans into the open door of the bus and calls to the other people. One by one they file out, all three of them. They appear healthy and well kept, in stark contrast to her father. The woman's dark hair is nearly black, touches of silver threaded through the strands at her temples. Her hair is pulled back into a neat, tidy bun. Her long dress comes almost to her ankles and reminds Reagan of something a schoolmarm would wear. She is tall and thin but seems healthy, which is good because they don't need any more germs brought to the farm. The boy is maybe in his early twenties or so and neatly dressed and turned out. He looks like someone her father would've had working under him in the Corps, like a young cadet. He is very tall and handsome. The girl is younger, perhaps early teens. She also has the dark hair of the other two, but it is cut into a short, pixie style. She is not dressed like a cadet. Her clothing is grungy and looks to be so on purpose. She wears torn jeans and a black leather jacket that is too big for her over a man's flannel shirt. Her hazel eyes regard Reagan with caution.

"Sir, I'd like you to meet my family," the Colonel says.

Nobody says anything. Everyone just stands there trying to pick their jaws up off the ground.

"This is Lucas, my son," her father says.

Grandpa extends his hand to the young man's already outstretched hand. Lucas has impeccable manners, nothing short of what the Colonel would expect if this is his son.

"And my daughter, Gretchen," he says.

"Just G," the girl corrects, earning a frown from her father. "Nobody calls me Gretchen, just him. Everyone just calls me G."

Reagan almost laughs. Gretchen obviously feels the same about the Colonel as Reagan does.

"Nice to meet you, dear," Grandpa says.

Reagan can tell that he's in processing overload; they all are. It's like the world tipped just a little off its axis while they were at the clinic today.

"And my wife, Lucille," her father introduces his supposed wife.

The woman shakes Grandpa's hand and greets him with a cordial smile. She must feel out of place.

"Wait just a goddamn minute," Reagan says.

"Still using colorful language I see," the Colonel remarks with a tight frown.

"Since you haven't been a part of my life since I was Sue's second to the youngest's age, I'll refrain from feeling put in my place by you, *dad*," Reagan says with a glower of budding hostility.

Her father frowns harder. This is the same frown that would've caused fear in Reagan's heart when she was a little girl.

"How old are you, Lucas?" she asks of her father's son.

"Um, hello, ma'am," he stammers uncomfortably and extends his hand which Reagan refuses. "It's nice to make your acquaintance."

"Don't call me ma'am," Reagan corrects angrily. "We're supposedly related. How old are you exactly?"

"Reagan, that is enough of the interrogations," her father warns.

"Excuse me?" Reagan counters. "Tell me this is an orphaned family you've adopted. Tell me this isn't really happening and you aren't related to these kids by blood, Robert."

"I said that's enough, young lady," he states slowly. "This is my family. You need to settle down."

"Uh-uh, I don't think so. You aren't getting off that easy. You think you can come home after how many years and stake a claim here and set up your family here like you have a right to?"

Everyone falls silent at this. John takes a step forward, a little closer to her, assertively showing his relationship to her.

"Oh, yeah! This is my husband," she states angrily and indicates with her hand toward John. "And the big guy? That's Hannah's husband. And they have a kid, and so do we. And Sue has three now. And we have a farm full of orphans. Some are even gone on a run getting supplies for us. Oh, and they're about to get into some shit with some dirtbags tonight, into an all-out military scale battle, but you wouldn't know that now would you? No, because you haven't been around too much for the last fifteen years or so. And no fucking wonder. You've got a whole new fucking family, don't you, pops?"

"That's quite enough now," Robert says with his own amount of anger aimed at her.

Sue asks, "How old is Lucas, Dad?"

She has apparently caught on to the point that Reagan is trying to get across.

"I'm twenty-three, ma'am," Lucas answers and looks at his feet.

Reagan is sure that the young man has no idea what is going on. He just knows that it is something bad and uncomfortable.

"Holy shit!" Reagan shouts to the heavens and hits her father with a venomous glare. "Wow, you are a real piece of work. Did you even wait for Mom's grave to get cold, you bastard?"

Grandpa comes over and rests a hand gently on her forearm. Then he looks at his son, fully expecting an explanation.

"Don't speak to me that way. I'm your father. Show some respect," he disciplines.

"Respect?" Sue whispers and turns her head away to shield her face.

"I loved your mother..."

Reagan snorts and laughs loudly at him.

387

"I did," he insists. "But when she got sick, I just… I couldn't…"

Reagan interrupts him in a lower tone and spits, "You're so weak. You ditched us. You ditched mom when she needed you the most."

"I did the best I could," her father admits.

"You left!" Reagan shouts through a haze of hatred. John pulls her closer and wraps his arm securely around her waist.

"But I'm back now," he says pathetically and hangs his head.

"Where have you been?" Sue asks.

Their father looks relieved for a break from her questioning. Reagan doesn't care. She'll get back around to that line of interrogation soon enough.

"When things started getting bad," the Colonel starts, "I was sent up to Colorado to make sure the President made it there safely."

"Did he?" Derek asks. "Because we had so many mixed reports even before we were released from service by the general."

"Yes, he's alive," he says. "He was air-rescued out of D.C. at the beginning. Some of his staff made it. A few senators. That's about all. The rest were killed."

"And that would've been right after, around March or April maybe? Then what?" Sue presses.

Her sister is holding her husband's hand very tightly. Reagan knows how upset she is about their father's appearance and, more importantly, about the appearance of his new family. What was just a short while ago a happy reunion for Sue has turned dark and depressing so quickly.

"I was ordered to go to Texas, but I couldn't," he tells them.

Derek says, "The last we heard of you, you were heading northwest. Did you go that way?"

"Yes, Derek, I did," he answers. "That's where my family was. I led a unit up there and left them to find my family once we got close enough."

"What?" Reagan asks with even more disbelief. This story just keeps getting worse. He ditched his men, too?

"I had to, Reagan," he answers rather testily. "I got word to Lucille, Lucy, that she should get the kids and head to a cabin we owned outside Portland. I knew it was gonna' be a crapshoot if she'd even make it. Things were falling apart fast."

"No shit," Reagan says. "Things fell apart fast for a lot of us. We all could've used some help."

"I'm sorry for whatever struggles you've all been through," he says. "But I knew you'd all make it here to the farm. My wife and children didn't have anywhere like this to seek sanctuary."

"Where were they living before the fall?" Sue asks. "We thought you were working in Germany."

"I was, for a short time," he answers. "My family lived in Tacoma. I mean Lucy and Gretchen were living there. Lucas was in Seattle. They met up and traveled to the cabin where I did meet them. It took a while for me to get to them, but we were prepared. We were sort of prepared. We had some food stores and supplies up there in the cabin. We were all right for a while."

"With no thought at all to your entire *other* family?" Reagan drills.

"That's not true," Robert argues with fatigue. "I had no way of communicating with you at that point. I knew my parents would be here for you. I knew Derek would make it home to Sue and their kids."

"He almost didn't," Sue says softly.

"And it looks like you are all doing a whole lot better than most folks out there. A lot better than we were," her father says.

Grandpa steps forward, snapping out of his quiet trance and says, "Why don't we go inside and discuss this later after you've all had some food and rest?"

"That sounds great, Dad," Robert nods with agreement. "There is so much more I have to tell everyone before it's too late."

"Before what's too late?" John asks.

Grandpa interrupts and says, "Let's just eat dinner and let them get showers. Then we'll talk once the children have gone to bed."

John nods, but Reagan can tell that he'd like to further question her father and get to the bottom of everything.

"It looks like Hannah's been cooking with Mom again," Robert remarks.

Little does he know yet that their grandmother has passed away. She knows how Grams always had a soft spot for her only son. Nobody breaks the news to her father that his mother is dead. The smile on his face is too hopeful.

"I sure am glad to see you again, Hannah," Robert says to her little sister, who just stands there beside her giant warrior wringing her hands in her pale blue apron.

"Colonel," her sister says, lifting her chin just a notch with nothing less than a haughty disdain. "I suspect we'll need a few more places set."

And with that cool greeting, Hannah turns and allows Kelly to help her back to the house. Kelly doesn't come back out. Everyone else slowly files in. Reagan notices that her father's new family doesn't bring in bags, luggage, boxes of supplies, backpacks, nothing. Even Paige and her friends had packs full of their valuables, which hadn't been much. They seem unsure of themselves. The kids whisper to their mother, who mostly looks at her feet and shakes her head. It almost makes Reagan feel bad. Watching her father hobble slowly on his cane with his son's help also almost makes her feel bad. And then she remembers that his son is almost the same age as Hannah and that her father was likely unfaithful to their mother during her darkest hours at the end of her precious life. So many times over the last four years she has wished for the comforting words or touch of her mother. She's never once wished for her anything from the Colonel.

Chapter Twenty-six
Cory

They make it to the Blue's bar and sack out to wait for the Mechanic's group. Cory is hoping they are able to work well together. They immediately unpack their gear and spread it out on the tables to take inventory and prepare for the coming night. Simon even takes their food out of the packs and sets the containers and bags on another table. Cory digs around until he finds a candle to light. All they'll need is the single candle. Anything more could draw attention to themselves, something they don't need.

Without preamble or circumstance, they sit down and Cory digs in. It's going to be a long night, and they'll need their energy. That's when Cory notices that Simon isn't eating much.

"You need to eat, bro," he comments toward his friend.

Simon just gives a lopsided frown.

"She'll be ok now," Cory verbalizes what his friend is stressed out about. "Paige is with her. Don't worry. They're safe."

"I can't believe we let that happen," Simon complains.

"We didn't let it happen. It just happened. That shit's always gonna' happen, man. There will always be dangers. Some of them we'll anticipate; some we won't. We just have to be more diligent when the girls are with us," he explains patiently.

"It just pisses me off," Simon swears.

Cory nods as he bites into his bread and slurps up some cold potted pork.

"I think those fuck-heads at the college may have been in on this, too," he confesses what he's been thinking.

"What do you mean?" Simon asks as he finally begins eating his equally cold food.

Cory sets his canning jar of potted meat and vegetables aside and says, "You see, I figure they set that trap on purpose for people at the college. If they eliminate the potential threat in a group and can get the women isolated, then they would have women to trade for shit at this barter camp we're about to blow open. Kill off extras, especially men, they get to keep the women for trade. They probably didn't figure on a woman falling through."

"I don't even want to think that could be true," Simon comments drearily.

"Me neither, brother, but I don't know if we can discount it. If those assholes were also bringing girls to this camp, we need to take care of them before we leave this shithole city," Cory explains.

"It's not a shithole city. Nashville used to be a nice city," Simon corrects him.

"Yeah, man, whatever. They're all shitholes now."

Simon nods solemnly and says, "You're probably right, though. We should check out that college before we leave."

"I don't want to leave that problem to someone else. Not if we can help to prevent it from happening to other people, especially women," Cory tells his friend.

"Careful," Simon warns with a grin. "People might start thinking you're a nice guy."

Cory snorts and says, "I don't think we have to worry about that."

"Well, my sister didn't seem like she wanted to tear your throat out today. That's an improvement right there."

Cory looks away quickly before his friend can see his guilt.

"Do you want to go over there or not?" Cory asks and tears into his food again.

"Yeah, sure. Of course we should," Simon agrees. "It's the right thing to do. Maybe we'll head over there tonight when we're done with Dave's group. Think we can handle them alone?"

Cory scoffs cockily. "Yeah, I'm about a hundred percent sure we've got this on our own. We'll recon it, but it didn't seem like that many dudes. Maybe a dozen or less."

"Good, I'm anxious to get back to the cabin," Simon admits as he stuffs a piece of thick bread into his mouth.

His friend is wearing his glasses, but Cory knows he'll remove them when it's time to go on their raid. They don't fit comfortably under his night-vision gear. He's plenty deadly enough without them.

"I know you are," Cory says. "Your girl's hurt. It's understandable."

Simon shoots him an impatient look and says, "She's not my girl. She's like my little sister."

Cory just grins and grunts at him. "I don't think you quite get the meaning of the brother-sister bond. I never looked at Em like that, and you don't look at Paige like that. Samantha is my little sister, too."

"I don't look at Samantha like anything," Simon argues with mounting irritation.

"Sure you don't," Cory counters.

"Let's just start going over contingency plans for tonight if it goes sour with Dave's group," Simon redirects.

Cory looks at him a moment longer, grins again, and grabs a scrap of paper and pencil from his pack. They finally agree to meet back at the Belmont Mansion if it goes south.

About an hour later, Dave's group shows up. It quickly becomes obvious that they'll mesh well with Cory and Simon. He's brought nine men and the woman that had been driving the minivan yesterday as a decoy. She's wearing all black and seems comfortable with the M4 she's holding. They all look high speed, low drag just like Simon and Cory, as if they are equipped for an intense mission and have done this many times. They all appear to be ex-Special Forces as they are squared away and intense. Cory feels better seeing men that remind him of Derek, John and Kelly. Dave greets them both by shaking their hands and introducing them to his men and the girl, whose name is Annie.

"We did a lil' recon on the way in," Dave tells them. "They're set up about two clicks from here give or take. Up north on the river is just a bunch of people living there in temp tents. We've seen groups of them before. I think they're nomads, though. This other place is more permanent, the one you guys wanna' hit. There's even some shacks built. Can't believe we haven't heard of it till now."

Cory and Simon nod.

"Are you guys familiar with hand signals?" Dave asks. "Have you been in a fight before?"

"Yes, sir," Simon answers for them. "John and Kelly trained us, sir. We've been in quite a few with them, and... a few on our own, too."

Dave turns to his men and explains, "John and Kelly were D-boys with me. These guys are good to go."

"What's the plan?" one of Dave's men asks Cory.

"We've got some ideas, but would like to hear what Dave has to say," Simon offers.

"What's up with this camp? John just said to get down here and lend a hand. Who's in there? Is this a snatch and grab, or are we just blowin' the fuck out of it?" Dave asks.

"No, sir," Simon says. "They've got a sex slave trade going on in there. They're selling women, prostituting them, trading them. At least that's how we've heard it."

"Really?" Dave asks as if he can't believe him. "Are you sure?"

Cory answers, "Yes, sir. We are."

Annie looks like she's going to be sick. Dave's a loyal friend to John and Kelly to agree to help, put his life and the lives of his men in danger to join a fight without knowing what they're walking into.

Dave says, "Fuck. That is bad. Is your source good?"

Cory chuckles and says, "Yeah, the source *was* good. He was also one of the turds kidnapping girls and delivering them to the camp. Tried to take one of ours."

Dave nods with the understanding that they've killed the source. If only they knew it was tiny Sam who did the killing.

He asks, "So, Cory, what's the plan you two have been working on?"

"Kill them?" Cory says simply.

They all laugh. Dave says, "Good fucking plan."

The woman says, "I think we need more than that, boys."

The men chuckle again. "Got it, Annie," one of them says to her. The young woman looks at Cory and grins. There is a spark of attraction in her eyes.

"Let's get to work, people," Dave orders. "We need to hash this out. I've drawn out the basics of this place. Looks like we're

394

outnumbered, but that's never been a problem before, right, boys?" His men call out a collective "hooah" in response. "My old lady advised me not to get my dick shot off, so we need to go at this carefully."

"Good advice," Cory jokes with a nod as Dave places his sketch on the table in front of them.

Dave laughs and says, "She's a smart woman."

One of his men says, "Not too smart; she's with you!"

Simon joins in and says, "Well, as the only surgeon on the team, I'm not sewing anyone's dick back on, so let's get a good plan going."

"All right then," Dave concedes on a laugh.

Annie mutters, "I doubt these creeps are good enough shots to shoot any of your little peckers, but let's figure this out, boys."

The men all laugh, Dave slaps her back and says, "Sounds good, little sister. What's your specialties, Cory?"

"Simon's our sniper. I'm just a grunt," Cory tells the leader of the group.

"We're all just grunts, brother," Dave says with a smirk.

"He's deadlier than he's letting on," Simon corrects. "He was out there alone for eight months and he's good with demolitions."

Some of the men in Dave's group regard each other with raised eyebrows.

Dave chuckles and says, "Oh, so you *have* been spending time with Harrison."

He's referring to John. Cory grins and nods. "A little."

"Good. Well, they've got shacks and tents set up in rows," Dave says, pointing to his surprisingly detailed drawing. "The river lays beyond the camp to the east, over here. There's a lot of activity going on in there. I saw guards, too. A gate here," he says, pointing. "More guards along the length of the fence. I did see women, too. Didn't know at the time what I was lookin' at."

"Have any numbers?" Cory asks.

Dave shakes his head and says, "Not really. Looked like at least a few dozen guards. Other men moving around that looked unarmed. Probably customers. Lot of confusion once we get in there. Shoot any men you see. If they're customers, then fuck 'em. They deserve it, too. Could be a challenge. Once we get in that gate, we need to keep the pressure on 'em. Don't let the guards or the men running the place regroup. Push hard. Push forward. Try to get those fuckers corralled into the center. Take 'em out. No prisoners."

Simon holds up his hand and asks, "Wait. How do you propose we get through the front gate?"

"Walk up and ask for admittance," Dave says with a grin. "Annie's gonna be the decoy."

Annie says, "Sweet! That means I get the first shot."

Cory and Simon smile with uncertainty at her. She seems way too excited about that prospect.

"Cory, you can pair up with Annie. You look… well, you pair up with Annie. Try to sell her to them. Get us in the gate. Once we're in, you two stick together. Everyone pair up with your battle buddy. Don't get separated. That'll help our snipers."

"We're gonna need to clear each row," Annie observes, pointing at the extensive camp.

"Right, Rick and Lil Joey will take the rear corner gate in the northeast as a blocking force, prevent them from sneakin' out the back like rats. At the go-time, they'll get a nice fireworks display burnin' back there for a distraction. The remainder of you will push in through the front with us. Snipers, you can perch over here on this building," he says, jabbing his finger at a roughly sketched building across the street from the park. "It's got the best angles for taking those fuckers out from high. It'll be long range, tough shots. Think you can handle that?"

Simon nods with certainty. Another man does, as well. Apparently he is Dave's sniper. He's carrying a Lapua rifle with a monster scope. He looks capable with it. He's a big dude, formidable, and he nods to Simon with camaraderie.

His commander bumps his fist before going back to the map.

Then Dave addresses the snipers, "Simon, you'll work with my sniper. We're gonna need anyone that comes out of there without their battle buddy taken out. Watch for us to be moving in pairs. Take out everyone else. Not the women. That would kinda' defeat the fuckin' point."

They go over the plan numerous times until everyone is on the same page before preparing to roll out.

"Everyone synch up," Dave orders. "Set your go time."

All of the men including Simon and Cory synchronize their watches to the same countdown.

They will jog in from their position at the Blue's club and leave Dave's pick-up truck at the restaurant in the back alley so it won't be stolen while they are gone. Simon and Cory stick together on the run to the camp since they normally work together. Once Simon's position is forsaken on the rooftop or if he can't make any more shots, he'll join the fight on the ground with them, paired up with Lucky, the other sniper. Two of the team are taking Third Street south and will flank the park where the camp is located. Everyone wears a headset for communication. When they close in on the park, they pause behind a building. The area is protected by guards and some half-assed, rigged together fencing.

"My team needs a few minutes more," Dave says, regards his watch and turns to Simon and Cory. "Once the shooting starts, take out the guards first and anyone armed. Annie and Cory get outta' the way and lay down some fire for us so we can get through the gate. Simon and Lucky, get to your positions now."

Simon bumps his fist against Cory's and sprints away with Lucky. Annie removes her coat, wraps it around her waist to conceal her hidden handgun. She lets down her blonde hair, giving it a good shake. She reminds him a little of Evie Johnson, but a lot harder around the edges and more capable of killing someone. Evie is just tender and soft, not a trained killer, not really capable of violence.

One of Dave's men, who is close in size to him, hands Cory his coat. He slings Annie's M4 behind his back and pulls the coat on to hide it. He hangs his own rifle from his shoulder. He's hoping they don't try to disarm him.

"Team Two, in position," one of Dave's team members says across the headsets. Cory isn't sure which one it was. They have only briefly been introduced, which makes it seem strange to be going into a fight with them. This is a tricky situation, though. They have to be careful not to get the captive women killed or accidentally shoot each other.

"Ready?" Dave asks him and Annie.

"Ready, sir," Annie answers and Cory nods.

He leads Annie down the street toward the park where they will need to get in that front gate. Without having a vehicle to ram through, they had to come up with another plan. Plus, they need confirmation of what takes place within that tent village. It may not have been accurately represented by those creeps that took Sam.

Cory tries not to think about that. It makes him sick thinking of his little adopted sister having to stab that bastard.

When they get within thirty yards, a man shouts from the other side of the gate.

"What do you want? Get the hell outta' here, asshole!"

Cory was designated to take on this role. He's unshaven, his beard coming in thickly again. He doesn't resemble a clean-cut, good guy. He knows it. So did Dave the Mechanic. It's ok with Cory; it wasn't an insult.

He yanks Annie's arm, hauling her forward with him.

"I said stop, asshole!" the man yells again.

Cory keeps moving forward but stops when he's close enough to see the man through the opening in the door where he has cracked it just slightly. Dave and the rest of Team One should be moving stealthily into position. He's a little on edge because he couldn't wear his night-vision gear.

"This the place that takes bitches on trade for shit?" Cory asks, doing his best to seem like a disreputable good-for-nothing.

"What's it to ya'?" the man with the long, tattered wool coat and beady, dark eyes asks. "Where'd ya' hear that?"

His evil eyes keep shifting to his right, and Cory knows the loser is looking to someone on the other side of the fence with him, perhaps someone who is in charge.

"I got this bitch I need to unload. Friends over at the school told me. You want her or what? She ain't no good to me no more, so I'm a figurin' on tradin' her for some shit," Cory slurs as if he's slightly drunk.

Furtive movement behind the other man skirts past Cory's line of sight. The man turns away from Cory to speak with someone.

"We might be interested," the scumbag concedes finally.

"Cool, man," Cory says with a lopsided grin. "Gotta get rid of her and get me some shit on trade."

"What kind of shit do you want?" the man shouts to him after a moment of discussion.

"Whatcha' got?" Cory asks with a grin. Annie makes a feigned attempt to free herself, forcing Cory to snatch her back against him roughly. He's not too worried about hurting her, though. Her upper arm is lean and muscular. She may be able to kick his ass if she wanted to. And he's quite sure she can certainly handle that

Beretta hidden under her waistband. His own rifle is casually hanging from his shoulder in a non-threatening manner. So far they haven't asked him to disarm.

"What do ya' need?" the man asks.

"Could use some food and ammo. Ain't had any ammo for this here rifle in a while," he lies smoothly.

"We might can work somethin' out. Not much for ammo, but plenty of food. The girls grow the food in here, so we've always got food. Depending on if the boss wants her, then we might make a deal," the man states.

Cory decides to press for further information, "She ain't much of a farmer if ya' know what I'm sayin.' She ain't good for much other than a lay."

"A sweet little honey like that, she ain't gonna be one of the gardeners," the man says, licks his lips, spits on the ground and grabs at his crotch.

"Oh yeah? What kinda' girls you got, mister?"

"About anything you could want," the man confirms. "Cooks, gardeners, sweet ho's like that one."

"Cool, man. Cool," Cory slurs again.

"We could make you a deal for a night with one of 'em in trade for that gun you ain't got no ammo for any know how."

Cory catches more movement in his peripheral vision before hearing Dave in his ear say, "Breach that gate. We need that door open, Cory."

"Yeah, maybe we could work something out," Cory tells the creep living on borrowed time. "This one ain't much to my taste, though. I like 'em a little younger."

The man cackles, pulls open the door a little further as if they are going to be great friends and says, "Yeah, I know what you mean. I like 'em young, but I might make an exception for that fine piece of ass you've got there. We've got a few of those sweet young ones, too. Got some for just about anyone's taste."

Cory walks without hurry closer to the man and has his right foot in the door when he asks the most important question, "How many ho's you got here? This place seems like a pretty good deal. Maybe I'll go into the business myself."

The man ushers them inside where Cory gets a quick glance around as best as he can. There are tents and ramshackle sheds everywhere. Men are loitering around. A few are armed, but some are customers because they are looking over a line-up of women under close inspection of a kerosene lantern on a pole. There are maybe a dozen men visible, but Cory is quite sure that others occupy the tents and shacks. Guards are posted every thirty feet or so around the fence. It's certainly not a fortress, but it seems well-fortified with manpower. There are torches placed every fifty yards down the fence line, but there are still too many dark, shadowy areas for his liking.

"I think at last count there were forty-two," the pervert says. "Forty-three with you, hotness," he leers at Annie.

"Who's in charge around here?" Cory asks.

"I am," a man says beside the beady-eyed creep.

Cory wouldn't have guessed this man to be in charge. He's short and thin, looks like a zero-threat factor. But his keen, pale eyes belie a savvy intelligence and a cool calculated manner. He has a .44 caliber revolver, damn near bigger than him, slung on his waist like he's in some kind of an old Western. Cory would like to ask him if he's overcompensating for something but holds his tongue.

Annie is still standing half inside of the door and half out. This is not by accident.

"We are in position," Dave says in his ear. "Make your move when you're ready."

The little creep strolls over to Annie and begins inspecting her as if she is nothing more than livestock.

"She got any diseases?" the man with the .44 asks. "We don't have anything to treat any V.D. anymore. I try to run a classy establishment here."

Cory would like to laugh or throw up or ram the butt of his gun into this puke's face. He's running a sex slave businesses and has the balls to call it classy.

"This is Slim," the pervert guard explains his skinny, devoid of all moral integrity boss. "He's in charge. Everyone just calls him Slim."

"And you are, my new friend?" Slim requests Cory's name with a greasy disposition.

Cory grins and moves his hand slyly to the grip of his rifle, which is loaded and ready. It starts ticking through the back of his mind that these men remind him of the ones who'd killed his little sister, that they could've been connected in some way. It's that same time bomb that ticks every time right before he murders people like

400

these. It starts out like a methodic, slow tick and gradually picks up pace until it goes off like a firehouse alarm. They don't know, but it's almost at deafening levels in his head now. It is a countdown to their doom.

"Well, you see, Slim," Cory starts with a smile, "my friends call me Cory. But you'll only ever know me as my call sign, the Death Stalker."

"What the fuck's that supposed...." Slim states with anger but is interrupted.

Cory swings on him with the rifle and fires a single cartridge into the man's bony chest.

"Hey, you fuckers!" the pervert guard screams.

Apparently his taunts and insinuations from a few minutes ago are more than Annie can tolerate because she whips out her Beretta and lightning-fast shoots the creep point blank to the face.

The fight is on, and all hell breaks loose. A loud explosion and an orange glow in the sky lets him know that Dave's two men near the river have created their diversion.

Cory and Annie jump to the side and dive for cover behind a rickety building made out of recycled materials. He throws down the borrowed coat and hands Annie her M4. Dave and the others push through the gate and begin rapid-fire peppering the area, taking out quite a few of the men, including prospective customers. A long-range shot cracks loud and clear through the night sky. Cory has no doubt that his friend has taken the shot. A man falls dead in his tracks. Definitely Simon.

It is a magnificent thing to behold, this battle taking place all around him. He wasn't with his family when they raided the Target store, so he missed all the excitement. Tracer rounds fly overhead, lighting the night sky like red streaks of angry lightning. The sounds are deafening. This is just like when he was rescued by his brother and the others in Arkansas. They'd made it as far as Little Rock when the shit hit. That's where they got into a battle in which Cory was sure they'd all die. It's also where he was shot for the first time when a bullet whizzed through his calf muscle. And they'd almost lost Derek. He remembers lying in the back of the Hummer shooting out the window as Kelly had instructed him while Em hid on the floor at his feet. His brother and John had used quite a few grenades just to get them the hell out of that city. This situation feels the same, only they aren't running from danger. They are the danger.

401

Dave the Mechanic is still near the front gate. He's barking orders in his throat mic and yelling them out to his men that are closer to him. He's got the knife hand going, slicing through the air directing his men right and left and forward. Hand signals are flying. His men are kicking ass and definitely taking no prisoners.

"Get that motherfucker, Lucky," Dave says into the mic to his sniper, which Cory and the rest of the group can hear. Apparently someone is trying to get away.

He continues on with his ordering and waving as if he is an invincible man standing there amidst the chaos as Cory and Annie lay down some suppressive fire so the rest of the soldiers can breach the front gate.

Annie taps his shoulder and indicates that she is moving to their right. Cory nods and follows while popping off some rounds at the guards scattering about. It feels strange following a woman, but this is the exact same move he would've made. They jog around to the other side of the building with four other men from Dave's group and fan out. Cory spots a creep a few yards away pulling up his pants leaving a tent. He takes quick aim and disables the jerk. Annie does similarly to another man as he runs toward them with a shotgun. They split off from the other four men and work together again.

This time, Cory signals they should move forward and to their left. This group of tents and sheds in the next few aisles is their assigned area to clear. Annie nods and follows him.

A creep jumps out of a tent in one of the narrow grass aisles and tackles Annie to the ground. Cory runs back and butt strokes him to the head with his rifle and then finishes him off with one shot to the chest and one to the head.

She is winded and shaken but is already back on her feet before saying, "Thanks."

Cory retrieves her dropped M4 and hands it to her. She nods before they move out again.

They pass close to a dozen small tents that are dark within until they come to one that is barely illuminated with a lantern. Cory pokes his rifle through and takes a fast glance. A woman is huddled in the corner with another younger woman. They are frightened and shaking. One of them is partially nude and trying to hold her hands over her bare breasts. Cory holds his finger to his lips, and they nod with fear. He and Annie move forward down the narrow row one aisle over. Long range shots ring out in quick succession, letting him know that Simon and the other sniper are still going to work on the camp. Any customers caught trying to escape through the fence were ordered by Dave to be sniped. Simon and his new buddy seem to be very busy. Other, steadier gunfire filters through the air, too.

They finally come to a clearing where a bonfire was lit earlier in the evening and has died down quite a bit. Cory catches the movement of shadows backlit on a cream-colored canvas teepee across the way and decides to pursue. Audibles are being called through their headsets, but he's in pursuit of the shadow man. A woman's cry of distress comes from the aisle where the man has gone. Annie touches his arm, letting him know that she'll flank.

He gives her a minute to get to the other end of the row before stalking the shadow. She isn't wearing night-vision gear, either, so the darkness makes moving fast more difficult. After a moment, Cory finds him. The man is holding a serrated dagger to a woman's neck and dragging her as he goes. She is begging for her life. She is also barefoot and scantily clothed. He is guessing that this is the john, and she is not a willing accomplice in his escape plan.

"Hey!" Cory shouts, causing the man to spin toward him.

"Get back!" he screams in a rage and terror. "I'll cut this bitch. Get back from me. I'm leaving, and you aren't stopping me."

"Ok, ok, calm down, man," Cory says, lowering his rifle. "I'm not gonna stop you."

"I am," Annie says from behind the man where she has crept up on him.

She fires a round to the back of the man's skull with her handgun. Cory is glad she's a good shot because he could've been hit if she missed. The perp lands with a thud on the cold, damp ground. The woman screams. Then she runs toward Cory and throws herself around his middle, hugging tightly.

"Get away, woman," Cory orders harshly and gives her a shove. "Hide. Go now! Don't come out till you hear an all-clear call."

The woman sprints away sobbing and wearing a splattering of the john's blood on the side of her face. The rage Cory felt earlier about Samantha being kidnapped is replaced with an even deeper anger at seeing this terrified, half naked woman running barefoot for shelter. It is cold tonight. He wonders if any of the women even have

403

winter clothing. Her face was gaunt, bruises marred different parts of her body, and she was filthy.

Annie indicates they should head to their direct left down another aisle of shacks this time. She holds her small flashlight while Cory kicks open the first door, finds it empty and moves to the next. There isn't much to the shacks- no running water, just single cots with dirty, musty bedding. The third hovel proves fruitful. They find a man cowering with his pants around his ankles and a woman cowering with equal fear under the bed holding her hands over her ears to block out the noise of the battle. Cory shoots him twice in the chest and orders the woman to run and find the others with whom she can hide.

"Got a runner," Dave says into their headsets. "He's heading east. Take that fucker out from the eagle's nest."

"Roger," Simon says calmly.

A moment later, his friend's rifle rings out loud and true. He doesn't often miss. Cory is quite sure the runner is now a daisy pusher. He also hears the occasional shot coming from the far eastern point of the camp near the river. He knows Dave's men who set the explosives are taking out escapees back there.

"Much obliged," Dave jokes over their headsets. Minus the unrestrained use of foul language, the Mechanic is a lot like John. He has a casual calmness about him and a deadly vacancy in his eyes when the battle was about to start. He'll sleep easy tonight, no doubt.

Shots pop off loudly throughout the expansive camp. Cory hadn't realized it would be so widespread on the park grounds. This would've been a green spot for the city, a space set aside for picnics, family reunions, city events and the like. There are cars and motorcycles, some that even seem to be in good working order, scattered around. Others have vinery and weeds growing out of them, but some appear useable. Multiple clothing lines are set up, most of which have articles hanging on them to dry. It is hard to tell if anyone lurks on the other side of the clothing which lends an eerie feeling to an already dangerous scene.

He and Annie take out two more assholes before connecting with the rest of Dave's group. He orders him, Annie and another guy named Skeeter to head west to work the next section. There are plenty more guards that took off to likely hide, and probably dozens more johns cowering somewhere. This is going to be an extensive, long search.

"Professor to Stalker," Simon calls through his earpiece.

"Go ahead," Cory answers into his throat mic as he and his group walk carefully down the next aisle, which is closest to the river and farthest from the entrance. It's also darker.

"Four dudes went that way before I could get them," Simon warns. "I think there were more over there, too. I'll watch your six. I'm in position."

"Got it," Cory acknowledges. "Head count change. My group now has three."

They are used to working together, so it makes an op flow more smoothly than working with complete strangers like Dave's group. Although he has to admit, working with Annie has been very easy so far. She's a tough nut. All of Dave's guys are trustworthy and reliable.

They find the first guard easily enough because he recklessly barks off a round as he runs straight toward them. Skeeter takes him out. Cory confirms it with a second round from his rifle as he steps over the body. The rest are hiding well, too well. It's a good thing he has a flashlight because there aren't any torches or campfires on this side of the camp. Skeeter is the only one of the three of them that has on his night-vision goggles.

Cory sees what looks to be the remainder of a garden to their right. The soft shriek of a startled woman comes from somewhere about halfway down that row. They jog as quickly as they can toward the sound. Annie shoots at a man to her right. She misses and the creep escapes. Cory raises his chin to indicate that she and Skeeter should pursue and that he'll keep going straight. He isn't worried about Simon shooting him. His friend already knows he's working this area. He was on his own for eight months. Another twenty minutes won't hurt.

He slinks closer to the origin of the sounds of the woman in distress. As he closes in, Cory can hear her whimpering inside one of the shacks. He slowly pushes open the door. A dark-haired girl that can't be more than fifteen years old is squatted in a shadowy corner. Cory motions for her to come toward him. The girl shakes her head and points to the floor. Perhaps she is afraid of him because of how he's aiming the flashlight at her. He lowers it, but she won't come to him. She points down again. Cory squats and looks under the shabby cot. Nobody hides there. He motions for her again. She just points to the floor three times with more urgency. Cory squints his eyes thoughtfully as he considers the salvaged wood of the floorboards. That's when he peers more closely and sees the two-inch circumference round ring that is bolted into the floorboards. It's concealing a trapdoor. He looks at the girl again who nods. Cory motions for her to come with him. This time she does so, tiptoeing lightly and trembling.

"Run," he whispers when she's stepped out of the shack. He pulls her a few feet away to speak. "Run to your friends or the other women. Be careful. We're here to help you but stay out of our way. Professor, make sure this kid makes it out safe."

"Roger," Simon answers.

Cory doesn't want to see her killed by some creep or accidentally shot by one of them. Simon can guard her from his nest until she makes it to the other women or out of the camp. She nods and takes off at a pace even faster than he would've given her credit for, especially since she is also barefoot. Keeping the women barefoot would've been beneficial to the dumbasses running this place. It would be difficult as hell to escape with no shoes, not through a city littered with broken glass, rusty metal, and sharp debris. Bloody footprints also would've made it easier for the creeps to track them. He understands this was by design. At least now he knows what they can do with all those shoes they took from the sporting goods store.

Cory steps quietly up into the shack and fires three rounds through the floor. A man screams, letting Cory know that he's hit his target. He yanks the steel ring, lifting the wooden trapdoor to reveal a dead man splayed on the dirt floor below him.

He immediately calls it in, "Be aware, the shacks have false floors. Check the trapdoors for groundhogs."

"Roger that. Dig 'em out, boys!" Dave orders his men. "Dig those fuckers out. No prisoners. No mercy."

Cory continues down the aisle, mindful that Annie and Skeeter haven't yet returned. They must be chasing down that creep.

"Move to your right a few feet, Stalker," Simon compels him.

Cory complies, jumping to his right against the wall of another shack. A thumping sound around the corner is followed by the report of Simon's rifle. Shouting somewhere else in the camp crescendos to deafening levels.

"You're clear," Simon tells him in his ear.

"Thanks, Professor," Cory says to his friend as he traverses the aisle again.

By the time he comes to the end, he's killed two more men, and Simon has taken out another. Simon tells him in his earpiece that the fighting has ended and to meet him at the gate. "All clear" calls come across his headset from the two-man teams. Cory sends out one of his own after re-checking the first aisle where a few shacks were located. He wants those trapdoor areas double checked. He doesn't find anyone. Dave's men have probably already covered this area. He crosses back toward the entrance of the encampment again. A few of the men have been taken captive and are kneeling. They are pleading their cases but not very successfully.

He finds Simon and the other sniper, and they wait as women come forward and Dave directs the chaos. A few of the women are very pregnant. Everyone raises their night-vision gear. Some of the soldiers light more torches and lamps, and others throw extra logs on the bonfire to help illuminate the area. A few of the younger women standing with the group of older women are as young as the girls on the farm, as young as Em was when she died. It makes Cory's stomach sick as he looks around at them dressed scantily as if they've been rescued in the middle of being violated yet again. Only two or three have shoes. The ticking in his brain has slowed again, but Cory still feels that unfettered rage.

Skeeter comes forward helping a hobbling Annie along. She's been shot it would seem. Cory rushes to her and lifts her gently into his arms.

"Bastard got me," she snaps angrily as she clenches her side.

"Well, I took care of him for ya,' little sister," Skeeter says with affection as he pushes hair back from her forehead. He obviously has tender feelings for her. Cory isn't sure she feels the same.

"Simon!" Cory calls to his best friend as he carries her toward a clear spot.

Simon is at his side in an instant. He pulls gauze bandaging out of his pack as soon as it hits the ground. Another one of Dave's men comes over.

407

"I used to be a medic," he offers and drops to his knees next to Simon. "I can help. We have others injured, too."

Simon has an IV needle with a saline drip in her arm in a matter of mere moments. The medic is pressing bandaging against Annie's side where a slow trickle of blood is escaping. Simon takes out another syringe and slowly pushes the clear liquid into her IV. Cory hopes for her sake it was some kind of painkiller. She's in pain, a lot of pain but trying not to show it. It looks like the bullet has passed through the fleshy part of her waist. Cory hopes it hasn't pierced an organ, whatever organs are over there.

"Can I help, sir?" one of the women asks. "I used to be a nurse here in the city."

She sure as hell doesn't look like a nurse anymore. The woman is short, small and petite and seems like she was once very pretty. She's maybe in her early forties. Simon's mom was also a nurse. The ticking gets louder again in Cory's head.

"Yes, ma'am. Hold pressure here. She's going to need medical care at our clinic," Simon says as he flings his night-vision gear to the ground. "So are some of the others. I saw a few of the guys get hit from my perch."

Cory knows his friend is in doctor mode and has left behind the sniper soldier he has to become sometimes. He is so much more suited to healing people than killing them. Cory, on the other hand, is quite at home with the killing aspect. The woman assists rather skillfully as Cory holds a flashlight for them.

"I can go with you to your medical clinic," she offers.

Cory says, "That'd be great. We always need help."

She looks so relieved to be getting a pass out of here that her eyes fill with tears before she looks away.

One of the bigger soldiers carries a young woman over to Simon and the medic. She is bleeding from her forehead and barely cognizant. She is perhaps twenty years old.

"What happened to her?" Dave asks with urgency as he comes upon them.

The huge soldier with the deep voice lies her gently on the ground and says, "I cornered the prick who had her. He clubbed her to the side of her head with something and tried to run. Lucky or Simon got him for me."

Simon mutters something under his breath. Cory is quite sure it isn't a pleasant comment. He's probably the one who killed her abuser. The girl is missing her pants. Her breath comes out in silvery plumes against the cold night air, and blood has dried in a long streak on her soft cheek. The soldier quickly pulls off his coat and covers her. She moans groggily as if she is still in pain but doesn't open her eyes.

"Sir, what are we supposed to do with the rest of them?" the big guy asks of the men they've rounded up.

"Take them to the other side of the wall where the women and... *children* can't see," Dave derides with a cool stare. "Do a quick questioning. I don't wanna' be here with our asses hanging out for long. Get what you can from them. We'll come back tomorrow to take what we can and deal with the stragglers. Finish it. We're movin' in twenty."

"Yes, sir," the other soldier says and jogs away to gather help.

Cory stays with Simon as he aids the injured people. Three of Dave's men have been brought forward for medical care. Two have been shot, and one has been stabbed. The stabbing victim is nearly passed out from blood loss. His wound is close to his heart or lungs. The others aren't in good shape, either.

Dave pulls him to the side and says, "We need to get these people medical care. I called in for back-up. They'll be here soon to do an evac. And we need to get these women the fuck outta' here. There could be other fuckers in the area that will regroup tonight. We don't need to lose any more men."

"Right," Cory agrees.

"I'm gonna have my men take the women to our town. But we need the McClane family's help with the injured. We don't have any doctors, just my medic and a dentist. I've got no way to treat them," Dave requests with a hand on his slim hip.

"Got it," Cory agrees and immediately gets on the radio.

They split up, corralling the women and young girls as shots are being fired on the other side of the fence just a short distance away. The execution of the remaining creeps is being carried out. Within a half hour, they are moving collectively down the street. Cory is carrying one of Dave's men over his shoulder who has been critically injured. He's not too confident that the man will make it. They are met by some of the other men from Dave's village who have stopped at the Blues restaurant to pick up their other vehicle.

They've also brought the deuce-and-a-half. They get the injured loaded first into the truck and then the women loaded into the deuce. They are going to be transported to Hendersonville where Dave's community will be welcoming them in.

Annie calls to him from her place near the back of the truck, so he goes to her.

"Hey," she says weakly.

Cory isn't sure what drugs Simon has run through her IV. She seems groggy.

"Thanks for watchin' my ass out there," Cory tells her gently and lays a hand on her arm.

"Thanks for saving mine," she says with a grin.

Cory smiles and says, "My pleasure, ma'am."

"Look me up the next to time you come to Hick Town," she jokes about her village in Hendersonville.

There is definitely an invitation in her glazed-over eyes. It was important enough to her to get this message clearly through to him or she else wouldn't have called him over.

"Will do, ma'am," Cory agrees and squeezes her arm before turning away. He has no intention of visiting Hendersonville to see her. He wouldn't want to lead her on like that. Even though Annie is an attractive woman, his mind has been fixated on another.

He radioed John to let them know that six injured people are coming to Pleasant View for emergency medical care while Simon prepared the people for transport. Cory's mentor was already awake and on watch duty back at the farm. John assured him that he'd awaken and transport Reagan and Doc to the clinic in town in time to meet Dave's caravan.

Cory stops the Mechanic before they leave, "Are you sure you don't want us to come with you to our town?"

"Nah, we got this. You guys get back to your women," Dave says, knowing that Sam and Paige are waiting out in the woods somewhere for them. "We'll meet up again soon."

Cory punches his fist to his new friend's. Dave the Mechanic is a hardcore badass with a lot of mileage on him, but he's also a good man at heart who is going to acclimate over forty women into his community without batting an eye. He's a hyperactive, fidgety and intense dude, a cusser that could give Reagan a run for her money, but he is steady and calm in the thick of it. Cory is glad for this new alliance.

"Thanks for the help," Cory says.

Dave shakes his head and says, "No, man. Thank you guys for finding this fuckin' hovel. I'm glad we could help."

"We owe ya,'" Cory acknowledges as he shakes Dave's hand.

Simon comes over and does the same.

"Ready?" Cory asks his friend.

"Let's roll," Simon says with an anxious nod.

Dave jumps into the driver's seat of the truck that will head to Pleasant View and to Doc's clinic. He gives a single wave and a curt nod and drives away.

"We still have work to do," Simon says as he turns to leave.

Cory follows and says, "You got enough ammo?"

"Yes, of course," his friend says. "I don't just go recklessly blasting away like I have no control."

Cory punches his shoulder.

Simon asks, "You?"

"I use more rounds 'cuz I'm in the shit, not perched on top of a building from afar like you, nerd. But I'm still good to go," Cory teases him.

Simon laughs and says, "Shut the fuck up."

Cory gives him a 'tsk-tsk' for the swear. He gets a return punch to his own shoulder.

They jog west toward Vanderbilt University and their Kappa Phi Asshole friends. Cory consults his watch, notes the time of oh-one-thirty. They still have a long night ahead of them before they return to the girls. Cory hopes that Paige stays diligent and safe.

Chapter Twenty-seven
Paige

After the sun goes down and the guys are long gone, Paige finally talks Sam into going inside. She'd insisted on standing watch with her own gun alongside Paige. She hadn't spoken, and they hadn't felt the need for conversation but, instead, kept to keen observation and alertness. They were both too jumpy to simply sit in the cabin complacently doing nothing until the men return. They stood near the front of the small cabin, sat on the small porch and returned to standing watch until the last bits of the sun's pink streaks faded from the darkening sky.

She starts heating water on the wood-burning stove that she first pumps into a metal bucket at the kitchen sink. The fire inside which still crackles and pops, provides warmth, heating the small cabin to toasty comfort. She also places jars of food on top of the little stove to start them heating. She carries more bucketsful than she can count to the small bathroom where she pours them into the tub. She has to make sure Sam gets as clean as possible and removes that man's blood from her body. She worries that her friend will get some kind of disgusting infection from that vile human.

"Sam?" she asks, jarring the other girl out of her trance. "Come with me and get washed up, dear."

Sam just gives her the thousand-yard stare, so Paige takes her arms and pulls her gently to her feet from her position on the bed. She doesn't want to put too much pressure on her hands because they are cut and likely hurt.

"Come on, honey," Paige orders softly.

She helps Sam get out of her clothing, mostly doing the work on her own as Sam just stands there. Then she assists her getting into the half full tub. There is a white ceramic pitcher on the floor next to the tub that Paige uses to douse Sam's long hair with warm water. She washes it for her, lathering it twice to remove the blood and mud. Sam reaches for the simple bar of homemade soap on the ledge of the tub and begins scrubbing at the skin on her face and forearms. Paige notices that she scrubs much too vigorously.

"Let me help you remove your bandages," Paige offers and takes the soap from her before she hurts herself.

She unwraps the gauze bandages and discards them along with the bloody pads on the floor beside her. She'll wash them later. She tries not to cringe when Sam winces at the stinging pain from the cuts. This may have felt a bit uncomfortable such a short time ago helping her nude friend take a bath, but Paige is mostly just concerned about her.

"I'll wash your back for you," she says to which Sam nods.

Paige lathers her hands and swipes the soapy suds over Sam's smooth skin. Sam draws her knees up and hugs them.

"I shouldn't have gone over there to pee," Sam mutters.

Paige pauses a moment in lathering her hands again. She's glad that Sam is finally talking. Maybe her state of shock is wearing off.

"I should've listened to you," Sam admits.

She just squeezes her friend's shoulder gently and reassures her, "It was just a mistake. We didn't know anything like that would happen. If there is one thing I've learned, Sam, it's that we all make mistakes from time to time. You survived it. That's all that matters. I'm just glad that nothing worse happened to you."

Sam nods and allows Paige to help cleanse her hands. Before long, she is clean, but Paige sees the remnants of the damage that man did to her. Sam's face has a purplish bruise on the crest of her right cheekbone. Her upper lip is cut but not bleeding anymore. There is a reddish-purple bruise on her left shoulder and another smaller one lower on her back. She put up such a fight. And thank God for her tenacity and spirit. That man could've killed her. If they hadn't got to her when they did, the other bastard that Cory took out

413

most certainly would have abused and then killed Sam for stabbing his friend to death. Although, Paige suspects he might not have come out on the winning end now that she's seen how lethal her little friend can be.

She helps Sam dry off and then redress in clean clothing. Paige is surprised when she rolls her soiled clothing into a ball and stuffs them into the wood-burning stove. She obviously doesn't want to take them back to the farm to be laundered. Paige doesn't blame her. They have plenty of clothing they took today from the sporting good's store that she can wear tomorrow. Together they manage to get her hands wrapped in the gauze that Simon has left them. She doesn't do as good a job as her brother, but she does apply the antibiotic salve, pads and wrappings as best as she can.

"Sam, the food's ready. Wanna' eat some?" Paige asks cautiously, hoping that whatever she does or says doesn't send her back into a state of silence and staring.

She gets a nod from her friend, so she quickly digs bowls and silverware out of the cupboards. Whatever is waiting for them in the hot jars of food seems like it has some liquid in it, so they'll need the bowls instead of plates. She wipes the dishes off with a towel from the bathroom because they are coated in dust. One of the cups had a dead bug in the bottom of it. Simon told her it's been a while since they've been to this cabin.

Paige tries to be optimistic and says brightly as she places the jars of food on the table, "Mm, this smells great. Wonder what it is?"

"Bean soup," Sam answers flatly. "They always pack soups or stews. It's the easiest to transport. Hannah and Sue make Grams's bean soup recipe just like she used to and can it like her, too. It's really tasty."

"I don't know if I've had it since I came to live on the farm. Smells good enough, though," Paige says as she uses a towel to lift and pour some of the soup into both bowls.

She then unpacks bread from the box of supplies Cory carried up to the cabin. She finds very small baby-food jars in the bottom and pulls those out, too.

"What do ya' think this is?" she asks Sam since she seems to have this all down pat.

"Probably some sort of fruit dessert," she replies. "Hannah always tries to pack us sweets. She says it's because the sugars have carbohydrates that our bodies need, but I know it's just because she wants us to have good food that reminds us of home."

"Think she's worried we'll run away?" Paige jests as she takes a seat next to Sam.

She actually grins weakly and says, "No, I don't think so."

Paige laughs and tells her, "Right. Like anyone would run away from the farm. Not with Hannah's cooking waiting for them."

"Reagan always says that's why Kelly married her. That she won him over by feeding him," Sam offers as she sips the hearty broth of the soup.

"She won me over, so I'd say that's probably true," Paige admits as she also tries the hot soup. It's heavenly. The flavors meld between the rich, pork-flavored broth and the grainy texture of the beans and carrots. It hits the spot. She even dunks her chunk of bread into the soup, letting it sop up some of the broth. "Who would've thought soup could be divine?"

Sam smiles gently and continues eating. That has to be a good sign. She's clean. She's eating and making a little conversation. God, Paige wishes that Simon was here. He's so much better with her. They both finish their entire bowls of bean soup, and Sam even has a second helping. Then Paige pops the lids on the small jars, curious at the orange-tinted contents.

"This is really good," Sam says as she dips her fork inside one of the tiny jars. "It's Sue's peach cobbler. She uses the canned peaches and Hannah's cobbler recipe. That was nice of Hannah and Sue to include this."

Paige's first bite hits her tongue with a sweet tang that is almost sinful. She just moans softly.

"I know, right?" Sam says, sounding more like herself. "Sometimes they put blueberries in it. That's good, too. The Reynolds have blueberry bushes. We trade strawberries for blueberries with them."

"Oh, right. I remember. Time flies on the farm," she reflects.

Sam offers a pained grin as if she is remembering something unpleasant. She doesn't want to push her. Sam seems to be good at compartmentalizing the bad in her life. Paige is certainly in no position to judge her or ask her to change just because she's uncomfortable.

"Do you think we'll always be able to live like we do on the farm? I mean, do you think the resources will someday run out?" Paige asks, trying to distract Sam from her woeful thoughts.

She frowns thoughtfully and says, "I don't know. I don't see how. Grandpa seems to have it all figured out. And the guys always come up with a plan when something seems like it's going to go badly or when things break."

"That's one thing that's definitely guaranteed, it would seem," Paige says.

"What's that?"

"Things always breaking," Paige allows with a chuckle.

Sam actually smiles after a moment of reflection.

"What are you thinking about?" Paige asks her.

"I was just remembering my mom and dad. Stuff used to break and my dad would get so mad. He was always working on something, a broken stall door, fence boards that needed replaced. He said our mini-farm was like having another full-time job."

"If it was anything like the McClane farm, then I'd say he was spot on," Paige says with a smile.

"No way. It wasn't anything like our farm. There is so much more work to be done on a daily basis. We just had a small horse farm. Not even that, really."

Paige notices that Sam says "our" farm when she means the McClane farm. It touches a soft place in her heart. She feels the same way about the family's farm. The McClane farm has a way of pulling one in for a long, warm hug and holding tight. It reaches deep, touching a person's soul. Sometimes she feels like she's never been so at home. It wasn't like that when she'd first come to stay there. She wanted out. She'd wanted to run away with her brother and friends. Not anymore. Now she just wants to run back there, tonight preferably, and never leave it again.

"What was it like in Arizona where you lived before you went to college, where your family lived? Simon never talks about it."

"Hot. Always hot. Our home was nice, I guess you'd say. It was big, Spanish style with lots of marble in the floors and in the entryway pillars. The homes in Arizona are a lot different than here or on the east coast. They use more cement and materials like tile and marble to help keep them cool. Our home was very nice but a little cold. My mom tried to make it homey and comfortable for us, but it still had a coolness about it that wasn't just from the marble. I think it was because it was so big and open, almost like a museum."

"It sounds pretty," Sam comments.

Paige shrugs and continues as memories assault her, "My dad would have government people over for dinner, so it had to be... I don't know, impressive? We had a maid. That was cool. I didn't know how much I'd miss that until I left for college. We had a cook for special events, but those caterers had nothing on Hannah and Sue. We were always having my dad's colleagues or his staff over for business dinners. Before an election, it was always crazy. I didn't like most of his friends, though. They just seemed like stuffy old fuddy-duddies, boring politician types that didn't seem genuine. I think that's why my mom worked so hard at the hospital. She used to always work over when Dad was having an event. It used to piss him off, too. He wanted her home or on his arm at an event or party to play hostess. She hated it. I know she worked extra hours sometimes so that she could get out of being around those people. Who could blame her? I hid in my room whenever I could unless we were forced to be present for something."

She pauses a long moment.

Sam says, "That's the most I think you've ever said about your old life. Do you miss it?"

"Sometimes. I miss driving a car or going out with my friends. But I don't miss my old life before I left for college. I just miss them."

Sam nods solemnly. Her friend knows what it feels like to lose both parents.

"Hey, maybe your dad's still alive," she says with a hopeful half grin.

417

"I doubt it, Sam," Paige corrects her as she begins clearing away dishes. "He was in London when it was nuked. If he wasn't immediately killed, he'd be dead by now of radiation poisoning."

"I'm sorry, Paige," she offers.

"Me, too. And I'm sorry about your family, too, Sam," Paige says. Sam's loss is so much harder than her own. Paige was separated from both parents when they were killed. She wasn't near them when it happened. Sam was on the property when her parents and siblings had been murdered. She would've heard the shots. And from what she's gathered of her life directly after that, Paige knows it must've been a nightmare.

She consults her watch. It's nearly eleven o'clock already. Heating all that water had taken a long time. She still wants to heat more and treat herself to the same, luxurious- or close to it- bath. She goes about tidying up after their dinner, insists that Sam just sit on the bed, cleans and organizes their gear and the cabin and finishes by eleven-thirty.

When she glances over her shoulder, Sam has lain down on the bed, but she doesn't appear to be asleep yet. Paige crosses the room, adds more wood to the fire, then sits beside Samantha on the mattress.

"When Simon comes home, will you let him sleep here with me?" she asks with her big blue eyes that have seen and endured so much pain and agony.

"Sure, Sam," Paige acknowledges. "I'll just sleep over there."

She tips her head toward the other bed. That leaves them with nowhere for Cory to sleep, but she isn't about to point that out to Sam. For some reason, only Simon can bring her comfort right now. Paige begins to rise, but Sam tugs her arm.

"Will you stay with me... just till I fall asleep?" she begs softly, looking like the porcelain doll everyone always accuses her of being.

"Absolutely," Paige says with a nod. "Let's get you tucked in, ok? I don't want you to get sick. Simon would never let me hear the end of it."

Sam smiles knowingly, and they pull the blankets and sheet back. Then Paige lies down beside Sam and spoons against her back, wrapping an arm around her small waist.

"Tell me more about your old life, your life in Arizona," Sam pleads.

Paige pauses and says, "Sure, no problem. My life before. Let me think. Sometimes it's hard to remember some of it. It seems so long ago. We had a pool. That was fun. My friends liked to come over. There was a guesthouse. Sometimes we had relatives or guests of my dad's stay out there. Then it sucked 'cuz me and Simon couldn't get in the pool. We used to have a lot of fun in it. Mostly trying to drown each other, of course."

"We had a pool, too. Sometimes after a horse show, my friends and I would cool off in the pool if my brother and his dorky older friends weren't in it," Sam says in a mournful tone of remembrance.

Paige can tell how much she misses her big brother. She knows exactly what that feels like. Getting home to her brother sometimes felt like that nightmare everyone has where they are running late and can't get to where they need to be. It was that same sense of anxiety every single day for three and a half years. But Sam will never get home to her brother. He's just gone.

"I'm sorry that happened to you today," Paige says with great remorse. "If it was anyone's fault, it was mine and I'm really sorry."

"It's not the worst thing that's ever happened to me, so don't worry about it," Sam admits sadly.

"I… know," Paige tells her.

"You do? What do you know?" Sam inquires on a yawn.

She really doesn't want her to think that anyone has been gossiping about her, so she needs to go about it carefully.

"Simon or Hannah or someone, I don't remember, told me that when you were traveling with my aunt's group that you were abused by them. That's all. I didn't want to pry."

Sam nods and sighs. Paige believes that she will just drop the subject and go to sleep, but she doesn't.

"One of the boys in that group. That's who did it. The other men were horrible, too. But he claimed me as his own and threatened them not to touch me. I don't know if it would've mattered, though. He was as cruel and mean to me as any of them could've been."

"I'm so sorry."

"I know. I don't talk about it because I don't like remembering it. But if it hadn't happened to me, I wouldn't be the person I am now. I wouldn't have been able to kill that man today. I just would've been his victim and probably the other man's, too. He was a cruel boy. Bobby was his name."

"My cousin. I know. He was a shit when we were young, too. Always in and out of trouble. Did a stint in juvey. My dad tried to keep us away from my mom's family. He didn't like them, especially not Aunt Amber and her son."

"I wasn't with them for very long, but it felt like a lifetime. Simon tried his best to keep me away from Bobby. He'd tell him that he needed me to help get water or do chores like the laundry or cooking. It helped. It got me away from him a lot. But it didn't keep him away from me completely. Simon even told me to tell Bobby that I got my period because he knew it would gross him out. It worked. But then the next week I really did start my period, and Bobby beat the tar out of Simon for it because then he knew Simon and I had schemed up the plan to fool him."

"Jesus," Paige whispers.

"I think he cracked two of Simon's ribs. His face was all black and blue. Bobby wasn't stronger or tougher than Simon, he was just meaner. Plus, if Simon fought back, the other men would hold him so Bobby could beat on him or kick him when he was down. It was unfair. I felt so sad because he was always trying to help me or Huntley and his twin brother, his brother who died. Simon is so good, so pure."

"Yes, he's always been like that. He has an old soul is what my mom used to say."

Sam nods and continues, "Then I got the idea to chop off my hair. It was even longer than it is now. I found a knife we used for cutting vegetables and sawed it off. I thought if I made myself ugly, he'd leave me alone."

"Did it work?"

"No, sadly it didn't. He just beat me for it. Then he beat on Simon because he figured it was his idea. Soon after that, we made it

420

to the McClane farm. We traveled around for a while trying to hook up with their friends, but never found anyone alive or still in their homes. Then Peter, Grams's brother, said we should go to his family's farm. That's how we ended up back down in this area. They weren't too smart. They didn't plan well or organize. They just kept trying to find someone to freeload off of. The men were going to kill the McClane family and take over their farm. I don't know how much Grams's brother knew of that plan, but he was a sick man, too, so who knows? They didn't think there would be Rangers living on the farm with Grams and Grandpa. Thank God they were. Simon and I could still be living under the thumb of those evil people if it wasn't for John, Kelly and Derek, even Cory."

"Yeah, it is safe. I like that I feel safe there, too," Paige says as she strokes Sam's dark hair back from her soft forehead. She is curious as to what role Cory played in getting rid of the visitor people but refrains from asking. "That's not something everyone has anymore. It's important to feel safe."

"It didn't take the family long to piece together what was going on in the group and get me and Simon and the twins out of there. They saved us."

"They seem to be good at saving people, huh?"

Sam says with a smile, "Right, the whole family is like an army of guardian angels."

Paige nods and smiles, but it disappears at Sam's next comment.

"Simon stabbed your cousin. Did you know that? Bobby attacked Reagan. He hated her. If Simon hadn't been more concerned about getting Reagan away from him, I think Simon would've done the same thing to Bobby that I did to that man today. I don't think he would've stopped with stabbing him one time in the back."

Paige lets out a shaky sigh at the disturbing image of her brother stabbing their cousin to death in a rage-filled bloodbath.

"I just feel sorry he got cheated that revenge," Sam admits before drifting off to sleep, her breathing becoming slower and deeper.

Paige slips away a few minutes later and starts heating water for her own bath. As she soaks in the warm water washing her hair and skin with the bar of beeswax soap from the farm and with her rifle and pistol within arm's reach, Paige thinks about her sweet-tempered, gentle-hearted, nerdy little brother with the auburn hair and freckles and reflects on how much he's changed since she knew him when they were both naïve young kids who liked to play Marco Polo in the family pool. She also reflects on what Sam told her about traveling with those people. Paige wishes she could've been there for him. If she had stayed in Arizona and been going to college there when the country fell apart, she wonders if they would've left with Aunt Amber's group together or if they would've stuck it out in their home. This also forces her to remember her mother, which is more painful than anything else. Paige could've discouraged her from going to work. She could've persuaded her to leave with them or to hole up and stay in their home together with Simon. Paige knows that most of these thoughts are naïve on her part, but remembering her mother and fantasizing about what could've been is all she has left of her. She misses her so desperately sometimes that it physically hurts.

She also misses the McClane farm tonight. It feels like her home now, or probably the only one she'll ever have. She misses the family, especially the children. Hell, she even misses Cory's mangy dog that follows her everywhere. A wash of homesickness comes over her hard and fast. And then she starts panicking about her brother and his safety.

He's been through so much. Paige is thankful he's changed and evolved as the world turned so malignant. His ability to shut down his emotions and fight for what he believes in, for what is right like defending Sam is such a stark contrast to the young boy he was when she left for college. Her brother has become a stone cold killer, and she couldn't be more pleased.

Chapter Twenty-eight
Simon

"Do you see that asshole, Cor?" Simon asks his friend, who should be moving in for a closer look.

They've made it back to Vanderbilt University and are scouting the area for those Kappa creeps. It hadn't taken long to find them.

"If you would be so kind, Professor, smoke 'em for me," Cory replies.

The man is armed, acting as a sentry, but yanking cruelly at the thin arm of a woman who clearly does not want to go anywhere with him.

"Roger," Simon replies and pulls the trigger.

They've been watching this group for about a half an hour since finding them. There is no doubt in his mind that they were also supplying women to the bastards down on the river. They found a room full of women and young girls, a locked room at that, on the first floor of the campus in one of the classrooms. They'd killed the two guards and told the women to head toward the Parthenon where Cory will have Dave's group come back for them. With all the work they have ahead of them still this night, Dave may not be able to send anyone for them until morning, but at least someone will and they should be safe there until they do. The windows of the classroom had been boarded up, the doors locked from the outside. They'd quietly questioned them and found out that they didn't know of any other women being kept anywhere on the campus. Then they had freed them and had continued searching for the ones who'd done this heinous deed. It had been difficult to leave them. Simon had just glanced at some of them but knew that they could use medical attention. He's hoping that he and Doc and maybe even Reagan can travel to Hendersonville in the next few days to check on all of these poor women and young girls. At the very least, most of them should be given a dose of antibiotics. He's thankful that Doc has been working on natural antibiotics with him. They will need a lot of it, and they'll need to make much more to get through the winter.

So far, he and Cory disabled four of the dirty bastards who've done this. Simon believes there are more lurking somewhere on the campus grounds. It's a big, spread out school, so it will be difficult to search it with just the two of them. He'd volunteered to go high and scout out through his night scope down on as much of the property as he could. Now he's going to join back up with his friend and begin a door to door kick-in if they must.

He climbs down the fire-escape ladder, landing softly on his feet. Jogging a block east, he makes his way toward Cory where they will meet at the hospital entrance. There is a good chance they will also find supplies that they could stash in their packs while looking for jerks who sell women and kids for supplies like food that they are too lazy to grow for themselves. He knows that Cory and his sister have already hit this hospital, but his friend was sure that there was more to loot.

Simon's mind has been deeply troubled all day. He knows it's because of Sam. He is worried about her, sick he let that happen to her, that she was almost raped again or possibly killed. His sister was right when she told him that mistakes happen. When he'd seen Sam on top of the dead man stabbing away, he'd wanted to go over and shoot him in the skull. If Paige and Cory hadn't been with him, he probably would have done so. He knew the man was already dead, but the blind rage he'd felt at the mistake, her kidnapping and her obvious attempted assault had sent him over the edge of sane reasoning. He's just not used to mistakes like that happening on his watch, and certainly not when he's also with Cory. They don't make stupid errors like that. It was an immature lapse in judgement to allow the girls to go to the bathroom by themselves, no matter how much they'd insisted. Simon has no plan on ever repeating such a mistake. He also doesn't want Sam leaving the farm again, preferably ever. His sister can park her butt there and stay, as well. He's pretty sure that this mandate isn't going to go over well, but, then again, his sister was pretty shaken up by the event with Sam.

"Ready?" Cory asks him when they have joined up near the front doors, both of which have been vandalized and the glass broken.

Simon offers his friend a firm nod, and they enter through the shattered glass panes of the sliding doors. Their night-vision gear will help considerably as the desolate hospital is black as pitch. Simon switches from his sniper rifle to his short-barreled shotgun and follows his friend through the main lobby. For being such a big man, Cory is quiet and stealthy when he wants to be. Most of the time, he doesn't give a shit if he's being quiet. But tonight, however, he must feel the need for creeping silently through the malevolent hallways of the hospital. They make a fast search of the first floor, don't find much worth salvaging other than a few bottles of pills and some bandaging which all gets stashed inside Simon's pack. They move on toward the building where those creeps had set a trap that almost killed Simon's sister. He still can't believe that happened, either. And on Cory's watch it seems even more ridiculous.

They find the spot where Paige fell through the floor, but the men who'd set the trap aren't anywhere around. Staring down into that dark abyss makes Simon feel a renewed sense of purpose and an untapped, violent rage. She could've been killed. Cory even grimaces hard, swallows and turns away from it. Apparently the terrifying, near-death incident is still weighing down his friend's thoughts.

They search two more buildings but find them abandoned. Pressing on is the only answer. These men must be found and stopped.

"Let's head around back," Cory suggests in a clipped tone. "There's a gymnasium back there. I wonder if that's where they've set up."

"Sounds good," Simon agrees as they leave the room of bad memories.

425

It doesn't take them long to make it to the gym, which lies beyond the stadium. They pause in the long hallway near the locker rooms so they can spy on the entrance, noting that no sentries wait there. If they are within the building, then they aren't too worried about guarding the place. These thugs apparently concluded that the few guards they had posted elsewhere were going to do the trick or else they are so foolishly confident in their ability to fight off attackers that they didn't feel the need for more sentries. Not too smart either way in Simon's opinion.

The door to the gymnasium swings open and a man stumbles toward the locker rooms carrying a bottle of what Simon can only speculate the contents by the manner in which he staggers about. Cory and Simon back up, slinking into the dark corners of the men's locker room. The inebriated man comes in carrying a lantern in his other hand and proceeds to relieve himself in one of the urinals. Simon wrinkles his nose. No wonder the smell is so bad in here. The plumbing no longer works, but they are apparently still using the facilities and have caused massive back-ups of the sewer lines. Cory nudges him in the shoulder, and Simon knows what his intentions are going to be toward this man. His friend sneaks up behind the other man and wraps his arm quickly around his throat, catching him in a choke hold. The man tries to struggle but the dagger Cory is pressing against his neck deters further fighting. Simon walks up to them and starts the interrogation before the man's friends discover his absence.

"How many are in there?" Simon asks impatiently.

The man spits at him, forcing Simon to punch him in the stomach. He doesn't like being this way, but if it means saving innocent people from being harmed, abused or killed by this man or his friends then he's willing to become a monster if just for tonight. The man has doubled over in pain, but Cory pulls him back upright and keeps the dagger trained on his carotid. His friend was right about these guys. This man seems well dressed and clean.

"How many?" he asks again.

The man is hesitant, so Cory nudges him to get him to speak. They get nothing again, so Simon punches him in the mouth. He has to spit blood this time.

"There's fifteen of us," the man says. "But we've got guards. You two are fucked."

"You mean the guards we killed?" Cory taunts.

The man swallows hard, his eyes full of genuine fear.

"Are they all armed, the men you're with?" Simon asks.

He shrugs, gets another encouraging choking from Cory and finally says, "Yeah, most of us."

Simon inquires, "What about the hole in the floor over there in one of the student buildings? What's that about? Did you guys do that?"

The yuppy thug shrugs, which is all Simon needs to know.

Cory asks, "Are there women or kids in that gym with you?"

"What? No, man. Just us. We don't want none of those whiners in there with us. It's just for us men."

Simon would like to remind this nefarious scumbag that men don't violate innocent women and young girls.

"Where's the rest of your group?" Simon asks.

"What do you mean? It's just us. We're all in there. Except for our guards. We take turns on guard duty."

"How many of those rooms full of women do you have around here on this campus?" Simon questions.

The man's dark gaze falls to the floor with defeat. He knows that he and his group have been outmatched.

"Just the one," he states. "I didn't want any part of that. It was their ideas. I'm just one of their friends."

"So you weren't participating in the group rapes that went on in that room the women told us about?" Simon asks, although he doesn't really need to. This man is as evil as the rest of his sick friends.

"No way. Not me. I'm not like that," he pleads pathetically.

"We done, Professor?" Cory asks.

Simon nods and turns away. By the sound of gurgling, he knows that his friend has slit the man's throat. It is no less than what he deserves for what he has done. His father was an attorney before

427

he became a politician. There aren't prisons anymore for men like this. There is no due process. He was never the kind of person before the apocalypse to believe in vigilantism, but his opinion has modified considerably since.

"I've got an idea," Cory says after he has dragged the dead body away, back toward the showers. The long trail of blood could still give them away.

"What is it?" Simon asks.

"Let's seal the doors and torch it. Shoot any of them that get out," Cory offers.

Simon considers this for a moment before saying, "Do you think that would work?"

"It's better than taking on a group that big by ourselves. No sense in putting ourselves in danger. We gotta' get back to the girls soon. We've been gone a long time," Cory adds with a thoughtful expression, one he doesn't often show.

"Yeah, you're right," Simon agrees. "Where do we start?"

A short while later, they have a steel bar threaded through the handles of the main gym entrance and an aluminum pipe blocking the other. One man door is left, which is the one Cory will use to make his escape after he starts the fire. He'll then seal off that door, as well. The windows are high off the ground, at least two stories up, surrounding the top edge of the gymnasium. Unless the men inside have ladders, they aren't escaping through a window. The only available exit will be the three small windows on the farthest east side of the gym where bleachers reach high enough to connect to them. Simon is positioned outside of the building in case that happens. Cory spied on the group to ascertain the man's story of the number and sexes of the persons inside. The details they were given are accurate. The women were detained in the rape room far away from the men, so Operation Torch is on.

"We're a go," Cory tells Simon in his earpiece.

A moment later, his friend is sprinting across the street to join him. Not many minutes after, a prophetic gray smoke begins billowing out into the street from beneath the door that Cory just came through and then blocked with a piece of lumber under the handle.

Soon the entire building is on fire, the red and orange flames licking the night sky. Two men try to make their escapes from the windows only to be taken out by Simon. Another tries to get out, and Cory shoots him. It seems a cruel fate, this killing of people by burning them alive. But, then again, what they did to those women and girls was even worse in Simon's opinion.

They wait until the heat of the fire is more than they can bear and nobody else tries to escape. The screams have stopped anyway. Simon knows they have most likely all succumbed to smoke inhalation. A glance toward his friend and he notes the thoughtful pursing of Cory's lips as he rubs the scruff on his chin. He seems unmoved by this murder scene. Simon isn't sure what his friend is thinking, but he almost never does. He looks like he's working out a difficult math problem in his mind. Cory is so guarded now, unlike how he used to be. Losing his little sister has changed him, darkened his heart, and made him more cautious about letting anyone in.

They double-time it back toward the cabin, stop at the creek to wash up, and jog in their damp clothing the rest of the way. Simon wasn't in too bad of shape, but Cory had blood splattered on his face and neck, likely from killing the man in the locker room. His sister is already leery of Cory; Simon doesn't want her to be downright afraid of him. It's important to him that they get along and seeing his friend covered in someone else's blood could turn her even more against him.

When they arrive at the cabin, they find Paige asleep on the front porch in a sleeping bag with her rifle resting beside her.

"So she needs some work on watch duty," Simon jests and barely gets a grin from Cory who seems more stoic and, strangely, upset at seeing her.

She snaps awake and scrambles to her knees as they climb the stairs to the front porch.

"It's just us, sis," Simon reassures her.

He reaches down and offers assistance, but she jumps up and flings herself against Cory, hugging him close. His friend appears as shocked as Simon and just stands there. Then he hugs her back with slightly less fervor but inhales deeply of her hair and neck. What the hell's going on? Simon's jaw flexes tightly.

"I was worried. Thank God you're back," Paige mumbles against Cory's chest.

"We're fine," Cory says quietly.

"Uh... sis?" Simon says confusedly. "I think you got the wrong guy."

"What?" Paige asks, stumbles back from Cory and sends and awkward glance toward Simon. "Oh...yeah. Sorry," she blurts and steps away from Cory. "I...I thought you were my brother. I was just disoriented."

Cory doesn't answer but retrieves her rifle from the floor.

"That's all right," Simon allays her humiliation, although she doesn't actually seem all that embarrassed after all. "Honest mistake. It's dark out here."

"Right," she whispers as she tries to slide past Cory.

"You shouldn't have been out here," his friend growls angrily and snatches her upper arm. "You were supposed to wait inside with the door locked."

His friend's concern is almost at dramatic proportions. He is more bent out of shape than Simon, and Paige is his sister. She doesn't answer Cory but yanks free, yawns widely and brushes past Cory into the cabin. She smells clean, her clothing is fresh and she has braided her long hair, which looks a little damp. Perhaps that is the reason for his friend sniffing her. It had better be the only damn reason.

Simon hopes she doesn't get sick from being out in the cold, but it's too late now to warn her. Her spirit is pretty tough. He's discussed with Paige some of the hardships she's endured on the road. Simon isn't so sure that his sister can't weather just about anything. Once they are all in, Simon shuts and locks the door. Cory places another log in the wood-burning stove while Paige sits on one of the chairs at the table.

"Shh!" Paige whispers and points toward Sam.

They both nod to her.

"There's a lot of food left," she offers.

Simon unloads his gear on the table, keeps his pistol on, and shrugs out of his jacket. He's looking forward to some sleep. Cory quietly allows his equipment to fall to the floor. Apparently his friend is also whipped.

Cory pulls his dirty, blood-stained shirt over his head, and Simon notices that his sister averts her eyes.

"Nah, beanpole, we're just gonna sack out now," Cory tells her, which doesn't get a response from Paige. "You can make us breakfast in a few hours, though."

She tosses a pillow at him. He catches it but doesn't give it back.

"Let me treat that wound before we sack out, brother," Simon offers, noting the fresh streak of red on the white cotton covering a small section of Cory's stomach.

Normally he'd get an argument, but tonight Cory just stands still while Simon disinfects his hands first and then the wound. Cory barely winces at the stinging solution. His gaze seems fixated on Paige, who is not looking at them at all. Simon is able to apply a clean bandage and tape to hold it down and keep it covered. Tomorrow when they get home, he'll have Doc or Reagan check it just to be safe.

"See, Professor?" Cory says as he turns away, not bothering with another shirt. "Just a scratch."

"I don't know about that, but I think it's gonna be fine without stitches. I'd probably advise you to take it easy for a few days so that it can heal."

"And I'd probably not take that advice but thanks anyways," Cory boasts.

Simon turns back toward the table where their belongings are being stored, removes his boots, pulls on a clean shirt and leans his sniper rifle up against the wall where the window is located.

"How'd it go?" his sister asks.

"Fine," they answer in unison, not wanting to give away the gory elements.

Paige pushes, "What happened?"

Cory says, "Everything went fine. We even made a stop at the school again. There won't be any more people falling through that

431

floor. They had women and girls stashed away there, too. It was a regular creep fest."

Simon interrupts before Cory gets too far into the details, "It's safe now. We took care of everything, and Dave's group is looking after the women from the river encampment. We sent a few injured people to Pleasant View to the practice and radioed the family to let them know. Everything's taken care of. Don't worry."

"Ok, sounds like it was dangerous. I didn't know you were going back to that college. I wouldn't have wanted you to."

"You wouldn't have wanted us *not* to if you'd seen the abused women and kids they had locked up there," Cory remarks as he wipes down his rifle and replaces the missing cartridges to the magazine. "I'm learning, beanpole, that you do have a pretty damn strong sense of right and wrong. And that fucked up shit at the college was all wrong. They got what they deserved and are in a lot hotter fucking place tonight than this cabin."

"Hey," Simon reprimands for the inappropriate language in front of his sister.

"Good, then I'm glad you went," Paige says softly and moves to sit cross-legged on the other bed. "I just wish you guys woulda' told me first."

"We're good, Paige. Just get some sleep," Cory says.

His friend's tone is kind and patient, unlike the way he frequently responds to Paige. Simon is glad to hear it. He's not so sure about that bullshit embrace on the porch, but he's happy they aren't harping at each other.

"Paige," Simon whispers to his sister. "Sleep with Sam. Let me and Cor have the big bed."

"I'm good with the floor," Cory says as he uses the same sleeping bag in which Paige had just been resting on the porch, spreading it out and plopping down with fatigue.

"Sam said she wanted you to sleep with her. I didn't feel like I should argue, so I didn't."

"But…" Simon tries to debate.

"She was really upset, Simon. Now shut up and go to sleep," Paige insists and rolls to her other side.

Simon slides in beside Sam but makes sure to stay above the covers. Her body heat immediately spreads like a low fire against his side. It's a lot better than sleeping next to Cory, he has to admit. He waits a while until he's sure Paige is asleep, knowing that Cory won't be yet.

"Cor," he whispers in the dark.

"Yeah?" his groggy voice returns.

Simon sighs a moment before asking the question that's been bugging him. "Have you ever torched a place like that before? I mean with creeps inside? You seemed like you knew how to do it."

A lot of time passes before Cory answers him.

"Yeah, it's how I killed the bastards that shot my sister. I locked them in, lit it up, and shot the ones who escaped."

"I thought maybe that might have been the case," Simon remarks without judgment. "I always wondered how you took on so many that night before John and Kelly got back to you."

"I could've probably done it another way, got a few here and there, waited. But I wanted them to suffer," Cory admits quietly.

Simon doesn't answer but eases onto his side so as not to disturb Sam. He is dismayed to find his sister staring at him from her bed. Her blue eyes are wide in the firelight, her expression troubled. Great. He wants her to like his friend, not despise or fear him even more.

To his surprise, Paige says, "Cory, it sounds like you did the right thing. If they'd killed my brother, I'd want a slow, agonizing punishment for them, too. Now both of you quit talking and go to sleep. This isn't a girls' slumber party."

They both chuckle. Paige rolls away from him and goes to sleep, and he's sure that Cory does so, as well, because his friend snores softly. Simon lies awake for a long time, though, pondering the dark stain on his soul that this night has blemished.

Chapter Twenty-nine
Reagan

Dawn is breaking on the horizon, the first drab gray haze of light filtering through the windows when she finishes with the injured and sickly women at the clinic brought there by her husband's friend, Dave the Mechanic. She sent Grandpa home a few hours ago with Kelly. She and John are still at the clinic with sentries, also sent over by Dave, plus their own town guards who are keeping watch over their little medical clinic until she is done. A few of the women have been put up in an old yet spacious Victorian across the street from the practice because they were too unstable to be moved to Dave's town. One of his men didn't pull through from his injuries. He'd been a type O negative blood, and they hadn't had a donor. He'd mostly bled out on the trip to the clinic. She may be less cynical since John has come into her life, but Reagan is also pragmatic enough to realize that the soldier may not have made it even with the blood transfusion. His friends are going to return him to Hendersonville for burial. He had a wife and two small children. Reagan hadn't taken it well when Grandpa had called it. She never takes failure well, but she's learning that it comes more often than not with post-apocalyptic trauma medicine. If she'd been in a working hospital, she could've carted him off to surgery with a room full of nurses, residents, equipment, an anesthesiologist and about six bags of blood. Survival and life is so fragile now. When she gets home, she'll sleep downstairs with her baby boy. She doesn't want to miss a single second of opportunity to shower that kid with love. She's caught

John many times standing over Jacob's sleeping body just contemplating. She knows what he's thinking.

John has mostly been outside on guard with Dave's men talking about the battle and the people from the river. She's heard snippets of the conversation and pieces of information about the battle from the women she'd treated. She's glad that Dave's men offered those bastards no quarter. Even the men who were just paying customers of the rats who ran the camp were guilty in her opinion. To be knowledgeable of such an encampment of evil where women and children were being used and hurt was cruel and sick in and of itself. They all got the justice they deserved for their sins.

She'd met Annie from Dave's group and had treated her gunshot wound. Luckily she hadn't needed a transfusion. She'll heal nicely if she takes it easy and doesn't pull out Reagan's perfectly applied stitches. Annie seems like a real pistol. Even though she was as pale as a ghost and going on her last pinch of energy, she'd volunteered to stay across the street at the makeshift hospital house to guard the women there. Reagan had chuckled at her right before hitting her with some medicine that knocked her out. One of the men had carried her out and placed her in the hospital house.

The rescued nurse from the river camp had been very helpful, after Grandpa had insisted that she scrub up well in the back room. She'd come back and quickly pulled on latex gloves and got right to work. The poor woman looked like she hadn't eaten much in a long time. She'd explained to Reagan while they'd worked in tandem on a young woman who'd been knocked clean out that the river camp was nothing more than a sex slave camp. She'd been a victim of that place for over three months. The girl they'd taken care of together is in a coma. They don't have CAT scan capabilities, but she and Grandpa had come to the same conclusion. She may or may not ever awaken. They will need to watch her for signs of bleeding on the brain or swelling of the brain or stroke. They don't have an ICU anymore. But one of the particularly fierce looking soldiers had carried her across the street and promised to stay with her and alert them over the radio if she comes to. He reminded Reagan of Kelly when he'd first come to the farm. He also seems like a man of great integrity like her beloved brother-in-law.

435

"You ready, babe?" John's husky timbre announces from the doorway.

"Just another minute," Reagan explains. "Putting things away and cleaning."

"Rough night?" he asks with the usual concern he feels for her.

Reagan turns and shrugs. "Typical, I guess. Gets old."

John crosses the room, slides his hands into the hair on either side of her face and pulls her up for a quick kiss. There isn't passion in the kiss but a comforting warmth. She can't believe she'd rebuked this man so many times. What was she thinking? That she could get through this disastrous life without him? What a fool she'd been.

John pulls back and kisses her forehead before stepping away. Reagan resumes wiping down the countertop and rinsing the rag that hopefully has enough sanitizing solution on it to kill whatever pathogens could be lingering. She drops her towels and soiled rags into the burlap sack. Without being asked, John takes the bucket of hot water and dumps it down the sink. Reagan hits the sink with some more bleach water spray and rinses again. He takes the sack out to the truck so that the linens can be laundered at the farm while Reagan stows away her equipment and the two boxes of supplies in the back room. When she returns to the waiting room, John is standing there leaning against the countertop where Grandpa's receptionist used to work. How can he look so damn good after pulling an all-nighter at the clinic with her? His tattered jeans are hanging just so on his slim hips. The sleeves of his button-down denim shirt are rolled back to his elbows, exposing his tan forearms. A lock of his sun-kissed blonde hair has fallen forward onto his forehead. Reagan steps closer and pushes it back only to have it fall again. He grins patiently and helps her into her jacket.

"You look like some sort of GQ model and I look like I got run over by a truck. Not fair," she complains as he tugs her hand, pulling her closer.

"This," he says, indicating toward the front of himself, "is no easy feat. It takes a lot of work to look this good."

Reagan rolls her eyes at his lopsided grin and teasing.

"But, ma'am, you look pretty darn sexy to me," John says quietly as he rests his head against hers. "And you smell good, too."

"It's the sterilizing solution," she jokes.

"Nah, my girl always smells good," John says and sinks a hand into the hair at the back of her neck, pulling her hair free of its ponytail. "Let's go home. You need some rest."

"I feel dead on my feet, but I also think I should just sack out at the house with the patients. I'm not sure it's a good idea to head back to the farm in case something happens with one of them."

"No way, boss," John says firmly and pulls her along with him out the front door of the clinic before locking it. "You're going home to sleep. Two of Dave's guys are staying over there. They'll radio if they have a problem. They're used to keeping weird hours."

"The sheriff's got a few guys over there, too. He stopped in earlier to tell me and Grandpa," Reagan says, although she's sure John probably already knows this. Not much gets by him when it comes to security.

"Good. That'll help," John says as he opens the driver's door of the truck and allows her to crawl in first to the middle of the front seat. Then he tucks his rifle in between his body and the driver's side door.

Once they are on the road and moving, John slides his hand onto her leg and gives it a gentle, reassuring squeeze. So much has happened in the past twenty-four hours. The biggest event was the return of her father. Grandpa hadn't pressed him for information about his family or his whereabouts for the past four years but had offered Cory and Simon's cabin to him and his wife. Reagan thought it was bullshit but had held her tongue. Now Cory, Simon and Paige will have to move their belongings to the house to accommodate a man who abandoned his own family during so many of their darkest hours of need. The two children of her father are sleeping in one of the bedrooms in the basement of the big house. They seemed very out of sorts and uncomfortable and had retired to their shared bedroom after dinner and hadn't come back out. Her father told them that there was so much he needed to discuss but that he was tired. When Sue asked him about the bruises and scrapes on his face and knuckles, he'd said they had journeyed a long way to come home and that the trip had been difficult and dangerous. Reagan had snidely informed him that his situation was no different than anyone else at the dinner table. His son also had the same matching scuffed knuckles. The wife and daughter had mostly remained silent throughout the meal. The mother just seemed exhausted. They were happy for the hot meal and very appreciative and thankful.

The girl was awkward around the family and had kept her head bowed throughout most of the meal. Her short black pixie hair, silver rings on multiple fingers, and the three ear piercings in each ear weren't something their father would've been happy about before or after the apocalypse. He'd always demanded that his girls dress and act conservatively so as not to reflect badly on him. Her father and his new family all showered and changed in the basement and had come to dinner clean and slightly refreshed. But Gretchen was wearing the same similar clothing style of grunge punk in the form of skinny jeans, a brown flannel shirt and matching hoodie. That is also not the tidy appearance their father would've approved before the fall. G has a definite sharp keenness in her pale hazel eyes and a very significant mutual disdain of their shared father.

The son, Lucas, had been slightly more vocal and obviously harbored respect for their father. Robert finally got the son he'd wanted to replace her dead, older brother. It was indicative in their relationship. There was still the missing element of fatherly affection, and it showed on Lucas's face. Reagan could tell that the young man had probably spent most of his young life trying to please the man. There was a desperation in his eyes for their father's approval. She'd like to inform him that it's probably never going to happen.

She'd also like an explanation about the new family, but it hadn't come last night. She's not done yet. She wants answers. She and her sisters deserve them.

After dinner they'd adjourned to Grandpa's office, but it was apparent that everyone was weary. Once he'd found out from her grandfather privately in his office that his mother was dead, Robert's demeanor had changed rather significantly. He hadn't shown it, but Reagan knows the loss of Grams hit him hard. The rest of the family had joined them after their meeting, but Reagan could see the defeat in his slumped shoulders. He'd told them very little, but what he did say before taking his wife to Simon's cabin was a confusing blend of information. What Reagan mostly got out of it was that her father had somehow managed to elevate his position within the government and had gone from being a mere colonel to an exalted general. She hadn't really been paying attention when he'd mentioned his elevation in rank because she isn't going to invest time and effort into the man who'd abandoned them. Reagan couldn't care less other than he may know more about the radio transmission that only Sam had witnessed in its entirety. His ambition is nothing new to her. He'd left the Navy to join the Marines and had given up his career as a doctor for what he'd correctly believed would be a more easily advantageous career in another branch of the military. Her father had been willing to sacrifice anything for his political ambitions. Even his family. Apparently someone has promoted him yet again.

She also knows that something is wrong with Robert. He seems ill. Grandpa offered to look at him and tried to discuss his health, but her father said they'd talk more in the morning, that he and his family were in need of rest. That isn't like the Colonel. He despised weakness of any kind and had demanded perfection in everything. Even admitting to fatigue would've been taboo when she was growing up under his heavy criticisms. She just hopes he hasn't brought some contagious disease to the farm.

His new wife had sat meekly, which is nothing short of what she'd expect from any wife Robert took, and again the woman said nothing during their brief discussion. She is an attractive lady but has seen her fair share of hard times. It showed in the wrinkles around her eyes and the pinched lines of her forehead. She doesn't seem old enough to have wrinkles. The new wife actually seems at least a decade younger than her father.

Later today when she and Grandpa have caught up on their sleep, she fully intends on finding out more about what's going on out West where her father had been living. He knows something. She could see it in his eyes when he'd evaded the questions coming at him from John and Derek.

"John, what would you do if the acting President called in the military?"

439

"What President? We don't even know for sure who the President is right now."

"I think my father does."

"Yeah, I think you're right about that. He's definitely got some intel the rest of us need to know."

"He wasn't a general before, so something has to have happened. Of course, this is my father we're talking about. For all we know, he could've appointed himself to a new position. His ego has never known restraint."

"He seemed pretty humble last night," John argues.

Reagan chuffs and frowns.

"You don't know my father, John," she retorts. "He's a real piece of work. I told you what he was like growing up. Hell, he was probably living up in the northwest somewhere running his own town or some shit. Control freak doesn't even come close to describing him."

"We'll find out more info soon enough, honey," John says with his usual optimism. "Don't worry about stuff we don't know yet."

"What if that radio message was about calling up all active duty soldiers to do something? Would you go?"

She doesn't like that he takes such a lengthy period of time to answer. He pauses to look out the window, slows the vehicle down to swerve around a fallen branch in the road. He sighs long and hard.

"Let's not worry about anything like that, ok, babe? I'm not going anywhere. You're stuck with me."

She nods but feels a certain dread building in the pit of her stomach. Reagan knows with absolute certainty that she made the right decision in not telling her husband about the entire transmission that Sam confided. She could never let him go, let him leave the farm and her and Jake. She'd rather die a slow, agonizing death than to say such a good-bye to her husband.

"No," she corrects as John pulls onto the rutted, hidden oil well road that will eventually take them home. "You're stuck with me, mister."

"I can think of worse places to be," he jests with a grin.

Reagan kisses his bicep and inhales deeply of him.

"Now just how tired are you exactly?" John teases.

She laughs and replies, "Are you serious?"

"Always," John says and squeezes her thigh.

"Yeah, right. You're never serious unless we're talking about sex. It doesn't always have to be about sex, ya' know," Reagan scolds half-heartedly.

John laughs loudly and pulls the truck off the road and into a copse of trees. He cuts the engine. They are in the middle of nowhere still miles from the Johnson farm, the first farm on this trail. They always drive slowly on the rutted path home so as not to tear up what few vehicles they have left.

"With us, it's always about the sex, my dear," her husband teases and pulls her close for a kiss that instantly has her squirming.

"What are you doing? Why are we stopped?" Reagan asks with confusion when he finally pulls back.

"Proving my manhood?" John says with a cocky smirk.

Reagan belly laughs and says, "I think you've proven that enough over the last few years, Harrison."

"I don't know," John murmurs as his hand slides under her faded green doctor's scrubs. "It's feeling a little affronted. I think I need to prove my point about our sex life."

Reagan chuckles and leans into him. Then he pulls her tighter, kisses her more thoroughly and presses her down onto the seat until she is lying beneath him and her smile has vanished. Clothes are shed, fires ignited, windows steamed up. And later as the depressing gray fades and the bright orange rays of the sun just begin rising over the treetops, they resume their trip.

"Promise me you'll never leave, John. That you'll refuse to go if they want you back," Reagan pleads.

"Right now, I'd promise to cut off my right foot for you, babe," he jokes, his eyes wide with exaggeration. "You have excellent timing when it comes to asking for things."

"I'm serious," she reiterates more emphatically, ignoring his insinuation about the sex.

"I'm not going anywhere," he swears and presses a kiss to the back of her hand.

441

Reagan rests her head against his shoulder and holds fast to his muscular arm. The next thing she knows, he is waking her and they are parked in the driveway by the farmhouse.

"Hm, you seem even more tired than when we left the clinic," John says with a smile from the open door of the truck.

"Wonder why," Reagan jokes with a smile.

"Come on, sleepy girl," her husband says as he helps her down. "I'm gonna' head out to the barn to talk with the guys. I'll be in shortly."

"'Kay, babe," she returns.

"You gonna' be downstairs with Jake?"

Reagan smiles softly. He knows her so well. She offers a nod, places a quick kiss against his smiling mouth and walks to the house without him.

"Hey, ya' lazy bastard," Kelly calls out as John approaches the barn. "Glad you could finally show up."

Derek soon joins in the hazing of her husband. Reagan just shakes her head and climbs the stairs to the kitchen. Hannah is there already, which is unusual. It's not even six a.m. yet.

"Want some breakfast?" her sister asks.

"Why are you up, Hannie?"

"Couldn't sleep. Kelly couldn't sleep either. He just kept tossing and turning worrying about everything. I gave up around five and just got up."

"Let me get changed," Reagan informs her. "I'll be right back."

She forgoes climbing the two flights to the attic and just strips out of her scrubs in the laundry room, unafraid that anyone will walk in on her this early in the morning. Opening the hutch, Reagan finds the stack of clean clothes always waiting there. She pulls on a pair of dark blue sweatpants and someone's hoodie. It must belong to one of the men because it hangs to her knees. She affectionately reaches out and touches one of her grandfather's freshly ironed and pressed shirts. This man, who was her real father growing up, who led her to become the woman she is today, still prefers an ironed button down and pressed dress slacks instead of anything casual like a t-shirt or jeans. He'll always mean more to her than her biological father.

"The kids are all right. Everything at the clinic went well… sort of," Reagan relates to Hannah when she returns to the kitchen.

"What's that mean? Who did we lose?"

"One of Dave's men. Also one of the younger women isn't doing well, but we're on watchful waiting with her."

"I'm glad the guys have made contact with this Dave man. Our family could always use more friends, especially ones with military experience. I can't wait to meet him. He sounds very kind and good."

"Careful what you wish for, sis," Reagan says as she slathers half of a biscuit with honey butter. "John says he cusses worse than me."

"That would be terribly difficult. He would have to be some kind of professional heathen," Hannah says with a sly grin. "Don't worry. Kelly already warned me."

"What was the Hulk worried about? The clinic or his brother?"

"He was just worried about Cory. He couldn't sleep until he heard from him."

"I always worry more about whoever Cory runs into," she tries at a joke.

"Reagan, he's getting better," her little sister reprimands. "Here, have a piece of sausage."

Reagan plucks the small, smoked link off of the extended fork and gnaws away at it.

"What about you, sis?" Reagan carefully asks after Hannah's health as she walks around the counter to stand next to her. "Are you getting better?"

Hannah stops what she's doing and stands there for a moment.

"Yes, I guess so," Hannie admits, knowing full well what Reagan means.

"It seems like you've been feeling a little better," Reagan tells her.

443

"It still hurts," Hannah admits with a frown, her mismatched eyes showing her pain. "I didn't know it hurt so bad."

"Me neither, sis," Reagan confesses softly and wraps an arm around Hannah's waist. "I miss Grams, too. Every day. And I think about Em every day, too. It does hurt. I just don't want it to consume you. We need you around here. I can't ever lose one of my sisters, ok? I'm sure as fuck not as tough as people think I am, so don't leave me again."

Hannah swallows hard and nods before whisking away a tear.

"I won't. I promise," Hannah tells her. "And don't make me get out Grams's rolling pin to use on you for swearing in the kitchen."

Reagan laughs and returns to her chair at the island.

"I have high hopes for you, but I'm not so sure about Cory," Reagan laments, too tired to express a different opinion about their adopted brother.

"I do," Hannah argues. "He's coming around. Someday he'll be able to remember Em without feeling so angry."

"Maybe," Reagan says just to be compliant. She decides since they are uncharacteristically alone, to broach the subject of their father. "How do you feel about Robert coming home?"

Hannah stops in the middle of stirring sausage gravy in the giant cast iron skillet. A cool expression comes over her fair countenance. She resumes swirling the thick mixture around.

"He's our father. He's the rightful inheritor of this farm. He has every right to come here."

"Those are all facts, but you haven't stated how you feel," Reagan reminds her.

Hannah sighs long and loudly and replies, "I always felt like I needed my father or a father figure in my life. I wanted him to come home so badly for so long. Now I just feel indifferent. I have my Kelly and our daughter. I have my sisters and all the children on the farm. And Grandpa more than anyone has filled the void of a missing father for so long now that I just don't feel much of anything toward Robert anymore. Maybe that's an unbiblical way of speaking, but as you like to point out, he did indeed abandon us."

Reagan is surprised by her sister's response. She would've thought Hannah would be excited by their father's return. This change in her is because of the unstable status of the country, her attack by one of the visitors, her loss of Grams in her life and so many other factors. But mostly, if Reagan was to guess, it's because of Kelly. He makes her stronger, and Hannah has more confidence in herself because of him.

"Yes, he did," Reagan agrees. "I want to know what his plans are, though. I want to know if he's staying or if this is just temporary. I want to know what he knows about the country. He has a lot of answers that he needs to give us."

"He's sick, Reagan," Hannah remarks.

"How did you know?"

Hannah sighs again, "When he hugged me before going out to the cabin, I could tell he was frail."

"I don't care how frail he is, I want answers. We deserve that much from him. If he came here to stake a claim on the farm, that's bullshit."

"I don't think he came here for that, but I could be wrong," Hannah says.

Reagan places a lid over the pan full of gravy and turns off the gas to that burner for Hannah. Her sister has other burners lit with food cooking in different pans. The kitchen has regained its usual wonderful, comforting smells. This morning, however, it turns Reagan's stomach a little. The stress of last night, lack of sleep and worrying about the kids being gone have run her ragged. She feels like she might just puke that biscuit back up.

"Then why do you think he came here? Why now?" Reagan asks her sister who is usually more insightful than her.

Hannah turns to face her and places the dishrag she's using to dry her hands onto the countertop. Then she feels around until she locates the dough she must've been kneading. A new line of distress blemishes the smooth skin between her eyes.

"I think he came here to die, Reagan."

Now she really feels like she's going to throw up. She hadn't expected that response. She also hadn't considered it herself. She was so pissed last night at Robert, has been so for years, that she hadn't really looked that closely at him. She'd noticed his weight loss, the graying of his hair, but she hadn't thought of him as being that sick. She'd thought maybe he was down with a bug or weary from road travel or something similar. She hadn't thought anything like this. Perhaps Hannah is right.

"Oh," is all she can manage for an answer. She's supposed to be the doctor, but Hannah may have intuited this one way before her. It shouldn't really be that big of a surprise. Hannah usually knows what's going on before anyone else, especially before her. She doesn't even know how to take this news. It may not be true. He may just be ill. They won't know anything until he talks with her and Grandpa. There isn't any sense in worrying about something they don't know yet. "I'm not sure. Let's just wait to see what he has to say."

Hannah shrugs and says, "Sure."

Reagan furrows her brow at her sister. She can tell that Hannah has already come to a conclusion on the matter.

"Well, I'm off to hit the hay unless you need my help."

"Burning food? No, get to bed," Hannah teases and waves her away with a spatula.

Even at this early hour, her sister is lovely and fresh in her long white dress and one of Grams's old white aprons dotted with purple violets. Reagan walks closer, slides her hand onto Hannah's over the dough and presses a kiss to her sister's cheek.

"Thanks for breakfast," Reagan says softly. "Love ya' you know."

"I do," Hannie says with a humble nod. "Get to bed. Your patients will need you later today."

Reagan smiles and walks away toward the stairs.

"Love you, too!" Hannah calls after her with a chuckle.

When she gets downstairs, Reagan passes Gretchen coming out of her shared bedroom. She is dressed in the same clothing from the previous evening. She also doesn't look like she slept much. There are dark circles under her pretty eyes. Her brother Lucas must still be asleep unless he's gone out with the men.

"Hey," Reagan offers cordially.

"Reagan, right?" G asks.

"Yep, that'd be me."

"You're the doctor?" she inquires.

Reagan says, "Yup. Just like our dad."

Gretchen scoffs and snorts in a most unladylike fashion. She's glad Robert had another defiant daughter. It's nothing less than he'd deserve.

"Yeah, right. He only uses that title when he's around people who wouldn't be impressed with his military ones," G expresses with a wrinkle of her pert, small nose.

Her short hair stands up on end in places in spikey disarray. Reagan doubts that she would care. As a matter of fact, she's pretty sure Gretchen would prefer it messy like that if it meant pissing off their father.

Reagan nods and smiles, "I'm sure. You can head upstairs. Hannah's making a huge breakfast as usual. Maybe you can help."

"Ok, I don't know much about cooking, though," she says and looks at her feet.

"Yeah, me either. But she'll boss you around and show you what to do. She's good at that."

G's head whips up with surprise and she asks in a whisper, "Isn't she... you know, blind?"

"She sure is, but don't let that fool you. And don't try anything on her. She also has ears like a damn bloodhound. She can be fearsome when she wants," Reagan says with a chuckle.

"Oh, ok. Sure," G says with a concerned expression.

Reagan would like to talk more with this step-sister of hers, but pure and utter exhaustion has officially set in. She offers a smile that probably comes off more as tolerant than friendly and turns to go. Gretchen touches her arm to stop her. Reagan turns back to face her.

"We didn't know you guys even existed till like three days ago on our way here."

"Are you serious?"

"I think my mom might've known. I don't know. She wasn't as surprised as us, so I'm just assuming."

447

"I would've figured she knew about Robert's other family. Maybe she didn't. Who knows?" Reagan speculates.

"Sorry we showed up like that out of the blue. It was a dick move."

Reagan has to hold back a laugh. Oh, hell yes. Robert deserves this kid. She'd bet anything that she drives him nuts with her language, her defiance, her appearance.

"Our dad said his parents were dead. He never told us he had other kids or anything," G explains and looks at the wall behind Reagan instead of making eye contact. "We're just as surprised by your existence as you were by ours."

"What the...?" Reagan asks of no one, especially not this young girl, who seems very vulnerable in this moment.

"Just one more big disappointment where the Colonel is concerned if you ask me. Seems only right that he'd have other kids. No sense in just makin' us miserable. Of course, my brother is one of those people pleaser types. He's a lot nicer about Robert. He doesn't like it when I... well, when I'm realistic about our dad. But I'm more used to being disappointed in him."

Reagan notices that G is a lot more talkative than she was last night. Perhaps it was the rest or the fact that G recognizes a kindred spirit in her and a mutual dislike of their dad. Reagan can definitely relate to disappointing the Colonel.

"Yeah," Reagan says on an exhale. This day has to get better. It sure as hell couldn't get worse. "Hey, it's not your fault. Don't worry about it. I mean about showing up here unannounced."

"Honestly, I'm glad we're here," G says and looks at her shoes again. "Even if nobody wants us here. It's still better than just being stuck with him."

"Nobody said they don't want you here. It was just a shock. That's all. Don't feel like that. Grandpa accepts everyone without question, especially his own blood. You'll get to know that about him."

Gretchen makes eye contact briefly and looks quickly away again. She swallows hard and frowns. Perhaps unconditional love is a new concept to this young girl. She certainly wouldn't have received it from their father. His love, which Reagan never earned, came with a lot of conditions and restrictions.

"I'm hitting the sack for a couple hours," Reagan says, excusing herself.

"Sure. Yeah, sorry. Didn't mean to interrupt."

"That's not a problem. We have a little boy who's been through a lot. We get a lot of middle of the night visits to our bed."

"I can tell you're a good mom. I can see it in your eyes."

Damn this kid and her seeking, light hazel eyes. She sees too much in people. Reagan would certainly not call herself a good mom, though. Hell, the raising of Jacob had been thrust upon her. She's probably fucking that kid up beyond even Freud's repair.

"Well, I also get called out a lot for house-calls at all hours of the night, too," Reagan says, deflecting her praise and changing the course of their conversation. Where's Sue? Her other sister would love this insightful, soul-searching little shit.

"Yeah, so are we. The bunker kept mega-bizarro weird hours, and there wasn't any light, so it was hard to tell if it was day or night. Super freaky," G says, showing her age and confusing Reagan even more about the whereabouts of her father for nearly four years. "Well, see ya.'"

Gretchen turns and trots softly up the basement stairs, leaving Reagan to stand there feeling very perplexed. What the hell did she mean about a bunker? A yawn escapes her as she sneaks down the hall and into the kids' room. She finds Jacob asleep on a lower bunk, Arianna above him and Huntley across the room on another bunk. They never know where the kids are sleeping from one night to the next with the exception of Huntley, who always sleeps in the same spot. Sue's kids are all over the place. Sometimes Ari sleeps in here, sometimes upstairs by Sam. She's a little nomad. Justin must be out at their cabin with Sue. He's not much better than his sister with the sleeping arrangements. And lately, Jacob thinks he's one of the cool kids and insists on sleeping down here when Sue's kids stay over.

Reagan climbs over her sleeping son and positions her back against the wall. She stays on top of the covers not wanting to disturb Jake further, although she's pretty sure a cruise missile could come barreling through the wall and he'd stay asleep. Just listening to the children's soft breathing and occasional snore is comforting to her. She does this sometimes when the shit in the world seems too unbearable. Last night had been pretty far up there on the scale of zero to unbearable. She hates losing patients. Hearing about the macabre scene at the river camp had also taken its toll on her moral conscience. The thought of young girls, some as young as her new step-sister, being abused sexually makes her sick. It also makes her feel violent, as if she'd enjoy returning the favor of torturous abuse by dealing with them the same way she dealt with the sick, malevolent men at her college who'd attacked her.

She wraps an arm around her son, takes pleasure in the even rise and fall of his bony little chest, and tries not to dwell on the disgust and filth of the world. It won't be long before the tantalizing smell of Hannah's cooking awakens the children and they sprint upstairs like they do each morning. That's fine with her. The basement is dark and cool, perfect for sleeping when the sun is up. She has no doubt that John will not be going to bed. He'll stay up with the men. She'll probably have to force him down for a nap later in the day. He thinks he's a machine. She has to remind him often that he's not. But for now, she'll sleep next to her little angel and try to focus on taking solace from the simplicity of snuggling with pure innocence and perfection and not dwell on men who are evil. Or absentee fathers who make sudden reappearances.

Epilogue
Herb McClane

He signs his name at the bottom of the amended document and waits for the ink to dry completely before folding it and placing it in the top drawer of his desk. He takes a sip of his steaming coffee that Hannah brought into his office a few minutes ago. Somehow she'd known he was up. No wonder the coffee was still in the back of a restaurant that Cory and Kelly raided a few weeks ago. It's some sort of frilly, frothy cappuccino something or other that tastes like cinnamon and pumpkin pie spice. He chokes it down and tries to tell himself to be appreciative, but it proves difficult.

Herb knows he's doing the right thing. He and Maryanne had discussed it a few years ago before she got too sick. Now that his son is home, this definitely needed done. He'll pull the kids into his office sometime soon and go over everything with them. He does not anticipate it going well with his son. Robert has always been a strong-willed man.

If an alien spacecraft would've landed in the middle of town yesterday, he couldn't have been more surprised. He almost hadn't recognized Robert when he'd stepped down from the bus. He hasn't seen him in nearly six years, and his son has changed considerably since then. He'd stopped at the farm one time on a layover. He was on his way back to London at the time. Herb had attempted to warn him about the dangers of being too high up in the government. His son had definitely not heeded his advice. He enjoyed the perks of a political military career. He was always a very driven person, even as a child. But Herb used to worry about his son's ambitions. He'd even given up on his medical career to further his military promotions. Herb always believed that Robert's heart was never in medicine anyway. It probably wasn't hard for him to leave it. His appointment to general isn't really much of a surprise.

He'd taken the death of Maryanne very hard. He's glad that he brought Robert to his office last night by themselves. His son deserved a bit of privacy away from the rest of the family and his own family to hear the news of his mother's death. He'd wept sadly and sat brokenly in one of the chairs in front of Herb's desk. Today, he plans on visiting his mother's grave.

He knows that his son has been privy to information that the rest of them need to know. Herb is planning on calling a family meeting, like they always do, and asking his son for some answers. Last night, Robert alluded to a sense of urgency. Tonight, he'd like to better understand why.

The young people Robert brought with him to the farm, his children supposedly, were an even bigger surprise. Reagan, as usual, had flown off the handle, which had made discussing it with his son more difficult. But he can hardly blame his tempestuous, young granddaughter. Their father did leave them, hardly ever visited, and apparently started a new life elsewhere if he is comprehending the situation accurately. He hadn't needed it explained, either. Both of Robert's children had some of his features. There was no denying that they belonged to him. He just doesn't like the secrecy behind his son's actions. Herb has always been the kind of man to judge people by the measure of their actions. This time, however, he fears his judgement of his own son may possibly fall lower than anyone else. Maryanne would be very disappointed in Robert. He's glad she isn't here to witness the tragic turn of events in their son's life.

He has no idea if his son and new family are planning on staying on at the farm permanently, but he'll find out from him today exactly what his plans for the future might be. Herb doesn't think it's going to sit well with the girls, Reagan especially, if Robert wants to stay. They would definitely need to get working on a cabin for his son and family. The wall build, clinic days, and everything else would have to be put on hold in order to get a cabin built for Robert.

Herb's just not sure if they can afford to do that, either. The town's security has to come first right now, especially in light of the recent burglaries.

Herb stands and arches his back, trying to work out some of the kinks. He downs the last of his mocha-crappa-latte and grimaces. Perhaps a hot tea might be better. The mouth-watering aromas of his little Hannah's cooking is permeating throughout the old bones of his house. He wanders over to the window and leans against the frame. Movement out of the corner of his eye catches his attention. He spies Gretchen sneaking to the side of the chicken coop. She obviously thinks nobody will see her there. Likely nobody would have, except for the fact that his office happens to face that side of the property. She's a cute thing, this new granddaughter of his, which is nothing less than what he'd expect coming from his bloodline. She has a feistiness and a whole lot more defiance in her than Robert could've ever handled. She reminds him a little of Reagan at that age. She pulls a pack of cigarettes out of her jacket pocket and lights one up. Herb has to suppress a smile. The poor kid looks stressed out. She leans her dark head back against the wall of the coop. Occasionally, she shakes her head as if contemplating something impossible. Herb finds himself feeling sorry for the young sprite. She is clearly tormented by her own thoughts, and he can only imagine what her young life has been like so far. Suddenly, she panics and stamps out her cigarette quickly and stashes her pack of smokes in between the slats of the chicken coop wall. A moment later, her brother, Lucas, comes over to her. She just hits him with an innocent smile that conceals her wrong-doing. Herb chuckles. Lucas is clearly on the naïve side. Her brother seems oblivious but also very protective of her. He must suggest a walk because they turn to go. Gretchen happens to look up and catches Herb watching her from his window. Her eyes grow large, but he places a finger to his lips and sends a wink her way. She grins unsurely and allows her brother to lead her away. They walk together over to the horse pasture and both lean on the top board to observe the animals. It makes Herb feel a touch of melancholy that he doesn't know these two, young people. They are his family, too, and he wishes Robert hadn't felt the need to

453

hide them from him. He definitely wants some answers from his son, even if he only confesses them to him privately.

He knows he should be sleeping. If Mary was still alive, she would've insisted on him doing so. But she's gone, and he hardly ever sleeps in their bed anymore. Too many memories. Sometimes she visits him in his dreams. She'll be there young and youthful, full of vitality and dancing with him at some fundraiser thing or another that she'd dragged him to. He dreams of her out riding with him like he used to force her to do when they were young, even though she was not fond of the horses. Sometimes he sees her bringing him lunch in town at the clinic and forcing him to take a walk with her. She was always good at getting him to slow down. But sometimes she is just a flash. Images of her braiding Hannah's hair, or teaching her lessons or the two of them working in the kitchen together, or helping Sue get ready for her wedding will come at him like a slideshow. Other times he remembers her as she was at the end, small and frail, like a withering leaf on one of her rose bushes, too delicate even to touch. His favorite visits are when they are together sitting on the swing watching the girls play in the front yard when they were younger, back before the world fell apart. He really hates those nocturnal visits when his Mary finds him in his sleep. He always awakens looking for her in their bed, searching for her hand to hold. Most of the time, he now prefers to sleep on the leather sofa in his den for this very reason. Too many memories.

So he takes his clipboard with patient notes attached to it and heads for his favorite spot, the front porch swing where he used to spend quality time with the love of his life discussing the girls, the state of the world, and anything else she wished to talk about. When he gets there, Susan is already perched on the swing. He joins her, and they swing gently together.

"Everything all right, Susan?" he asks and takes his oldest granddaughter's hand in his.

"Sure, Grandpa," she replies. "Just worried about the family that's not here. Always do."

"We all do, dear," he admits. "They'll be fine. What else is troubling you?"

She regards him with her soft, brown eyes and smiles.

"Just thinking about Dad coming back."

"I figured," Herb admits. "How do you feel about it?"

"I'm not sure how to feel about it. At first I was happy, but now…"

"I know," he says. "We'll get it straightened out. I'm calling a family meeting tonight if we can. I want us to all be present. I have some important things to go over with you girls and your husbands. I'd like Robert and his wife to be present, as well."

She cocks her head to the side with puzzlement.

"What are talking about, Grandpa?"

"You'll see. Don't worry, honey," he allays her fears. "It's nothing bad. I just want everyone present so that there isn't any confusion later on."

"Okay, we'll be there."

"As for your father's return, I don't care how you girls feel about him or even his wife, but I'd like everyone to be kind to his kids. Or if kind is too much, then at least courteous and tolerant. This isn't their fault."

"I agree," Sue acknowledges. "I'll talk to everyone about it today. I think we all feel the same way, but I'll make sure to discuss it with them."

"Well, it looks like you have another sister and brother."

"Yeah, Grandpa, I guess we do. Strange," Sue says with a wrinkle of her forehead as she contemplates this.

"It'll all work out," he promises. "You'll see."

Sue tries to offer a smile, but it doesn't come off of as completely genuine. Herb feels the same, so he chooses to look down at his notes instead. He doesn't like false illusions between them. He's always been open and honest with the girls, even when the world fell apart, even when the truth was going to be harder to take than a falsehood. He makes a note on one of his patient sheets to distract himself from having to look at his lovely granddaughter, who has chosen to stare off into the distance. He can only wonder if the promise he just gave his granddaughter will prove true.

CPSIA information can be obtained
at www.ICGtesting.com
Printed in the USA
FFOW03n1430210518
46818574-48981FF